FIC
BUN

THE
PROTEST

Dianne Kozdrey Bunnell

THE PROTEST

WORDSMITH PUBLISHING, INC.   *Washington, USA*

AUTHOR'S NOTE

The Protest is a work of fiction. All of the characters are the product of my imagination, and their actions, motivations, thoughts and conversations are solely my creation. I've drawn inspiration from my own experiences, but the characters, the situations in which they find themselves, as well as the locations, real and fictional, and the non-existent religious sect, The Fellowship of the Holy Bible and its minister and members, are not intended to depict real people, settings or events.

THE PROTEST

Copyright © 2003 by Dianne Kozdrey Bunnell.
All rights reserved under International and Pan-American Copyright
Conventions. Published in the United States by WordSmith Publishing, Inc.
in the state of Washington, one of the most well-read states in the nation.

Grateful acknowledgement is made for permission to reprint from the following:
Steven Hassan's *Releasing the Bonds: Empowering People to Think for Themselves* (2000)
and *Combatting CULT MIND CONTROL* (1990).
Richard Gardner, M.D.'s "Psychotherapeutic and Legal Approaches to the
Three Types of Parental Alienation Syndrome Families" from Chapter Nine of
Family Evaluation in Child Custody Mediation, Arbitration and Litigation and
The Parental Alienation Syndrome, Second Edition,
Cresskill, N.J. Creative Therapeutics (1998).

Cover design by Rohani Design, Inc.

FIRST EDITION

Library of Congress Cataloging-in-Publication Data
Bunnell, Dianne Kozdrey.
The Protest / Dianne Kozdrey Bunnell — 1st ed.
p. cm.
Includes bibliographical references.
ISBN #0-9723498-8-X
1. Child rearing — Religious aspects — Fiction.
2. Custody of children — Fiction. 3. Parental alienation
syndrome — Fiction. 4. Schizophrenia — Fiction.
I.Title.
PS3602.U846P76 2003   813′.6
QBI33-771

No part of this book may be reproduced or transmitted in any form or by any means,
electronic or mechanical, including photocopying, recording or by any information
storage and retrieval system, without permission in writing from the publisher:
WordSmith Publishing, Inc.
P.O. Box 1576
Yelm, WA 98597

Printed in the United States of America

For

My Daughters

Contents

Foreword

They Thought They Were Saved

Times were hard. As soon as I graduated from high school, I enlisted for six years in the Navy, before the war started, and became an electrician. My tour of duty started at Newport Beach, Rhode Island. I got aboard the USS Yorktown, a ship over a thousand feet long, carrying about 250 planes, fighters, bombers and torpedo planes. We were in Pearl Harbor about a month before the bombing, but pulled out, went through the Panama Canal and began convoying ships in the Atlantic along with the British, where they were being attacked by German wolf packs, submarines, that is.

Our ship eventually ended up deep in enemy waters. The first battle of WWII between aircraft carriers, only, occurred at the battle of the Coral Sea on May 8th, the date of my 21st birthday. Torpedoes very narrowly missed our ship. At one time we had planes coming in at us, about 25 bombers and 25 to 30 torpedo planes. We were hit by a 500 pound bomb, which plunged through the decks and was finally stopped by 5-inch thick impenetrable metal, where it bounced between the fifth and sixth decks until it exploded, killing about 50 men and deafening the rest. The USS Lexington was sunk in that battle. We went to Pearl Harbor to get the ship repaired, which was full of holes from the attack.

After 120 days out to sea, it took us a while to load up on food and supplies, but soon we took off from Pearl Harbor for Midway. About 15 to 20 Japanese battle ships, cruisers, carriers were all headed for Midway at the same time, while they also sent a diversionary task force to the Aleutians. We had five carriers and they had five. It was a terrible battle. We lost almost all our planes. The Japanese also had heavy casualties. They say the water was blood red because of the thousands and thousands who were killed that were supposed to go ashore and fight, but never did.

Since we'd been partially damaged from the battle in the Coral Sea about a month before and it was more difficult for us to maneuver, we were set about 100 miles back from the other carriers to be safer. But the Japanese found our ship and came at us with about 100 to 200 planes torpedoing, fighters strafing, and started dropping the bombs. We weren't quite so lucky this time. Three bombs hit and two aerial torpedoes hit, one right after another, so the first one opened the ship up and the second came in and blew the hell out of everything. There was an enormous roar, the kind that makes you think it's the end. You can't believe how terrified you can get with bombs falling everywhere and you know you're facing, possibly, your last moments of life.

I was in the emergency diesel generator room, five decks down, toward the stern. When the torpedoes hit, the ship literally flew up into the air, and threw us up about a foot and a half, then we came crashing back down on the metal floors. They told us to lay down, because they knew if we got hit and were standing, it could break our ankles.

Our ship was then dead in the water. I came up to about the fourth deck, where I found there were a few night lights on, blue and red, everything else was pitch black. Other guys were starting to come out from the main generator room and the damage repair crews. It was deathly quiet. We climbed the ladders up to hatchways and on up to topside. When I got up on topside, I couldn't believe what a beautiful day it was, until I noticed hundreds of men dead; most piled up against the stack of the carrier. Others were still sitting in the gun turrets, with half their bodies blown away. The ship was listing at about 40 degrees. I got to the high part of the flight deck and listened to the captain tell us through a blow horn that we had done a good job, but needed to abandon ship.

I was quite late coming up from so deep in the bowels of the ship, and since it was pitch black down below and we couldn't see and didn't know we would be abandoning ship, all the life jackets were already taken. So I lowered myself over the side and into the water without a life jacket. I swam toward a ship, and on the way, I ran into a couple guys with life jackets who were swimming. I asked if I could rest on them a minute, and one of the guys pulled out a knife and told me to get lost. So I swam off toward another destroyer with a line over the side. I grabbed a hold of it, along with ten or fifteen others.

Just as we thought we were going to get pulled up into the ship, the Japanese fighter planes came back for strafing and the ship with the rope we were holding onto took off. Soon it was moving pretty fast. All the guys ahead of me who were holding on were forced off the rope because of the pressure of the water against their life jackets. I kept pulling myself up further and further as these guys got knocked off, until I was number one. I wrapped my legs around a young guy who was crying, terrified, thought he was going to get killed, and we held on that way, just the two of us. Everyone else was washed off. Finally, the ship stopped and they dropped a rope ladder over the side. I tried to climb up it, but was so tired I couldn't. I just put an arm up and two or three guys grabbed me and threw me onto the deck.

—Edwin Martin Kozdrey

Acknowledgments

When I was in the fifth grade, I wrote a ten-page story for a school assignment that made my dad laugh; great big belly laughs that rolled out of him, the sweetest sound in the world. My writing career was born in that moment, and nurtured by the many nights I made up bedtime stories to tell my six younger brothers and sisters, who amazed me by their voracious appetites for my creations. To my mom, whose love was always good and pure and generous, and Dad, and my brothers and sisters, I am forever grateful.

I would like to thank my husband Ernie, whose love, generosity and faith in my ability sustained me, and whose rare gift of insight into people, their reactions and dialogue helped make this book more richly realistic; also, thanks to my daughter, Anna, for choosing to love me and for supporting this work of fiction. Heartfelt appreciation to Sandi Ludescher for her belief in me and tirelessness in the novel's early stages as she critiqued chapters hot off the keyboard. Thanks also to my step mom Pam Kozdrey for reading the manuscript and offering love and encouragement. Many thanks as well to Dr. Richard Gardner and Steven Hassan for their generosity in allowing information from their books to be used in this publication. And special thanks to Anais Rain for her generous donation of herself to serve as model for the cover.

Professionally, my heartfelt gratitude is tied to Tuesday nights spent in the company of the Eatonville Writers' Workshop, whose members taught me more about writing than I knew was possible, including workshop leader, Don McRae, Sr. (who attended a writing workshop at which I was reading and started this whole novel-writing process by saying, *You don't want to write a short story. Where's the sense in that? You have to turn this into a novel. Come visit our group next Tuesday night.*), and his son, Don McRae, Jr., Lee Hodges, Jim McDaniels, Bill Nicholls, Vicki Di Giulio, Gail Haines, Carol Kaiser, Vern King, George Webb, Beverly Vines-Haines, Dean Hooper and Bill Cross. Irene Wanner gave what I *thought* was my finished manuscript such a thorough going over that the story was more compelling than ever for her insights on pacing and cutting extraneous information. My appreciation to Brygitta McDermott's women's group, a forum for reading, discussion and critiquing; and to Mary Armstrong and others I've lost touch with of the Whitworth College writers' group for their critiquing as I honed my emerging writing skills—and thanks for not kicking up a fuss when my girls attended a session or two on evenings I couldn't get a sitter.

Also, thanks to Jim and Carol Bartley, who were willing to share details of the *real* house made from a barn, upon which I based the description of Dallas' home.

Thanks to George Hobart for loaning books and promotional materials and DeLynn Hobart, for assisting through George, to me, in tech support. Thanks, also, to John Nunes for his computer expertise, used to help a desperate writer with formatting problems. And thanks to Dodie and Jerry Ruzicki and Sandra and Gary Worthington, who encouraged me concerning the promotional plans for *The Protest*, based on their own experiences with their books.

And finally, I'd like to thank each and every one of my students over the years who've heard the first chapter of *The Protest* and learned a little about how literature is put together. Thanks for your love of me as your teacher, and your encouragement to keep on with the writing.

To those whose contributions I have neglected to include here due to failure of memory, please accept my apologies. I owe all a great debt.

One

*Feminism causes women to abandon their husbands,
commit crimes and perversions and become lesbians.*
— Reverend Logan Churlick, 2003

Summer settled with a vengeance on the dusty little town of Rathcreek, a dry August heat eastern Washington was known for, the kind that wrung sweat and energy from everything living. By nine o'clock in the morning, the clapboards of the Crownhart home were seared in dust.

Janey Crownhart Powers stood at the kitchen sink peeling potatoes. A shaft of sunlight bore down on her from the skylight, and the long chestnut hair shone in a neon halo of copper highlights. Her open face wore mischief like a jaunty hat cocked as if nothing would ever knock it off. The nose, too long and narrow, gave her a knowing look, like a fox. But the look was redeemed by compassionate, almost ethereal eyes.

Janey rinsed off the potato, took aim and lobbed it into a large pot. Water splashed over the counter and dripped onto the floor. She glanced at her sister, Louise, who was chopping onions and wiping her eyes on her sleeve. Except for the musical jingling of the potato peeler and steady beat of the knife striking the cutting board, it was quiet, the practical quiet that accompanies working women when the conversation lulls.

Dragging the peeler across the brown skin of another potato, Janey broke into a mournful, throaty song. "Sum-mer ti-i-i-i-me—and the peelin' is easy—"

Hardly skipping a beat, Louise belted out, "Potatoes flyin', cotton soaked with sweat—"

"Eyes are cryin' 'cause the onion is slaughtered—"

Louise sang lustily, "You ain't seen nuthin' like Weezie's 'tato salad yet! Oooh-wee! God, I've missed you, Janey. Why'd you have to marry that asshole? Oughta leave him, come back here and have breakfast with us every morning."

A smile touched the corner of Janey's mouth. She whispered, "Louise, he'll hear you."

"No he won't. He's watching a church program with Dad. As if they won't get enough today." She stepped back and peered through the doorway. "Oh, sure. The asshole who really needs saving is pretendin' to watch t.v. He's reading want ads, while Dad, who's already 'bout as born again as you can get, is overdosing on his evangelical drug of choice." Her large gray eyes turned squinty. "Son of a bitch! What—? Hell, he's readin' personal ads. God awmighty, Janey—with a highlighter."

Louise slid across the floor on her stockinged feet to block her sister's charge. "Wait!" She held up her hands. "Joke. Sorry, sis." A smarmy grin appeared.

"That was not funny, Louise."

"Mmhmm," she murmured, back to her onions. "Too close to home?"

Janey stroked sure along the rough hide of the potato, turning it glistening white. "I wouldn't put it past him, you know. To get back at me."

"Jesus, Janey."

"We all have our moments of depravity, but most of us don't pledge allegiance to 'em like some flag."

Louise glanced sideways. "I tried to warn you. Ye shall know them by their fruits. Know what I mean?" She arched her eyebrows. "The far-flung influence of the CIA."

Here we go, Janey thought.

Suddenly, Louise squatted and yanked open the cupboard doors. She rotated cans this way and that. "God damn CIA. Puttin' things in your food, into your head, always tryin' to get to you."

She held up a can of beets. "Aha!" Mumbling about red dye, she tossed it into the trash can.

"You listen to your big sister. Things are not always the way they appear. And you, little sister, are a babe in the friggin' woods. You gotta understand one thing: there's Christians, and there's *Christians*. You listen to me. The CIA is alive and well." She gave Janey a nod in her way of conveying mystery out of madness.

Genius glittered around the edges of Louise's mental illness at times. As Janey sifted through the jumble today, however, she was simply inscrutable.

"Well, I don't know about the CIA, but I sure do understand 'by their fruits.' I've had a bellyful of Jake's using scripture to make me submit. Dad rules the house, but he loves Mom." She picked up another potato. "When do Mom and Dad leave for church?"

"After Dad's morning constitutional. He's just biding his time till Mom gets out of the bathroom. He swears that with all those vitamins keepin' him regular, he's gonna live forever. And if he doesn't? He's covered himself with," Louise dipped, "*Je*-zuz."

Janey said, "When I called the other day, he tried to get me to take a thousand milligrams of 'C' four times a day for my scratchy throat."

"No way!"

Janey giggled. "You know how gassy that much 'C' makes you."

Louise nodded.

"Anyway, he took that much last Sunday when he felt a bug coming on. Said he took acidophilus with it so when he farted, they were so mild no one even noticed."

Louise broke out in wild laughter. Her hand flew up to cover her mouth. Janey liked her sister's laugh. Spontaneous, robust and convulsive, there was always the feeling she might not get it under control.

"I know. I know," Janey said. " 'What's so funny?' he wants to know. 'Dad,' I said, 'do you think maybe it was because the people at church, unlike the hard hats you work with, were too polite to say anything?' "

"What'd he say?"

"What could he say? He was busting up."

Life was a serious matter to Joe Crownhart. A place where, sooner or later, dreams withered and died. God, vitamins and a tight budget were all that pulled them through. These essentials, and the luxury of humor. All the family was blessed with the gift of a quick laugh. It was this faculty that gave balance to the seriousness of living.

The timer on the stove buzzed. Janey took a pan of hard boiled eggs from the burner and ran them under cold water. "Dad still on his diet?"

"Well, until today. You know he had a bet going, didn't you?"

Janey shook her head.

"With the guys at work, to see who could lose the most weight in a month. Been starving himself, really. But today it's over. Sure got his eye on that pie Mom baked."

The apple pie sat on the kitchen table. Sugar crystals sparkled on the flaky, golden crust. Janey bent and sniffed the cinnamon, broke off a piece of crust and popped it into her mouth. She crossed the room, pulled out a drawer and rooted around for a pencil.

"Weez, what do you think Dad would do if his pie didn't make it to the picnic?"

Louise stopped her chopping. "Oh no, Janey. This is serious stuff." She glanced at the doorway. "Fifty-fifty?"

Janey was writing now, then she held up the note:

If you ever want to see your apple pie alive again, leave $100,000 in small bills in a bag on the kitchen table.

Louise covered her mouth with both hands; only wickedly gleeful eyes showed. "No, no, a hundred thou' is too much. Not subtle enough. Make it an even hundred."

They heard the click of the bathroom door.

Janey pulled a piece of tape off the dispenser. "Hide that pie in the picnic basket. And put a sack on the table, would you?"

Louise saluted. "Yowsir."

Janey hurried into the hallway and met her mother leaving the bathroom, which smelled of lilac and toothpaste.

"How's lunch coming, honey?"

Dressed in her Sunday garden variety print, Mary Crownhart was slender, a faded version of Janey, but with more red in the shoulder-length chestnut hair she wore pulled back. A mild soul who took her husband in stride, taking vitamin C when he pushed it on her, doing without because of his tight-fisted ways, Mary wore submission as a mantle of devotion to God and her mate. A woman could lose herself in such humility and the thought frightened Janey.

Impulsively, she hugged her mother.

The soft, brown eyes opened wide in surprise and pleasure.

"Louise is working on the potato salad. Tell Dad I'll be just a minute, would you?"

She stuck the note to the mirror, flushed the toilet and opened the door to her father, who was standing on the other side, wearing a look of annoyance.

"Hurry, Dad, or we'll be late." She brushed past him. "Jake and I'll be in the car."

"Glad someone's on the ball around here. Mary?" he shouted. "We're going to be late."

Out in the old station wagon, Janey and Jake sat in the back seat.

A few years ago, Jake Powers had been a force at Rathcreek High. Not due to blonde hair and blue eyes, but catapulted to popularity by a bad-boy mystique. Rath High prom had been held free in the school gym as far back as students could remember. But the principal, in a financial scrape, claimed that that year's dance had ruined the floor. Amidst cries of outrage, the thousand dollar charge for a new coat of gym seal was stuck to the junior class. The following year, Jake Powers inspired the seniors with a plan: not even a nod to the tradition of a senior class gift to the school. In a fit of righteous indignation, valedictorian Janey Crownhart announced to Board members, the principal, and the Rathcreek community sitting on bleachers in the gym that fine June day, "This year's graduating class would like to present as the senior gift a plaque commemorating *last year's gym floor*."

But somewhere between their collaborated rebellion and a year of married life, they had faltered in their devotion to each other.

"Ransom note?" Jake asked.

"Uh-huh. Isn't it fun? I wonder what he'll do? You never can tell with Dad." She peered out the window toward the house.

"I don't get it. No one's gonna pay a hundred bucks for pie. You can buy one for less than ten in town."

She said gently, "That's the joke," and decided to leave it at that.

He shook his head and opened a soft leather-bound Bible.

Mary bustled down the walk, arms filled with flowers for the church. Joe followed, carrying a Bible in one hand. In the other was a small sack.

Doors slammed. Joe started the car and turned to face the back seat. He held out the sack. "Here. This is for you."

It rattled. Janey grinned at Jake, who rolled his eyes.

With a look, he'd ruined the joy of it, and the bag sat unopened on her lap. Janey trained her gaze out the window to avoid her father's eyes in the rearview mirror. The car pulled into the street.

She wished Louise were there. If she were, the mood would lighten, she could breathe easier. But Louise could not attend Fellowship services, even if she wanted to. Disruptive behavior, brought on by her schizophrenia, which refused to be banished by faith healing, brought banishment of Louise from church instead.

Finally, Janey's curiosity was too much. She opened the bag. Inside was a note. Removing the slip of paper, she glanced at the rearview mirror. Her father's droll eyes were on her.

Here's the hundred dollars in small pills. That pie better be at the picnic. No double crosses. P.S. This is B complex. Take it once a day for stress.

In a low, hard pew of The Rathcreek Fellowship of the Holy Bible, Janey fanned herself with a service bulletin. The odors of mold, wood polish and perspiration hung in the air. Moisture gathered on her neck and dampened the back of her light cotton dress.

She glanced at Jake's stony face. Was she imagining his moodiness? Uneasiness gnawed at her. The pie ransom? Or the scene outside the church earlier?

That morning, devil's tails had whipped up dirt in the gravel lot, lifting the hem of Janey's dress. She was standing in the half-shade of the mighty split oak, which was rooted near The Fellowship of the Holy Bible, and had been there at the time of the building's beginnings, so that one seemed a part of the other. Lightning had struck the tree, rending it into two trunks. One part had died, but the other trunk had somehow survived. Janey stood in its shade, and the breeze felt good in the eternal heat. She hadn't resisted the skirt's billowy sail. But Jake had been displeased by her immodesty.

What was so wrong? It was only the wind, and a glimpse of her knee, nothing unnatural about that.

But she should have known better. The slight frown, the way Jake avoided her now. Why was it so difficult to be good? Other wives didn't seem to struggle as she did. What was wrong with her?

A voice caught Janey. She looked up, and as always, Reverend Logan Churlick claimed her, along with the rest of his followers. The wild black eyes, the voice. No ordinary human, Logan Churlick possessed the cool sense of purpose and towering strength of a giant Nordic god. Even when he had been jailed for an incident involving faith healing gone wrong, the guardianship of his flock was so important, he sent taped sermons back with Mrs. Churlick for each Sunday's service. Even in jail, he seemed always everywhere.

Like Jonah's whale, Logan Churlick had swallowed all of The Fellowship, and for the most part, they lived happily in his belly. Imposing, not with the bland hair, the watery blue eyes of the Norse, his black eyes reached deep into The Fellowship's subconscious pool of guilt. Now, clapping, smiling, he sang,

"Satan's a liar and a conjure, too!
If you don't watch out, he'll conjure you . . ."

Mrs. Churlick's hands pranced over the organ keys, her strident voice above the rest.

When the singing ended, the congregation settled into its seats, revitalized, full of spiritual juice. Jake and her parents were to Janey's left. On her right, her best friend, Margie, and nephew, Nathan. In the stale air, the little boy fidgeted.

Margie whispered, "Now you be quiet, honey. Shhh," and gave the boy her keys. He settled down, then the keys clattered to the floor. Nathan stood on his sturdy two-year-old legs, turned and waved at Mrs. Scanlan in the pew behind. Margie pulled him to her lap. He howled and several heads turned.

"Nathan, the devil's got into you this morning!" Margie scolded. "Why can't you sit still?" He struggled, then slipped to the floor, where Margie, unable to quiet the child, left him to whine. She gathered up her belongings and prepared to gather her nephew.

A paper airplane glided past Nathan, a service bulletin folded to a point, wings flaring with church announcements. The little boy looked with wonder in the direction from which the plane had come. Janey waved with a finger.

Then, Jake squeezed her other hand, and she let out a little cry. More than the pain, she felt the sting of her husband's rebuke. Hers was not exactly church conduct, but she had helped quiet the child, hadn't she? With Jake, she was to have no mind of her own, no will, no ambition, but to be the perfect wife, with a personality of paste.

Well, you can take your paste and shove it, Janey thought, sick of it all, and with a sudden impulse to be free, snatched the Bible from his lap and whacked his hand.

"You b–," he exploded, wrenching away. Janey caught her breath. His gaze darted from face to face, then at her. She read his smoldering anger as *Wait till later.*

Finally, she returned her attention to the little boy. "Pssst!"

Nathan watched her dig through her purse, find a roll of Life Savers and pick out a red one. Lifting an eyebrow to the boy, she inched the candy along the seat back, around his aunt, slowly, slowly making its way toward him.

He crept up onto the pew and watched the red jewel. He pounced on Janey's hand when it stopped, peeled the fingers from the candy and put it in his mouth. His lips clamped shut. He turned and sat down, clonked his feet together.

"Thank you," Margie whispered.

Reverend Churlick's baritone filled the small sanctuary. "In Joshua 5:14, Joshua was told to remove his shoes, for the very ground was holy in the presence of God's messenger. Can you imagine?" He smiled, his brows relaxing. "This church is holy ground, did you know that? It is, because we do God's holy work here. And we need to get in touch—with our bare feet—with the awesome responsibility God's laid on our hearts."

Something in the image struck Janey. The verse had never seemed so personal. She reached down to unstrap her sandals and wriggled out of them.

"Oh, that's good," she murmured. "Definitely holy." Her feet, crossed at the ankles, rested on the smooth wooden floor. A light perspiration left imprints of toes, soles.

The preacher slid easily from God's holy work to the work of marriage.

"Just this week, I received a call from a desperate man who was joined in holy matrimony a year ago in this very chapel. Already, he's disillusioned with marriage."

Janey and Jake had been married in the church a year ago. A year of struggle and adjustments. Jake taught her there was no romance in real life, and already, she had quit expecting it.

She fidgeted, stealing a glance at her husband. His eyes were on the preacher. The thin smile on his lips made her uneasy.

Then, as he sometimes did, Reverend Churlick opened the forum, calling on parishioners to unburden their hearts.

Jake stood.

Paralyzed, on the verge of tears, Janey gazed up at him. As he spoke, her heart raced and a thin trickle of sweat streamed down her side.

"So I'd like to take this up here and now," Jake declared. "My life sure isn't what I thought it'd be. I wanted a wife who'd put me first, but she's too stubborn to properly submit." He cleared his throat. " 'Specially in the most important way."

A murmur rippled through the congregation.

"Oh, my God." Janey shielded her eyes. Embarrassment ran up her neck and cheeks. She made herself turn to face him. Staring straight ahead, he continued, voice unflinching. As her disbelief gave way to betrayal, she blinked back tears. She knew he was unhappy, but how could he let the world know what went on in their bedroom?

Reverend Churlick waved his hands. "Whoa, Jake! Don't need to make this so personal. We can unburden without details, brother."

"But I thought you said to. . . ."

"No, no, no, not like this. Not to hurt Janey, but to help."

Jake picked up the Bible, doggedly thumbed through it. "The Bible talks about it, so I don't know why we shouldn't. First Corinthians 7:4 says, 'The wife *hath not* power over her own body . . . *but the husband.*'"

How could she forgive him? These people would never know what she had to put up with. The way he belittled her, criticized her friends, pressured her to limit contact with her family, saying he hated her overbearing father and joking about her crazy sister. Yet, like a time clock, every Friday night they punched in at Jake's mother's house. He insisted they have dinner with her, to keep her occupied and out of the bars. Then, there was the way he was incapable of making love, demanding sex when she was sick or upset. Sex, the "cure." Of course she had refused him.

For all the confidence Reverend Churlick usually possessed, he appeared uneasy now. "God bless you, Jake. You got a heavy heart, as anyone can see. But maybe we can talk this out later. I can't say I know what's goin' on in Janey's mind. Maybe the poor thing's just scared. Everything's new. Maybe she just needs some reassurance. Well, Jake, if I had a wife like her," the preacher's dark eyes shone, penetrating her with sympathy, "I'd do everything in my power to make her happy. Bringin' the problem to light is the first step. Now talk to her."

"Amen!" came from the back of the chapel.

Janey had the fleeting feeling they were all on a talk show, and the audience was squaring off, taking sides. She looked up at Jake with hope.

"I can't talk to her. I can't do anything right. I'm tired of it always being my fault." He sat down.

The reverend said, "You know, Jake, before a woman can be properly submissive, you need to love her. Like Jesus loved the church, eh?"

Yes! She clenched her fist. Gratitude fortified her. She soaked up his advocacy like honeyed ointment.

Gripping both sides of the lectern, the preacher lowered his chin and looked out over the top of his glasses. Then, letting his benevolent gaze fall on her, he pulled back. "Nothin' to be ashamed about. All marriages have their ups and downs. I guarantee you, though, this marriage can work. God don't believe in divorce.

"Janey, honey, Jake, come on up here. We're gonna pray for this couple. An' I saw lots of head noddin' goin' on while he was talkin'. Anyone else with problems, we'll pray for you, too. The Lord lo-o-o-ves longsufferin', but you've suffered long *enough*. Who believes in the power of prayer? Who *knows* that God answers prayer?"

The church was abroil in "Amens!" and "Hallelujahs!"

Jake took her hand and pulled.

She drew back. "Jake," she whispered, "I can't. Please don't make me. Jake!"

He pulled. She stood, and the roll of candy fell to the floor. He moved her up the aisle, her bare feet sticking to the wood. Panic gave way to bewilderment, and she followed, eyes never leaving the floor.

They stood before the members of The Fellowship of the Holy Bible. Others joined them. The minister placed a hand on both their heads and recited scripture. Hands clasped in a ring around them. They prayed for Jake and Janey and others. But the scandal belonged to Jake and Janey Powers. Their marital problems would be the ones buzzing behind doors that night. And in a church where submission of women was paramount, she would be cast to blame.

"Someday, Jake," she said under the cover of praying and wailing around them.

He frowned. "Huh?"

"What makes you think I'm going to. . . . to keep taking this?"

"You'll take whatever I tell you, *wife*."

Sick with resignation, she said, "Someday."

Hands pushed her bowed head and the air was sweaty with lamentations. Close, hot words of comfort and coercion. Reverend Churlick's arm clasped her waist.

The prayers and crying and entreaties to God went on. Her throat spasmed as she fought for control. Someone took her hand, squeezed it.

"Mom!" she sobbed.

"Oh Janey," Mary cried. "Now don't you worry, hon, everything's gonna work out. I asked the reverend if you can see him for counseling and he agreed."

Janey's tears started up again. "Can I come live with you and Daddy till Jake and I work this out? I. . . . I just can't go back."

"Is that a good idea, hon?"

Before Janey could answer, the minister put his arms on her shoulders. She was surprised to see his red-rimmed eyes.

"It's not supposed to be like this." Then for the benefit of the congregation, he said, "Janey, honey, Jake, George, Shirley, Stan and Debbie, let's have you make a public confession of your sin an' ask the Lord for forgiveness."

She shook her head.

"Come on, hon," the preacher urged.

Janey reached up and cast moist hair away from her neck, pushed it behind an ear. The tight collar of her dress choked her. Unsteady, she let Reverend Churlick lead her and the others before The Fellowship. She stood at his side facing every friend and relative she had ever known.

"For all have sinned and come short of the glory of God!" Reverend Churlick shouted. "Reject your sin! Repent before God and this Fellowship."

One by one, the sinners repented, crying, faces red. They were broken and rebuilt, to the cheering of the congregation. At last, Janey's turn came.

She stood, silent, looking from Reverend Churlick to the eager crowd, faces raised heavenward, hands like antennas to receive God's signal. Margie, little Nathan, her father, all of them waited. But she could not confess. She could not tell them about a sin they would not understand.

Always his need. "Forgive her, Lord!" Never hers. "Heavenly Father!" For affection and respect, a marriage of partnership, the way it should be. "Sweet Jesus, Je-sus, *Jee-zuz!*" Her emotions blistered by remarks like nettles: "You're always over-reacting. Crazy bimbo. You're crazy, just like your sister."

All eyes were on her.

She opened her mouth to speak, wanted to tell them she was the one who was wronged, but the words were not there.

"C'mon, Janey," the reverend whispered, breath hot on her ear, "we don't want to have to cast you out of The Fellowship, dear."

The air was heavy with the odor of perspiration and worn hymn books. It was all she could do to keep from being sick. Her throat tightened. She tried to swallow, but her mouth was dry.

Oh, God, she thought. *Oh, God, no.*

Reverend Churlick put up a hand to silence the congregation. He waited, eyes glistening, searching hers.

She knew what came next.

Voice shuddering with emotion, he said, "Janey! Don't make me do this. Please." He waited. Reluctantly, he turned. "Janey's made her choice, and so we must make ours."

He shouted, "We rebuke and discipline you in the name of the Lord!" Reverend Churlick turned his back to her. "It's with a heavy heart I lead this society of Christians in shunning Janey Crownhart Powers."

Two

*The wife hath not power of her own body, but the husband:
and likewise also the husband hath not power of his own
body, but the wife.*

I. CORINTHIANS 7:4

A week later, when Janey entered the duplex she used to share with Jake, she breathed a quick prayer, thanking God that Jake was at church.

She took a framed greeting card that Louise had given her off the wall. Earth below, dark star-studded sky above, the woman, head back, held the crescent of the moon in her hands, and drank the milky way spilling out of it. The Earth Mother taking the galaxy in her hands had helped Janey through a particularly bad time with Jake. It went into the paper bag she had brought.

While she considered being ousted from The Fellowship bothersome, one aspect she relished: the forbidding of a shunned spouse from engaging in sexual relations. The strange edict had infuriated Jake, but for Janey, it more than made up for the rest.

In the bedroom, she flipped the light switch. It felt eerie to be back where she had suffered so much at the hands of a man who was supposed to love her.

She threw clothes into the grocery sack: underwear, sweaters, socks.

Strange, she thought, *It's like some big, cosmic joke. All my life I was scared to death, thought I'd be damned without The Fellowship, but the only thing I feel is relief.*

Being cast out gave her a clarity of vision that was completely foreign—foreign, because hers was a religion based on violent emotions, one in which blind faith was its native son, and logic a heretic.

Amazed at how strong she felt, she had quickly gotten over the shock of being ostracized. Just one week ago, she and Louise had gone into the Rathcreek drugstore. The man at the cash register stared at the items she had placed on the counter. She handed him a five dollar bill.

Arms crossed, he stepped back. "I ain't touchin' that."

"What?"

"Any money from your hand's unclean. I ain't touchin' it."

Janey withdrew the bill, unsure what to think. "I need those things. Where am I supposed to go?"

He stared at her.

Louise, who was approaching, would be no help. She had been shunned years ago.

At the counter, Louise took in the situation, held up her hands. Putting Milk Duds and a *New Woman* magazine onto the counter, she fished in her purse, wadded some bills and threw them at the man.

"Oooooh-wee! Don't take money from this filthy heathen hand, or you'll burn."

"Now, dang it, Louise . . . "

"Burn, baby, burn!" Louise shouted. Several customers looked their way. In her finest slow pitch, she hurled Milk Duds at him. The magazine fluttered over his head. "I'd like these bagged, Carl. If you don't mind."

She pointed. "Money's still on the floor. Better to stoop low, than take it from the hand of a sinner like moi. Or my sister."

The scowling man scooped up the candy, magazine, wadded bills, rang the sale and bagged it. Janey watched, fascinated. The money of a shunned person was all right; but he couldn't take it directly from her hand.

As Janey thought back to those scary first days of ostracism and Louise showing her the ropes, shunning seemed a silly, empty punishment that made her want to laugh rather than be taken back into the fold.

She went to the closet, took down an armload of dresses and tossed them on the bed, then staggered back. "Jake!"

Jake perched on an elbow, stared at her through sleepy eyes. "Hello, sweetheart." He rubbed them, pinched the bridge of his nose. "Goin' somewhere?"

"I thought you'd be at church."

"You mean you didn't want to run into me. It's okay. Maybe we can talk now, since you're not takin' my calls." He cleared his throat. "I know I been a son-of-a-bitch. Never shoulda brought you up in Fellowship. The Reverend told me he'd handle everything so you'd come running back to me," he mimicked in a soft drawl, "like the good little Christian wife you are. I think he suckered me."

No, just brought things to a head sooner, she thought. "Is that why you're not at church?"

He winced. "No. I'm not feelin' so good."

"You're hung over!" Jake had his faults, but drinking was not one of them.

"Been hittin' it a little since you left." He smiled his little boy smile, squinting blue eyes over big white teeth. He turned on the bedside lamp, and shading his eyes, pointed at the ceiling light. She went to turn it off.

The dim light made the room morose, a reminder of many nights she would rather forget. Jake's shadow was thrown across the pale blue wall. She focused on his face, away from the muscled arms and torso.

He patted a place for her to sit.

"No, I've got to go. I just need a few things." She glanced at the closet.

"Jeez, hon, you treat me like I'm some kind of leper or something." He sat up, winced, then grinned. "You did this to me." It was the kind of smile that used to make her lose her grip on everything save carnal instinct.

She couldn't help herself, grinned. "You deserve it."

Again, he patted the mattress. She shook her head.

"It's a shame we come to this. Can't we work it out?"

Janey looked at her watch.

"Go ahead. Get all your shoes. No sense makin' another trip."

A part of her wanted to comfort him. Instead, she gathered some things off the closet shelf and the few pairs of shoes she owned. When she turned to stuff them into the sack, she caught her breath.

Jake stood, holding the bag like a fig leaf.

Damn! I should've known. She stepped back. "C'mon, Jake, quit playing games. I've got to go."

"You're the one playin' games." He placed the bag on the floor, his nakedness unavoidable now. "C'mere, baby, let's see if we can't work this out."

Shit! Should've run when I had the chance. She measured the distance to the door. An old fear shifted her heartbeat faster, faster.

"Did ya forget? I'm still your husband. Just 'cause you're taking a little vacation at your folks' doesn't mean we're not married anymore." He came at her.

Her insides turned to liquid. She broke for the door.

Jake lunged and his arm bit into her waist. He yanked her back into the room, tearing her fingers from the door jamb.

They wrestled roughly toward the bed. Panic tore through her, paralyzed her.

Janey screamed, "Jake! No!" He muffled her with a hand. She twisted against him, tried to jerk her arms free, but even with one arm, he held her with an incredible strength. Suddenly she felt hot with nausea. The thought of his touching her filled her with revulsion, of his being in her. . . .

They toppled onto the bed, Janey pinned under him.

"Stop it!" she screamed. He caught her wrists and laughed, which made her more furious, until her anger dissolved into tears. Breathing hard, he glared down at her, victorious.

She lay there, panting. *God, don't let him.*

To be raped by him again. A part of her was terrified of the violation. Then, a moment of calm enveloped a larger part of her. This would be the last time. She could see it, now. Finally, her ugly marriage would end.

He bent to kiss her. She turned away. His warm tongue wet the side of her face. She closed her eyes and lay still.

Straddling her, he put both her wrists into one hand and caressed her face. "You coulda had anyone. So pretty—classy."

Her voice was ice. "Classy? You mean I wouldn't go to bed on the first date."

The vivid blue eyes crinkled. "Yeah, there was that. But I mean the way you talked. So smart. Valedictorian. I was lucky to graduate." His hands played with her captive fingers and he whispered, "So how'd I get so lucky?"

His phony charm enraged her, and she yearned to wound him. "How does it feel, big man, to know you have to force your wife to be with you?"

With a dead calm, he studied her. He leaned down, close enough that she could smell his sour breath. She cringed, fear mounting as the long moments slipped by with Jake hovering just above her face. His blank eyes filled her with dread. Suddenly, he took her face in both hands, cheek covering her nose, and bruised her mouth with a long kiss.

Suffocating, she clawed at his back, until finally he pulled off.

She gasped, "You bastard!"

"Yeah, probably." He shifted his grasp to her wrists. "You played hard-to-get for the last time. Now I'm takin' what's mine."

"I'm not *yours*."

She struggled to keep her legs closed, but his thigh parted them easily. Lust made his breathing raspy. "I'm gonna take you to paradise. How 'bout it? Could be heaven."

The sardonic edge to his voice made her shudder.

Without waiting for an answer, he ripped off her panties. She squeezed her eyes shut and made her mind go somewhere else. For the last time. From far away, she felt herself shoved toward the bed's head, elbows and buttocks burning from the hard thrusting against the sheets.

A few hours later, Janey skidded down the steep bluff, lost her footing and half ran, half stumbled down the slope. She caught herself on a tree.

"Son-of-a-bitch, Jake, you son-of-a-bitch. Never again. Never. Never. Never!"

The rough bark stung her hands. It hurt to walk, to move. And it was dangerous to gather too much speed. Gingerly, she worked her way down the hillside, grasping branches of bushes and trees, pausing now and then to wipe her forehead, pull out her blouse at the neck, fanning it back and forth, trying to cool down.

The Spokane River roared below. She was taken by its magnificence, glistening, as if God were shaking out a blanket of diamonds. Trees stood out on the bluff above and the late afternoon sun threw shadows that covered the opposite bank with a wall of darkness.

Flinching from the soreness between her legs, Janey moved slowly.

"How could he do that? And think I'd ever come back to him?" she asked aloud. "How could I be so stupid? And how on earth did he get to me in the first place? Sure wasn't his brain."

So what did attract me? she wondered. *Danger? Breaking the rules?*

On the surface, Jake was devout, but underneath, a 'bad boy.' She had longed for a man who could take her outside the tight confines of Fellowship, family. Jake had been that vehicle. It wasn't long before he turned on her, though, when his ego became lost against her high-spirited intelligence, dissolving into impotence unless he was flailing her against her will, feeling savagery to feel anything at all.

Far below the bluff overlooking the Spokane River, Janey was a speck far away from Rathcreek in a dark valley cut into the thousand-year-old ravine.

At first he seemed so strong, she thought. *I guess I was like raw nerves. I felt everything. He was never out of control, so cool, never felt anything.* She picked up a stone, rubbed the jagged edge with her thumb, then threw it as far as she could. The water swallowed it, and moved on as if the rock had never existed. Jake was like that, swallowing her, then blaming her because she was no longer his light.

She stopped at an enormous fallen pine jutting into the river. Suddenly, she saw everything clearly: Jake made snide remarks about her, but he needed *her*. Needed her emotions, burning, painful, like fire, because it was impossible for Jake to ignite the fire. He couldn't, because he was not alive. He had nothing to do with life, but was a kind of death, trying to find life, in her.

"My God," she whispered, "for a year I've been raped by death."

Gnarled, exposed roots anchored the giant to the earth. Violence everywhere. Water rushed through the branches, eddying in the hollows of the tree. Smaller limbs were bent, or broken and gone; larger limbs, patches of bark beaten off, withstood the pounding of the swift current.

Janey climbed onto the log, arms out, walked along the trunk until she emerged from the shadow of the bluff above and reached the warmth of the sun. Water splashed her shoes, legs, soaked her skirt.

Feels good, she thought. Testing a limb, she sat, dangling her legs in the river. Water swirled, yanked her skirt, tangled it around her legs. She hiked it up—a scandalous lack of modesty by Fellowship standards—and smiled. She could be her own vehicle to danger, she supposed. The river splashed against her back, slapped the tough branches. She and the tree waited in the hot sun, cooled by the water.

"Janey!" Reverend Churlick held open the outside door to his study. "Your first appointment isn't till next week." His eyes narrowed. "Come in, child. What's wrong?" He helped her to a leather couch.

"Thanks." Janey sat down, spreading out the still-damp skirt, and surveyed the room to avoid him. His office was nothing like what she had expected. Dim, the only illumination the small lamp at his desk and narrow bars of sunlight through the blinds on the window. No pictures, other than one of Jesus on the cross which hung behind a large mahogany desk along with the minister's certificates.

"Are you all right?"

Gazing down, she shook her head. Shame burned in her; no matter that she had resolved a few hours earlier to confide in her preacher, she could not do it.

"Relax." He sat next to her on the couch. "Let's just talk. Is this something to do with Jake? You know it's not my job to blame. My job is to fix what's broke."

"There ain't no fixin' this, I'm afraid." She mimicked the soft Texas drawl of his that still lingered after twenty years away from the South.

He rose, walked around the couch and rubbed his hands, which made a dry, papery sound.

"May I?" He pantomimed massaging motions.

She shrugged.

His large hands were warm through her blouse, and the strong fingers worked her muscles, slowly pulverizing the knots of anxiety. Gently, he rolled her neck, hands working relaxation into Janey by the force of his fingertips.

"Oh, that feels so good."

"'Course it does." He smiled, returned to the sofa. "Muscles started out like concrete, now they're just plywood. You're one of the most intriguing members of my flock. But it does seem to me your stubbornness gets in the way. Like when you wouldn't speak in Fellowship?"

"Louise is every bit as stubborn. Do you think I'll end up like her?"

"Like Louise? No. She's not as smart as you, and she doesn't have your heart." He shook his head. "Louise thought she could get over your brother's death by makin' her own rules. But she didn't get over David, and now she's lost to all of us."

Janey knew it would have taken a miracle for things to be different. The sister she loved so much, and resented for going crazy, leaving it all up to her. The first born, Louise had always had pressure on her. *You're too rebellious. God commands girls to have submissive hearts. What would Jesus say if he saw those grades? You're the oldest, you should be setting an example for Janey and David.* Between the belt and the Bible, Louise was poised to rebel. For three years now, after David's death, her rebellion had taken the form of a mild schizophrenia. On her good days, she laughed too loud, had a few nervous tics and no government spies poisoned her food. On her bad days, there was so much Thorazine coursing through her system, she walked sideways.

Janey recognized that her job, now, was to be perfect, to make up for the psychological indiscretions of her sister. For Janey, unlike Louise, this was no chore. Out of a finely honed sense of idealism, the kind of pressure Janey routinely put on herself was what diamonds were made of.

"Must be a gift we Crownharts have. First David dies, then Louise goes loony. Now me, lost to the wages of unrepentant sin." Suddenly bitter, she asked, "How could David's diabetes be a sin?"

A shadow flickered across the minister's face. "You miss him, don'cha, hon? Me, too. I don't like losing one of God's little lambs. But who are we to question God's will?"

He retrieved his Bible from the desk. "Got two years for criminal mistreatment, but I'm not complainin'. Preached the gospel while I was in jail, even won over a couple souls. Truth is, your brother was to blame for his own death." He held up the book. "Faith healin's according to scripture. Seems to me if I had diabetes, I'd renounce my sin and allow the healin' power of Jesus to claim another victory. God knows we prayed till we were prayed out over that boy."

There was no sin about David that Janey could see. If she were the idealist, he was the innocent. There was something wholly good about her little brother's heart, even as nasty, mean and torturous as she knew a boy could be. As she'd told him once after a ferocious fight, *I love everything about you, Dave, even the bad stuff.*

Reverend Churlick sat on the arm of the couch. "But I have the feelin' you're not here about family. How's it goin' with Jake?"

The mention of his name made her aware of the dull pain in her groin. She shifted on the couch, to better see his reaction when she answered.

"I loved Jake once. I don't anymore." That was enough for a start.

Reverend Churlick reared back. He went to the window. In the harsh light, his hair looked blue black. "He hasn't exactly been careful of your feelin's, huh?" he asked, facing away. "Sounds like it's mighty close to bein' too late."

It is, it is, she wanted to say. But she knew what the Bible said about God hating divorce.

He strolled over. "A wife has special duties to a man—and for his part, he needs to be considerate. Then it's easy to love back. I know you're a very loving woman, I can tell these things. My Lord, if you were my wife . . ." He smiled. "But maybe the chemistry isn't workin' like it used to. Who's the real Jake? Have you really looked at him?"

From an inch away, a few hours ago, she thought. Too ashamed to voice her humiliation, she said, "Yes, I've looked into his eyes. They're cold as death."

He flinched at her bluntness. "Maybe you're not seein' his essence. Look at me." The playful grin, just for her. "I bet it's been a while since you looked at each other like the early days. Practice, okay? Now, I'm not your minister, I'm just a man. Can you see the real me?" He took her hands and rested them in his.

She stared, unwavering, into intense black eyes. Eyes so deep, she felt lost, as if they held the very last of all emptiness. A black hole that pulled things into it and devoured. Dark eyes fastened on her timid gaze until she pulled back.

"That wasn't so bad, was it? You're special, Janey, not just any parishioner. I've known it for quite a while, since before you were married. I think God has something special in store for you, and you're going to be blessed in ways you never imagined."

Three

Louise lay on her bed. Fingers laced behind her head exposed glistening, unshaved arm pits. "God *damn* it's hella hot for September. So, you gonna tell me what's wrong before I slip into a heat stroke?"

Janey lay on her bed, ankles crossed in the air. "Shhh. You want Dad in here?" She got up and switched the fan to high and stood listlessly in front of it, hair streaming out, then falling to her back as the blades oscillated.

Louise's room was a work of art in progress. Copies of *National Geographic* covers marched in perfect order around the upper edges of the walls. The rest of the room, a bright collage of magazine pictures and epitaphs: CAUTION: *Women at Work*; Through the LOOKing glass; Burn Your Romance Novels; Conceal Your Emotions; What the HELL Have You Been Smoking?? Forget About Slipping by UNNOTICED; Cult of Personality—CIA!!! It was childhood to chaos captured by art.

"As always, right again. It is stinkin' hot." Janey flicked off the wall switch and doused the room in a cooler half light.

She nodded at a magazine picture of a handsome man, arms resting on the back of a sofa, legs spread comfortably. "I always feel like I should wash my hands after touching that switch." He wore a huge smile and gazed at something out of view. The picture was positioned with the light switch situated in the crotch of the young man's slacks.

Louise prided herself on the art of vulgarity, an expression of her repugnance to the world's values, which were, she was fond of saying, sicker than she was. To Louise, obscenity was not off-color words, but a bloated, greedy corporate America underpaying people and justifying huge profits. Using the name of God in vain was so-called Christians doing dirty to others.

Louise glanced with a fond smile at the picture. She sat up, legs parted carelessly and dirty feet smudged sheets of the unmade bed. "Well? You gonna spill?"

Janey drew in a long breath. She wanted to open up to Louise, but was afraid. No, she couldn't turn back now.

For the past week, like a thick, rank smoke that ruined everything, she had thought of leaving The Fellowship. The church would never let her divorce her husband. No, the reverend would hate her and she couldn't bear that. Her father would never forgive, and that terrified her. Instead of relief now, thoughts of rebellion choked her.

"I'm going to leave Jake."

"Well, I'd like to know who's been sharin' my room the past month? I thought you already left him."

"Funny. I mean for good. I'm getting a divorce."

"Well, praise the Lord!" Louise beamed. "No good son-of-a-bitch! Never did like that sorry excuse for a husband."

Janey sighed. "You think I don't know what a mistake I made?"

"You only get one life—if you had to do over again, would you choose Jake?" Louise sat up straight. "You better say, hell no!"

"Yeah, but how am I going to do it?"

"What are you talkin' about?"

"Divorce him. I'm scared. What about Mom and Dad?"

"They'll live. We'll all live, hard as it is to believe."

"It's so selfish. The worst thing I've ever done." Twenty-one and divorced. The old sermons came up again and her stomach churned until she was sick with the feeling of failure. Shamed before God, the church and in her own eyes.

"Jee-zuz H. Christ, Janey! Quit torturing yourself. You made a mistake, huh? You're not the perfect Crown-heart after all, which I, personally, find refreshing." At her sister's silence, she said, "Well, I'm not married to him, so I don't have to be decent about it, but you go right ahead. One sorry son-of-a-bitch. I say good riddance and hallelujah!"

Louise wasn't even a legitimate test. An inmate in her own reality—chains of insanity rattling around her brain—naturally, she would back her. Telling Mom, Dad, The Fellowship, would be different.

Louise picked up her journal and a pen off the bedside table. "That man changed you. You packed part of yourself away when you got married." A sly look appeared. "I went underground, too, you know." Then she blurted, "Wanna know something?"

Janey looked up.

"CIA's definitely infiltrated The Fellowship."

"Oh, c'mon, Louise. You and your CIA."

"Man, Janey, are you blind? Don't be so naive. CIA's got 'em all right. Bunch a candy-assed holier-than-thou back stabbers. Serves 'em right." She laughed, too loud.

Janey walked to the closet and gazed at the dresses.

Louise glanced up from the notebook balanced on her knees. "Where you going?"

"Counseling appointment in twenty minutes."

"You sure as hell don't need the goddamn CIA breathing down your neck." Louise flipped furiously through the journal. "Don't you realize how strong you are all on your own? Remember how you did your commando thing at Dave's funeral?"

"What'd you do, write it down?"

"'Course. I record all the important goin's on in this family." She traced her finger over the page and laughed until the fit doubled her over. She wiped her eyes. "What a strong-willed little shit you were!"

Janey blushed, then giggled as only her sister could make her.

"That minister at Dave's funeral, the one that took over for Churlick when he was in the hoosegow. One thing I always wondered about. How'd you get the balls? Only eighteen, but out of all of us, you stopped it."

The memory emerged from behind its dark curtain. Janey said simply, "He cheapened Dave's death. He turned our brother's funeral into a circus. Get your salvation, get it while it's hot. *While every head's bowed and every eye's closed, anyone here like to give their hearts to Jesus? Nobody knows when their time will come, just like poor David didn't, God help him.*"

"*That* was enough to set Mom and Dad off," Louise said, then softly, "I'd never seen Dad cry before. So how'd you do it—you little goody two shoes?"

"I don't know."

"Oh, c'mon."

"No. Really. Sometimes you just get a feeling you can't put into words. You just know something's so wrong you've got to stop it."

"You, singular, get a feeling. Not everybody, little sister."

"Maybe we don't always listen to it. Anyway, I looked to see if anyone was buying. Nobody. That so-called man of God, running his alter call at David's expense, trying to scare us into salvation. It went on and on. It still makes me crazy."

Louise chortled, waggling the notebook in the air. "Just like Jesus an' the money changers." She read, "'Scuse me.' Suddenly every head was up and every eye in the place on you. You stood up. 'This memorial is about David. I'd appreciate it if you'd quit implying he's gone to hell, unless you've been there yourself and can talk to the fact.'"

Janey took over, "'Now young lady,' he says, 'I've been invited to speak, and I think . . .'"

Louise broke in, voice ringing out as it had in the church, "'No, you *didn't* think!'

"That stunned him," Janey said. "You couldn't tell I was so angry I was shaking?"

"No way. It was awesome." Louise's arm shot up. "A core of strength. Absolute core—they could sharpen tungsten on you."

Louise laced her fingers behind her head again and leaned back, ankle resting on knee. Her black soles seemed almost like the smooth veneer of leather. Sturdy ankles ran up to trim, tan thighs. "Power. Control, Janey. That's all the asshole wanted. Careful, Churlick's the same way."

Janey took a navy and white cotton striped dress from the closet and slipped it on. The fan's breeze hit her, stirring the light material against her calves.

She considered defending Reverend Churlick, thought about how helpful his counseling was. He had worked the truth out of her about her marriage, then, pronounced Jake guilty of some mistakes. The preacher was kind and understanding, and with his help she was building herself up out of the rubble.

But, she couldn't talk to her sister, they would only argue. Louise hadn't trusted Churlick since David's death. Her parents pardoned the reverend for his part; still looked to him as their spiritual leader. At eighteen, how could she love Mom and Dad and not do the same? Janey forgave and survived. David was dead. Holding grudges wouldn't bring him back. Louise couldn't forgive, and look what it did to her.

Janey slipped on sandals. Each woman existed in her dark privacy, the fan's rhythmic gusts the only sound. Louise scrawled on the page and Janey studied her.

Louise was solidly built, like their father. She had the Crownhart gray-blue eyes and their father's square Polish jawline. The fan's breeze riffled the pages of the journal and her hair, which she kept short because of dyes put into their shampoo by the CIA.

There had always been no nonsense and no giving in about Louise or their father. Now, studying her, Janey found herself wondering again about the perversity of someone so strong giving in so completely. When Louise took vitamins, she was functional; walking schizophrenia, Janey called it. Thorazine for emergencies. She'd learned over time, how not to aggravate her sister's paranoia, how not to be taken as the enemy. There were also the good moments, when they still related, and she cherished them.

Louise gazed up from her journal. "You lasted longer than I thought you would—with Jake, I mean."

"When have you ever known me to give up on love easily?" Janey took her keys from her purse. "You've got to keep this thing about Jake and me a secret. I can't stand for anyone else to know yet, okay?"

Louise smiled. "CIA couldn't pray it outta me."

"You mean pry?"

But Louise was writing again.

Logan Churlick measured water and iced tea mix into a glass pitcher, dumped in ice cubes and stirred with a long, wooden spoon. He placed the pitcher and two tumblers on a tray and carried them down the hall to his office.

Elbowing the door shut, he checked the lock, set the tray down and turned on the desk lamp.

A vase of lavender dahlias sat on the coffee table surrounded by professional journals and a small African fertility idol, a gift from a visiting minister. The coffee table, desk and book shelves shone from recent waxing. Logan approached the air conditioner, which was vibrating with a ferocious effort, and turned it down till it hummed.

Where was she? Forefinger and thumb cracked open the window blinds. The glare dazed him a moment, and he squinted. Heat made the ground shimmer. The blinds clinked shut. He picked up his Bible and settled onto the cool leather couch. Scanning the words, his thoughts wandered and the thin page trembled in his fingers.

Logan noticed he'd left the spoon in the pitcher, and leaned forward to get it out. He studied the spoon through the glass and ice and the amber tea. It looked warped, the wooden handle bent. Little bubbles had gathered along the handle. Removing it, he stuck it back under the edge of the sofa.

The thought of Janey left him vaguely uneasy, but he dismissed the feeling. In that one moment of clarity, that split second when everything crystallized into understanding, he chose to understand nothing but her. As if mind and monstrous conscience had sunk far beneath the surface of the amber water of the warped images. There was a time he might have seen things for what they were. But not for a long time now.

He recalled Janey's smell, an odor deliciously fresh, virtue mingled with the delicate acrid scent of perspiration, so sultry and challenging it made his mouth water. Each time she moved, her fragrance, warm and rich from the curves and hollows of her body, infused him with agony. Sometimes he would massage her—ah, the subtle rising and falling of her breasts when he kneaded her shoulders. Her skin, so cool and firm, her muscles, at first so taut, would give in, finally submitting.

Then there was the smile, radiant, holding nothing back. Chased by the glimmering laugh. The wry hazel eyes, incredibly alive eyes, so unlike Dolores'. He pictured his wife's faded blues, bleak with fear, empty. She always tried to hang him with those eyes.

In the beginning, he had rescued Dolores, like a knight, and that was enough. In the rescuing, something grew animated in him. But, eventually, the feeling turned into resentment at what he could have had. Her insipid giggle, the docile, imitative, dull conversations. His emptiness was fed by the knowledge that life without Dolores could have been a splendor.

His throat tightened and pulse jumped at the quick rapping at the outside door. He exhaled a low, nervous chuckle at his rubbery knees. The quick tapping again. Logan took a deep breath, breathing in a new world of possibility, a new existence. Now, splendor was before him.

Four

The thousand subtle manipulations of a religion are powerful. Even questioning and doubt are tricky ful-crums with which to break from a faith, because while they can spring the soul to freedom, they can also ensnare.

In the twenty years since Reverend Logan Churlick had founded The Fellowship, he had never known a woman ostracized from an element so integral to herself, yet who so retained her integrity. He had never known a woman like Janey Crownhart Powers.

Logan, knees inches from Janey's, blinked rapidly, like a string of flinches. "What do you mean, you'll think about it?"

Janey sat in the overstuffed chair, her youth, her quiet determination undoing him. The dim light of his study masked her expression until she raised her head to face him. Her hair, the room's light seeming to concentrate on its glory of flecked copper, slipped back to let him see those eyes. He trembled, staring back at a look of self assurance that scared him to death.

"I don't know if I want to come back to The Fellowship, even though the two months of shunning is over. Why should I? I mean, where does this leave me with Jake? In the eyes of The Fellowship, I'm still wrong, aren't I?"

He forced himself to speak, but it came out blustering nonsense. "Wrong? How could *you* ever be wrong?"

"I can't be a part of something not right. Jake's the one who needs to ask forgiveness. But that'll never happen. The Fellowship doesn't have a place for women who've been wronged. Our place is only to make men feel good, right or wrong."

She's changed, he thought, and cursed his part in it. He felt moist palms, along with the weight of the catastrophe he had begun in building her self esteem. He hadn't calculated on this tendency toward martyrdom and principle.

Logan picked up his iced tea as he considered what he stood to lose. Before, he had admired only her beauty, the carefree swing of her walk. And her emotional resilience. He had tested her during one of their sessions, asking how she would handle Jake's continual nagging about her appearance: the scar on her knee, her slenderness that could not be coaxed to the voluptuous look Jake had always coveted, the spray of summer-begat freckles across her nose she refused to cover with make-up.

She had laughed and said, "I gotta have some meat on me to be pretty? Louise called me a skinny lil' bitch the other day—a compliment. When Jake told me I was ugly and skinny and willful, it was his way of controlling me. But no more."

After two months of counseling Janey, the sound of her voice and laugh, coming to know how she thought and felt, addicted now to her magnificent, burgeoning strength, he knew he had to have her.

She was everything he could want. Gracious, intelligent, even deferential—but not submissive. The challenge of bending this woman to his will fascinated him. Now, gone?

How can she do this to me? He sat on the corner of his desk and took strength as he noted her growing discomfort. *This isn't easy for her. Praise God! Deep down she knows where she belongs.*

He struggled to breathe evenly while he tried to think. *Today's her last session. What if she won't come to church anymore? How will I see her?*

Giving up the only bright spot in his life, going on with no one but Dolores to fill the dark void? Unthinkable. His mind searched for the words to make her stay. If he had learned anything at all about Janey's abusive situation, it was that her soft heart was her greatest weakness. If he could just figure out how to approach her. Keep it low key so she would never sense how she had become a consuming need to him.

"You must be either the bravest sinner or weaker brained than I gave you credit for." He noted with satisfaction that the remark stung. "Sittin' there so calm, tellin' me you're giving up your God?"

"Not God," she answered, her look faltering, "just The Fellowship."

"Just The Fellowship." He paced. "Always starts out innocent enough.

You don't agree with church doctrine. Pretty soon you're hanging out with non-believers. Starts out with small sins, then you don't care what anyone thinks, and . . . "

"No!"

He had hit his mark. He almost went to her then, in his urgency to possess her. But he knew more hurt was necessary. He approached the couch, put his glass down and stood above her.

"After the habit's broke, you come back once in a while, out of guilt, but really, you're done." He bit off the words, "No better than one of those C an' E Christians."

The most detestable of church attendees, he had often ridiculed Christmas and Easter Christians from the pulpit as an affront to the church, with their hypocritical show of piety twice a year.

"It's a cruel, carnal world out there, Janey. An' what do you think is gonna happen? You think Satan's just gonna let you go? 'Course not. Just the fact that you're questioning right now, doubting. You know that's from the devil, don't you?"

She lowered her head and said nothing.

He wanted to dance around the room. Praise God for years of sermons. Those frightening messages could not be underestimated. In a solicitous voice he said, "I pity you. Not a shred of love in your life, Janey. Not from your father, who you've shamed, from your husband, who you've all but abandoned, or from me, who you've betrayed."

She shook her head, wearing an expression of wounded confusion.

"Bet it feels a little bit like Judas, don't it? I loved you like a father since you were a little girl. I always thought of you as my special one." His voice caught, and it surprised him how the words unlocked an ache, a picture of a kind-hearted little girl who was loved by all and who loved everyone; his Janey, his delight, skinny legs, arms around his neck, exuberant, high-pitched giggle, teeth too big for her small face, now gracing that smooth-skinned beauty of a woman who sat before him. Hope tormented him, and he longed for her now. "I always loved you, Janey. I thought you loved me, too."

"I do," she cried. "You know I do, Reverend Churlick."

Joy flooded through Logan's veins like a burning intoxicant. She loved him. He had known it, and now she said it for the first time. He would remember this moment forever: the broad bars of navy and white of the striped dress, the chestnut hair, the exquisite anguish he read in her face. He would never forget her shy admission of love, her surrender. Never.

Crossing his arms, he leaned back into the cool leather of the couch and said, "You have a funny way of showin' it."

Janey swallowed, trying to hold back the knot of grief that threatened to choke her. Shamed, speechless, she stared forlornly at Reverend Churlick, the quiet depth of his expression, brows slightly knit, eyes searching, wanting. With all his authority, he was appealing to her now with such gentleness and patience. And she, the cause of his sorrow. It was unbearable.

He took off his reading glasses and rubbed his eyes. Dark hairs covered the thick wrists. The material of his white broadcloth shirt strained at the shoulders. Solid fingers combed black hair from his forehead. He looked older than his forty years at that moment. But then, to Janey he was ageless. In the years she had known him, he had become mythic.

My marriage may be over, but how can I leave the church? I can't do it. I can't. Doesn't he understand how I hate Jake? He has to know that by now. How can I stay when the church won't allow me to leave Jake?

She made up her mind, then, to go through the final step of her shunning by making a public absolution in church Sunday. Above all else she could not stand the thought of hurting Reverend Churlick, or worse, that he might be angry with her.

Forearms on knees, he leaned forward and said softly, "Have I been wrong in loving you? Maybe I overstepped my bounds. Maybe I loved you too much."

"No! I mean, of course not. I wanted your love." She looked away, suddenly bashful. "It was good you were always there for—us."

If she could have told the truth, she was flattered, no honored, at his lavish attention over the years. Although he had a way with all children, he had chosen Janey, Louise and David to take on fishing trips and outings that their father thought expensive or a frivolous waste of time.

When Logan reached for her hands, his touch gave her a warm thrill. "That's all I can ask for. As long as we have love in our lives, we're livin' in God's grace. God's eyes are on us. He's pleased to see the deep, abiding love we have for each other . . ."

The voice filled her. The silence. His touch.

"My love for you is so deep, Janey. Inexpressible—absolutely inexpressible."

The look was so intimate, so starkly yearning, she was overwhelmed by a delicious confusion. A primitive gut reading, and suddenly, a stream of disquiet trickled through her happiness. That childish security she had always enjoyed in his presence was gone. She straightened and pulled back her hands.

He cleared his throat. "So. You goin' through with your repentance on Sabbath?"

She nodded.

"Good. That's my girl. It's important you finish this shunning up and come back into the fold. We'll worry about Jake later. We both know you had good reason for sayin' no to him. But denying a man's needs is one of the worst sins. An' this church stands behind him."

"Why does it have to be so unfair to women?" she cried.

"If a woman's not taking care of the needs of her man, it means she's not submissive to man, and if she's not submissive to man, how can she be submissive to God?"

She looked into his eyes, eyes like an ancient bird's, set back in hollows and shadows, reflecting the flat, black obdurance of his beliefs. They held a depth of understanding, ages of understanding.

"How can a woman commit her heart and will to such a big thing as obeyin' God when she can't even obey a man?" He asked. "That's your burden. Mine is to know how God would have me command you."

He leaned forward, body taut. "Do you trust me? To lead you in God's way?"

"Yes."

"Do you know how difficult this is for me? Knowin' all along the reason you couldn't repent was because you couldn't submit?" His gaze was preoccupied, remote. "And knowin' I'm the man," his look was sharp then, "I'm the instrument God wants used in teachin' you to submit?"

Janey pushed back her hair behind an ear. She took up her iced tea and drank deeply, staring at his features, bent by the rim of the glass. A vague fear settled over her. Instrument? Despite the air conditioner, the room seemed close, as if the blast of autumn's Indian summer were pushing against the walls.

"I guess you can imagine what it's like bein' married in name only. Dolores an' me are so pathetically unsuited to each other. It's so hard on a man, livin' like brother and sister. She's a good person and all, but she's like a little girl. Everything's kittens and puppies, know what I mean?"

The confession surprised her. Why was he telling her this? She nodded, uncomfortable at being put in the position of her minister's confidante.

"At last it all makes sense. You with your pain and me with mine." He smiled, tearful, so that he blinked rapidly, bird-like, crepey-thin folds of skin puckering around smiling eyes.

He said solemnly, "All our years of pain—your pain and my pain—have led us to this, Janey. I see God's plan now. He's given me the answer."

His shaky voice faltered. The face, unmoving, except for the ridiculously toothy grin, as if the smile's intensity were enough to carry her along, enough to make her leave reason behind. But his gaze held her: intense, compelling, an expression more ancient than a bird's. Reptilian.

"Don't be scared, Janey, don't be scared. God's guiding us now. You can feel it, can't you? My love—and the power of Jesus?" He touched her, his fingers lingering.

The room suddenly seemed airless. What at first had been fascination gave way to a frightening awe. Frightening, because she felt herself responding to the power of God, and to the power of this man. She could not help herself. Both excited her, entwined as they were. Crazy. Her breathing was shallow. She shrank back into the bulk of the chair, afraid of wanting what he was suggesting.

He fell to his knees, took her hand and pulled her down to the carpet where they both knelt. A cool, musty breeze moved around them.

"Father, we know Your eyes are on us, now. If it's Your will, use me, Lord, to help this woman, teach her the yieldingness she lacks. Help me minister to her, Lord, so she can find her way back to the path of righteousness. Help her give up her will to Yours. And let it be with a willing heart, Father. In Jesus' name we pray, 'n the Father, the Son an' the Holy Ghost."

Logan stroked her hair with a trembling hand. She shivered.

"Hallelujah, praise Je-sus. Je-sus, Je-sus," he said in a teary voice.

Then he was pulling her to him, and she let herself be led, incapable of arguing with the divine authority he wore, or with the resonant voice that vibrated her blood and bones and the air she breathed.

"Thank you, Father. That's right. Let me hold you a minute. Jesus loves you. An' I've loved you so long. All for this moment."

Something in her fought the mesmerizing softness of the deep voice. *Oh, God. What's happening? What am I doing?* She shuddered, then struggled against him.

"No! It's not right. We shouldn't be . . ."

"Don't you see, Janey?" he cried, face bright with conviction. "Even if it was wrong, in God's eyes, the worse our sins, the bigger His forgiveness." He licked dry lips. "But it's not. I know it's no good for us to fight this. You hafta learn submission, and God wants you to learn it from me."

Kneeling there in the dim room with his arms around her, she could no longer manage to make the right response. She couldn't deny he'd made her want him, fiercely, like an animal with its nostrils flared, catching a scent that brought juices to its mouth, strength to its legs. Suddenly, she did not know why the image should come to her just then, but she thought of Jake. Their last time together. She tried to imagine what he would do if he knew she were with Logan Churlick. If he knew she were with someone who could really love her.

Tears welled in her eyes. A small voice whispered that it was wrong. It was wrong, she knew it was wrong. She quieted the voice to hear Logan's. He was right in the only thing that mattered. She longed to be loved. It was all she ever wanted.

He whispered, "You are the most beautiful, perfect woman I ever laid eyes on. Jake never saw that. He couldn't love you the way you deserve. I love you, Janey. I've always loved you."

He loves me. Logan Churlick loves me, she thought in wonder.

"Janey?" Tentatively, he tightened his embrace.

For a long moment, she was perfectly still, as she had been during his most disturbing sermons. Fire. Eternal damnation. If she was perfectly still and not afraid, God would tell her what to do. Her Heavenly Father loved her. Logan wanted to love her now. He gazed down at her, holding his breath, fear of her refusal standing out in every line of his face. That tender yearning, almost a submission of its own, made it possible for her to yield. Solemnly, almost reverently, she yielded.

"My God, my God," he murmured, staring at her as if she were something sacred. "Such a woman — a gift from God. You're everything to me, Janey. Everything."

She gave herself completely to the way he needed her, loved her, had always loved her. She lifted her face to him. Hungrily, he kissed her mouth, her neck, the curve of her breast, leaning her onto the couch. His grazing mouth rained relentlessly over her until her mouth obeyed. His palms caressed her breasts gently, worshipfully.

Janey could do nothing but submit. His desire raised her own fury of desire to an unknown plane, a different mode of existence. Taboo. Rage against her husband. God's will. And the drunken mystery of the flesh. These were the elements of her world now.

Five

For a while, Janey convinced herself of the rightness of her love and Logan's. Long enough to be welcomed back to The Fellowship at the following week's service. Just long enough to rebuff Jake's "Welcome back." But the hypocrisy, facing Logan, facing her God in His house, she couldn't go again after that day, and so for almost three months, had stayed away.

At night, a sharp, relentless dread would haunt her with images of Churlick's dark study, the tangle of flesh, the leather couch and the odor of sex.

Vivid dreams often woke her, sobbing, from her sleep. One, particularly frightening, she dreamt over and over again.

She was water skiing, leg muscles sore, hands cramped. As she prepared to drop, something from the green-brown water bumped her.

Crocodile.

Screaming, she cut hard, trying to shake the beast. He angled sharply, cavernous jaws coming to devour her.

The boat racing toward shore. The closer she drew, the more desperate the croc, his burning breath inches from her calves. Rubbery legs, heart pounding. Numb fingers clenching the line. Terror beating down fatigue.

Finally, close to land. The crocodile, like a razor, slashed her thigh. She screamed, clutched her leg, hot blood spilling through her fingers. Slick red trail, like oil, on water.

Land would save her.

Ropes of blazing lights, criss-crossing the dunes and pampas grass. A streak of black lightning. In its wake, smoke, then the rasping, crackling sounds of grass bursting into flame. The roar of fire, like a thousand voices.

Then she saw the snake. Fire in his wake, he blazed to position himself where she would land. The boat raced and made the snap to propel her to shore.

"No!" she cried. "Oh my God!"

The length of rope snapped taut. She had to make a decision, but couldn't grab at any thought to save herself.

"You gonna finish that, hon?" her mother asked.

Janey yawned and irritably pushed away a half eaten piece of toast. "I'm not hungry." A feeling of impending annihilation remained of the nightmare, and when such times were upon her, it was all she could do to be civil.

"You feeling all right?"

Mary's soft voice filled her with apprehension. Did she see through Janey? She tried to act normal, but it was an effort. Everything she did seemed weak, insubstantial. Her guilt, the only reality.

"Maybe I should ask the reverend out for a layin' of hands."

"No," Janey said, voice sharper than she intended, "there won't be any laying of hands on this Crownhart." Then seeing her mother's expression, she softened. "I'm fine, really, just a little stomach bug. Nothing to bother Reverend Churlick about."

Mary scrutinized Janey a moment, then spooned honey over hot oatmeal. "Do you feel good enough to come with us to the clinic protest?"

Before Janey could answer, Louise shuffled in, scratching her thigh. She wore a satin bed jacket and woolen leggings. Taking a bowl from the cupboard, she felt under the lip, then turned it over and examined it thoroughly. She exchanged it for another and went through the routine again. Finally, one pleased her.

"Breakfast of champions!" she chirped, pouring milk over Wheaties. Nose raised, she sniffed the pungent odor of coffee, and asked, as she did every morning, "Got any—java?" The pause, the slightly bemused grin, inspection of the cup before pouring coffee, was vintage Louise.

"Actually," Janey said to her mother, "since I've been allowed back into service, it feels strange. I haven't gone because I don't feel like I belong anymore."

"Honey, that's not true."

"All I knows," said Louise around a spoonful of cereal, "is that she's been clean of the GDA couple months now."

"GDA?" Mary asked.

"God Damned Agency."

"CIA," Janey clarified.

"Louise!" Mary said with half-hearted indignation. She turned to Janey. "Is it because you'd see Jake there?"

Janey had an opening, and Louise for support, such as it was. Now was the time to let her mother in on her decision to divorce Jake. She tried to organize her thoughts, but found she suddenly had to have a cup of coffee. Strong, black coffee. Such an unnatural hankering. In the past, if she drank coffee at all, it was with plenty of cream and sugar, more a hot milkshake than the fine, acrid jolt she now craved.

Pouring herself a cup, she returned to the table. "I've never really told you much before, Mom, but Jake wasn't very good to me." She let her hand drift over the worn table. The texture of the raised grain seemed new to her, though she'd sat at the table thousands of mornings.

"Did he hurt you?"

Janey lowered her eyes. "Sometimes, if I wouldn't do what he wanted, especially, well . . . he never beat me up or anything. He didn't have to. He's a man, Mom, he can intimidate me with a look."

He crushed any shred of happiness I could've felt as his wife. He raped me—she shuddered—*and enjoyed it.* She knew she could never be honest about such things with her mother.

"What is it?" Mary asked. "Is this what you've been so upset about?"

Her mother's perception startled Janey. So her turmoil was apparent. "No good son-of-a . . ."

"Now, Louise, Jake may have his problems, but he's still Janey's husband."

"Mom," Janey whispered, "I'm trying to tell you something. It's important."

She looked over her shoulder at the kitchen doorway. Her mother waited, lips pursed in the way she had of taking in bad news.

Her voice cracked. "I'm not going back to Jake. I'm getting a divorce."

Mary Crownhart stared at her daughter as if the word hadn't registered, or perhaps was not in her vocabulary. Then, she looked horrified. "My Lord! My Lord, Janey, you can't. We've never had a divorce." She wrung her hands. "Honey, it's a sin. God hates divorce." She clutched her worn bathrobe at the throat and spoke as if to herself, "Lord, what'll The Fellowship do? Oh, Lord, your father . . . "

In the heavy silence that followed, Janey thought, *If you only knew, Mother. Divorce is just half my problems. Adultery, divorce—how much more damned can I be?*

She let her gaze travel over the kitchen, the painted white cupboards, bright yellow countertop, the chip in the kitchen sink where she'd dropped a heavy frying pan when she was ten. In the corner stood the water heater wrapped in thick insulation. Somehow, now, it all seemed small.

"I'm just trying to survive. Everything's changed. I'm going to do this."

"Cut the asshole loose," Louise grumbled. "Sorry excuse for a husband."

"Now, Louise," Mary said. "Dear, you gotta give it a chance. You gotta start seein' Jake again. Prayin' over it."

Janey stared at her. "M—" she started, but the word in her mouth felt thick, the lips over teeth seemed exaggerated in the effort to bring them together to make sound. She started to break up. Gulped air. Tried again. "This marriage is killing me," she whispered. "My soul. You don't know how desperate he makes me feel."

Mary glanced nervously at the doorway.

Anger, guilt and self reproach boiled up. "Don't you do this to me, too. I expected it from Dad, but not you. You're all I've got against the world, Mom, against The Fellowship." She wiped at tears that sprang to her eyes. "There's nothing a child can do to make her mother give up on her, is there? Isn't that what you've always taught us? Even if I make the wrong choices, terrible mistakes, you'll always love me. Isn't that right?"

With shallow breath, Janey watched her mother's silent struggle.

Eyes lowered, Mary shook her head.

Janey's chest felt empty, as if the life in it had dried up.

But then, finally, Mary raised her solemn face and nodded. Janey stared at her in disbelief. The tears in her mother's eyes broke her heart. The whole of her life seemed at that moment to come down to a nod of her mother's head. And written in Mary's eyes, eyes that were strangers to heresy, was the full knowledge of the serious breach this mother was committing against her church by siding with her daughter.

Mary's eyes flickered over Louise. "Some of us get so broken, we don't get fixed, no matter how much we pray." She whispered, "I don't want you to break."

Numbing bliss flooded Janey then. She had always thought of her mother as a simple woman with black-and-white beliefs. The depth of such a faith. Janey didn't want her mother to have to choose, but of course, she must, and that choice was what made the sacrifice so reverent.

Throat tight, Janey reached across the table and took her hand. "Thank you, Mom. I hope I can be as good a mother someday."

Mary smiled, squeezed her hand. She glanced at the clock on the stove. "Lord, look at the time. I better get your dad out of bed or we'll miss the demonstration." She rinsed her bowl. "He'll be mad at me if he took a day off work and I let him oversleep. Reverend was counting on us being there, and he 'specially asked us to bring you, Janey, since you been missing service." At the doorway, she stopped. "You coming?"

"Yes, ma'am!" Louise saluted. "Wouldn't want to miss the Lord's army against poor pregnant women gone astray."

Mary's look shifted from Janey to Louise, then back to Janey.

Guilt exploded in the pit of Janey's stomach. She swallowed; nausea, the bitter aftertaste of coffee. She panicked at the thought of facing Logan.

Questions she had asked a thousand times raced through her mind. *Why? Why did I do it? How could I be so weak?* And the unanswerable, *How could he?* She was not sure which was worse, fear of being found out, or fear of succumbing to him again. For nearly three months now, that one mistake defined every living moment.

She sighed. "I'll come. To keep Louise company."

Churlick stood in the back of a pickup truck and barked through a megaphone. "How will these misguided women answer God when He asks what happened to the soul He entrusted them to bring into the world? How will we answer when He asks us why we stood by and watched it happen?"

At the rear of the group, Janey stood with Louise. Despite the cold, she was uncomfortably warm. Try as she would, she could not help being moved by the passionate voice. His pleading filled her with the memory of a tormented, hungry desperation to reclaim his manhood in her. For that, she could almost forgive him. It was cloaking his desire in God she could not forgive. Over the weeks, she had come to realize this man of God and his self-serving ministry simply used the Almighty to sweep aside her resistance. Churlick had carefully dictated only one choice for her.

"Ours is a vengeful God. Nuthin' will save us from His fury if we turn our backs and do nuthin' to keep this abomination from happening."

A gust of wind tugged at Churlick's coat and he shoved his hands into his pockets. "Let us pray." Thirty or so of The Fellowship huddled in the brisk November air, protecting their placards from the shifting wind. His deep bass voice raised in prayer resonated torment in Janey. Once a call to faith, now it was a reminder of lost virtue, but to the crowd, her parents included, it was a beacon in a sinful world.

When the crowd sang "Washed in the Blood of the Lamb," hands waving in the air, Janey noted for the first time how ridiculous they looked. Some, fingers extended toward the heavens like divine antenna picking up God's signal, others like a confab of waiters, palms up, hoping for the Father to fill their platters. Her new-found irreverence still felt strange, but she couldn't help herself, in fact did not want to. How ironic, she often thought, that she had lost her faith in God through a man of the cloth.

Louise nodded to Janey. "Sinner at three o'clock. They'll be nabbin' her any minute now."

A young woman lowered her head against the stiff current of the wind as she made her way past the group toward the entrance of the Spokane Women's Medical Clinic. The crowd's clamoring rose, and at Churlick's direction, they closed in.

Churlick jumped down from the truck, but instead of joining his soldiers of God, he caught sight of Janey and Louise and began making his way toward them.

"Janey, good to see you," he said. "Hello, Louise. Haven't seen you in a while."

Louise's hand flew up to the brim of her fedora to guard it against the wind. "Probably because you banned me from service. You kicked me out, remember?"

Churlick blanched.

The momentary fear made him a little more human, loosened his grip on Janey's slippery nerve. But knowing that he was human did not calm her, it merely made her wary. He looked uncertainly from Louise to Janey, a wan smile plastered over his discomfiture, then gazed up at the leaden sky. "Good day for a protest, isn't it? Guess it's always a good day for doin' the Lord's work."

A gust caught Louise's hat, and she snatched at it, but missed. Like a Frisbee, it sailed away. She chased after it, grumbling loudly, "Goddamn CIA."

Reverend Churlick seized the opportunity, and casually, as if discussing church business, took her by the elbow, until they stood sheltered from the wind between cars and trucks parked in the grassy field next to the clinic.

Logan opened his mouth to speak, then paused. Tall and strong, he seemed unbalanced by a sudden awareness of what a pathetically weak position he was in. This vulnerability saved Logan. Janey had contemplated leaving him without a word, but at the sight of his silence, pity stopped her.

He took her hand in his moist palm.

She jerked it away. How could he assume he had the right to touch her, when she had avoided him for months? Did he have no decency? His possessiveness galled her.

"Where you been? I-I missed you at church."

"Good God, Logan! I can't believe. . . . You just think. . . ."

"Wait-wait! Just hear me," he begged. "Never in my life have I felt the way I have with you. Never gave better sermons, never touched people's lives so profoundly. It's all you, Janey. I'm nothing without you. An' since that day we were together, well, I'm just dyin'. I don't hear from you. You don't come to church anymore. I don't know anything except you're all I ever wanted. All I ever needed."

In a coarse whisper, she replied, "I've never felt worse, Logan. Can't eat. Can't sleep. I take showers with the water turned up full blast, trying to wash until I feel clean again. But I can't. I can't wash away how dirty I feel."

"It's Dolores, isn't it?" he said, not skipping a beat. "I'll get rid of her. She means nothing to me. It's you, Janey," he said, taking her by the arms. "I have to have you."

Shocked, she backed away. He hadn't heard a word. He only said what he thought would sweep away her objections. His callous reference to his wife appalled her. Where was his remorse? After twenty-odd years of marriage, did Dolores mean so little to him? And what about The Fellowship's sanction against divorce?

"Get away from me! Where's your conscience? Don't you ever feel anything a normal person feels? I can't even bring myself to be around you, knowing we've been intimate . . ."

"What the hell's goin' on here?" Louise bellowed at Janey's elbow.

"Louise! How long you been there?" Churlick asked.

"Long enough."

"Now, Louise, if you know what's good for you —" he started.

"You got nerve threatenin' me," she said. "Come out here today, gettin' Mom to do your bidding so you could work on Janey."

Churlick's face broiled into an open flame of hate, a look so intense, showing no fear of retaliation, that even Louise was shut up.

But before he could respond, two members of the congregation ran up. "Reverend! We need you." A man gestured at the woman outside the clinic entrance. Several of The Fellowship were standing hand in hand, barring her from the neat brick building. "What do we do?"

Churlick collected himself, then ran off without a look behind. Louise and Janey were silent a long moment.

Louise put her arm around her sister. "The reverend poked you? Why'd you let him do that?"

"I-I thought I . . . I don't know. I really don't."

Gusts buffeted them. The clear sky of morning had forsaken the day. Wind was rounding up clouds, corralling them into a gray bank of thunderheads.

Janey pulled up the collar of her coat. "Let's go. I don't want to have to talk to him again."

"I'll just go tell Mom and Dad you weren't feelin' good after all. Simmons can take them home."

They drove in silence for a while.

"What're you gonna do now?"

"I don't ever want to see him again. I'm done with The Fellowship."

"No great loss, believe you me. Fellowship's not the only way to get to God. They'd like you to believe that, but it's a bunch of horse shit."

"Louise! You never talk about God anymore. What's all this? You still interested in making it to heaven? Without The Fellowship?"

Louise fixed her with a cynical look. "Trust me. We just moved up from coach to first class."

Louise, pursuing her private thoughts out loud, said, "You know, it's bad enough he got into your pants. How do you know he didn't get you pregnant?"

"Don't be ridiculous!" Janey snapped, stomach suddenly threatening again. She felt weak and small, as if the pool of her nausea had sapped all her strength. *I'm not! I can't be,* she thought, strands of fear winding through sinews, tightening around her mind until she couldn't think, until she was all wretched feeling.

Whenever the possibility of pregnancy surfaced in her mind, she shoved the tightness away. By the time Louise spoke again, the possibility would not leave her alone.

"Hey! What about this stomach flu? It's been more than a week with no appetite." Suddenly, a schizophrenic intensity leapt from her startled gray eyes. "When was your last period?"

"Shut up, Louise! Just shut up!"

Louise raised her eyebrows. "All right, sure. Everyone loves a surprise."

"My God, Louise! I can't be, I can't. After just once? How is that fair?" She hid her face in her hands, temples pounding, and a sob rose in her throat, guttural, full of fury. "My God, don't do this to me! Please don't let this happen to me."

Louise let her cry. She drove past the Lion's Club sign welcoming visitors to the town of Rathcreek. Before they reached the street that would take them home, Louise pulled up to the drug store. She left the car idling while she ran inside. When she returned, she handed Janey a bag containing a pregnancy test kit.

When they arrived home, Janey headed directly for the bathroom. For a while, she read the directions, but nothing registered. Finally, she called Louise in to help, followed the simple steps, and with her moral support, waited for the results in the kitchen. Resting chins on hands, they watched the litmus betray Janey.

"No!" Janey hid her face in her hands and wept.

Louise touched her arm. "What're you gonna do?"

Janey wiped at tears. "I'll tell you one thing. I'm not having his child." A sob caught. "I don't know how, but I'm not having his child."

Louise's mouth opened, then snapped shut. "How? Holy shit! You talkin' about abortion? You thinkin' of going to that clinic we were at today?"

"I'm going to do it, Louise, don't try to change my mind. I'm going away and never coming back. Someplace where no one can find me. I can work. I can take care of myself."

"Sure you can."

Janey slumped over the table. The enormity of leaving made her stomach plummet.

"How much you got saved up?" Louise asked.

"Not much," she admitted.

"We'll figure out how to get you money. We can get the money," Louise said. "But you can't do this alone, Janey. It's too hard to go through alone."

Her laugh was brittle. "I have a whole lot of choices, don't I? Who? Mom? Dad? They'd never believe me if I told them the reverend got their little girl pregnant. That's if I survived Dad. Then Mom'd probably have Churlick over to lay hands on me, anoint me again with his holy oil."

Louise tried not to laugh, hands over her mouth, but she failed. Her too-loud laughter filled the room, and rang against the silence. Then her eyes snapped naughty and bright. "Hey! I got it!"

"What?"

She went for the address book. "Someone who's wicked enough to help you."

"Who?"

Louise grinned conspiratorially. "The black sheep of the family."

Six

That Sunday, the angry dawn broke ranks with the night. An icy Canadian wind drove black clouds across the Rathcreek sky, and a cold, hard rain rapped on windows and roofs.

Janey packed some clothes in an old suitcase.

Louise watched. "You're gonna go to Churlick's turf?"

"I have to."

"There are no have-to's unless we make them ourselves," Louise said mildly.

"I told you. I can't just leave without saying good-bye to everyone that's ever meant anything in my life. I can't just leave my past behind like it didn't exist." She threw shoes into the suitcase. "I'm not going to let him take that away from me, too."

Louise fished something out of her pocket. "Good. Here."

She held a gold ring that was thin as the carpet thread in her mother's sewing basket. But the stones were a brilliant design of rubies and diamonds.

"Louise! Where did you get this?"

"It was Grandma's. She gave it to me 'cause I'm the oldest. You oughta be able to hock 'er and get enough to help some."

"I can't take this, it's yours."

Blue-gray eyes regarded Jane with exasperation. "You can't? You can't? What else can't you do today?"

Janey waited.

"I've about had enough whining, haven't you? What is it going to take? I really could give a shit whether you go off and have an abortion or have this baby and name him Junior, but you'd better not get passive in my face any more.

"Sometimes you gotta throw a brick and break the pane, just to be. You better know, really know, what it takes to be alive, before you choose *can't* all your life."

Her sister's words pumped adrenaline directly into her blood, her lungs. Breathing hard, Janey knew she was right.

Louise dropped the ring in her palm. "If you don't take this, I swear I'll sneak over and drop it in The Fellowship's collection plate."

Janey closed her fingers around it. She embraced Louise, burying her face in the stale odor of her hair. For the most part, since her illness, hygiene was lost on Louise. Janey was simply thankful she was herself today: hard, cynical, saying aloud what Janey had always secretly believed were the mysteries of her mental illness.

"Better get going. I don't want to be late for church." Janey took down the last garment hanging in the closet and, with grim determination, made herself ready.

The church was bedecked with pointsettias, children's artwork of baby Jesus in His manger, and donated food for the needy. Despite the storm outside, the festivity, the closeness of times past with these people she loved, the overwhelming nostalgia in this final Sunday before Christmas almost made Janey regret having come.

Janey squeezed her best friend's hand. She and Margie sat in a pew as far from the pulpit as they could get, hoping to go unnoticed by Churlick. But his gaze roamed over the congregation, as if by ritual, until he found her. His face broadcast the shock of finally seeing her again after three months.

His reaction affected her more than she thought it would. First, because she did not want to know again, undeniably, that he had been waiting for her to return, as he knew she must. Second, it was plain he still wanted her. But, also, because her self assurance—perhaps only daring masquerading as self assurance—vanished. Every nerve screamed for her to leave. If Margie's hand were not in hers . . .

Dolores began, like a switch turned on by her husband's slight nod, playing a piece of music, low and moving. The melody repeated, louder, over the thunder and the wind's howling. All together, the storm, the music, the singing, rattled the hollow doors of the church. Then, the sermon began.

"Sounds like a war out there," Churlick said, pausing to hear the steady rainfall. "Let's talk about silence in here. God's word. In First Corinthians 14:34, God spoke to Paul. 'Let your women keep silence in the churches; for it is not permitted unto them to speak. They are *commanded* to be under obedience, as also saith the law. And if they will learn anything, let them ask their husbands at home; for it is a shame for women to speak in the church.'"

Janey glanced at Margie, who gazed ahead. Rain pounded the roof, then a thunderous concussion shook the building. The sermon went on, but Janey paid little attention. She noticed a discolored ceiling tile, its lacy design of concentric brown rings. She tried to see the roiling storm through the window, but there was no seeing out the narrow panes, the stained glass yielded nothing but a dim ghost. Eerie, to feel so separated from the natural world.

Strange to be in church at all. Besides wanting to avoid the man himself, her metamorphosing beliefs kept her apart from The Fellowship. Once the crack in her beliefs began, it widened rapidly, as if by its own natural law. She now saw divine order with a cynicism clear as any heathen's.

Part of her mind wandered over her plan to leave Rathcreek that day. She had come to service only to see her friends for the last time. Safety in numbers. Churlick would not dare approach her today.

Churlick removed his glasses. "I don't know why God led me to that passage, but He always has a purpose. I wasn't sure I even understood it. I thought to myself, the women of The Fellowship will never go for this!"

"Amen!" a young woman in her pew interjected. Janey smiled.

The lights dimmed. Rain drummed on the stained glass. Churlick searched the ceiling as if to find inspiration, then crooked his finger at Dolores, and she came to stand beside him.

"I value women's opinions. Kinda gives a fella a little perspective — amen?"

"Amen!" shouted the congregation on cue.

"So I asked my wife what she thought of this passage." He waved her to the pulpit. "Honey, why don't you tell them? You say it best."

Dolores approached the podium. She wore a pleated pastel skirt, a neat blouse and matching sweater, and as she gazed out over the congregation, her stooped shoulders belied her fear. For a moment, she looked shrunken against her husband's power. She brightened, then, too bright, a powerless woman basking in her moment of power.

"I guess what I'd have to tell you is just what me and Logan have been talking about. Why would God want women silent in the church? He asked me how I would be able to accept such a thing. I think we got it figured this way: it's not just that God wants women silenced. He wants men talking. It's a way to keep our men involved in the church. You see, women just have a natural tendency to talk . . ."

Churlick's hand shot up, puppet-like. "Yada, yada, yada, yada."

The congregation chuckled.

The artificially soft, high-pitched voice made Dolores sound more like a child than a middle-aged woman. " . . . and if we're talking, men can't get a word in edgewise. Give us half a chance, and we'll take over the church. Where does that leave our men?"

Resentment grew in Janey with every word. As if that kind of power could ever fall into the hands of the women of The Fellowship. The irony of mousy Dolores proposing such a possibility, discussing the merits of women taking power by talking.

Dolores said with fervor, "We say we want our men to stop drinking, we say we want them to spend more time with the family—amen?"

"Amen!" came the rousing chorus.

"We want them to follow God—amen?"

"Amen!"

"Why should they, if their authority, their rightful place at the head of the church is usurped? If women submit and are silent the way the Bible says, the message is loud and clear they're needed to run the church. And God'll come into their lives."

Then she prayed, hands raised, words spilling from her, face ecstatic. She stepped down, eyes averted, humble, and in a moment, music surged through the chapel. Under Churlick's guidance, voices rose. "Lead me, lead me to a rock that is higher than I."

Janey watched the singing, smiling faces and shuddered. The idea of these people—all friends and family—embracing such a sham made her feel sick. And the women, not one of them self assured enough to cause a man to be uneasy. Especially Churlick.

Then it hit Janey: only her self assurance was a threat. Her senses fluttered between revulsion and addiction to the scene around her. Watching Dolores was like watching a prostitute doing dispicable things, betraying her sex, because she was paid. A thought stopped her. She had been paid by Churlick, too, hadn't she?

What am I doing here? she thought. *What was I thinking? That I could just sit through this bullshit and not feel anything? Just come and say my goodbyes? I can't. I can't anymore.*

Churlick descended from the platform and mingled among the pillars of the church in the front row of pews. He sang and clapped, smiled, rested a hand on their arms, whispered to one person, nodded to another.

"Lead me, lead me —"

Was this the same man who had gasped in ecstacy, who had shuddered in her arms? Was she the same woman? She, too, had been whispered to, and felt the warmth of his approval. She had been transported by his powerful magic. Now all she could think of was that she'd like to tell them all what the real Churlick was like.

She wanted to deliver a sermon of her own: *I see God's light without Churlick's help. I trusted the slimey message he fed me. Now it's growing in my belly. He's replaced your common sense, just like he did mine, with an oozing rhetoric, mindless submission. Can't you see?*

Churlick said, "I hafta agree with Dolores. It's a battle to keep men interested in The Fellowship. Because we haven't been followin' God's plan." A thumb jerked to his chest. "That's when I always get in trouble, when I think my plan's better'n God's."

Good-natured laughter answered.

As he waited for quiet, he zeroed in on Janey, staring until she felt her pulse rise.

"As Christians, we hafta believe every word. Every 'i' dotted an' every 't' crossed, isn't that what God tells us? Not just some of the Bible, but all of it. Amen?"

"Amen!"

"I've prayed about this, asked God to guide me in the way He would have us go. I trust God to lead us. Do you?"

"Amen! Hallelujah! Yes! Praise Je-sus!"

Churlick spoke in the practiced voice of a leader, deep bass of authority which would not be questioned. Benevolence in his look, his gestures. "I believe with all my heart that God led me to these scriptures, and as shepherd of this flock, I have to lead you. So here it is: women will maintain silence in service."

There was no turmoil, no questioning. The air was heavy and still in the church. Outside, the wind was sighing, pushing, nosing around the building. Trees creaked and groaned, and a little crashing explosion of shingles accompanied the roar of thunder.

Shortly, a murmuring mounted, as wives turned to their husbands and daughters looked quizzically to their fathers. Soon, quiet returned.

Stunned, Janey glanced around her, waited for dissent. In the answering stillness, Churlick's eyes, bright with disdain, captured hers. His amused, hard look said he knew she was not caught up in the hocus-pocus.

The proud angle of his head, the self-righteousness were to hurt her. She knew it instinctively, and understood, then, that his victory was hollow. In his face lurked the most terrifying of hungers. Still powerful, he could not have the only thing he wanted.

He stared at her. "It is a shame, from this day forward, for any woman to speak in church."

Is this for me? she wondered, astounded. *Silence Fellowship women to keep me quiet? He's doing this so I can't tell them about us!*

Her eyes stung. It was as though he'd struck her. A gag—or perhaps punishment for rejecting his love. The idea of this catastrophe befalling the women of The Fellowship—her mother, all her friends—as her legacy, needled through her brain.

Suddenly, she was on her feet, feet on holy ground doing holy work, feet that took her slowly, dream-like to the front of the church.

Churlick reddened and bellowed, "Mrs. Powers, sit down! Sit down, I said!" In a rage, he pounded the podium and ordered her father to do something.

"Janey!" Joe Crownhart shouted. "So help me, sit down!"

Janey spoke in a hard, trembling voice. "I have something to say."

"Sit down!" Churlick roared.

Janey's voice rose over his and her father's. "I'd just like to say *good-bye.* I'm moving out of Rathcreek."

The news plunged the church members into new consternation. Janey pushed her hair behind an ear. She was close enough to see beads of sweat collecting on Churlick's forehead and nose.

With a rude laugh he said, "Naturally, you'd want to leave, now that the heat's on. Now that it takes some kind of courage to be a real Christian woman."

"Courage? That's what it takes to walk out of this place, which is what I'm doing now." She turned to go.

"Of course," Churlick said.

Joe Crownhart stood again. "I'm sorry, Reverend. I don't know what's got into the girl. Janey, you get back here. Reverend Churlick doesn't deserve that kind of disrespect."

She slipped totally out of control. "Oh? What kind of disrespect does he deserve?"

Churlick answered with a derisive chuckle. "Only you would know."

Cheap and effective, the remark knocked the wind out of her. No one else could put meaning behind his tone; he had meant only her to read it.

Numbing outrage shook her. Before, she had only wanted to get out. Now, she only wanted to wound him.

"Oh, one more thing." She pushed her hair behind both ears. "I want to let you all know before I leave . . . I'm pregnant."

A confusion of grins and congratulations broke out around the chapel in response to the glad news of a supposed reconciliation. Jake stood, his features a puzzle of disbelief. In his look, Janey read that it was too long ago since he had taken her against her will. A man, all smiles, slapped Jake on the back. Another shook his hand.

She waited for the commotion to die down, then turned to Churlick, who stood before her, gaunt face reduced to dark, regal eyes that damned her. She pointed a trembling finger.

"And *he's* the father!"

Seven

Reverend Churlick, a tangle of emotions, stood paralyzed, mouth flaccid, until shock gave way to a kind of reconstitution. His slack lips pulled back, a taut rubber band of hate.

"Liar!" The word rang out. Churlick leaned over the pulpit trembling under his grip. His tongue touched dry lips, then another fiery, "Lies! She's bein' used by Satan!"

Janey stood there, finger pointing, numb. There was no sound from the membership, not a cough, not a rustle. Only the storm raging outside. Angry faces, frightened, confused. They waited for the punch line to this sacrilege, an explanation of such poor taste. She never thought she was a woman who would not stand by truth, but she could not speak further. She hardly knew how she'd gotten there.

Then, The Fellowship came to life. Confusion. Hostility. The shock and disbelief swaying between her and their leader. Finally, settling by the power and conviction of Churlick's presence. How dare she bring such filth into the House of God? A true exile, now, their yabble spewing forth, cleansing The Fellowship, banishing the filth of her.

Mouth opened to speak, she realized there was no talking over the congregation and the thunder that seemed directly over the building. She searched for support. Her father's expression was a chilling mix of mortification and contempt. Her mother's face was a study in suffering. She sought out Margie, Sandi, Sue, all solid friends. They looked anguished, confused, witnesses of heaven and hell colliding.

She stared at Reverend Churlick and saw he had recovered. Unsmiling, the color normalizing, his look hurt and accusing, an act. How could she have expected him to admit to his part in the craziness she had begun?

Oh, God, how she wished he would have taken out his wrath on her, rather than these people she loved. What could she do now?

Suddenly, Louise's words, her indignation, were with her. *You better know, really know what it takes to be alive, before you choose can't all your life. Don't you go gettin' passive on me.*

Strength returned to her heart, her lungs, her legs. Lightning flashed in through the stained glass. She turned and walked down the aisle.

Churlick's terror of her abandonment, his roaring need of her came out as divine authority, to everyone but her. "You better stay, Janey Powers! You're on shaky ground. A sinner can't do God's work in Satan's world."

"I'm *doing* what God wants." She yelled over thunder that rattled the windows, and walked on holy ground, out of The Fellowship of the Holy Bible and into the storm.

By that evening's special service, he was ready. The rain wept softly.

Reverend Churlick looked out across the faces of the congregation. Sweat prickled the back of his neck and his heart pounded. The church was full, they hadn't given up on him. Expectancy filled the small chapel in the seconds that slid one into the next. He gathered his courage. *Holy Father, help me. With Your help, I can do this.*

Suddenly, he turned to his wife. "Come on over here, sweetheart."

Dolores stiffened where she sat at the organ. She hesitated, then came to him.

He put her hand in his, and the congregation waited.

"Remember Joseph, son of Jacob?" His voice was soft and resonant. "He was a good man, and God caused him to prosper. Was considered quite a catch in his time. By one woman in particular: his boss' wife. You see, the Egyptian's wife wanted Joseph, wanted him bad. Tried to seduce Joseph over and over. But he said no. So, she accused him of having his way with her, and Joseph was thrown into jail."

Both hands grasped the pulpit. "Did Joseph deserve to be sent to jail? No!" Without looking at her, he reached, again, for Dolores' hand. He said quietly, "But he *was* . . . all on the accusation of a woman who was only interested in her own desires."

He mopped his face with a handkerchief. Dolores, at his side, moved her fingers in the hand. He gripped her tighter, glanced at her, and though her whole body appeared to ache with the pain of ruined dreams and faithlessness, still, she was with him. She would always be with him, he realized, which yielded him no comfort.

Lord, help me. I deserve a chance. If there was one woman on earth, Lord, it was her. You know she was meant for me. This shouldn't never of happened this way.

"We had a similar scene acted out in our church this morning. A member of our congregation accused me of being the father of her baby."

Whispering through the rows of church members.

Churlick patted his wife's hand. "Dolores and I been married for —" he paused. "Goin' on nineteen years, isn't it, darlin'?"

Mrs. Churlick's brief, pained smile turned demure. "Twenty, dear."

A titter rippled through the congregation.

He beamed. "I stand corrected. Twenty years we been happily married."

He grew serious, held his wife's hand to his lips and kissed her fingertips. "I wouldn't trade this woman for anything in the world. Not anything or anyone. She's my helpmate, confidant, means everything to me."

Dolores stood in the way frightened people hold themselves, shoulders raised without being conscious of it, slightly hunched.

Heads nodded and benign smiles lit up like soft yellow windows dotting the countryside. The endorsement gave him courage.

His deep voice rose into a cry, "I'd do anything to keep Dolores from being hurt. Lay down my life for her, an' she knows it."

Her sardonic look stopped him. He checked the crowd's response. One look from her had turned them against him—or was he being paranoid? Calm down, calm down. They were with him to that point, he would get them back. He squeezed her hand, not hard enough to register on her face, but steadily tighter.

Dolores changed her mind then, her demeanor saying to the congregation, Yes! Yes, he would lay down his life. Yet, he knew she viewed the claims that fell out of his mouth like the poisoned apples that fell from the Queen's tree. Twenty years of rotten truth. He smiled at her, and she smiled the rueful smile of a woman stuffing her pockets full of the only apples she would ever taste.

"Sometimes, though, we unintentionally hurt the ones we love most." He pointed randomly at the members before him. "I'm right, aren't I? I've listened to you all pour out your troubles to me. Amen?"

"Amen!" from a few faithful friends.

"Janey and Jake Powers brought their problems to me. You probably figured out, Janey is one mixed up young woman. I was workin' on patchin' up her marriage, but I mights well tell you, she's lookin' for a divorce." He nodded toward Jake, "Sorry, Jake, but we gotta tell 'em the truth."

Jake, every pore the victim, cried, "I know, Reverend, I know what you told me—now tell them. Tell 'em about her!"

A grumble of shocked disapproval passed through the membership.

Churlick pinched the bridge of his nose in aggrieved concentration, unsure how to go on. Then, after a quick prayer, convinced the spirit moved him, he spoke.

"Janey was unhappy and confused. I think I represented some kind of happiness and stability, and she wanted that more than anything. But she gave up wanting it from her own marriage." His voice grew faint. "She wanted it from me." Louder now. "She let me know she wanted something from me I should never of given her."

The congregation sat before him like angry masks, like strangers he never knew, a jury to convict this killer of the strange, singular faith that was their ticket to heaven.

Logan's voice cracked and he cried out, "Oh, Jesus! Jesus," in agony, he looked aside, "this is so hard. Give me strength, Lord, to do what I gotta do." He wiped his eyes.

"I come before you, my beloved Fellowship, to confess my sin." He was filled with the regret of someone caught. Why did the only woman he could ever love have to ruin him? The pain of losing her was killing him. And now this. It wasn't fair. The unfairness caused him to weep. Tears of anguish flowed down his face.

"I wisht I was Joseph. Lord knows I wish I could be strong like Joseph. But I wasn't." He ran trembling hands over his face, smeared the tears.

"No, I wasn't. The woman who came to me had her way. I'm guilty. Guilty of being a weak man. Now, I've asked Dolores to forgive me, Jake, Janey's parents —"

He caught the eye of Joe Crownhart, who sat alone, stoic, no wife by his side.

"I've asked my God to forgive me. And tonight—" He raised outstretched arms and cried, "tonight, I'm askin' *you* to find it in your hearts to forgive this sinner. He who is without sin—" He broke down, then. Hands over eyes, sobbing. Dolores, crying as well, held her husband. The congregation shuffled in their seats.

The response seemed to begin with a collective breath. Then, the rhythm of breathing broke into audible pieces, scattered and merging into elemental emotions hammered at the fire of their emotional hearths. Hammered by the smith who had woven gossamer wings of salvation to take their deepest yearnings for immortality to the heavens, to take their dirty little lives, scrubbed clean, and transport them to another realm, higher and guaranteed, than the Christians in the next town who didn't know the Lord through his mouthpiece, Logan Churlick.

Men and women moved uncertainly, at first, to the pulpit. Then the church was in an uproar. "Let the one without sin cast the first stone . . ."

They crowded around their preacher. Weeping and singing, they gathered around him. Voices rose, then floated down to blanket his grateful murmurings, the murmurings of a sinner, like they were. The murmurings of a victorious man.

"Amazing grace, how sweet the sound, to save a wretch like me . . ."

Eight

Janey exited I-90 at Division Street, got mixed up and took a loop through the heart of downtown Spokane. Rain pelted the windshield even more heavily at that moment and she swore, then laughed.

Still giggling, she squinted at the foggy glass. *Am I becoming a real heathen?* The perversity of swearing, breaking from Fellowship decorum, got her sniggering. *What would Jesus say? Jesus who? Churlick's?*

Downtown Spokane. Would her life have been different if she had been exposed to the sophistication of a city? She remembered Christmases past and the twinkling trees lining Riverside Avenue. Feeding the ducks, riding the carousel in Riverfront Park. But today, puffy, miserable, suddenly on the verge of tears, she could not think of happy moments without feeling as though they would never come again.

Grand Avenue took her past Sacred Heart Medical Center, the city's premier healthcare facility. Sacred Heart was a two hour drive from Rathcreek. David would have gone there for treatment of his diabetes, had modern medicine been given a chance to debunk The Fellowship's faith healing.

Oh, God, I miss you, Dave.

A sharp ache stirred at his memory. Odd. Until she had been cast out, she had not thought of her brother so often. Somehow, the memory had become bigger than he was, standing for so much more than his short life, now that hers was ruined.

Now, she was rocked by the loss of her whole community. The scene from that morning played itself again. Why had she told them about Churlick? Even as she spoke, she knew the truth meant disaster, but was unable to stop. The careful plan to just say her good-byes, Churlick goading her on, then finding herself at the front of the church in a nightmare of accusations and being thrown to the devil.

She stopped herself. Nothing could be changed.

Somewhere in this sprawling city an abortion clinic would perform a procedure to save her. The blasphemy of abortion meant emancipation from the past and the future. A new beginning, or was it her end? Hard to feel relief, though, hard to feel anything at all. Nothing worthwhile anymore. She had thrown away everything that meant anything to her. Threw it away when she became Logan's woman, accepted the cool leather of his couch, his hands, accepted him. Oh, God, had she actually reached for him?

A horn blared. Janey swerved to miss a truck. Heart pounding, she took a quick look around. Where had he come from? She caught a glimpse of a red light in the rear view mirror. Shaken, she pulled off to the side of the road.

Where am I? she thought. Nothing looked familiar.

She gazed blankly at the address on a piece of paper. Louise liked Ruth and Bob, and she could always count on Louise's assessment of people. Still, she felt nervous. What were they like, these black sheep? Who could possibly accept her?

Thunder rumbled. The wipers slapped back and forth across the windshield. From where the car idled, she could just glimpse the Spokane River as it made its way through the city built along its banks. Watching the swollen river flow by, she waited for the jitters to leave.

How do you get out of sin when you reached for it?

Janey rested her head against the cool window, wanting nothing more than to be done with everything. There was no way she could bring herself to face these relatives Louise was sending her to. For long moments, a perfect stillness lay over her. Hand to belly, she pulled out into traffic.

She pulled into the parking lot of the Liberty Bell Hotel, a grand old brick structure with a long, curved drive. At its rear, a beautifully landscaped lawn ran down to the river. A few marmots courageous enough to brave the weather grazed there.

After being shown to her room, she gave the bellhop a generous tip and closed the door. She gazed out the window to the gray sheet of sky and the city beyond, seeing nothing, feeling nothing. Somewhere in the complex, a baby cried. She was slightly dizzy with detachment.

Soon, the steamy water of the bath opened her pores. In the seamless porcelain tub, she could no longer outrun her thoughts.

I can do this. I can do it. Nothing mattered but her mantra, nothing existed but the words that blotted out the pain that would not leave her alone. If only she could rinse the shame and loneliness and horror of her situation down the drain with the soap scum.

"Why'd this have to happen to me?" The pathetic self indulgence rebounding from the walls let loose her tears. She was afraid and lonely and could not stop crying. Driven from her home, relegated to distant relatives who could assist her in committing yet another sin, now she sat in this old hotel with walls so thin she could hear that damn baby still crying somewhere.

She ached for the infant she could never hold, her baby, and a profound sadness settled on her.

What kind of life does a child have whose mother hates it? she thought. *I won't bring this child into the world. His God damned child. I won't!*

Her arms crossed over her chest and she slipped deeper into the water until it was just under her nose. She felt weightless, floating in liquid space. Then, she slid under.

Churlick was there, waiting. Maddening replay after replay, his naked body, his moaning, the orgiastic spasms that sent her shuddering long after he had rolled over and lay panting. Shameful that she had enjoyed their love making so much.

Suddenly, she lunged to the surface, air bursting from her. Panting, raging, crying.

Finally, limp and drained, she felt the subtle ache to be done with it all stir again. Impatience, the knee-jerk reflex that made decision making so automatic, was a well-known blessing and vice to her, and it nagged her now. Right or wrong, she was never indecisive.

Janey stared at the razor on the tub edge, picked it up and examined it, wondered how hard the pressure would have to be. It was very sharp. Would cutting through her skin be like butter? Or tough, like a dull-bladed knife trying to cut a tomato?

She ran a thumb along the razor's length; a thin ribbon of blood beaded into the grooves of her fingertip. No pain. But she wouldn't have minded if dying were painful. Self-loathing was now so complete, she didn't care about anything anymore. She wondered about this for a moment, the unnaturalness of not caring, then let it go.

Idly, she turned her palm up, stared at it for a while, then began tracing the network of tiny veins at the wrist, thumb worrying them like fingers over a rosary. When fear invaded her thoughts, the repetitive motion neutralized it.

She imagined where the artery was, how easy it would be to make one quick cut. Numbness overtook her then, pulsed out from deep within, from her marrow, worked its way out into individual cells until she felt wooden.

She imagined herself dead. Better off. Everyone would be better off, including the damned baby. She wouldn't have to make that horrible choice. God damn Logan! She had been stupid to imagine The Fellowship could believe her over him. Nobody really knew him. Even she didn't really know him, though she knew him more thoroughly than anyone.

Janey put the razor above her wrist. One quick cut. She practiced in the air above, drawing the razor across, then brought it gently down to the skin and softly, softly, let the edge rest there. One - quick.

Her mind filled with details: wide, translucent red ribbons in the water, pumping, oozing, the bath water becoming darker and darker; the maid discovering her naked body. She shook off a violent shudder and imagined instead what it would be like for her problems to be over.

She pictured her parents' grief. Imagined her life wasted.

Again, a baby's wail carried through the wall. Hunger, or loneliness, maybe. The crying went on and on. She listened to it, grew more and more agitated. What would make a baby cry like that? Isn't anyone with the child? Why don't they pick it up? Come on, get the baby. *Get the baby.*

Fist raised to bang on the wall, mouth opened to shout, she paused. The crying had stopped abruptly. Started up again, then stopped for good.

Good. Finally. Someone's feeding the baby, or maybe just holding it.

She thought of the baby, wondered what the child looked like, the powdery smell of its skin and hair, its tight balled-up fist. She looked at her fist, thought of the beginning of her life. Life. It might be good again, if she could just start over.

She looked at the razor blade in her hand, held her arm out over the edge of the tub and let the blade slip from her fingers to the floor.

Nine

Janey reached the Buena Nueva development by midmorning the following day. The houses sat on two acre lots, surrounded by trees on a bluff overlooking the Little Spokane River. Janey stared at the numbers: 7718 Haveteur Way.

Mom's sister? Jesus, if this is the reward of being heathen . . .

Pale sunlight filtered through gray upon gray, and a transient sun collided with clouds across large bay windows like water reflecting darkness and light. She opened the car door, hesitated. Louise hadn't told her they were rich.

Damn it! I hate being Little Orphan Annie, come to live with Auntie and Uncle Bucks. Frowning, she slammed the door with determination. *What choice do I have?*

She lugged her suitcase across a long wooden bridge that led to the spacious front porch. On either side of the bridge were ferns, saplings, verdant undergrowth. Splashing beneath the wooden planks, a small stream, like suppressed mirth, spilled to an expanse of neatly trimmed lawn.

A small blonde woman opened the door wide to her knock. "Jane!"

The woman called inside to her husband, then threw her arms around her.

Janey hesitated, unsure how to react. She felt awkward at such an exuberant welcome. This stranger, her nice house; Janey was certain her aunt wouldn't want to dirty her hands with the problems she had dragged with her from Rathcreek.

Her petite aunt was lovely to look at: blonde hair bobbed shoulder length, the same soft, brown eyes as her mother's, but different. Her mother's eyes wore perpetual worry, and there was none of that in her aunt's.

"Hello, Aunt Ruth," she said, smiling with a shy liking for the way this woman had made her at ease with her affectionate welcome.

Ruth took Janey's suitcase and arm and brought her in.

"Thank you for having me. I feel like a total stranger you're opening your home to on faith. Louise told me—"

"We're not exactly strangers," Ruth said. "Don't you remember—"

"Remember what?" came a sharp, clear voice from behind her. "Uncle Bob?"

"Hi there, squirt! Well, not so much squirt anymore, is she?" he said to Ruth.

Bob was a compact man with curly brown hair and athletic looking, except for a high forehead that suggested bookishness. But blue eyes, intense and shrewd, eyes that crinkled sparks of wry amusement when he grinned, held Janey. That voice, those eyes, why did they seem so familiar?

Years ago, inklings of joy and magic and terror. A violent flash of memory, and Janey knew, she knew who these people were. Aunt Ruth and Uncle Bob had stayed with her family when she was a child.

Janey had fallen in love for the very first time. Sweet and affectionate Aunt had left a special mark on her, but Uncle. Uncle! This young, outrageous, cigar-smoking, fun-loving uncle had charmed them all, but especially little Janey, who had stood entranced, watching her uncle snap open the black case, and then tune up his violin in their kitchen as her mother fixed breakfast.

The other children, sleepy-eyed at so early an hour and drawn by the wonderful, strange sounds, wandered into the sun-filled room. It was the first—and only—time there had ever been live music in the house.

The sight of the dashing young man! In a plain white tee shirt and plaid pajama bottoms, he sat on a kitchen chair, legs spread wide, violin tucked under his salient chin with morning stubble unshaved, bow drawn and ready. He winked one of those snappy, conspiratorial eyes at the adoring girl of seven, who was already, at this tender age, constrained by Godliness, goodness and obedience. The wink filled Janey with an elation of anticipation.

And then he began to play. The music, with a life of its own, leapt from one note to another, high and lilting and jaunty. In a moment, Janey was pulled into a world of pure sensation and pulse. An animal in her belly and heart, in her legs and thin arms came alive and catapulted her out of shyness and goodness. She moved to an unknown longing, to break free of all the pent up unnaturalness of the life her loving parents had led her to believe was "the way." She was dancing, this quiet child, so unexpectedly caught up and propelled by fierce, powerful, commanding notes, exuberance radiating from her.

She knew one thing: she wanted to love this man with all her heart; a god who had created her in his image. The spirit of a new self, a true self burst out of her in a rush of freedom, pure joy, sensations and feelings, no thought, no reasonings, no prohibitions of her natural state in favor of the canned contrition for what, she did not know. Original sin? No, original goodness and sensuousness and grace. It would be a long time before she would love herself again this way.

Eventually, Louise, nine, and sweet, five-year-old David joined with her in a world of sensation, so that all the children were out of joint with the normal sense of things done in this serious house, and the roomful of adults broke into laughter and clapping.

Janey barely heard them. She barely saw her brother and sister. She heard only the sounds coming from the violin, saw only the sweet straining grin of her uncle's upturned chin and the vigorous flailing of his bow arm across the instrument of agony and delight. There was nothing in its free-wheeling fancy that was regulated or measured, nor certainly nothing restrained as in the "live" music she heard at church every week. The music played by Mrs. Churlick was dead compared to these sounds which lifted her from her mother's kitchen to heaven! Uncle stood, kicking over the chair, back bowed, sawing the fiddle into fiery notes that bantered and soared and lifted everyone up, even her father, who tapped his toe at the kitchen table and sipped his coffee as he watched his children dance.

Later that morning, after Uncle had put away the magic instrument, and stood at the kitchen sink shaving himself, looking into a little, round silver mirror suspended from the cupboard above, she still hung around him, shy now. He talked to her, Adam's apple bouncing under the thick white shaving cream, laughed, and fixed her, occasionally with those sharp blue eyes.

Her mother rushed over, grabbed her arm away from Uncle as Janey giggled at him, shaving a small swath on her forearm.

"Bob! Stop it! You want to have her looking like a gorilla? It'll grow back all thick there. Stop it. Now, Janey, you go sit down and eat your pancakes."

Then, later, there had been words, terrible words. She never found out what it had been about, but remembered her father shouting, Uncle swearing, and herself jumping out of bed, running down the hall and standing on shaking knees, hardly daring to gaze through the slats of the wooden venetian hall door, yet not able to tear herself away. Heart beating, swelling the veins on either side of her neck into pulsing, agonizing knots of certainty: her father was kicking Uncle out, and he and his beautiful wife, her Aunt, left.

Uncle Bob and Aunt Ruth. She knew, now, it was them.

Later, after pleasantries had been exchanged, Janey was taken to her room down a long hall, a bright room in lime greens, white wicker, and yellow. Ruth cranked open the white wooden blinds, and the fresh, cold breeze sifted through the slats.

When she was alone, Janey took her nightgown from her suitcase, breathed in its scent, the smell of home.

She touched the small dark tuft of little hairs on her forearm. For many years, she had taken to fluffing the hairs after a shower in the morning, so they melded better into the soft, sand-colored hairs. In the summer, she had even taken to bleaching them, and the dark hairs truly disappeared in those golden months.

In her room, the room she would live in, in Uncle and Aunt's home, she gazed at her forearm where the hairs called attention to themselves, stroked them lovingly, then pulled out a short sleeved blouse.

Ten

Janey was glad of the fresh start Uncle Bob and Aunt Ruth gave her. She, alone, was free to make the decision of whether or not to have the baby. They even advised her to attend a pregnancy crisis group, which she had done during her first few weeks in Spokane. Disaster.

A mix of heathen and devout, all victims of various forms of, as she told her aunt and uncle, rape or lustful stupidity, each member of the group grappled with the decision to carry out her pregnancy or end it. During her last session, Janey had turned the gathering into a free-for-all that strained the counselor's last nerve and caused a schism between the Christians and those, like Janey, who knew for the first time they were not simply a shadow thrown against the church wall.

There was a time she would have joined in the protests with her pregnant Christian companions against those despicable women, those baby-killers. It was not until later, when it was her life, her body, being invaded by an enemy, that Janey could conceive of doing as men who fight wars do, and summon up the courage to join forces to obliterate the enemy invading the precious land within herself. Like all who have fought in war, life would never be more real than in that time, and she would never be the same afterward.

She knew there had to be pro choice people in Rathcreek; it was a small town, but not that small. But she did not know anyone who was not "pro life." There were no gray areas within the family of The Fellowship. Only Louise had publicly maintained her views, and her self, in the face of Churlick and his pervasive Fellowship.

"God damn! Says here another doctor butchered by the Christ

lovers," she would say, reading the newspaper over breakfast. "Murderin' fanatics. Think they've been appointed deputies."

From the time Janey had fled to Ruth and Bob's, she drank only the intoxicating nectar of an unimaginable view of reality till she felt that slow, smooth burn of a fresh perspective clearing her senses, her brain, till she knew, without a doubt, that it was Churlick, her parents and rest of Rathcreek who were the Mad Dog 20/20 that, had she swallowed one more bellyful, would have left her blind and gnawing on her own arm.

"I'm a mess, coming apart at the seams," Janey said to Ruth and Bob at breakfast one morning. "Think of it: how perverse is God if *we're* created in His image."

"I'd be surprised if you weren't a mess," Ruth said.

"Ah, theology at breakfast!" Bob said. "I'll take some jam with mine."

"Have you thrown in the towel with the group?" Aunt Ruth asked.

"I'm done. It just became a war between the Christians and heathens. Besides, I've made up my mind. Made an appointment for Tuesday."

"For an abortion?" Ruth asked.

Janey replied, it seemed her voice was always trembling when the talk came to this, "I'll be able to have children again." She knew she didn't need to voice arguments made in the dead of night, many nights, pacing, swearing, weeping. Men went to war against terrorists threatening their homeland, their freedom and pursuit of happiness. This was woman's war, and she was not going to lose.

"I've made up my mind," Janey said. "Is it selfish to want the same freedom *he* has, because biology says he can't carry his own bastard child?" She stopped suddenly, conscious of her filthy mouth, then smiled sheepishly, knowing the emphasis was not taboo in this house.

"Is it selfish of God to allow spontaneous abortions—miscarriages?" Ruth asked.

"Are souls recycled when God brings about their end, but not if these tadpoles are called home early by another means?" Bob wondered aloud. "How fair is that?"

"Those are questions we'll never know the answer to," Ruth said.

"Fairness has nothing to do with it," Janey cried. "Is it fair that one of the girls in the crisis group was *twelve*, raped by her stepdad? How fair is it that Churlick used God to get into my pants? After buttering me up for weeks of counseling, probably drooling every session, waiting for the right time to get his hooks into me? God told him to teach me yieldingness? How could I believe that? No one on earth could be so naive. No, life isn't fair. And when it comes to times like these, the best I can do is look at everything without The Fellowship telling me what to believe, and just know I'll have to live with the consequences."

With fierce savagery, she said, "I'm not bringing another *him* into the world." Suddenly defensive, and feeling morose because there was no need for defensiveness, she fought to keep from breaking down completely. "I going to get my life back, whatever it takes."

Bob cleared his throat in a way that suggested an emotional tidal wave threatened to engulf him, grabbed a piece of toast and began slathering jam. "Jesus, you're brave. You know we're with you."

Ruth nodded.

Uncle's music had put her in touch with something sacred that could never grow in her parents' home, and now this environment of trust in her instincts was more her real home than that alien place of her youth twisted by Churlick's religion.

She looked at them squarely, having already decided that everything must be honest and open and real now, no matter how ugly, or what was the use of all the pain?

Janey woke abruptly Tuesday morning from a dream she could not remember. The dark room, like a somber gray compress, weighed heavily on her. She gagged with the urge to be sick. A veteran at morning sickness, however, she waited to see if the sensation would leave before running for the bathroom.

Bleak morning seeped in through the window shade, the same dim gray as the night her brother died, the kind that gave night an ashen pallor. The dream was about David. She still couldn't remember it, but the thought of him made her sad. Had it been four years since he had been alive? Suddenly, Janey missed him fiercely.

She recalled the moonlit night he had played his last prank, in a lifetime of close calls. The pale face, the dark circles under sunken eyes. Even on the verge of death, he knew how to love life.

Sitting on the edge of his bed, she had been playing chess on a tray set up between them. After moving her rook, a stack of school books on his desk caught her attention.

"Pretty slick way to get out of homework. I think that's mate, by the way." She ran a hand through his crew cut, loving the feel of the bristles, like a soft brush.

He said nothing, but concentrated on the board. Then he groaned, scrambled up the pieces and said, "Lucky."

Though she didn't know it, juvenile diabetes was consuming David without treatment. But his mental state frightened her most. The sickness sapped his energy, and without energy he had no enthusiasm for even the things he loved. In the past, he was often gone most of the day fishing or playing baseball, when he wasn't in school. The last few days, he had hardly gotten out of bed.

"C'mon, Dave, you gotta get better so you can kick butt at knowledge bowl."

"I'll leave that to you," he said. "You're the one in a couple years who's gonna get gold cords at graduation." He leaned back in bed and sighed. "I can't even remember any more how it feels to be well."

"You gotta pray, and . . ." the look said he had heard it before, plenty. "Okay, so what do you want to do now?"

"You still owe me two bucks, don't you?"

"What are you talking about?"

"Two bucks you borrowed. Big time interest, sis."

"I'll have it for you next allowance, okay?"

He tapped his tooth with a finger. Rubbed his hands together. "Big time."

"Okay, fine."

He grinned slyly. "Know what I miss?"

Janey waited.

"Outside."

"Are you crazy? It's freezing out there! Snow's a foot deep and it's pitch black. And you're sick. Are you crazy?"

"Yup. Big time. You said."

She studied the pale, almost transparent skin, the thin frame and the boyish smile, hope lighting him like a Chinese lantern. Then weighed the chances of their getting caught. Couldn't believe she was even considering such a loony scheme.

He sat up. "I got it all figured out."

In the end, she couldn't resist. It was the first time he had been excited about anything in weeks. Janey went to her room and put on a heavy sweater, socks, long underwear and mittens, then opened the door and peered down the long hall.

She knew it was crazy, knew their father would kill them if he found out. Kill her. David was ill; he wouldn't get punished. And he wasn't supposed to be outside of bed, let alone outside the house. At night. In the freezing cold. He wouldn't go through with it, she told herself, but knew she would find him bundled up and waiting. A shiver of excitement ran through her. The danger of it, all for the sake of a kooky dare and nothing more, was so like her brother. It was the challenge, the exhilaration of being outside the ordinary that mattered. She loved that in him.

The television blared in the livingroom, and she pictured her parents and sister in front of it. She tiptoed down the hall and hesitated outside his door, hand on the knob. Then, out of no where, a solid thunk, thunk on her shoulder jumped her heart beat to the pace of an electric bongo.

"What's up?" Louise stood behind her, holding a dish of ice cream.

"Louise! You scared me to death!" Janey pulled her into the bedroom.

"Hey!" David said, poking fingers into mittens.

"What are you two dressed so weird for?"

After Janey and David spilled everything, Louise whined, "*I* wanna!"

"No! You keep watch. Dad'll kill us. David's supposed to be resting and praying."

"I don't know about this prayin'," Louise said. "If he was gonna get well by prayer, he'd be cured as a Hormel ham by now. There's another prayer meeting tonight."

"Where?" David asked.

"Here. Eight o'clock." Louise placed her hands on Janey's shoulders. "Okay, okay, I'll keep my eyes open. Now get out there."

The three made their way to the coat closet. They worked desperately not to be discovered, clapping hands over each other's mouths, Louise, on scout, flinching at the doorway every time their father's recliner squeaked or the pair giggled.

David held out their mother's thick wool coat. "Here. Put your arm in this sleeve and I'll put mine in the other. And then we do like this." He slipped his other around her waist. And she put hers around him. They marched out the door into the night.

Scrunching holes in the shin-deep snow, they tromped around the house, a two-headed snow creature. David laughed, because they had gotten away with it. Laughed so hard they staggered and fell in the snow, drowning each other in white mounds. Then they got up and marched some more in the warm camel colored coat.

David was not afraid of getting caught; he was being bad and he was free. There was nothing they could do to the sick boy who flaunted all their concern. What, put him back to bed? But Janey was afraid. Her heart pummeled her ribs at the thought of her punishment if they were found out.

"Freedom! Independence Day! Yahoo!" he shouted.

"Shhh!"

He flung out his arm, lost his footing and whumped to the ground, yanking her with him. Their cackling laughter startled the snow-muffled quiet. Darkness lit by the faint moon outlined their teeth, dim faces and reflected the vast whiteness they were a part of.

"Quiet! They'll hear!" he commanded, laughing and out of breath as they wallowed. He tried to rise to his knees, but fell back into the mangled snow, where they flailed a two-headed angel.

"Shhhh." She held a snow-caked finger to her lips, and they laughed in billowy clouds.

Their wrists were raw. Snow was down their necks, in their boots, in the creases of their stocking caps and their coat sleeves. They struggled to their feet, and with numb fingers, brushed themselves off.

"Janey."

She looked up to see the ghost of his words drift into the air. Snow muffled every sound and the sliver of the moon wrapped them in its ashen night light. David passed his hand over the white landscape.

"It's beautiful," he whispered.

She nodded.

As they walked toward the house, trying to keep their balance by stepping into the boot holes they had already made, a car pulled up.

The frigid air pinched their noses and ears. They stood watching, frozen with fear as the car lights blinked out. Another car followed, pulled up, lights out.

"Reverend Churlick! They're coming to see you. C'mon!" Janey whispered, half dragging him away from the front of the house to the back yard.

For a short distance he kept up, then slogged through the snow, until he stopped, panting. "Too tired."

"David!" She caught herself at the sound of car doors slamming. In the light cast by the livingroom window, she could see he was in no shape to move quickly. If he hadn't been sick and lost so much weight, she wouldn't have been able to support him, but she hoisted him onto her back and struggled to carry him the short distance to the back porch.

He slid from her back and she helped him up the icy steps. It was no fun now. Janey felt the bitter cold through the soles of her boots, in her finger tips and face. She was afraid one of them would slip, lose their balance and bump into one of the monstrous icicles hanging from the roof. If it broke off, she was sure it would kill them.

She cupped a hand around her eyes and looked in through the kitchen window. Holding her breath, she tried the door. Locked.

Nothing left to do but throw themselves on their parents' mercy. David leaned against her, strangely quiet. She rapped on the door, urgently, and imagined how she would explain things, how she had, no doubt, caused his condition to worsen. She imagined the reverend and the prayer group making their way up the walk.

The door creaked open, throwing out its shaft of light. Louise, beside herself, yanked them in. Eyes wild, she whispered loudly, "They're here, they're in the front hall!" She peeled the coat off them and said, "What's wrong with him?" Then, "Never mind—hurry!" Half dragging their brother between them, they made their way to his room. Their parents' voices and the voices of The Fellowship could be heard.

Janey tugged off mittens and boots, then tore back the sheets and Louise poured him into bed and brought the blankets up under his chin to hide his clothes.

"Jeez, Dave, you look like something out of the frozen food section." Janey giggled, and brushed the tips of his frosted crew cut.

"Tonight was a new record. Best home run I ever made," he said.

Best home run. David could be so corny. The memory made Janey smile. She blinked at the light now streaming through the window shade. Still smiling, she realized that it was two hours before her appointment. The procedure that would change a life she couldn't even recognize anymore. The little girl in the camel coat got out of bed, walked to the dresser, and putting on dark glasses, stared at herself in the mirror, feeling all in holes.

Eleven

Consciousness leaps and
    another curdled Emmenthaler breaks,
    fresh, pungent, pulsing stew of promise
    reduced, breeding glory.
    The green wheel,
    stranded on its earthy atoll,
    worked on by forces,
    strong brine and this paradise's sun,
    cures into a Swiss cheese existence.
Ripe eyes open.
A whole, all in holes.

The Eastside Women's Clinic was a rundown building in a poor part of town. Picketers marched past. Janey knew none, yet was grateful for Ruth's suggestion that she wear sunglasses. They made her feel anonymous as she faced the black-coated accusers pushing gory pictures of fetuses at her, screaming that she was one of Satan's chosen. Bob threatened the mob so they could enter the building.

Inside, Janey handed a slip of paper certifying positive proof of pregnancy to a woman behind an orange counter.

"Okay, hon, I'll let the doctor know you're here."

Janey sat in a nubby oatmeal-colored chair. Her uncle, for the first time, seemed unsure, and handed her a magazine. Ruth patted her arm.

Janey glanced at the other patients. Some young women, like herself, alone, others with boyfriends — or husbands?

She leafed through the magazine. Scolding voices in her head. They berated, cried, and the pain swirled around in her brain and moved to her belly, where she knew *it* was growing, developing, more every day.

But she wanted her life back. She wanted to be somebody significant. College, a career. She wanted a husband, babies to love, not this reminder of Churlick. She had always wanted children, but not this way. Not by him.

"This is so hard," Janey whispered. "Man, I wish I didn't have to make this choice. I wish it would all go away."

Ruth squeezed her hand. "It would be hard no matter which way you chose."

"And it doesn't mean you're doing the wrong thing, either," Bob said.

"It doesn't?"

"You're going to have grief if you give up having a baby, and there'll be grief if you have the child."

The thought shook her resolve. He was right. If she ended this child's chance at life, she would always have the pain of that decision. And a different pain of going through with it, keeping her child, having her own baby to love. *Jesus! Stop it,* she told herself.

"If there's any question in your mind," he said, "you can still give it up."

She knew that would never happen. Even the crisis group counselor maintained that 95% of those who went through with pregnancies ended up keeping their babies.

"Or you can keep it. We told you we'd help, and mean it. Now this isn't supposed to feel like pressure . . ." He looked distractedly around the room, ran a hand through his hair. "It's just—it's not Rathcreek. Tell her, Ruth."

"He can't stand to see a woman in turmoil. He's got knight-in-shining-armor-itis worse than most men. He just wants you to know we're behind you."

Janey said, "I've made up my mind. It's better this way, it's just hard, that's all."

She gazed out the window at the busy downtown traffic. A bus rumbled by. Picketers milled around the building. People hurried by in the bracing wind, heads bent. She watched the picture without sound, people going forward with their lives.

When the nurse called her name, Janey went to the desk.

The nurse led her to the back where she changed into a gown and went through the check-in routine. Finally, the doctor arrived.

Dr. Leander was a middle-aged man, his manner comforting as he made small talk and described the procedure. The nurse busied herself at the counter. Janey sat on the table clothed in the open air gown, all goose-bumps. She hugged herself.

"Any questions?" he asked.

Janey shook her head. Couldn't think. Numbness had set in, and everything seemed dull and flat. The only thing she was aware of was that time moved slowly, drawing her closer to the moment becoming part of her past, and the movement of time linked her to things of substance: nurse, doctor, implements lined up on the silver tray.

Lying back on the examining table, a sheet draped over her stomach and legs, Janey let the doctor guide her feet into the metal stirrups. She shivered and stared up into a field of butterflies in a poster taped to the ceiling.

I can't believe I'm really doing this, she thought. *Is this me? Is this something I would do?* But nobody was holding a gun to her head, were they? Still, it took all her courage not to jump off the table and run from the room.

The doctor began the pelvic exam and she jumped a little.

"Sorry, guess I'm nervous." Tissue paper crinkled as she scooted back into place.

"Just try to relax," he said. "I'll go slow." His gloved hand was gentle. Head tilted, absorbed look on his face, he called out information that the nurse noted. Janey stared at the ceiling. Something like the butterflies in the poster beat in her chest. And as the examination came to a close, panic stampeded through her stomach.

What's wrong with me? She began reciting her litany to herself. *I don't want this baby. I hate him for making me go through this. I hate him. Hate him.*

Her mind pulled away, back to a little boy in the waiting room who looked so much like her brother, back to her memories of David.

Janey, Louise and David. Guilty as sin when the door of his room swung open and their parents and church members filed in. Janey, cheeks still numb with cold, ice crystals clinging to her pants and in the creases of her sagging socks, burned with fear.

The discovery came, of course. How could it not, when the laying of hands revealed David's chilly temperature, his ruddy cheeks? None guessed the full truth and so punishment was overlooked. Besides, they were more concerned with the task at hand.

In silence, Janey watched the faith healing.

Reverend Churlick prayed, one hand on David's head. He tipped a small bottle, dipped a finger, and called for David to cast off the sin of his illness. He touched the boy's head with his oiled finger. Janey squeezed her eyes shut and mouthed an urgent prayer. David prayed. Louise's lips moved. Her parents, Reverend Churlick, members of The Fellowship. They all prayed.

When Janey opened her eyes, she gasped. Reverend Churlick's face, filled so recently with reverence, was taken over by an anger shocking to see in a man of God. Hands under her brother's pathetic arms, he shook the boy, who simply looked at him in astonishment with the terrible innocence of such a faith.

"Don't make me do this, son! Repent this sin!" he shouted. "Repent!"

Then in a deliberate move, the reverend turned her brother over his knees. His large hand chopped the air. Her brother's body jerked under the blow.

She couldn't believe Churlick had actually struck him, not enough to hurt, but to stun. But the boy's wounded face revealed another kind of bruise that she knew would never go away. Then she realized: *the faith healing was not working.* She twisted to see her mother, whimpering, chewing at clasped hands. Her father, on his knees, hands also clasped, cried out "Jesus!" at every blow.

Why? Why was no one stopping him?

A shrill scream exploded from Janey. "What the *hell* are you doing?" Lunging forward, she felt a hand stop her. Her father's tight grasp. Her mother's eyes held agony.

Janey twisted, unable to get free. "Stop it! Someone stop him!"

Louise, shivering violently, suddenly lashed out with a string of horrible filth, fled the room and slammed the door. The invective that followed from the hall went on and on, amidst sobs and what sounded like the fury of fists hitting the wall.

Janey's hand clutched her mouth. *My God, my God, my God.*

Crying, hand pressing hard against her teeth, she watched, until her father forced her from the room. It was the last time she had seen David alive.

In the procedure room of the clinic, butterflies swarmed above Janey in a blur.

My little brother. Oh, David, I miss you so much, Janey thought. *More than I ever realized I could. I've wanted to tell you how much I loved you for*

so long. But it's too late. I didn't know I wouldn't see you again. I didn't know.
They didn't know. I'm sorry, David. I should've done more to save you.

Her chest heaved and she opened her mouth wetly in a silent grimace.

"Are you okay?" Dr. Leander asked.

Janey shook her head, and the tears streamed from her. She had not been okay since her brother's death.

The doctor stepped back, signaled the nurse to stop the procedure.

Finally, the all-encompassing sadness she had resisted for years claimed Janey, and the silent weeping turned to sobs that shook her. In the span of twenty-one years, she had suffered a beloved brother's death, her sister's mental illness, and now, her parents, her sister, her friends, gone. Even a husband she had hoped would bring love—all gone.

So many losses. Janey wondered if she could take one more. Would abortion free her from the past, from Churlick? At that moment, she no longer knew. What was most true for her now was that she had faced the loss of David's death. She could not fight the God-given sanctity of her brother's life, mixed up with the life not yet bulging under her fingers spread over the white sheet. She glanced at the doctor, staring at her, his expression perplexed.

Be rational! she told herself. *This is Churlick's child!* She breathed. *And mine.*

Some women know when they are called to motherhood. Janey knew she was destined to love with generous affection, laugh often and believe in the goodness of her creation. Fate had caught her up with her deepest truth.

The unique soul she carried, never before on the earth. Her, its mother. Finally, in her bones, everything she wanted was in this one chance at love that God—who else?—had placed agonizingly within her grasp.

In the waiting room, Bob and Ruth were puzzled.

"Everything okay?" Bob asked.

"Yes. It's okay now." She took their arms, tucked them under hers and sank into a chair between them. Squeezing their hands and leaning forward, she smiled slowly, shyly, trying to find the words.

Voice full of awe, she said, "I'm going to be a mother."

Twelve

In the six months since Janey's decision to keep her child, along with the freedom she felt from her divorce of Jake, she experienced trimesters of worry and doubt. Fear was loose inside, raw and wanton with her imagination. Miserable misgivings, resentment of stolen freedom. And worse, she worried her baby would have Churlick's nose or eyes, and wondered how she could bear to look at, much less love the child.

She could not be at peace until the day she made an inner vow, a covenant with her unborn child, that he or she would never feel the hatred that belonged to Churlick.

In the beginning, for three months, she was deathly sick, then, suddenly voracious. And the cravings made no sense. Strong coffee. Sickeningly sweet praline ice cream. An entire pizza in a sitting.

The first fluttering movement was dismissed as indigestion. Then, little frogs hopping, playing in the gigantic proportions her abdomen had assumed. Squirming, definite, elbows and butt and head. She imagined the strenuous movements must surely mean the baby was already crawling, at least up on hands and knees, teetering under the tight dome of its home. When her moods allowed, Bob played his fiddle and teased her with impromptu songs about the only reasonable pregnant woman to ever exist, who had a craving for nothing more than toasted snow. Lying in bed, Janey would imagine a strong, healthy child. Her child. And she felt a joy so shining it was almost unbearable.

Now, in the attic of Ruth and Bob's home, Janey watched her aunt tidying up her old painting studio, which would soon be Janey's bedroom and the baby's nursery. She locked her hands across the vastness of her belly and pushed with her bare foot against the floor. The bentwood rocker creaked. Coppery highlights shone in her hair from the strong spring light flooding through a nearby window.

Janey flipped through the pages of a baby name book in her lap.

"If it's a boy, I'm naming him Luke, light giving. And if it's a girl . . . I've always liked Rebekah, since I was a little kid. You know, all those bible stories about the maid of beauty, modesty and kindness who married Isaac."

"So what does Rebekah mean?"

"Hm. Says tied, knotted." Jane looked up from the book. "Strange, huh?" She turned more pages and ran a finger down the names. "I really like Darcy, too. From the stronghold; dark one. Sounds like a corporate CEO to me. Don't you think?" Janey squirmed, trying to find relief from the ache in her lower back.

Ruth placed a hand against her niece's swollen belly. "They're both beautiful."

"And I think the middle name will be Dale, after grandma Crown-hart." Janey thumbed through the book. "Dweller in the Valley. Did you know Grandma Dale?"

"I met your dad's mother a few times before I left the fold. Delightful Polish woman who married Joshua Crownhart. Boy, could she cook. Everyone loved her. Hey, what's going on in there?"

"Basketball game. I think the little guy's at the free-throw line," Janey said and rubbed in circles where her belly suddenly poked out.

"What's your name mean?" Ruth took the book. "Jane. God's gracious gift."

Jane laughed. "This does beg the question, am I going to need God's grace?"

"Remains to be seen. You could do worse."

"I like Jane. Think I'll update little Janey."

"It suits you." Ruth raised an eyebrow, thumbed through the book. "And what does Logan mean?"

"Fang, of course."

"I don't believe it," said Ruth. "Logan means little hollow."

The corners of Jane's mouth turned up in wicked gleefulness. "So. There it is."

Laughter rolled from them, echoed off bare walls. They protected themselves in fortresses of laughing, of wisecracks, of anything to blunt the truth of their fear of him.

Jane shared everything with her aunt, including Logan's persistent letters. After the divorce, Jake had never spoken another word to her. Pride, she supposed. But Logan's letters were almost pathological in their fervor, in the way his declarations of love and decency supposedly made up, now, for all his past mistakes. And the checks. Sent with the letters, via her mother, for the sake of the baby. Jane, consumed by curiosity—what the hell does he have to say to me?—at first read each one, fascinated and repelled, then returned them with the checks, as Bob and Ruth advised.

What did the letters mean? Was he daring her to send these Lotharion proclamations back to his wife? To the congregation? She had responded once, in order to clearly, finally, reject him. After that, what could be his point? Offerings to assuage his conscience? He needn't have bothered. Thank God her mother had not given Ruth's address or phone number. Jane was sure he had tried to wrangle it, but his scheming failed, even with her submissive, God-fearing mother.

She missed her mother. After the baby was born, Jane would make amends to her parents. She would blunt the fury and shame she had brought her father with the cherubic smile of his grandchild. In the meantime, she was grateful for the only contact she had.

Lately, however, not even Jane's fascination with Churlick's strange and chilling declarations, this odd obsession of a married man, no, not even the compelling pull of morbid curiosity saved the letters from being returned. Unopened.

In the birthing room, Jane sucked in air, held her breath. She clutched the metal bed rail.

"Focus, hon!" Ruth cried. "Breathe! You've got to let the air out, Jane!"

The words mingled with some loose remnants of logic retained during labor at its height, even allowed that her aunt meant well and was absolutely right in her coaching.

Impossible. The pain. Like an animal, grunt, pant, pant, pant, until the pain released her. Fingers tingled from hyperventilation and she lay limp and damp in the bed. Only will power enabled Jane to stifle the urge to shriek at Ruth's supreme correctness.

She managed, "Ruth, can you—I mean, it's just—"

Louise picked up the thread, "Just shut up for now, okay?"

"Okay, okay," Ruth said. "Don't breathe then. Sorry. Just doing my job."

They waited for the next wave of pain in an awkward silence. The birthing room was a classic study in maternal happiness. Pink and blue. Print of a mother nursing her child. Floppy-eared bunny and blocks with big letters. Sappy. Happy. What Jane wasn't.

What they needed here, Jane had decided between contractions, in a room filled with awful fears about surviving the pain her body took her through, pain she had never even had a hint existed before this day, what they needed, instead of the floral wallpaper with the small sprinkling of blues and pinks and the wainscoting imbued with its golden glow from the tasteful lamp she'd like to hurl through the window, was a rack, with gynecological leg and arm straps. Bring it on, Lamaze.

Ruth reached into a cup and fed her a few ice chips, stroked her hair.

"How far apart?" Louise asked.

"About two to three minutes. It won't be long," said the nurse.

Louise asked Ruth, "Why don't you take a quick break and let Bob know we're almost at the fourth quarter?"

Ruth looked at her doubtfully.

"You'll be back in time for the fireworks."

Ruth handed Louise a brown paper sack, kissed Jane on the cheek and left.

In another moment, the labor was on Jane, and she braced against it, made herself breathe steadily, willed herself to stare at the lamp. Outside the intensity of the light, the room grew black. Light burned itself in through her eyes, to her brain's pain center. She tried to hold onto the brightness that obliterated the pain.

When the contraction was over, Jane sighed. "Poor Aunt Ruth. Don't run out on me if I get pissy with you."

Louise smirked. "Wasn't invited to the conception, so I wouldn't miss this for anything."

"Dad let you come?"

She snorted laughter. "Dad don't run the universe. Maybe Mom feels like she has to listen, but I'm back on my feet again, so he can talk all he wants."

Louise showed up at the hospital shortly after they arrived, in response to Ruth's call to alert them her time had come. For months, Louise had been absent from her sister's life, as well as much of her own. Since their brother's death, stress was no friend to Louise, and Jane's leaving had been stressful.

The pain was mounting again. Muscles that gathered in the fury of childbirth broke over Jane. She stared into the light, *Deep breaths, now let 'em* — Out of control again, gasping, until she was hyperventilating, then, all pinpricks.

Louise looked to the nurse. There was no command to breathe from this coach, only paralysis. Finally, the contraction over, the nurse instructed Louise to offer her sister the bag. Jane breathed deeply into the crumpled sack until she could feel her limbs again.

Closer now. A minute apart. The doctor came in again and stayed this time. Ruth returned, and Louise snatched up the brown bag and gave it to her. Ruth took her place on one side, Louise on the other.

All at once, the urge to push, that wholly engulfing prompt of nature, came over Jane. More overwhelming, even, than contractions. She grit her teeth and bore down.

After several minutes, the doctor said, "It's crowning. It's coming!"

Jane's breath came in gasps. The pressure was here again. She squeezed her eyes shut and pushed. Finally, the sensation subsided. Quickly, once more, it took hold of her, and she bore down, until she thought she had no strength left.

A lusty cry pierced the room.

"Jesus, Janey, you did it!" Louise cried. "Our baby's here!"

"This one's not going to be ignored!" said Dr. Leander. He held the baby up for Jane to see and the nurse swabbed the infant's eyes. The newborn was coated in a white, waxy finish like some half-baked mottled bisque, squalling, pink, beautiful.

"A girl!" Jane cried. "Hello, Rebekah," she said in a voice thick with emotion.

"She's beautiful!" Ruth stroked the babe's dark, moist fuzz and took inventory of fingers and toes.

Rebekah was laid at Jane's breast where she quieted immediately and began to nurse. Jane opened her daughter's tiny fist, and it closed around her finger. A naked, shining, new contentment wrapped around her. She sighed, shut her eyes and savored the child's warmth on her flesh.

A shock, like electricity, went through her again, from crown to the balls of her feet. The urge to push. She groaned and, having no choice but to obey, bore down.

"Wha—? Oh God, what's this?"

Dr. Leander peered at her. "Huh. Very rare. Apparently, undetected because of the way the babies were situated one behind another instead of side by side or on top of each other. I never got more than one heartbeat."

Babies? Jane looked at him with fright, then tensed again as the electric current to push pulsed through her. "I can't do this," she whimpered through clenched teeth.

"You're doing fine, Jane. It'll be easier this time," he said.

She waited for the urge, then strained with everything she had. Rebekah was forgotten. Strength was dwindling. Only the urgent command to push this child down the birth canal. Breathe. Push. Breathe. Push.

Finally, the doctor held up the infant for Jane to see. Rosy, quiet, peaceful.

"What's wrong?" Jane cried, lifting up on one elbow, holding Rebekah to her. "Is it all right?"

"She's fine," he said. "Look at the way those little black eyes are so alert already." He placed the child on her mother to nurse, than busied himself with the umbilical cord.

"Je-zuz Jehosephat!" Louise cried. "Two of 'em. We got two babies, sis!"

"There'll be plenty to go around," Ruth said. "And look at that auburn hair."

"Darcy," Jane said, breathless and filled with wonder. "Beautiful, peaceful Darcy. Bekah and Darcy, all mine to love."

Thirteen

Logan Churlick sauntered up the narrow walk of his modest two story. He had separated the newspaper before he reached the first step.

As he seated himself at the kitchen table and spread the paper open, Dolores said, "Your eggs are gettin' cold."

She filled the espresso machine and set out two cups, then watched her husband spread open the *Spokesman-Review,* but he hardly noticed.

He adjusted his glasses, scanned the vital statistics. Then his mouth dropped open, and what he saw transfigured him forever.

Steam exploded from the Krups coffee maker and the hot, dark liquid hissed out.

Elated, Logan gazed at Dolores. "Praise God! The baby's here! A daddy at last!"

She said nothing, but her features contorted and her teeth chattered until she ground them still.

Her reaction provoked him. She knew he had recently subscribed to the Spokane newspaper, and long before this moment figured out what he looked for everyday. He was single minded in the ritual. She was not stupid. Why so shocked?

He picked up the paper and re-read the information. Read it again. Incredible! He laughed with delight and looked up.

Dolores was holding onto the counter.

"*Two* daughters! Praise *Je-zuz—two! Thank* you, Father!"

"*Two* girls?" his wife cried.

The despair in her voice irked him. Logan perceived her anxiety momentarily, not really seeing, transfixed as he was by things she was not a part of. Then, it occurred to him: his daughters. She was jealous of his baby girls. And it irked him to realize that while Dolores understood only too well that first place in his heart could at times be a cruel honor, it was all she had ever wanted.

She turned from him and finished making coffee. Steadying her hand, she brought a cup to Logan, watched him a moment, then retrieved her own and sat down.

"All these years we been together," she began slowly, as though his happiness this morning had shaken her lose of her wits, as if everything she lived for was hollow. "These should be *my* children. Yours and mine. Over twenty years, I stood by you. Even your bad luck held us together. When you were in jail for the Crownhart child's death, didn't I stand by you?"

He watched a sob gathered force in her chest, tighten into panic, and saw her squeeze it back. He frowned. She knew he hated scenes.

She was right, of course. But what did that have to do with anything? Yes, she was his helpmate, his loyal messenger to The Fellowship with taped sermons, his advocate, his cheering section, and finally, the force behind the warm welcome when he returned. And he had loved her for it.

But this is different, he thought.

She collected herself. "The only sure, soft thing about you is with kids. You'd do anything for other people's kids. Because you know they'll love you, no matter what. No demands, just the way you like it."

The truth shocked him a little—and irritated him, but he forced himself to say, full of cheer, "Delight thyself, darlin', our prayers have been answered—in duplicate."

"Our prayers? You mean your prayers. How'm I supposed to compete with two squirming little brats?" They were mean words, edged in hardness, the little girl voice gone.

He eyed her sharply. "What're you tryin' to say?" The look, the tone, were meant as a warning, but her expression told him caution had run away this morning; Dolores was beyond herself, scared to death.

Her high voice trembled. "Yippee, I'm so happy for you. Your adultery with that slut's produced two bastard children!" And she screamed, "What am *I*, Logan? Chopped liver? Where do I fit into this big, happy family?"

It took a moment for him to master his anger and revulsion. Then his chair scraped and he lunged around the table, grabbed her hard by the shoulders. The rough seizure threw her to the floor.

She screamed, instantly terrorized, as if her heart were water, and he had spattered it, sizzling, over the kitchen.

"Shut *up*, you stupid cow! If you *ever* talk about my daughters like that again," he shook her where she leaned on an elbow on the floor, "I swear I'll . . ." The stark cannibalism of his voice caught him. He stopped, ran a shaky hand through his thick hair.

"So what am I supposed to do?" she whimpered. Then the bitterness edged back. "You can't expect me to just accept these kids. How do you know they're yours, anyway? Could be her husband's."

"They're mine, all right. I didn't counsel Jake for nothin'. I know when's the last time they were together."

Pained at having to explain any of this to her, he tried to control his harsh breathing. *Stop talking, you idiot. Just stop talking.* He put out a hand. She put hers slowly into it, and he lifted her off the floor, guided her to her seat. In a moment, he was massaging her shoulders, as if nothing had happened.

"Right now, I need you, darlin'. More than ever."

Under his hands, she seemed scarcely to breath. Then she said, "To use me, you mean."

His hands stopped their kneading.

"What?" she challenged, and twisted to stare up at his face. "To you it's ego. You want these kids to show the world what a good daddy you could be. To undo the things your daddy did to you."

Logan studied her with sardonic interest, head nodding. "That's right. Blame everything on him. Dad was tough, all right. He was one tough son-of-a-bitch. Used to beat sense into me with his belt, coat hanger, whatever he could get his hands on." Pride came into his voice. "But he never beat me 'less I deserved it. I was a rotten little shit, and he was just enough rottener to make me come around. He's the reason I'm the man I am today. God-fearin' Christian."

For a moment, he was lost in memories, then focused. "Even when he locked me in that basement, snakes everywhere, just one bare bulb, it was for my own good. I might of went a little crazy, but once I calmed down, I finally called upstairs and asked Dad to forgive my sins." He gave a short nod. "He always did."

He squeezed her shoulders. "This is just the beginning of what God has in store for m—us. He's multiplied our blessings. Now don't make me angry, Dolores." He gripped her tense muscles.

She began to tremble under his touch. The pressure on her shoulders was not painful, but firm. The voice was not harsh, but cold. His punishing ways were subtle and devastating. Hundreds of times, perhaps thousands, he had put her through his silent blackmailings. Her fruitless pleadings, his pitiless rejections. He knew that his silence, when she moved through the house like a ghost, where the only sound at meals was the clink of silverware on plates, always killed her.

"I - I just don't think I can."

Sweet Jesus, help me, he thought. *Bitch!* The strong hands bore down. "You stand by me—you stand by me, or . . ." Then, he let go, and laughed. "You want to know who's the slut? *You're* the slut. Barren slut! You're the reason we can't have kids, now aren't you? Aren't you? Say it!" He bellowed, "Say it!"

"Stop it," she cried, hands over ears. "That was before we ever got married."

"You weak, stupid woman. You ran around trying to find love in anything that would have you. That's all it took to get your tubes scarred."

"Kill me then! Push me out a window. You know I deserve it; but I'm too big a coward to do it myself. I'm good for nothing. Don't know why you ever married me, dirtied goods that nobody else wanted. My good is as filthy rags."

He came around, grabbed her jaw and whispered, "Shut up! What kind of fool do you think I am? You screw this up and I swear you'll regret it. You'll never understand how much I love these girls. *My* girls! You better get it through that thick head what this means to me, and *play your part!*"

Face inches from hers. His thick fingers clenched her cheeks, and he knew her teeth in this grasp were shredding the tender insides until they were bloody. She cried, writhing in his grip. He flung her face away.

"An' I better not hear a word about my—affair. It's over. You, of all people, have nothing to hold against me." He stood with his back to her, looking out the window.

He could hear the clock on the old stove ground out one minute after another, black numbers flipping into place.

Her voice sounded as though now, more than anything, she wanted to live. "Play my part? Then you still want me?"

He turned to her. "Why do you have to make me so crazy? Can't you see this is part of God's plan? Yes, the barrenness is your fault, but a blessing anyhow. This is the only way I could ever be a parent. Any other kids would be bastards, but not these. These are sanctified." Voice a tense whisper, he said, "I was God's *inst*rument. You're His instrument, too."

"It was a miracle when The Fellowship forgave you," she said, caught up in the craziness, softened by his awful sincerity.

"Treated me like a hero, didn't they? It was part of His plan. It had to be. And you're part of the plan, too."

"God's plan?" She looked at the fat hands resting in her lap, each knuckle pocketed with dimples. She pulled her robe tight and re-tied the belt.

"Born again in the blood," he said in his baritone.

Dolores went to Logan and tucked her arms around him. "My lord. Oh my lord. Such an important man, and you chose me. Of course you want me to accept your own flesh and blood. I'm ashamed."

He stared down at her in silence.

"I'm sorry," she said in a small voice. "I'll stand by you." She laid her head against his chest. "I'll be better. Promise." And she said in the little girl voice, "Love me?"

Fourteen

In her hospital room, Jane shifted to get comfortable and hummed a little song, soft and maternal. She wondered at this seduction from normalcy she had become used to over the past 24 hours. Babies wheeled in for feeding and cuddling, then wheeled away until she was ready for more of them, which was often, especially with Ruth and Bob anxious to escalate the spoiling of her daughters.

"Jane?" A nurse called from the doorway.

"Oh, hi, Nina."

"It's your sister. She's been out here since before visiting hours, and now she's, well—" the nurse hesitated, trying to choose her words, and gave up in an exasperated sigh. "She's weirding us out, out here."

A slow grin slipped into place and Jane asked, "Paranoid? CIA?"

"Yes!"

"It's okay. She just has a hard time in waiting rooms, hospitals, airports, dentists' offices. She's harmless. But she won't come unless the CIA isn't around. Tell her they're up on Orthopedics."

Nina shook her head, mumbling as she left.

In a few moments Louise appeared, wearing a tee shirt and tight jeans. Dirty heels hung over the ends of her thongs, and toenails painted red wiggled like hounds trying to pick up a scent. She brushed short hair that looked newly self-butchered out of her eyes. Recognition of Jane ignited a rapturous smile.

"How the hell's the mama?" Louise strode to the bed, took Jane into her arms and they clung to each other, Louise's pungent odor barely endurable.

Jane patted a place on the bed and Louise sat next to her. "Have you seen the babies today?"

"Yeah, they smiled and waved at me. One of 'em said Weezie, I swear! I could read her lips. That one—Bekah—looks just like your baby pictures. Adorable!"

She grinned. "Yeah, yeah, gorgeous. Gerber's already asking for photos."

"And that other one, Darcy, is so sweet. Much mellower than her sister. Those long, dark lashes and rose petal lips. What a heart breaker she's gonna be. Except for the red hair, looks a lot like Churlick, doesn't she?"

Jane wanted to protest, but couldn't. Darcy wasn't like most babies who were born with blue eyes. Hers were black like the night. Intense, serious eyes, like her father's.

"So how do you keep getting out to come see me without a war with Dad?"

"He said no Janey and no red toes, but I got my ways." She gazed with satisfaction at the bright toenails. "They go under cover in my tennis shoes when he's around . . . and he hasn't even seen my new tattoo." She lifted her tee shirt and turned around. On the entire upper portion of her back, Salvador Dali's "Temptation of St. Anthony" sprawled.

Stunned by the artistry, Jane said, "It's unbelievable."

"Something about that scene, the Jesus freak holding off the circus, where everyone's having fun, with his pitiful, stupid cross. It reminded me of our lives, how much we missed out on, on account of God and the goddamn CIA." She pulled her shirt down. "Been having dreams lately. A lot of trouble comin' from the CIA."

"Yeah, so's everyone," came Jane's automatic reply.

"No, I mean it. Something's gotta break soon."

"Weez," she said, full of tenderness, "what makes you think the CIA is heating things up?"

Louise snapped to attention, a cunning smile shaping the corners of her mouth. "Oh, it's true, now that the babies are here. We gotta be careful, sis. Can't be too careful. Anyone who lets a dog lick his toes—and I'm not talking just a quick little doggie kiss, I'm talking major toe jam wash, here. First one foot, then the other, five minutes running. You gotta know someone that perverted will go to any lengths."

"What are you talking about?" Jane could not imagine such a scene. It struck her that this was the first time Louise had personalized her CIA imaginings to a single person.

"Sure. Remember the time we went over to the Reverend's when we were kids? That dog, Pooky or Pukey, something like that, kept sniffing his feet, whining, until ol' Churlick finally decided it was okay since it was just us kids—couldn't a been more than eight at the time, and you were six—so he whips off his socks and let ol' Pukey go at it?"

"Churlick?" Jane asked, incredulous. "I don't remember that. Well, maybe . . ."

"Mrs. C was pretty uptight, but he just laughed, said nobody'd believe us."

"Wait. What does that have to do with the CIA?"

"Everything." Louise stared at her, face calm. "Yeah, about time. God damn CIA."

"Churlick?!"

"Sure. You know, C.I.A., Churlick. Is. Antichrist." Louise hiked her eyebrows and gave a nod of significance.

Jane was confused. Was Louise hearing voices again? Voices connecting Churlick to the Central Intelligence Agency? All these years of paranoia—was it a mixed up delusion about the CIA based on her distrust and hatred of Churlick?

"You're talking about the C.I.A. of the United States? What does the CIA have to do with him?"

Louise snorted. "You gotta be kidding! Everything! He has everything to do with those sons-a-bitches. Church. Is. Angry. Cross. Isn't. Against. Christianity. Is. Abusive."

Jane could not have been more surprised if she had found out their family was part of the witness relocation program. She broke out in giggles.

Louise's frown lifted, and in a monotone she recited more acronyms. "Churlick. Is. Amoral. Churlick. Incurable. Adulterer. Churlick. Impious. Asshole. Church. Is. Anal."

Jane laughed, then said, "You haven't been taking your pills, have you?"

"'Course not. Can't see when I'm on those damn things."

"All this time, the CIA was Churlick?"

"I can't say no more, sis. You know I can't let you onto my source. You just gotta trust me."

Jane nodded.

"When you been burned by that church as much as our family has, you can't be too careful." Louise raised her shoulders, like a cat hunching its back, and turned to the door.

Jane gasped.

Jane had forgotten how impressive Logan Churlick was. His dark figure filled the doorway, wide shoulders narrowing to a slight paunch. His thick brows arched in surprise, as though startled that Louise should be there. The dark hair was peppered with gray, something she hadn't remembered. But the penetrating black eyes were just as she recalled: intense, confident.

She knew she would run into Logan again some day, but she was not ready—not now, so soon. Her stomach tightened.

"How did you get in here?"

"Is that any way to greet me?" But under her withering gaze, he added, "Nurses are real busy, said just knock and go in. Hello, Louise."

Louise scowled, crossed her arms and muttered, "God damn CIA."

His hand went to his pocket, then, jingling coins. He glanced at Louise who had picked up the phone and was dialing.

"Hello, room service?" she asked loudly, her back to him. "We need a bouncer. Can you send someone up?"

"It's all right, Louise," Jane said, and took the receiver.

Louise winked at her, sauntered to the door and opened it, crossed her legs at the ankles. She hitched her thumb and sang loudly and with gusto, "Hit the road, Jack, and don't you come back, no more, no more, no more, no more . . ."

"Louise." Churlick went to her and spoke in a hushed voice, and she quickly turned from him and hurried down the hall.

"What did you say?"

"Nothing. She's fine. Just taking a peek at the babies."

"What do you want?" Jane asked.

"Is this the way you address your minister? I came to congratulate you on the birth of your daughters."

"You're not my minister."

"Okay," he said, deadly quiet. "But I am the father of your children."

"You don't know that. They're Jake's."

"There are tests for fixin' paternity. But I'll just take your word for it that day in church so long ago." He gave her a patronizing smile and moved toward a chair.

"Don't sit down. You're not staying."

She watched Logan struggle with the shattered belief that he could still control her. Fear came into Logan Churlick, and she wondered how such a man could fear her. In a rising exhilaration, she felt free. Here was this man coming to her. No longer the voice piece of God, no heavenly authority on earth. A mere man. It was powerful to know she was important to Logan, who was not important to her at all.

"I'll go. Just give me two minutes."

She crossed her arms. "Is that a promise I can trust?"

He nodded, sat. "You never answered my letters."

"What's to answer? Come off it, Logan, what're you doing here?"

"What do you think I'm doing here? I'm the father," he said. "You never even called to let me know."

It was the only thing he could have said that could puncture her hostility. She wrestled with her compassion. Tears in his eyes, then. Shit.

To hell with this man. He had *seduced* her with his God and his manhood. The counselor she had seen said it amounted to rape, because she had no chance against Logan's manipulation of God.

Voice soft, persuasive, full of amusement, powerful again. "You're a mean little thing, aren't you? Keepin' 'em all to yourself. Well, my beautiful, sweet Janey, there's no way under heaven you got pregnant by yourself."

She opened her mouth to reply.

In a rush, he said, "I had to see my children. You, of all people ought to know how important each and every baby is to me. I weep every time we lose a soul to abortion. I wondered for months if you'd even have my children."

She turned away in disgust.

He took her chin and made her face him. Like a child.

Something snapped. She yanked her face away, then raised her fist and he caught it. For moments, they stared at each other.

Finger raised in caution, he loosened his grip and put her hand down.

"These babies are *ours*," he said fiercely, "put on this earth by God. You can't change that now, and you can't change that I love 'em."

She watched his mouth as it formed the words in a rasping whisper, "I love you."

"God *damn* you. You think because you made me a mother, you're a father now? That wasn't God, you bastard!"

"Janey, listen. God used us. And He meant our children to have both parents." Churlick's words were frantic. "I swear, I'm down on my knees here, beggin' you to come be with me, be my wife. We'll have lots more children. As many as you want."

She shrank back. "You are a lunatic!" She reached for the call button.

He wrenched it from her. "I'm askin' you to be my wife!"

"What are you talking about? You have a wife. Or did you forget?"

"I don't love Dolores, haven't for years. But you are the love of my life, my only love." He went on, oblivious to anything outside his crusade. "You liked it, didn't you?"

She stared at him in horror.

"I know you liked it. You wanted me as much as I wanted you. That was burnin' up love, little girl, an' it don't happen every day." His fingers touched her thigh.

She snatched up a pen on the night stand and drove it into the back of his hand.

He cried out and jumped from his seat. The pen stuck from him, and he held the hand, staring at it in disbelief. He grabbed the shaft and yanked it free.

"You touch me again, and I'll scratch your eyes out. Now get out!" Shaking with rage, she shouted, "Get out! Get *out* of here!"

"Janey! Honey, what did I—"

But the crying, the voice cracking through the tears. She had heard it all before. On Sunday mornings the weeping sounded so natural, so convincing. Here, outside its natural setting, canned, pathetic.

"Get the hell out of here!"

"Now listen—"

She spoke slowly, and the sound came from deep in her throat. "Leave."

Stunned, he backed away. "You can't take a man's children away. It's my God-given right." He shouted, "You can't take 'em away from me!" Holding onto the door frame, he lurched into the hall.

Fifteen

In the quiet light filtering into the loft that was now Jane and the twins' bedroom, the old bentwood rocker creaked in the easy cadence a mother falls into when holding an infant. Jane nursed Bekah while Darcy, with her round, full belly, lay asleep in the crib. One of the ways Jane's babies had changed her was rhythm; she often moved even while standing still, in the universal swaying of mothers.

At midnight the night before, and two, four and six o'clock, the twins awoke, howling to be fed, as they had for the past three months. Today's feeding, though quiet and uneventful, wore Jane out. Exhaustion ate away at her romantic sense of child rearing. Some days, between feedings, laundry, diapers, bathing and caring for her babies, she never changed out of pajamas.

The workings of Bekah's mouth were sporadic now, as she dozed in and out. Jane kissed her daughter's head and savored the talcum smell. She rose from the rocker, then froze and held her breath, praying the rocker's creak would not wake the child.

Darcy was so easy. But Bekah, wiry and active, needed little sleep. Worse, it seemed her tiny radar responded to the least suggestion of abandonment. Ruth and Bob's attempts at comforting the baby helped little; she wanted only Mama. Bekah's red-faced hysteria perplexed and frightened them all, resulting in a bonding so complete between mother and child it was crazy making at times.

Jane lowered Bekah to the foot of the crib, as far from Darcy as possible. Bekah started, waved her arms. Jane held her breath. She gently rubbed the tiny back. The baby's eyelids flickered open, then closed, the small fists relaxed. Jane backed away to the other side of the room and sank into bed.

Deep rhythmic breathing. Cool, dark, restful. Shortly after the watery deep of sleep soaked into her, restoring her, Bekah's piercing wail brought her back. Jane lay there, and finally opened scratchy eyes. Now Darcy squalled.

Jane sat up, woozy, defeated.

"Go to sleep, babies!" she croaked. "Let me sleep." Part of her wanted to comfort them, but fatigue had wiped out the power to move.

Bekah and Darcy bawled, and Jane found herself crying and overwhelmed by self pity. Shaken by her inability to cope, she felt like a child, not a mother, and wanted nothing more than to rest.

What am I going to do? I need to sleep. God, I need sleep, she thought. *Other mothers don't go round the clock like this.* Then, worry seeped in. *What's wrong with Bekah? Maybe I should call the doctor again.*

Mom. The name came to her suddenly. But she recoiled from it. Often, during the past year, she had wanted to contact her mother, but each time she went to the phone, she tensed with anticipated rejection. When she tried to write, no words came. In all that time, her mother had not been in touch.

She clamped her hands over her ears to shut out the screeching, wanting her mother now with fierce longing.

Wiping her eyes, Jane picked up her daughters, whose faces, by now, were blotchy red. She tried to shush them, talking in a low, melodic voice, but the babies continued to scream. With grim determination, she got them ready, and with Bekah in one arm and Darcy in the other, headed out the door.

On the freeway, she could think. The motion of the car lulled the children to sleep in their car seats. Her eyes flicked occasionally to the rearview mirror to check on them.

I should just put them in the car for their naps. But that doesn't help me. I need to rest.

Angelic. Her parents couldn't possibly reject them. She caught herself. No, it wasn't the girls she wondered about. It was herself. She tried to picture the expression on her mother's face when she answered the door. For a year now, she had avoided Jane, lacked the strength to stand up to her husband and fight for Jane. Her father's temper, like a troll under the family bridge, kept them all tiptoeing. No one, not even Louise, though at times she enjoyed taunting him, wanted to anger the ogre.

Air roared in through open windows. Verdant eastern Washington conifers sped past with a cornblue sky overhead. The interstate traffic kept her busy enough to put aside her mental wanderings. Her lip stiffened, she took a deep breath and pushed the needle of the old car's speedometer up until the vehicle shuddered.

Two hours later, she pulled onto a familiar street and slowed. It seemed strange to be back in Rathcreek after being away so long. She turned a corner, and felt fear.

What if Mom wants nothing to do with me? How will she react when she sees her grandchildren? She noticed her grasp of the steering wheel and loosened it. *What if she turns us away?*

Jane let the car drift past the tidy beige house. She jammed on the brakes and thought, *This is ridiculous!* then, threw the car into reverse. *I'm going to get my mother back.* She pulled into the driveway, turned off the engine and glanced at her watch.

Good, Dad's still at work. First, Mom, then Dad. Jane took a deep breath.

Bekah and Darcy stirred in their car seats, awakened by the lack of motion. Bright, round eyes opened wide, and Bekah's and Darcy's faces broke into gummy grins. Jane held out her arms and the babies strained toward her. The grip of anxiety loosened.

With a baby in each arm, she made her way to the front door.

"Jane!" Louise cried, and awkwardly, they hugged around the girls. Jane flushed with gladness at seeing her sister's happy face. Louise clapped her hands, and, palms up, waved Darcy toward her, well aware that Bekah would have no one but Jane.

Jane was relieved Louise had answered the door. No military uniform or combat boots, make-up tame and hair clean. Louise wore large, silver peace symbol earrings and a red halter top—only because it was verboten in her father's house, no doubt. Yes, Louise seemed to be having one of her good days.

Jane took in the surroundings. Everything as it always had been. The worn, plaid couch, her dad's rickety recliner, the television's soft whining. All her life in this home, she had been prepared for nothing resembling real life: divorced, mother of two children by another man, an outcast of her family and friends. Back among the things of her past, her life was like a Picasso among Norman Rockwells.

"Mom, look who's come to dinner!" Louise called.

Mary Crownhart came from the kitchen, and stopped in the doorway.

After her initial surprised "Oh!", she wouldn't look at Jane. Pale as the faded carpet, eyes to the floor and up, floor, up, like an abused dog.

Jane's throat closed. She labored to breathe. Didn't know if she was alive or dead. Louise had gotten it wrong when she reported a nasty fight between their parents over Jane. It wasn't her father at all, but her own mother who didn't want the daughter who had disgraced the family.

With effort, Mary lifted her head. Her eyes glistened. Jane reminded herself to breathe. She said in a thick voice, "Mom?"

Mary seemed unable to move. The soft brown eyes looked to be a sad sign of welcome. Her mouth moved without words, just trembling lips.

From the couch, Darcy, propped up with pillows, chortled. The lamp shade over Louise's head tipped back. "Peek-a-boo!"

Mary's gaze went from Jane to her granddaughter. Louise was blowing on the baby's round belly now, making loud, rude noises. Darcy giggled, and the sound, like electricity to a bulb, illuminated Mary's face with soft joy.

Jane cleared her throat. "Thought you'd like to see your grandchildren, Mom."

"Janey," her mother cried, the sound, to Jane, the sweetest pain.

Then she knew there was nothing that could kill the love between this daughter and this mother. There was no sin beyond the power of love to heal.

The two came together and clung, tears wetting their cheeks. Jane held her tenderly, fiercely. Her mother's frame was slight, like her own, yet seemed more fragile. When Bekah let out a squeal, they laughed and parted, both wrung out with relief.

"Watch that little one in the middle," Louise called from the couch, where she was playing pat-a-cake with Darcy. "She's a real mama's girl, and has nothing to say to you or the CIA, thank you very much."

Jane wanted never to let go of this moment. Mary's eyes had not wavered from her face. For a time, they stood, just looking at each other.

"I-I'm so sorry, sweetheart." Mary pulled a tissue from her jeans, dabbed her eyes, and, as if not believing her daughter stood before her, ran a hand over her hair and down the curve of her cheek.

Jane took hold of it and nodded.

They spent the afternoon playing peek-a-boo and pat-a-cake and tickling the dark, dimpled Darcy, who captivated everyone. Bekah's reserve finally broke down and, feeling at ease in experienced hands, let her grandma hold her. They looked through boxes of old photos, comparing the twins to Jane's baby pictures. Jane told her mother about Bekah and asked how to get the child to sleep.

Mary laughed. "You're not going to like what I have to say."

"What do you mean?"

"You have such a tender heart, you won't like my advice. You got to let her exercise her lungs. She needs to get used to entertaining herself, like Darcy does. Start with small doses. Leave her crying in the crib five minutes a few times a day, then go in and pick her up. Then, ten, fifteen, thirty minutes, an hour. And for heaven's sake, put the girls in separate rooms. Divide and conquer."

"It's so simple, Mom. Why didn't I think of that?"

"Because you're tired." Mary fluffed the sparse hair on Bekah's head.

"You mean exhausted. Was I like Bekah?"

Mary grinned. "You had your moments, but, no, not like Bekah. She's more sensitive than most. And there weren't two of you."

Jane winced. "I don't know if I can stand to hear her cry that long."

"You're a good mother, sweetheart. That's why it's tough. But sometimes, they got lessons to learn."

"Even at three months?"

"Even at three months. You got your share. I had to go to the other end of the house and turn on the radio. Looks like you turned out all right."

Warmth flowed through Jane. Her mother loved her, had always loved her and always would.

Later, Jane nursed the babies, and afterward helped Mary set the table. Bekah played with a set of keys a few feet away in her carrier. Louise sat at the table jouncing Darcy on her knee.

"Can't wait to see Dad's face," Louise said, glancing at the clock on the stove.

Jane looked at her mother. "What do you think, Mom?"

Mary shrugged, and put broccoli into a pan of boiling water. "I hope he can see he has a daughter and two beautiful granddaughters and put an end to this."

"It's just the sex," Louise said.

"Louise!" her mother said in a warning voice.

"What do you mean?" Jane asked.

"Well, lessee." Louise turned her attention from the baby to Mary. "Mom, you know how Dad gets all blustery and flustery whenever the idea of Jane and the rev doin' it comes up? It's like sex is the top ranking sin. I mean, Jesus, she didn't kill anybody. Me thinks he doth protest too much."

Mary said stiffly, "Careful, Louise. There is no top-ranking sin. You know good and well that blasphemy against God is the only unforgivable sin."

"You mean like using God in vain? Like taking advantage of Janey in the name of God?"

Jane had to smile. Louise was in prime form.

Mary took the salad to the table, her movements bristling. "Don't you bait me, young lady. I will not be drawn into where this discussion is going."

"Okay, okay. But you gotta admit that sex is the uncomfortable sin for Christians." Louise moved her shoulders and her breasts jiggled.

"Louise!"

Louise put the baby's hand to her mouth and blew her pursed lips. Darcy squealed and pulled away. "I wonder how many of The Fellowship had sex before they were married? Did you and Dad—" She glanced up and didn't finish, then asked in a tone suggesting safe ground, "It's righteous to hate the homos, though, huh?

Good God! Careful, Louise, Jane thought, stifling a giggle. Phil, one of Louise's best friends, was homosexual.

Mary was silent.

"But what about regular ol' adultery, like Janey did?"

Jane felt herself blush. Mary's lips were a tight line, as if she knew Louise had to play herself out.

"Whatever. Remember when God forgave David not only for plankin' that guy's wife, but for killing her husband, too? So what are we worried about?"

"Nothing. Absolutely nothing," Mary said. Trying to keep the lid on Louise was impossible, but she made an attempt anyway. "Hush. You don't know how your father will react today, none of us do."

"My money's on Jane staying with Aunt Ruth." Louise tilted her head side to side for the baby, who opened her mouth in a soundless smile.

"Aunt Ruth and Uncle Bob said I could stay as long as I want." Then to Louise, "You'd never know they're Christians, it's so peaceful there. But I want to get a place of my own as soon as I can get out and get a job. Find some daycare." Her smile slipped from her face. Her father's old station wagon was pulling into the driveway.

In a few moments, the kitchen door slammed behind Joe Crownhart, dirty and tired-looking in his work clothes.

He was a tall, solid man with graying hair, wide shoulders and strong arms from years of construction work. When Jane was a girl, he used to make her laugh by putting those massive arms behind his head and flinching the huge muscles, making them dance.

His gaze took them all in, the babies, Mary, Louise and finally, Jane. It seemed to Jane, that the sight of her babies, the only grandchildren he would likely ever have, surged over him like a riptide, and his silence and the helpless look on his face felt to her as though he was drowning in the swell of his emotions.

They were absolutely beautiful. He had to see that. She wondered how anything could go wrong out of this moment of finally coming face to face with his own child's children, two of them, the continuation of his blood line, and wondered if his knees were as weak as hers were.

Then, she saw the resentment flooding through him, as if this joy were rendered unnatural, these children conceived in sin. Jane, always heralded as the brightest, the best, his last hope of bringing honor to the Crownhart name, hung her head, seeing in his eyes that she had only brought disgrace. How stupid she was. How adolescent to believe a couple of Gerber babies could wash away her sin. Jane looked up at him, and her look wrung out the pride from his face, until only disgust remained.

"Hi, Dad," Jane said in a controlled voice.

Ignoring her, he walked to the stove and lifted the lid of a sauce pan. A cloud of steam escaped. "You call the repairman about the oven?" He replaced the lid with a clatter of irritation.

Mary looked at him in supplication.

He was unyielding.

Louise, with Darcy at her shoulder, sauntered to the cupboards, opened one, found what she was looking for. "No, she didn't, Dad, but I called Olan Mills and set up an appointment for a family photo session." She waved a package in front of the infant. "See this, sweetie? This is *jerk*-y."

Joe bellowed, "Louise, that's enough of your smart mouth."

Louise shrugged.

Mary went to Jane and put an arm around her, pushed the long hair behind her ears. Mary studied her face, the face they both knew so strongly resembled Joe's: the narrow nose, sharp jawline, high cheekbones.

"I've invited Janey to dinner," Mary finally said, shepherding her daughters to the table. "Please, Joe, sit down and let's eat before everything gets cold."

He walked across the kitchen, shoved his lunch pail onto the counter and glared at the women. "I'm not hungry."

Louise and Jane exchanged glances.

"Can I have yours?" Louise asked, voice snide, eyes narrowed.

"Who do you think you're talking to?" he roared. "As long as I pay the bills in this house, you'll show respect. Go to your room!"

Louise looked as if to respond, but changed her mind and turned to go. The babies were crying now.

"Please, Joe, you're scaring the babies." Mary took Darcy from Louise as she stalked past. She held her against her shoulder. Jane shushed Bekah, but it did no good.

Mary spoke over the babies' crying. "Joe, it's time you talked this through with Janey, see her side of it."

"I thought I told you, we have no daughter by that name."

Mary's face clouded. She pounded the table. "These are our grand-children!"

He lashed out at Jane. "You had to come, didn't you? Now look how you upset your mother. Think you can just waltz in here with these - these *kids* of yours."

Jane, holding Bekah tightly to her, shouted, "Don't you speak about my daughters that way! Don't you dare stand there, when I know you still go to his church, believing him over me, when you never even asked what happened. Your own flesh and blood!"

"You dirtied the Crownhart name," he replied, drilling the words at her. "You've done nothing but bring shame on me and your mother and the Lord our God."

"David's dead!" she screamed at him. "Logan seduced me! Why can't you see?"

Joe didn't say a word. Jane watched her father, the head of a respectable family, a God-fearing man, blind to his dead son, his schizophrenic daughter. And saw his pained look turn to one of revulsion.

"Awright, you want to know? You made your choices. And they *were* choices. Yes, David's dead. Reverend Churlick and I talked that out, man to man. God's will. Not his *choice*. So you up and *choose* to back out of your marriage vows with that boy. Jake was a fine husband. And you go traipsing around, get yourself pregnant, and expect me to believe *your* word against the reverend's? He's already said you seduced him. Already asked forgiveness of this family, Jake, The Fellowship. How am I *supposed* to look at it? Who would you believe?"

"I wish I could make you see that things aren't what they seem." *But then*, she thought, *Churlick's so damn good at shaping everything into the way he wants us to see it, as far away from God as it can get.* She wiped her nose with the back of her hand and asked softly, during a lull in Bekah's crying, "Wasn't there ever a time you needed to be forgiven?"

She could see, even through the veil of tears, that the plaintiveness of her voice startled him, haunted him.

Her father's mouth twisted. "Yeah, I been forgiven. For sins you never heard of, before you were born. Your mother's never heard of 'em, neither. And you're not gonna hear about 'em now." He licked his lips, his eyes vacant, back to another time. When he focused on her again, he was angry. "Logan Churlick made me into a new man, a stronger man, an' my core belongs to God. But you, you rejected the church. My church. My faith. My God. The one that saved me. So now you're askin' me to choose you over my God. Well, I'm not about to do that."

His words wounded Jane deeply. Yes, she had rejected everything he hung his soul on, but she was his loving daughter. And yet, he chose Churlick's God.

"All right, stop it! Stop it!" Mary's voice was strong, stronger than Jane had ever heard it, and her face was like granite. "For a man who helped in the making of her, I think you've done enough to destroy our daughter for one day."

Joe was so surprised, he simply stared at her.

"I gotta go," Jane said, lips tight. She gathered the babies' things, while trying to quiet the child on her hip.

Mary nodded. "I'll call you soon. This is something your father and I have to work out."

He swiped at the air with a huge paw. "Work out, nuthin'. And you're not callin' her if I have anything to say about it."

"In the name of almighty God, Joe! Will you *shut up?* I won't have you upsetting our daughter and grandbabies one more minute."

Joe's mouth fell open.

Jane, her heart throbbing in her chest and in her temples, turned from him, and followed by her mother, left the house.

Soon, the old Ford idled in the drive. Mary leaned on the open window, grasping Jane's hand.

"It's going to be okay, now. Really. And if you hadn't come, if I hadn't seen you and these babies, I don't know how long it would've taken me to do what I should've done a long time ago. You have so much courage, my darling girl."

Jane squeezed her hand. "I'm not letting him take you away from me again. Are you sure you'll be all right?"

She nodded, lifted Jane's hand to her lips. "Jane. He can't tell me how to feel or how to think. But you have to leave this to me. This is something between a husband and wife. Now you go on and leave it to me."

Jane watched her mother go back to sit on the porch step. She waved good bye, then saw her father open the back door and call out, "You coming in?"

Jane put the car into reverse, waved again. Mary's eyes didn't leave her. As she backed slowly down the drive, she heard her mother say, "Joe, did you see those babies? That little Bekah looks just like you."

Sixteen

Jane fought the first battle for her children with her parents, and eventually there came an uneasy truce. She did not know, however, that the war was only beginning.

By the time the twins were toddlers, Jane's life was full and happy and busy. She was the center and meaning of her children's existence, and they had become the sun of her orbit. Jane raised her girls with a firm tenderheartedness, which produced happy and cheerfully dutiful children in everything a parent could ask for. Everything except bedtime.

Bekah and Darcy sat on either side of Jane cozied between them on the big bed. She flipped to a page in a Mother Goose book and read:

> The Man in the Moon looked
> out of the moon,
> Looked out of the moon
> and said,
> "'Tis time for all children
> on earth
> To think about getting to bed!"

"No!" Bekah yelped, holding her ears before the poem had finished. She dove under the covers.

"No bed!" Darcy brought the covers over her head in imitation of her sister.

In her best crusty pirate voice, Jane said, "N-o-o-o-o-w, I wonder whar those kiddies could've gone? Whar could they have dis-ca-peared to?" She lumbered out of bed, taking the comforter as a cape, and through one squinted eye, glanced around the room. "Could they b-e-e-e. . . . in th' *closet?*" She scrambled over. "Flibber me gibblets. Get away from *me*, will they? *I'll* find 'em, or they'll be Cheetos to pay!"

The blankets giggled.

"Uh? Aaaarrrgh. Not there," she muttered, and swung around to survey the room with her good eye. "Whar *else?*"

The blankets shivered in excitement.

"Ah ha *ha!*" Jane croaked and hobbled forward, cloak dragging. "Aye know whar those girlies went. Right *here!*" she cried, and yanked back the bedding.

The twins erupted in screams.

"Aaarrrgh! Now I've got you, my little girlies!" She snorted and lunged across the bed, pulling one girl by the foot, then the other. The girls squealed and scrambled madly to the safety of the pillows, only to be dragged back again by a foot.

Finally, Jane stood and announced that it was bedtime. Really.

Bekah pouted. Hazel eyes downcast, face framed by a wispy halo of sandy curls. Darcy, round cheeks dimpling, checked with her sister, then shrank back into the pillows. Her thick auburn hair, static electrified, reached for the ceiling.

"You had snuggle time, reading. Time for bed now," Jane said, voice firm.

She picked Darcy up, nuzzled her soft neck with kisses and arrrghs, then tucked her into bed. Darcy's arms went around her neck. The little girl kissed Jane. Arms around her neck. The kiss. The look in her daughter's eyes. Tenderness blew through the room, and the petal of Jane's heart floated to the floor.

"I love you, Mama."

"I love you, too, more than anything." She smoothed the child's round cheek, feathery strokes that brushed its softness. A physical tightness took her breath away.

"Mama!" Bekah called, impatient.

Jane turned. Bekah scrambled down from bed, then the wiry child's footed pajamas, fffph-fffphing across the carpet. She looked back at Jane, and raced for the door.

Jane dashed, swooped her up. "Got you! *You* are a stinker!" She poked her stomach, and the little girl grabbed her belly and laughed.

Bekah tucked into bed, smiling angel now, pooched out her lips. Jane bent and kissed her headstrong child.

"Hug!" Bekah demanded, thin arms outstretched. Held in love's headlock, Jane received a moist, artless kiss, the kind she would remember always.

Still, Bekah held her, prolonging the parting. She whispered, "Mama, you're my best friend." Jane bent forward, touched her forehead to Bekah's.

"I love you, too, Bekah. More than anything in the world."

Downstairs, Jane collapsed into the softness of the old second-hand sofa and pulled a couple of throw pillows over her head. The furnishings were meager, as was the old duplex on the south side.

For a while, she went a little crazy, with no job, no prospects and two kids to feed. Ruth and Bob had asked her to stay, but pride wouldn't let her, at least not any longer than necessary to prepare a decent future for her kids. So she brushed up her secretarial skills, unused since she was married to Jake, and lucked into a job that let her quit the WIC program. She was a low level secretary in the Spokane school district. The salary was decent, and she was out of Rathcreek. With a steady paycheck and a few months longer with Ruth and Bob, she was able to save up enough for first, last and damage deposit. It was not easy, and she missed her kids insanely in the beginning, but it worked better than the church had ever given her to expect the single mother routine could.

The phone rang.

"What's up?" Ruth asked.

"Hi, Ruth. Not much." Jane paused, then plunged ahead with a problem that had nagged her all day. "Well, actually—I was thinking of calling you tonight. You know how Churlick's been pestering me, turning up the heat lately, trying to see the girls?"

"Yes. Just a second, hon," Ruth said. "Bob? You need to get on the other phone."

"Three cheers for the easy payment plan for the lawyer you got me."

"Maybe not the best, but definitely affordable," Bob said.

"Good enough that he's been stalling Churlick's lawyer for almost two years now: illness, continuances, whatever he could come up with. Anyway, I got a letter today. I'm served with a summons and petition, and I have to respond within twenty days. Judge . . ." she scanned the envelope she'd pulled from her pocket. "Barker is calling for a command performance on September 15."

"Son-of-a-bitch," Bob said. "We knew it would come."

"Thank God they've been able to live in peace this long," said Ruth.

Cordless phone to her ear, Jane walked to the window. The evening sky was bright with colors that washed the pines on the hillsides cupping the run-down neighborhood.

Her thoughts spun into the past, the way her little girls giggled when they had plundered the berries in Ruth and Bob's yard. Purple hands held out for Mama, Aunt Ruth and Uncle Bob to see. Peace, happiness. All that was threatened.

The death of summer. Bare branches and gray clouds on gray skies. Harsh, soul-chilling Spokane winters, dark and depressing. Rain, fog, and finally, snow that blotted out everything, and made it seem as if the blank world had started over.

She turned from the window, tried to sound matter-of-fact, but her words were tremulous and she was close to weeping. "Something about a paternity suit. My lawyer said that means they'll take a blood sample and determine if Logan's the father. And when they do," her voice faltered, "he could be awarded joint custody of my girls."

September 15th. An edgy, tension-colored day. Electric black, crackling under the surface of Jane's thoughts, guided by a mind there and not there.

Straight-backed, shoulders tense, Jane sat in the third floor courtroom of the Rathcreek Courthouse feeling as insubstantial as fog laced with fine particles of fear. Her attorney, Oliver Sanchez, was on her left. Ruth, Bob and her mother behind. Logan and Dolores Churlick sat at another table with their lawyer, Dick Moore.

Judge Hellen Barker presided. Even expressionless, a scowl that cut a permanent line on either side of Judge Barker's mouth gave her a judicious air. In her black robes, she commanded respect to the office of judge of the superior court.

Finally, the court clerk called Churlick versus Powers. A summary of the relationship between Jane and Logan was made by Mr. Moore. Information concerning the children's names, ages, birthdates was entered into the record. Mr. Moore submitted exhibits to the court concerning the determination of parentage, the DNA lab reports that would prove Logan Churlick was the father of Bekah and Darcy Powers.

Bekah and Darcy Powers. Jane's children. Her life. And now, Logan would enter it, as if he had simply been gone on a long trip.

After the swearing in, Mr. Moore asked, "Reverend Churlick, how long have you known Janey Powers?"

Logan smiled pleasantly and spoke in the resonant voice that she had heard most of the Sundays of her life. "Since she was old enough to wet my knee."

Mr. Moore chuckled. "Since she was a toddler, then?"

"Yes."

"And what has been your relationship to her?"

Logan took his eyes from the attorney and fixed them with benevolence on Jane. "I've been her minister, minister to her entire family for these twenty years."

"Reverend, now tell the court about your relationship with Mrs. Churlick."

Logan grinned like a school boy. "She's the love of my life. Married twenty-two years, an' there's nothing I wouldn't do for my wife. We have a strong, committed relationship. Even stronger since this, ah . . . indiscretion."

Jane glared at him. Still vivid were his desperate pleas in her hospital room, his throwing Dolores away, his proposal to Jane.

Mr. Moore said, "I realize this may be painful, but can you tell the court what's been your recent relationship with Ms. Powers?"

Logan was silent.

Judge Barker asked curtly, "Did you hear the question, Reverend Churlick?"

"Yes, Your Honor, I heard. It's just hard for me. Not something I'm proud of." He nodded toward his wife. "I'd do anything to spare Dolores havin' t' go through this again." Then he straightened. "In all the time I've been in the ministry, I've never met a more openly seductive woman as Jane Powers."

Jane's mouth fell open. In a moment, her astonishment abdicated to stark fury. She pounded the table, but was checked by her attorney's grip on her arm. With an abrupt, definitive movement of his head, he cut off her words. She shot a look of cold hatred to the wooden box at the front of the courtroom, then slumped back in her chair.

"I always prided myself on bein' a man strong in the spirit, and strong in the flesh, but I'm here to tell you, there was nothin' any man coulda done against her cunning manipulations." He turned to the judge. "She says she came to see me about counselin', but there wasn't no counselin'. I'm enough a professional to know that's against the law."

"Then what happened?" Mr. Moore prodded.

Churlick hung his head. "She seduced me. I swear I didn't want to. I was a happily married man! But the way she had about her, the way she used me to get back at her husband. And now she's divorced, and I'm doin' the best I can to rebuild my marriage."

Jane felt Oilver Sanchez's hand on her arm, and realized she was standing, mouth opened, a quick breath taken to speak. He pulled her back into the chair.

Lies! Lies! she scribbled on a legal pad.

Sanchez whispered, "We'll have our turn. Stay calm. Judges hate emotional outbursts."

"How many times did you and Ms. Powers have sex?" Mr. Moore asked.

"Let's just say lots. Whenever we could get alone for a little bit." He hung his head again, then looked up. "We were lovers. That is, till she found out she was pregnant. Then she went a little crazy. Guess we both went a little crazy, being as I was the spiritual leader of my church, an' Rathcreek's a small town. We knew it had to be my baby, because she was separated from her husband long before this time. Whenever I tried to talk to her about it, she refused, said it was God's punishment. Poor li'l thing was so mixed up. Seriously unbalanced at this point, I'd say. Wouldn't let her parents or anyone else help her or talk sense to her, only her schizophrenic sister, I guess." He looked at her, effecting a perplexed sympathy.

"Then she ran away to live with her aunt and uncle. Now they think they're just tryin' to protect her fragile mental state, but they've done a whole lot of harm standin' in the way of us workin' this out."

Jane felt the threat of tears and struggled for control. Trembling, she turned to her lawyer.

Sanchez frowned and shook his head in a short, swift motion.

She sat back, feeling doomed, her children doomed. Their beautiful faces, arms around her neck as she kissed them good-bye that morning after dropping them off with their *schizophrenic* Aunt Louise.

Light-headed, Jane was startled when the courtroom was suddenly enveloped in surges of fear and anger leaving holes in her hearing. And so with her half-hearing, she took in the sounds, surges playing over it all, and tried to concentrate on what she would say when her turn came.

Mr. Moore outlined Logan's conduct since the birth of the babies, his regularly sent support checks for the girls, which were returned, trying to talk to the children's mother at the hospital, contacting her by letter, and finally, appealing to the court.

"I'd like to be a daddy to my daughters, Your Honor. I deserve that. I *am* their father. Even though I'm sure Janey's doin' a good job raisin' 'em so far, I don't think she should be allowed to use these girls to get back at me."

Mr. Moore thanked the reverend, gave another report to the clerk, a psychological profile of the Churlicks certifying their suitability as parents, then said he had nothing else.

Cross examination by Sanchez yielded nothing. Logan stuck to his story, elaborated on it, even, and denied assertions that he had mentally coerced Jane and forced her into a single sexual encounter. The judge excused him, and Logan ambled to his seat, took Dolores' hand and kissed it.

Feeling translucent, Jane was called to the stand and sworn in. She drifted in and out, recognizing that her life could be destroyed by this con man's story. Her children could run into the arms of this man, laugh and be nurtured by the same breath that was hot on her own ear. And she understood that she, the unbalanced, assassinated mother of these happy children could sing Truth from the rafters, but only God could protect them.

Oliver Sanchez talked in a comfortable, languorous manner. "Jane, Logan Churlick has told this court he's minister to your family. Would you say he had authority over everything that went on in your life for as far back as you can remember?"

"Yes."

Sanchez nodded and strolled to the corner of the polished oak table. "Jane, you had problems with your husband, Jake Powers, is that right?"

"Yes."

"Problems you went to see Mr. Churlick about?"

"Yes."

"And how old were you when you went to see Mr. Churlick for marital counseling?"

"Twenty-one."

"Twenty-one. And Mr. Churlick answered earlier that he was in his early forties. So you went to see this man, *old enough to be your father,* a trusted counselor and spiritual guide for help in putting your marriage back together?"

"Yes."

"And did Mr. Churlick, forty-some years old, hold any physical attraction to you?"

"No!"

Sanchez said quietly, "No, I don't suppose a young woman *would* find a man her father's age attractive at all, under normal circumstances. But then, these are not normal circumstances, are they?"

"No."

"So when and how did things change?"

Jane drew a breath and let it out slowly. "I. . . . I'd been to see him several times, and then one day—" She looked away.

"Yes, go on."

"He said God had appointed him to teach me 'yieldingness.' The problem with my husband. . . . oh, God, I can't even *believe* I used to be this way. But, I *believed* him. Honest, Your Honor. And here's *why* it could happen." She turned in earnest to the black robe on the bench. "It's drummed into you that you're not to question God, not to assert yourself, but let *His* will be done. His will, as related by Reverend Logan Churlick. Any need to question why, and you're not a believer. You don't have faith. Question God? Not if you want to belong . . . and more than anything in the world, you *want* to belong to this church, belong to God. Question God's man, Reverend Churlick? It just wasn't done. By anyone. He said God told him he was to minister to me to teach me yieldingness to my husband."

"Objection, your honor!" Mr. Moore called from the opposing table. "We didn't waste time going over details of the seduction, which are not important to the question at hand. The focus of this inquiry is not a pornographic recounting of who seduced whom, but rather the fate of the children which resulted from their union."

"Your Honor," Mr. Sanchez appealed, palms wide, "this establishes the father's moral depravity. I'd never have my client re-live such a traumatic episode if it weren't crucial to establishing the overall character of a man who could be raising these children."

Jane was horrified. The judge couldn't throw Churlick's character out. Their case depended on revealing him as morally corrupt and dangerous. Churlick's story, of Jane as a woman of loose morals, a seducer who was crazy like her sister, had been allowed to be established, and lodged in some pocket of the judge's mind. It couldn't be fair.

Hellen Barker considered a moment. "Overruled. The question of whether both parties are suitable to care for these children can only be established if I hear enough testimony regarding Ms. Powers *and* Mr. Churlick's character to make a determination."

Jane let out her breath.

Mr. Sanchez said, "Thank you, Your Honor." Then to Jane, "How did the seduction happen?"

Voice subdued, eyes lowered, Jane drifted back to the study, the cool darkness with the furnace of August outside, the leather couch, the rug's texture against her knees, their praying, hands clasped, then hands on her breasts . . . "He told me God wanted me to submit to Jake, and he was the one who would teach me to submit. Then he kissed me and told me he loved me, and God loved me . . ."

She leaned forward in the chair. "All my life, my minister was the spokesman of God to me. I trusted him. He took advantage of me when I was vulnerable, thinking of divorcing my husband. But most of all, he convinced me it was God's will to submit to him and honor this love God had allowed to happen."

Oliver Sanchez shook his head. "Incredible. This preacher took advantage of his position of authority, manipulated you via God's will, until he had total control of you in the privacy of your counseling sessions."

"Session. We had sex once. I never went back. The next time we had any kind of conversation, it was at the hospital, the day after I had the babies. He came to my room, told me he wanted to be a father to the girls, wanted to - to—" She glanced at Churlick's wife. A part of Jane hated to hurt Dolores, who, she believed, was also a victim. After all, nobody in all of Rathcreek really knew how sleazy, how self-serving and manipulative a man Logan Churlick was. But Dolores surely knew, as the job had always fallen to her to cover up the slimy mark he left behind.

"He wanted to marry me, so we could both be parents to the girls."

Churlick whispered to Dolores.

"I told him he was sick and to get out of my room," said Jane.

"Would you tell the court in your own words the reasoning behind your spurning any moves by Mr. Churlick to co-parent?"

Jane drew herself up. "I gave up a lot to bring my daughters into the world, and I love them with everything in me. He manipulated me into having sex. He knew and I knew it was wrong. That's not belief in God. It's not even normal. And how normal is it for a man to come to a woman's hospital room and beg her to marry him? To throw his wife away?

"Look," she pleaded, "Just because he's persistent about his rights doesn't make him a good father. It makes him a fanatic. He was involved in my brother's death and he seduced me . . ."

"Objection!"

"Sustained. Keep to the pertinent facts, Ms. Powers."

Unrepentant in her heart, she could not contain her fear. "He's asking me to offer up the two most precious people in the world to him. After what he did, which practically amounts to rape in the name of God, he doesn't deserve to be a father to these children."

"Objection, your honor!" Mr. Moore shouted.

"Sustained," Judge Barker said. "Ma'am, your testimony has unraveled into a diatribe, and I don't think I need to remind you that my courtroom is not an appropriate place for name calling. Is your client finished, Mr. Sanchez?"

Straight to hell. That's what she'd done. Sent her darlings straight to hell. Maybe Moore was right. Maybe she was unhinged. Oh, God, what had she done? Why hadn't she shut up? Limp and lightheaded, Jane rose to leave the witness box.

"Mrs. Powers," Churlick's lawyer began, approaching her. "I know this has been difficult, but I have a few more questions."

She sat down, suffused with a new fear.

"Mrs. Powers, are you asking the court to believe that Reverend Churlick, a man of the cloth who has never had a shred of indecent behavior leveled at him by any other member of the congregation, except for you in your attempt to thwart his attempt at . . ."

"Objection!" Sanchez charged.

Judge Barker sustained.

"My apologies, Your Honor." Moore turned to Jane. "Do you believe Reverend Churlick is a rapist?"

The judge raised her eyebrows, but Moore held up a hand.

Jane felt trapped by the question, which, she was sure, was his intent. Not, did he rape you, but *is* he a rapist, like he does it every Sunday evening after a rousing sermon.

"A rapist? You mean like someone who stalks young women jogging in the park?" she asked in a cutting tone.

Judge Barker said curtly, "Just answer the question, Ms. Powers."

Jane sighed. "I swear before God and this court that Logan Churlick mentally coerced me into having sex with him."

"But you were twenty-one years old, is that correct? And married?" Moore smashed his fist on the railing. "And a willing participant!"

"No!"

"Then you attempted to get away?"

"I. . . . I struggled. I told him no. But he . . . he wouldn't, and I couldn't . . ."

"Did you scream? Did you scream so that someone, maybe Mrs. Churlick, might come into the reverend's study and interrupt the so-called rape?"

Oh, God, he *had* trapped her. She lowered her eyes. "No."

"So you lovers were simply enjoying yourselves?"

Jane was silent. In his office, Logan had been so convincing, and she had felt such shame at her lack of faith. But here, in this court of law, the lawyer had twisted one of the most powerful moments in her life. Now, God's instructions, Logan's declaration of love, had become all rubbery and farcical. How could she tell them he had mesmerized her? His eyes, those intense, black eyes she stared at now with loathing, and felt his victory glinting back at her. Those eyes were magic.

"I couldn't scream," she said, "I was afraid of offending God. Reverend Churlick said my refusal would offend God. You have to understand how it was—" She glared at Moore. She had never hated anyone as much as him at that moment. He was working to take away her children and give them to Logan.

"Mrs. Powers," the lawyer breathed in exasperation, "did you report the alleged 'rape'?"

She was dumbstruck. Her stomach, like a rollercoaster, clicked to the top, then plummeted. Sweat trickled down her sides.

"Mrs. Powers?" Mr. Moore was insistent. "Did you report the alleged 'rape'?"

"No."

His face was a picture of incredulity. "May I ask why?"

Exhausted, Jane's head pounded, a tight squeeze of thudding pain behind the eyeballs and along the back of the head, down her cramped shoulders. "I didn't report it because I didn't want to have to go through all that with the police and examinations. I was too torn up emotionally." The dark paneling of the courtroom seemed to close in on her, and the windows emitted little light, and no air.

"So, you became lovers . . ."

"No!"

" . . . and then you moved out of reach when you found you were pregnant and refused him access to his children."

"Ob-jection!" Sanchez cried.

"I withdraw the question," Moore said. "No more questions, Your Honor."

Seventeen

After her dealings with the halls of justice, Jane was known to say that fairness was a dangerous philosophy. She lost her children to joint custody with Churlick, weekly visitations, Father's Day, Christmas, the regular splitting in two of children whose parents are enemies.

Logan existed on the fringe of their lives and made his presence known by his growing influence over vital parts of his daughters' flowering childhoods. By the time Bekah and Darcy were three, they were singing, "Jesus loves me, this I know . . ." and bringing home Sunday school papers with Joseph and Mary glued next to little baby Jesus. By four, they would wake with headaches and stomach aches, recounting, in their limited way, the fiery devils and demons learned at their father's knee.

Jane seethed. All the pains she had taken to protect them from the dangers of organized religion, wasted, because she could not control the most harmful contaminant. Like sludge from the sewer, Logan, pure and unadulterated, flowed freely into their uncorrupted minds every other weekend. Attempting to reason with Logan, she had learned over the years, was like trying to grab at yellow, sulfurous gas; besides being a waste of time, it always left its stink.

But, the girls' goodness and love for her were unchanged, and their sweet ways always moved her. Sometimes it was hard to believe something so beautiful as her daughters could come out of something so ugly as her relationship with Churlick.

Life went forward under a heaven indifferent to Jane's calamities and ecstasies. She dated on and off over the following six years. Recreational dating, she called it, and closed herself off from anything more than companionship. Kissed a little, necked a little, allowed herself the pleasure of a man feeling her body on the dance floor, or feeling the crush of his ardor afterward on the couch. But she never let it go far, and never let herself take it seriously. She did not trust herself to choose the right man after Jake and Churlick, and it brought out a tyrannical cynicism of the heart that bred fine green vines criss-crossing her emotions until they were encased in a living sarcophagus.

One night when Logan had the kids for the weekend, Jane went out on the spur of the moment. She stood with her ticket behind a woman in a purple coat in the lobby of the Garland Theater, waiting for the late night showing of *Citizen Kane*. A man who introduced himself as Theodore struck up a conversation with the two of them, which the woman in purple took over.

Jane nodded good-bye and found her way into the dark theater, then was amused as she noticed the man's look when he realized she and the other women weren't together. After the show, Theodore lost the purple, waited outside, and asked Jane to accompany him to the Milk Bottle Cafe. Normally, she was more cautious about strangers, but his soulful expression, along with his panache of suggesting an analogy between rose bud and the terrorists of September 11, intrigued her.

Later, they sat in her livingroom, having tea.

"You know what confuses me about you?" Theodore asked.

She waited, wondering at the somber expression on the moon shaped face.

"You laugh. All the time, about serious things—I don't know—how they are funny? Please tell me, do you take anything seriously?"

Jane grinned, sipped her tea. "What? You don't have jokes in Romania?"

"Sure, sure. But—how you say? Pick and choose? About government, mainly, in order to survive. But life! Life is full of sorrow. Americans push sorrow out of their minds; it is too real, too difficult. They distract themselves, they laugh, they drink. And so, they lead such shallow existence."

This man's company was enjoyable. But, no spark. It didn't matter. Someone to take her out of herself was enough. It had been so long.

She glanced out the window through the loose weave of the curtains. Hushed snowflakes shone silver in the beams of distant street lamps. Light from the livingroom windows lit the yard, but where the street lamp had burned out in front of her house, it was black.

A car. Instead of slowing to take the turn at the corner, it stopped behind Theodore's parked Acura. Its lights went off. The vehicle, a dark stain that stood out from the snow-covered yard, continued to hold Jane's attention. She waited. It didn't move, no one got out. No dome light. Someone had to be just sitting in it. In front of her house. She reached over, and holding a finger to her lips, pulled the tassel on the lamp.

Logan Churlick sat in the black abyss conjured by his horned madness over Jane, and stared at the car in front of him, then at the house. He jerked when the lights snapped out. Mittened hands that clutched the steering wheel fell helpless into his lap. His face was gray as ashes. The snow sifted down onto the warm hood and melted at first, then concealed the black. The snow thickened and the air in the car grew colder as he waited for inspiration. He didn't know what he could do, but he had to stop his woman from committing this betrayal.

In the back seat of the car were the forms of his sleeping daughters under mounds of blankets. He shivered, soaked with sweat inside the great black wool coat. The coat had been his father's, thick and nubby. It was very warm, and when he moved, the heated air wafted up from the coat's recesses into the frigid car. His breath hung in turbulent clouds of smoke around him before disappearing. He had spied on her many times before, most of the time to no avail, but tonight, something told him to come to her, and now he saw he wasn't crazy. Here she was, with another man. His mind raced, and he rubbed his fist in circles against the dull burning in his chest, trying to quell the pain.

The street lamps were too far away to provide light. He found the darkness soothing to a brain that seemed on fire. And when a final judgment was reached, blackness suited him. He pushed the button on the glove box and groped for the cell phone.

Theodore, mistaking Jane's meaning when she extinguished the lamp, moved closer. "Well. Dis is serious?" He put his hand on her thigh, moved it tentatively.

Jane stopped his hand, slid a foot along the floor, feeling for her shoe. "No, it's just that something's . . . I thought . . ." She couldn't say anything. It would sound too bizarre.

The phone rang.

"It's wrong number," he whispered.

"No. It could be my parents. Or my kids. Just a minute." And she went in search of the phone.

"Hello?"

Churlick's strangled voice. "Do your children know you're having an affair with another man? Do they know the meaning of 'slut'? Someone'll have to teach them."

"W-What? Logan?"

"You think you're pulling something over here. Well, the Lord's eyes and ears are always open."

"What the hell are you doing parked in front of my house? Where are the kids?"

No response. Then, "They're with me."

"What?"

"Here, wanna talk to 'em?"

She could hear him rousting them from their sleep, hear their protestations against the cold. Finally, she heard Darcy's sweet, high voice.

"Hi, Mommy."

Jane tried to sound calm, but felt as if a hand were squeezing her vocal cords, forcing the words caught in her throat from her an octave higher than normal. "Hi, sweetheart. What're you doing?" She was moving through the darkened house, now, until she stood gazing out the living-room window to the street.

Theodore said something. But more importantly, Logan was talking, muffled, no doubt, by his hand on the phone.

"Mommy," Darcy yawned, "why don't we move in with Daddy?"

"Good God!" Jane cried. "What's that? His idea of a joke?"

She pictured Darcy's earnest face, her fearfulness at the harsh sounds, pictured her handing the phone away, heard the sounds of Logan's voice and Darcy's.

Then Bekah took over, her voice bold. "Why do you have to be divorced? God doesn't like divorce. Other kids have a mom and dad in one house. Why can't we?"

In a slow progression through the synapses of Jane's brain, the words and all their meaning flowed out and through her.

My God, she thought, *the kids know I'm divorced, but not from Logan. Of course, this is the way they put it together. It's the way he's put it together.* In the next instant, she realized she couldn't correct the picture. How could she tell ten-year-olds that she'd never been married to their father, that they were illegitimate? Not now, like this. She swallowed and stared out at the black car covered in whiteness.

When she regained her voice, she said, "Bekah, most parents who live apart never get together again their whole lives. In your dad's and my case, it's a guarantee. Besides, what would happen to Dolores? Is he gonna hang her from the rafters in the attic?"

Bekah answered promptly, the words close at hand. "Just get rid of her."

"Get rid of her?" A dread was building in Jane, something was not right. These were not values she had taught her daughter about kindness and consideration.

"Yes."

Jane could see Bekah's guileless attempt at persuasion with this bright, single word. "You won't tell, will you, Mommy?"

Jane's mouth gaped a little, allowing the shallow breath to pass her dry lips. She shook her head slightly.

Bekah continued, "Daddy says it's our secret because if we told Dolores, it would make her sad. He wants to marry you, but you won't . . ."

Jane looked at the window stupidly, her emotions like a rope around her neck, squeezing off the air.

What *was* this unending fantasy of his? It was beyond anything she had ever heard of, way beyond. The girls were ten years old. Could he really be so obsessed with her? It was so twisted. More importantly, what did it mean for her children every time they went to their father's house?

"Put Logan back on."

"Huh?"

"I said put him. . . . never mind." She threw the phone down, ran to the door and flung it open.

"Logan! You son-of-a-bitch! You coward! What are you doing to them?"

She ran down the porch steps, but her feet slipped in the deep snow, kept her from the target she wanted to hurl herself at. She grabbed the railing. The cold stung her hands, snow piled up her sleeve.

The car started and its lights went on.

She screamed, "Leave them out of it, you slimy bastard!"

Logan took off, wheels whipping the rear of the car back and forth on the snowy road.

"You leave them out of it!" She stood there, ankles raw, cheeks icy and stinging, wiped at her runny nose, stared after them. And knew the scene would never leave her.

Eighteen

Obsessions, Jane found from her research at the library, were tricky. Some went on for many years, the unrequited lover playing the martyr. Fantasies replaced reality, and any rebuff of the advances of the obsessed only served to feed his ardor. Sometimes the rebuffs resulted in stalking and threats. A crisis, such as the object of desire moving away or becoming involved with someone, could bring the obsession to the surface, along with bizarre behavior. Jane asked herself who would believe this about Logan Churlick, then let it go.

For several months after the incident that winter, Logan seemed to be on his best behavior. Then on a Sunday in April, he decided to take his daughters' visitation schedule into his own hands.

"I thought I'd call to let you know I'm keeping the kids tonight," Churlick said. "They're going to evening service with me."

"What are you talking about?" Jane asked. "I called your house three times this afternoon, and no answer. Finally, Bekah called and said they'd be home soon. You get them over here. I've just started dinner. I've made their favorite cake."

"I said I'm keepin' 'em. I'll drop 'em off at school tomorrow morning."

"What the hell are you talking about? You can't just keep them. The visitation plan says they're to come back after church service Sunday morning. You'd better get your sorry, late ass over here with my girls."

"But they want to go to church with me," he said reasonably.

"They *hate* going to church with you," Jane cried. "Anyway, that's beside the point. You don't decide when and how long you'll have them. The court does. Now you get them over here."

The girls didn't come home that night, but Jane figured a scene at the church as they played tug-of-war with their daughters wouldn't be the wise answer to this power struggle. So she waited.

Monday evening, the fragrant smells of Mexican food threaded through the house. She was chopping cilantro, then putting together tacos, piercing the spicy, meat-filled corn tortillas with toothpicks to make them ready for frying.

"When's dinner ready?" Darcy asked, looking up from where she and Bekah worked on homework at the kitchen table.

"Not too long."

"Can I have Christina over?" Darcy asked.

"And Leia?" Bekah added.

"Well, I don't know," Jane answered. "We have some serious stuff to talk about."

"About Dad?" Bekah asked.

"Yes, about your dad. Besides, you love my *ta*-cos, ya see," she said, pronouncing the long *a*. "I'm not so sure about Christina and Leia. These are different from the regular variety. Big as bull frogs." She squinted one eye. "Have Christina and Leia ever eaten bull frog-sized *ta*-cos?"

Darcy smiled, shook her head. Bekah giggled.

"There you go then. Tonight's private for dad-talk and bull frog *ta*-cos."

An extra child or two at dinner happened often. Along with the bustle, noise, the dog and cat. Jane loved it all, needed it, like blood coursing through her. It baffled her how some friends at work complained about fussing and straining with their children, when for her, her girls provided the daily infusions she needed to stay alive.

Some days the mounds of dirty clothes and bickering children were a trial, but these tedious, trying details of raising her girls were simply the cost of living. Fulfilling, as nothing else she had ever experienced. And many times, wrapped in ordinary days, a sweet, loving moment lifted her above the mundane.

She cut an avocado in half and scooped out the tender green meat. Mashing it with a fork, she added sour cream, salt and onion powder, simple but good guacamole. Tacos sizzled on the stove.

Bekah and Darcy set the table, and soon they were feasting, the table raucous with girl talk. Their dog, Lucy, sat with her head on first one lap, then another, waiting for hand outs. A chocolate cake waited on the built-in sideboard.

"Well, I'll make this short and sweet," Jane said. "Your father thinks he can remake the visitation plan handed down by the court, according to his whim. That's why he kept you for church last night. Against my wishes."

"We *hated* it!" Bekah said. "We didn't want to, but he made us."

"It's so boring," Darcy added.

"And it's not right. But your dad thinks there's nothing I can do about it." Jane paused. "And I'm here to tell you, he's wrong. Here's what I'm going to do, and I need your help." She looked from one child to the other. "If he wants to play that game, I'm taking the time out of his next visit with you. So if he keeps you over Sunday, I'll keep you over Friday night, and take you to his house on Saturday." She saw the shock. The twins looked at each other.

"Don't you think he'll go ballistic?" Bekah asked.

"I'm scared," said Darcy. "He's going to be mad at *us*."

"Yup, he'll probably flip out, but he won't be mad at you. He'll be mad at me. And maybe he won't be mad at all. If he follows the plan, he has nothing to worry about. I think he'll come around pretty quick."

They ate in silence. The twins shared worried looks.

Bekah said, "I was scared when he wouldn't let us come home last night. Darcy was crying. I wasn't, but we both wanted to go home."

"Yeah, I hate Sunday night church service. No kids but us. It was so boring I fell asleep. Then I got in trouble from Dad," Darcy said. "And I missed you, Mommy. I told him I wanted my Mom."

A lump rose in Jane's throat, along with the protective rage. Her plan was the best she could come up with, and not jeopardize the girls' emotional well-being.

Bekah chewed a mouthful of taco, swallowed. "I have something important to talk about tonight, too."

"Shoot, sport," Jane said.

Bekah's and Darcy's eyes met in the conspiratorial way of twins. Bekah was silent a moment, then blurted, "Can we get our ears pierced?"

Jane's taco stopped in mid-air. She stared at Bekah for a long moment, and Bekah returned the look, unwavering. Darcy also waited.

These cherubs, innocent girl-childs. Ear piercing at ten years old? What next, tattoos? Jane observed her daughters, really looked at their faces. No longer the pudgy cheeks, the overall babyishness. When had that happened?

She understood then how much the twins yearned to grow up, were beginning to take steps that would bring them to womanhood. She also realized, achingly, how much she wanted Bekah and Darcy to stay little girls, innocent and protected by their mommy.

Her usual answer to such questions was rejection to any speeding up of her daughters' headlong rush toward adulthood. Soon enough, they would be wearing and saying things reeking of peer pressure.

Bekah asked again.

"I heard you. I'm thinking," Jane answered. "Who's getting their ears pierced?"

"Everybody."

"Everybody? You mean if everybody jumped off a bridge. . . ."

Bekah and Darcy groaned. "*Mom!*"

"We'll talk about it later, when I've had time to think about it."

After cake, the table was cleared and they sat around the livingroom. Darcy had found an old picture album, and plopped down beside her mother.

She laughed. "Is this Aunt Louise? She looks really weird."

"Some things don't change, hm? And this is you two. Little squirts."

Bekah joined them. Darcy flipped through the pages, Jane commenting on the pictures. Darcy stopped, looked up quizzically. "Who's *this?*"

The girl in the picture couldn't have been more than fourteen, and was sporting her mother's infamous crooked scissor-cut bangs. Young, slender Janey wore shorts that ballooned out, making her long, awkward legs look even more spindly. But the most unfortunate part of the picture, the part that made Jane laugh out loud, was her tortoise shell cat-eye glasses.

Jane chuckled. "That's me."

Bekah and Darcy appeared staggered by the revelation.

In a worried voice Bekah said, "But, Mom, we didn't know you were retarded when you were little."

Jane broke down then, peals of laughter coming from her, until the twins lost their worries in laughter of their own.

"Oh my! That's the best I've heard," she said, and between giggles, let her girls know the circumstances of her appearance.

"Well," Darcy said, "you look much better now."

Jane wiped her eyes. "Thanks. The contacts help, huh?"

She told the girls funny stories about when they were babies. About the time she had fed them strained green beans for lunch, and how later that day it made its way out of the corner of their diapers, down the leg of each and into green mounds on the floor.

"Gross! Tell another one!" Darcy demanded. "About me, this time."

"Like how you loved baked beans and ate them with your whole face?" Jane pointed at a picture of baby Darcy holding an unused spoon in her fist, her bean-covered face beaming above the empty bowl on her high chair tray.

"Now me!" Bekah said, and Jane told her one.

"Now me, Mom?" Darcy begged. "Just one more?"

It was a pleasure to see her earnest Darcy letting herself go. Jane wanted to hear her carefree laughter, but she suddenly didn't feel well. She put a hand to her forehead. Was she feverish? Some of the staff at the office had the flu. Had she caught it? There was a school board meeting tomorrow. With her advancement to mid-level secretary, she couldn't afford to be sick; she had important responsibilities now. Tomorrow night she was supposed to fill in for the Superintendent's secretary and take minutes.

"Alright, girls. It's getting late, and tomorrow's a school day. Time to put your bull-frog bellies to bed."

Bekah and Darcy moaned.

Bekah looked at the clock on the mantle. "But it's only seven-thirty. We always stay up till eight."

"Okay," Jane said, not feeling strong enough to argue.

"What's wrong?" Darcy asked, coming close.

"I don't feel very well. Think I'll rest on the couch a while."

Jane dozed lightly, and was awakened by earrings being gently removed. Her shoes. She smiled. A blanket was carefully draped over her. It seemed almost enough to make her well, her heart was so swollen with love.

Later, when she awoke, Bekah disappeared, then returned, holding out the cordless phone to her.

"We called Aunt Weezie for you, Mom. Thought it might make you feel better." She tried to sound casual to make her love and pride not too sappy.

Jane blinked, hardly able to keep from crying. Never, never, had she felt so loved, so indispensable to her daughters' happiness—as they were to hers. She held out her arm, and from her reclining position on the couch, embraced them both.

"Hello, Weez," she said, laughing. "I'm calling from Little Shriners. Got two of the best doctors in town working up this special prescription: phone medicine. Guaranteed I'll be better by morning."

She was better by morning, apparently victim of a twelve-hour virus. As she rushed to pack lunches and get ready for work, Bekah and Darcy came into the kitchen.

Darcy asked, "Did you think any more about our ears?"

Jane had thought about it, and felt firm about her decision. "Yes, I have. Thirteen strikes me as a good age to get your ears pierced."

The girls crumpled.

Jane held up a hand. "Wait. Hear me out."

Darcy handed her a brush. Jane took it and drew it gently through her long, fine hair, careful not to pull the tender scalp. Nobody could brush Darcy's hair but Mom.

Jane said in a soft voice, "Thirteen's a magical age. It's the first time you're called teen-agers, and lots of changes are happening then, because you're starting to grow into women. It's a time when you get more privileges, and you've got more responsibilities, too. That's where the ear piercing comes in."

In a tone of confidence, she said, "Thirteen is the age I've always had in my head for you to start wearing light lipstick and maybe some blush, if you want." Not much of a concession, since most girls she had seen at that age were beginning to experiment with enhancing their looks. Some well before that age.

The girls looked at each other, smiles breaking out.

She had beaten them to the punch, made the upcoming transition more of a rite of passage, with all the trappings and privileges of womanhood.

She said, "You may even start wearing bras then, if not before."

Two mouths pulled open in shock and delight. "Mom!" they chimed, awed and embarrassed by the visual she had conjured up.

Jane flipped a silken bunch of hair over Darcy's shoulder, then sectioned off another part of the tangled mass and carefully brushed.

"And by the time you're thirteen, you'll be old enough to take proper care of pierced ears. It's a lot of work, making sure you put peroxide or alcohol on them all the time. If you don't take good care of them, they get all infected and filled with puss."

Their eyes widened.

"Didn't know that, did you?"

They were quiet when she finished, offering up no pleas, no bargains, no complaints. They knew their mother had made her decision with her heart. And Jane knew she had given her girls one of life's rare gifts: something solid and magical to look forward to about the scary prospect of growing up.

Nineteen

Giant ponderosa pine, red cedar and western larch crowded the lush mountains surrounding Lake Pend Orielle, except in the rough, bare granite patches nature had worn into sharp spires and ridges. The rugged points held little to sustain life, save the tenacious vegetation and rusty-colored lichens. The dark peaks reflected like sharp, inverted v's in the pristine water of northern Idaho's largest lake. The August sun blazed over the mountains and the thousands of shimmering reflections in the restless water below.

Waves sloshed against the side of power boats and canoes docked near the shoreline. A hundred feet from shore, an American flag fluttered atop a tall pole in a compound of bunk house cabins, a cook house and an open air craft center where The Rathcreek Fellowship held its annual church camp. Some lingering children, their sunburned cheeks and shoulders glistening in the sun, played in the water, but most of the campers were already cleaned up and assembled under a large, striped tarp for the afternoon testimonial.

Under the canopy, eighty evenly spaced chairs lined up in such precision that from any angle the geometric design marched to its vanishing point. And while children, ages nine to thirteen, from Rathcreek and surrounding areas were regularly sent here each summer by their parents to be immersed in a week of Christianity, to come home cleansed of their childish inadequacies, this was the twins' first summer Bible camp. It was the first time the courts had mandated summer visitation for the girls with their father.

Reverend Churlick approached the altar in his flowing robe and multi-colored stole. He smiled at his daughters, pleased to see them sitting near the front as he had arranged. He noted other eleven-year-olds, children of church deacons and elders, seated with them, laughing, talking.

"Look, there's Daddy," Darcy said, and waved.

He nodded and surveyed the growing crowd. The music started up softly, gained volume, and the children began to sing. More parent helpers and children migrated into the tent until it was jammed, a roiling hubbub of heat, music and closeness.

Mrs. Churlick, at the piano, trilled,

"Rise and shine, and give God your glory, glory,
Rise and shine and give God the glory, glory,
Rise and shine and - clap - give God your glory, glory . . ."

Logan grinned when he saw Bekah's head bobbing to the catchy beat and heard Darcy's clear, high voice above the rest. Rhythm was powerful.

As the music died away, he paused, then spread his arms in a wide welcome.

"Hello and God bless!" he boomed into the microphone. The children responded in low murmurings, in the way of pre-adolescents trying to be cool.

Logan held up a hand to his ear and cocked his head. "Eh? Was that some mice I heard? I said hel-*lo-o!*"

The children roared their response.

"Now, that's more like it!" He chuckled. "And that's what we're doin' here—givin' *God* the glory! Hallelujah! Let's hear that last part again," he called to Dolores.

She turned back to the piano and banged out the refrain. The children sang louder, and the ebullient feeling of family seeped into the campers, bubbled out from under the tent, and pleased Logan.

"Now, that's *some* vocalizin'!" his voice rang out. "I never knew you kids could sound so good! How come you don't let 'er rip like that back at Rathcreek?"

Giggles rippled through the crowd. He gazed out into the sea of bright faces. Catching his daughters with a special wink and smile, he felt their girlish laughter as a chord plucked in his heart.

He bowed his head and prayed, "Almighty God, You love these children and I love these children. Bless 'em, Lord . . ."

Loving other people's children had always been Logan's strength, a way of filling emotional needs he could never trust in a mature relationship. Some of the youths, relying on him as their main source of affirmation and affection, flourished under his attention. Even more gratifying, however, was that he could feel his daughters being won over, influenced by their Fellowship friends who genuinely loved him.

Over the years, no matter how he struggled to install himself in his daughters' hearts, the girls resisted with an animal-like wariness. A part of Logan acknowledged this had to be a result of his constant pumping them for information about their mother, listening in on their phone calls to Jane, all the ignoble acts they were forced to be a part of. A major defeat, however, was the revelation of "the ugly lie," as Jane called it: his blaming her as the reason they couldn't marry. Yes, she had confronted him in their presence, without revealing to the twins they had never been married. He had backed down, admitting that dumping Dolores was not exactly Christian behavior. They must have secretly hated him for that.

Yet, this summer, their self protective reserve seemed finally to be weakening, due to his powerful sway within the community of their church friends, envoys who brought to the twins a new vision of their father. Spiritual counselor and listener to broken-hearted girls, he could understand. But, he could hardly believe when word filtered back to him that he was considered a Mac Daddy.

Soft music played, a cotton batting muffling the outside world. The children's singing was pure and good. Logan's thoughts rested, again, on Bekah and Darcy. He swallowed, emotions overflowing. He would bring these two special souls to Jesus.

The music quieted, Logan bowed his head and led the invocation in his baritone, smooth and benevolent and strong. He asked God to make this wilderness experience a pivotal one in their relationship with Him, asked for forgiveness for their sins, and to make them worthy of His love. Another church camp revival was launched.

Life for the campers over the next week was a dervish of activities. By the dozens, elk, bear or eagles and their teen counselors communed in daily devotionals. They were submerged in wild strawberry hunts, swimming and water skiing, horse rides, sing alongs, nature walks on miles of trails disappearing into the saintly aspens. Awards hung from cabins' flag poles, and each day ended with camp fire vespers at sunset with Logan's Bible stories and more singing. The exhausted, happy youngsters were packed, day after day, and long into the night, with sugar-coated cereals, candy, soft drinks and God.

On the last night of church camp, a huge bonfire snapped and popped in the clearing, and the night was balmy with pine and wood smoke. The air vibrated with the steady hum of a generator. The group of nearly eighty children, counselors and parent chaperones, once separate individuals, formed a semi-circle around the fire as a new unit forged by their strengthened faith, the week's experiences and love.

Bright yellow flames danced, pagan-like, in the blackness. Behind an altar, Logan stood with arms folded. In a large picture propped on an easel, Jesus hung from a crucifix. Full spectrum spot lighting shone on the Christ behind, and on Churlick in front, and cast a long undulating shadow along the packed earth.

A special joy possessed Logan that evening. His lips moved, "Almighty God, grace my tongue tonight, give me the words to finish the job You've begun in my girls. Amen."

Bekah and Darcy sat in the front row, tired and happy, faces sun-burned, eyes shining in the firelight. They had opened up during the course of the week, offering testimonials along with their friends and praying with arms outstretched. If the twins had been inhibited at church in Rathcreek, this week had broken their reserve. They were ready.

"You remember the story of Nebuchadnezzar?" Logan's strong voice quieted the few stray pockets of conversation. "Listen," he hissed.

"The Bible tells us Nebuchadnezzar was a great king, a powerful king. And one night, he had a dream about a statue: gold head, silver chest, bronze loins, iron legs and feet of iron and clay." He hunched his shoulders. "But nobody knows what it means. So what do they do? They get this guy, Daniel, out of jail to interpret the dream.

"Daniel says the gold head stands for the great king, Nebuchadnezar, the silver chest stands for another kingdom trying to take over the gold head. The feet are Rome, and they're gonna break into ten toes, or kingdoms." His voice built, "Then, out of the sky, this big ball strikes the statue and grinds the whole thing into dust."

Logan raised his arm toward a giant gold papier maché figure, crowned, which stood above the blaze. Just barely visible by the light of the fire was a wire running from the statue upward to a pine tree just outside the circle of illumination.

Suddenly, a heavy sphere, about the size of a bowling ball, rushed, humming, down the wire. The ball slammed into the belly of the statue, exploding in a brilliant shower of fireworks, and sent the figure crashing into the fire. The younger children screamed and covered their faces, at the clash and noise and sparks ascending into the blackness. The teens exclaimed, "Cool!"

The large amounts of phosphorous turned the bon fire into a pyre that consumed the royal effigy in a crackling roar of leaping flames. The fire and the darkness all around the children were scary, and counselors and parent helpers comforted the children until they felt safe in the ring of light.

Logan fairly quivered at the effect, had thought of the spectacle himself, and an urgency and excitement made him jumpy inside. The microphone amplified his voice and sent it into the expectant children and into the darkness beyond. He came around the pulpit, and as if in confidence, stage whispered, "Well, ol' King Nebuchadnezzar doesn't like that interpretation. Oh, no!" He mugged, "SO, WHAT DOES HE DO? He decides to build the statue his way, all gold, so his kingdom isn't threatened, and then commands everyone to come see the statue and show homage by bowing to it.

"But there were these three Hebrew kids, Shadrach, Meshach and Abed-nego, who wouldn't bow to the golden statue. They were sharp-faced, with clear eyes, quick minds and spirited. These young men were heroes, champions of their Lord. Still heroes to us today." The words flowed from him now; almost without effort, he had the youngsters. The blaze of the fire lighted their faces, which shone upward at him, excited, waiting.

They're mine! he thought. *It has to be the Lord's anointing.* Then he was all over the platform, appealing to the boys, then the girls, "Would you be scared? How about you? Would you bow down?" They giggled and shook their heads. Adored, he was father of them all.

"So the king has them arrested. Eventually, throws them into this fiery furnace." He climbed down from the altar and came as close as he could to the blazing bon fire. He held up his arm against the sheets of fire, heat searing the side of his face. Sweat stood out against his forehead and he called out in a voice booming like thunder, "Well, God don't like this. Don't like it at all. So what happens next? You wanna know, don't you?"

The children clamored for him to go on.

"Well, they open the door, and the blast of the furnace kills the guards. Then, King Nebuchadnezzar looks into the furnace and what does he see?"

Backing away from the fire, Logan put a hand above his slick brow and peered at the blaze. "What does he *see?*" He backed further away, scrunched his eyes against the flames, and feigning disbelief, turned to face them. "You're not gonna believe this!"

He clasped his hands in the air, walking up and down the perfectly lined aisles, talking to this child, then that one. "You won't believe it. No! Shadrach, Meschach and Abed-nego! Unbound! Walking around! *Inside* the furnace!"

He snapped his fingers. "King's changed, converted—like that! Sees with his own eyes the *power* of God Almighty. So, he lets those three boys go."

Logan tripped lightly back up to the pulpit, wiped his brow and put the microphone back into its stand. "Whew! That's hot!"

Relishing the awe he read in their faces, he waited, knowing he had them now. "What are we supposed to learn from this story? I'll tell you what we're supposed to learn. God the father punishes those against Him and protects those who serve Him. God will protect you if you stand strong and face His enemies.

"Sometimes it's hard to tell who His enemies are. They can be anybody. Your friends at school that lead you off the path of righteousness, teachers that talk about myths, about Darwin and monkeys bein' your ancestors. Even your own parents, if they cause you to go astray from God." He let it sink in.

Music started, soft from the piano, building, like sticks on a fire, until the beating rhythm emitted its own heat: "Onward Christian soldiers . . ."

"God wants you to stand strong against His enemies, and He will give you the strength, I promise you that. His enemies are your enemies, and we have to remember *we* are the only soldiers He has."

Arms wide, music pounding, he sang, "With - the - cross - of - Je-sus . . ."

Logan raised his fist, "Who's God's soldiers?"

The children roared, "*We're* God's soldiers!"

His other fist shot up. "*Who* is?"

"*We* are!"

Both fists in the air "Let's hear the army ROAR!"

They roared and screamed and cried and shouted hallelujahs while he raised and lowered the volume, squeezing it until he'd wrung the last bit of emotion from the half-crazed children.

He motioned for them to rise. "All right, you daughters and sons of God, you soldiers who've taken the vow to serve. Stand up and let's sing so that God can hear us, hear our answer to His call for soldiers to fight the evil." Their voices joined together, ringing sweet and pure from the circle of light through nature's goodness and the night's blackness.

After the singing came testimonials, each gaining from the previous in emotional intensity.

A young girl of fifteen, one of the teen counselors, stood up and in a quavering voice said, "I've been bad, I-I've been, um, I've been bad in the world." She studied the ground, then, eyes glistening, looked up. "Jesus, forgive me!" She choked up, was silent a moment while she collected herself. Reverend Churlick made his way through the straight backed chairs and laid a hand on the girl's head. "You're a good girl, Charlene, and God loves you and I love you. Let's pray for Charlene, shall we? God answers prayers, let's take it to God and ask for His strength."

All heads bowed, and he prayed, eyes squeezed shut, a cry in his voice. The children's murmurings followed where he led. The girl smiled up at him.

"Thank you! *Thank* you, *Jee-zuz!"*

The excitement of absolute control surged through him.

He returned to the pulpit, gazed at the swell of expectant faces lifted to him and wallowed in the ecstasy; his flock, his daughters, they all held him in adulation. The very notion pumped him and gave him an almost erotic feeling of controlling destiny. He hadn't been so charged since the time he took his father's car up to ninety one night on a deserted freeway and got an erection.

His breathing was rapid and shallow. He licked his lips, trembling with the excitement he always felt at the wrap up of a revival. Children, hands raised, danced in place with a sort of frenzied, unselfconsciousness that comes only to those moved by the spirit. The fever pitch, the pulsing piano, made Logan tingle.

They're waiting! Waiting to subject themselves to my will. Waiting for the miracle I can give 'em. They're mine, now, Father. I can bring 'em to You."

He held out both arms, and the wide sleeves of the robe fell back to reveal the black hairs of his bare wrists. The children quieted. The stage lights blinked off, and blackness surrounded him. His voice rang out, a Niagara of emotion.

"We've all done things we shouldn't of. But God loves us, each and every one. Even if we don't deserve it. An' He kin make us whole again."

His lips parted into a rubbery smile at Charlene. "Like Charlene here, no longer a worthless sinner, but born again in Christ's love. An' all we have to do is love Him back. That's not much, is it? Can't you stand up for Jesus, who died on the cross for you?

"I know there's more of you just wanting to get clean. Know someone else in your life needs prayin' for, too? Your brother? Your mother, maybe?" He stared at Bekah, then Darcy, narrowed eyes daring them to resist him now.

They looked afraid, confused. He grimaced in the hot firelight, sweat like oil on his face. Fright shot through him. What if he lost them, just when he had almost won?

The girls huddled, clinging to one another, crying, not out of fear, he saw, but the wail of the repentant. The sight sent a hallelujah bursting from his lips.

"IS THERE SOMEONE YOU LOVE WHO NEEDS PRAYIN'? WHO HASN'T COME TO JEE-ZUZ?"

Bekah's hand went up, seaweed waving in a gentle current, lips moving in a hushed prayer. Then, Darcy, tears trickling down her cheeks, raised her thin arms, palms up.

Logan moistened his lips and panted in his excitement. He walked back and forth, grasping the microphone in his slick hand, barely hearing the general wailing or the music, hardly seeing the throng. The girls were his now. They were God's and they were his. And now, he knew, Jane would be, too.

He gave the signal and Dolores picked up the volume of her chording, chords to tear at the youngsters' hearts, and he led them in, "Now I Belong to Jesus."

Then he went to his daughters, put his arms around them, and they allowed it.

His voice sunk low. "You wanna give your hearts to Jesus tonight?"

"Yes, Daddy," they cried as one.

"Lord Jesus, I pray for Bekah and Darcy, and for their mother. They give themselves to you now, Lord, hearts and souls. We pray You work a miracle in their lives and in their mother's life, to spare her from damnation of a fiery hell." Bending his head to nuzzle their hair, he said, "We ask, sweet savior, that You make Your presence known to Jane, save her, Jee-zuz. And make their lives and mine whole again. Amen." He looked up. "Amen, girls?"

"Amen!"

At the altar call, Bekah came forward without hesitation and Darcy followed. Then others came in a rush.

"Who can pray with me now for these girls and these boys?" Pink-faced youngsters came up, some running down the aisle, not wanting to be left out, and the altar was crammed with children. Counselors surrounded them, helping, "Iloveyou,Jesuslovesyou, hallelujah,praiseGod, doyouwantmetoprayforyou?"

When there were no more coming forward, when they were all joined together, all crying, all hugging, he knew it was time to give his Thankyou-Jee-zuz speech.

"Do I hear amen? Do I hear thank you, Jee-sus?" he finished tearfully. "Is there anyone here who wants to say thank you, Jesus? Raise your hand—He'll see you."

A chorus of "amen" and "thank you, Jee-sus" reverberated out into the darkness, through the ancient trees, to the godly hills beyond.

Logan sat on the plywood stairs covered with cheap carpeting, wringing wet with sweat, and giddy with joy and fatigue. Tears dribbled down his face. Never had he felt such complete victory, such holiness.

"Now you're in His flock, all of you." He smiled at Bekah and Darcy, and the tears of love kept falling. "You belong to Jesus now, and He belongs to you. Your personal savior. How's it feel to be like Shadrach, Meschach and Abed-nego?"

Darcy, drained, merely nodded, leaning her head against his side.

Bekah answered brightly, "Good, Daddy!"

To those children blanketing the steps of the altar, he said, "Tomorrow your parents'll come, and you'll all go home. But you won't go back the way you came." He smiled down at his daughters. "Because now you know who you really belong to, heart and soul. Now you can't ignore your responsibility as God's soldiers to go home and fight the good fight and be counted when the day of judgment comes."

Twenty

Three weeks later, Labor Day
Priest Lake, Idaho

Margie met Jane coming up the steps to the cabin where the annual Rathcreek school district picnic was held.

"Jane!" Margie hugged her. "You're just in time for lunch. Where are the girls?"

Jane pointed to a group of shrieking children playing in the water, hers among them. Brightness bathing her, she lifted a hand to the brim of her hat. But before she could beckon Bekah and Darcy, Margie called to them. The twins waved.

It felt complicated and weird that Margie knew her children, had seen them over time, more than Jane and Margie had seen each other. Every other Sunday for years, her best friend had watched Bekah and Darcy grow in The Fellowship.

Churlick was the reason Jane had decided to attend this year's picnic. She noted with horror since her daughters' return from church camp, Churlick's Jesus, his Bible and politics had turned the girls. Jane was not godless, she knew goodness and truth; they were part of her. But when she tried to tell her daughters their father was frightening them into his religion, they refused to believe her. Jane quaked at the Jesus that stalked her once again. She had to talk to somebody who knew Churlick and knew her. Margie.

They walked along the broad porch toward a picnic table laden with food.

"And this is Dallas," Margie said, nodding toward a man holding a plate in the throes of collapse under the weight of chicken, potato salad and cake.

"Dallas Boulder?" Jane asked.

The man tipped his cowboy hat. "Pleasure. And what a lovely welcomin' party she is, Margie. A far improvement over last year's. 'Course, last year, Sergeant was the welcoming committee, and he just peed on my tires."

Jane and Margie loaded their plates.

"Jane Powers, recently transferred to the district office from Spokane. Don't I know you? Weren't you at the board meeting just before the school bond was up?"

"Yup, made me famous."

"Oh, Lord," Margie said. "That would be Dallas."

Jane said, "I had to change the minutes three times before the superintendent would let 'em fly. 'Tone down that Boulder bullshit,' he told me. You started a war!"

"And it ain't over yet!"

Jane stuck out her hand, and Dallas high-fived it.

"I don't get that kind of admiration every day. Wanna get married?" he asked.

The man's wide nose looked as if it had been broken, and the unruly blonde hair suggested no hint of pretension. When the smile broke over his face, the mischief and irony coalesced into an exploding cigar kind of attractiveness.

Jane laughed, shaking her head. "What kind of wild man are you?"

Margie asked Dallas if he would take an empty tub to the kitchen and refill it with ice and beers.

Jane watched him go and though she was having more fun than she could remember, decided to take advantage of the privacy. "I don't know how to say this, but I need someone to talk to about Logan."

"Reverend Churlick? What do you mean?"

"Well, you still believe in him. But things are not what they seem, Margie. You don't know the real Logan."

"What do you know about my minister that I don't?"

"I should've let you know a long time ago what was going on."

"What? What's going on?"

Jane studied her, then said, "He spies on me, pumps the kids for info on who I'm seeing, how serious it is . . ."

"What's the deal? Why's he interested in who you're dating?"

"What if I told you he was obsessed? About me."

"What? Get out of here. That's too strange!"

"I can hardly believe it myself." She told Margie everything. "The kids are different since they came back from camp."

"How?"

"They asked me the other day if I believed in New Age. They don't even know what it is, really, but Logan's filled them with this book, *This Present Darkness*. Anyone whose faith isn't fundamental has Satan and sulfur-breathing demons inside them, clawing through their brains."

Margie was stunned. "That's terrible, scaring children like that. How do you know what the book's about?"

"I borrowed it." She smiled sardonically. "Unfortunately, it got lost. In the trash."

Jane told her the rest, about his waiting outside her house, kids in the car. How, when she had picked up the girls, she faced their father, his conniving out in the open. Had to listen to Logan accuse her of heathenism, look into the girls' beautiful faces, broken by grief. Was forced to explain that the dream he had seeded in their minds for Mommy and Daddy to get back together was never to be. She watched them, put in the middle of their parents' war. Sweet daughters, victims of her and Logan's bloody upbringing.

Perhaps the stormy battles within the church over the years had already begun weakening Logan's credibility. Perhaps he'd had too many tearful confessions, like the one about Jane, from the pulpit. Too many times he had called from on high to put women in this twenty-first century church in their place. Whatever the cause, Jane assumed when Margie took her hand, squeezed it, that she accepted her truth. To Jane, her touch was a transfusion of hope.

They looked out at Priest Lake. A tattered flag beat the air above a skiff some children played in.

A group of boys and girls squealed and caught Margie's attention. Jane turned and saw a short distance away a pair of pants sagging around white calves that towered above the children. The legs belonged to a man standing on his head on a bunched up sweatshirt.

Margie glanced at Jane, nodded. "Remember him?"

"Ought to try standing on your head sometime," the man said. "Good for your health. Gives you a whole new perspective."

"Really?" Jane said. "Would you mind holding my dress up for me while I try?"

The legs swayed, then buckled. The children clapped, clamored for more. The man told them the show was over, then, sitting Indian style, he turned to see Jane. A hand went absently to move the hair back into place. He said nothing, taking in all of her, face assuming the look of a teacher who's seen too many faces over the years.

The beard, mustache, the sharp blue eyes; the name came to Jane's lips the same instant the man smiled.

"Saint Bernard!" Surprise and joy crowded her heart.

"Jesus," he said softly and rose to his feet. "After all this time. God, you look wonderful, Janey."

The softness of his look, the emotion, caught Jane unprepared. The familiarity of the teacher-pupil relationship dropped away, and an awe of this impressive man filled Jane.

"And that's Mr. Saint Bernard to you." He said to Margie, "Why didn't you tell me she was coming?"

"Same reason you're here. She's staff. Works in the district office now. Transferred over from Spokane to the head spot when Sal left. And got a hefty raise, I hope?"

Jane nodded. "Only reason I'd come back here, big Rathcreek moola."

Margie said, "You're still the wildest English teacher at Rath High, Bolivar, but honestly, sometimes you gotta take your head out of the books. And what's with the Saint Bernard bit?"

Jane lowered her head, grinned. "Mr. Bernard was more than my English teacher, he was my St. Bernard, tromping through the snow to save me. When my brother was getting really bad, I spent most of my lunch hours in his room—"

"Crying on one helluva soggy shoulder," he finished. "Glad to do it."

Bolivar began piling food on a plate. "So, did you marry that worthless Jackal, Jake? Hope he's treating you alright."

"Should've listened to you," Jane said. "We've been divorced quite a few years now. I have two beautiful daughters, though. Bekah and Darcy. They just turned eleven." The evasion made her cheeks and neck grow warm. She gave Margie a look that warned her not to elaborate. "They're down at the lake somewhere." They walked to the edge of the porch and she pointed. "There they are. I'll call them over. I want them to meet you."

Bolivar put a hand on her arm. Like the photographer who waits for the natural pose in favor of something staged, he observed them.

"They're beautiful, Jane. You did well. Very well."

For all the mistakes she had made in her life, in these two children, she had, indeed, done well, and it pleased her to have Bolivar acknowledge it.

He said, "Mine's around here somewhere. Probably found himself a filly, and they're neckin' in the woods. Been tryin' to marry him off for years. None of my students would have him, though. Too smart."

Dallas appeared, lugging a tub brimming with beer and ice. He said across the tub to a fellow coach, "That little sophomore, Kristin, knocked one clear down this poor lil' gal's throat. Won us the game. God, what an arm. If she wasn't so young, I swear I'd marry her just to dip into her gene pool."

"Jeez, Dallas," said the coach, "You tryin' to get yourself fired?"

Jane said, "Hey! I thought you just proposed to me."

Dallas' grin widened. "Can I take that for a yes?"

"Can't a girl be indignant without getting engaged?" Jane asked.

"Well, hell, okay. Never did like the coy type." He opened a beer and took a swig. "What's this, Bo? You been making time with my bride while I was gone?" Dallas stuck his hand out, and Bolivar shook it.

Jane reached into the tub for a beer.

"You drinking beer now?" Bolivar asked.

"Don't act so shocked," Jane said. "I threw off the yoke of the church years ago." She studied her teacher. She didn't feel the difference in age, in fact even as his student, had always considered him a friend. Like family. And family was more valuable to her than anything in the world. How lucky Mrs. Bernard was.

"Janey! Well, well, isn't this providential. Where's the kids?"

The shock of hearing that voice made Jane's knees buckle. Slowly, she turned to face Logan Churlick. For a moment, she only stared, heart pounding, stomach plunging into a cold pool of dred.

The truth had come to claim her. Bolivar knew of her relationship to Reverend Churlick only in regard to the faith healing and David's eventual death. The pride she had felt at Bolivar's compliment of her children vanished. He had assumed her ex-husband was the father of her children, as she had wanted. She looked to Margie, who returned her hopeless gaze.

"Logan," Jane said, trying to calm her voice, "I'd like you to meet my high school English teacher, Bolivar Bernard. Bolivar, this is—"

Dallas was about to say something, but Margie shook her head.

Logan, hand extended in a show of cordiality, interrupted, "We already know—"

"We've met," Bolivar said tersely. "Board meeting not long ago. Almost got me fired for teaching mythology. Thank the gods, his tentacles don't reach far enough—yet. Campbell and I, scourges of the Christian world."

Jane hardly heard. "Bolivar! Listen."

He turned to Jane, ignoring Logan's still proffered hand.

"Logan is the father of my girls."

Bolivar looked like a person who had taken a bite of something awful, and was trying not to spit it out. He offered no comment, only wiped his hand against his pant leg.

Tears came to Jane's eyes, and she fought them. She remembered once hearing that of all creatures, human beings were the only ones preferring death over embarrassment. At that moment, watching Bolivar put it together, she would have gladly died.

Dallas grabbed a beer from the ice and handed it to Bo. "Here. You need a brew."

"Thanks, man." Bo clapped Dallas on the shoulder, pointed the bottle at Churlick. Sarcasm edged his words. "I've got to go find Simon and see that he has his prophylactics on him. Hate to see him get some poor girl pregnant for lack of a rubber. Right, reverend? Yup, Simon's seventeen now—almost a man. Almost."

Logan, face crimson, was speechless.

Bo turned to Jane. "Been a pleasure, Jane, as always." Then, he was gone.

Jane, Margie, Dallas and Logan stood in uncomfortable silence. The heat of Jane's cheeks faded. She let out a shaky breath.

Dolores Churlick appeared with two paper plates laden with food. Her face was flushed with the heat. "Lunch, sweetie?"

Logan winced at the little voice. The look of humiliation at Bolivar's hands still fresh upon him, he answered in a controlled rage, mimicking her, throwing up his hands, "No, I'm *not* hungry, sweetie." A hand caught the corner of a plate and sent it cartwheeling through the air. Chicken and potato salad, cake and blueberry pie rained down.

"Oh!" Dolores cried. "Oh, Logan!"

"Oh, man," Dallas moaned, and turned away.

Logan, unmoved, watched the blue rivulets running down his wife's blouse.

Jane's heart went out to Dolores. Then she shuddered. She caught the look on Logan's face, there only a moment, and knew she would never forget the look of primitive hatred that blamed Dolores for everything.

Twenty-One

"Mom! Look, Mom!" Darcy cried.

"Kids've been keepin' me pretty busy here," Bolivar said, buried from neck down.

Jane nodded. Fondness for this man filled her.

"Can we bury your face now?" Bekah asked.

"Sure!" Dallas said, sidling up. In ski vest and swim trunks, he was muscled more like a laborer than a teacher and coach. His fair skin was burned, and he wore a ski glove on one hand.

"Been skiing, Jane. Water's fine." He stooped and tousled Bo's hair. "Don't think this guy's goin' anywhere soon. Wanna ski? Margie says you used to."

"Used to love it." She looked up at the boyish grin, then went back to patting the round, gray belly of Bolivar. "Thanks, but Bo's already invited me."

"Oh. *That's* what Margie meant. She said to go get you and Bo for the next turn. They'll be back in a minute." Dallas grinned.

"You ol' bandit," Bo said.

"But you said we could bury your head," Bekah wailed. "You promised."

"So I did. I think we have time before the boat comes around again," Bo said. "Let your mother be in charge, though, so I'm not killed in the bargain."

Bekah rounded up a snorkel and Jane folded a beach towel to cover his face.

"Now, you let us know by wiggling the snorkel once in a while that everything is okay," Jane said.

He placed the snorkel in his mouth and wiggled it.

The burying went smoothly, and soon a worthy sarcophagus appeared. Piled high and smooth, it was a sand casket of notable proportions. Bekah and Darcy walked, giggling, over trunk and limbs. They danced little jigs on the bulge that was Bo's stomach.

"You still there, Bo?" Jane asked. The mound was still as a tomb. They waited.

"Bolivar! Quit playin' around," Dallas said. "Wiggle the damn snorkel!" They stared at the tube in the sand. Dallas looked to Jane. "C'mon, this isn't funny, buddy."

The ground was still. The mid-day sun had dried the sand to the color of cement.

Heart pounding, on the verge of tears, Jane shouted, "Bolivar! You come out of there! Come out, *now!*" Dallas had already begun clawing at the sand, and she, ready to throw herself into it also, when she noticed the snorkel wiggling.

She shut her eyes and thanked God.

A hand cracked through the surface, then another. Bolivar struggled to unearth himself. He was still too deep, however, so they all set to work unburying face and torso. Jane carefully peeled away the towel and he spit out the snorkel.

"This must be heaven." He sat up and rested his eyes on Jane, then looked toward the sound of slow chugging of an outboard motor. A ski boat idled its way through the swimming area toward the dock.

Bo stood and brushed himself off. "Let's go, Jane."

Dallas tossed his ski vest at Bolivar. "Don't worry about a thing. Uncle Dallas will watch over the children." Noting Jane's skeptical look, he added, "Really."

In the ski boat, Jane sat next to Margie, while Bolivar sat up front with the driver.

"Why didn't you warn me?" Jane whispered as the boat maneuvered slowly away from the dock.

"I didn't know," Margie said softly, glancing at her husband behind the wheel. "I didn't know Michael would invite *him* when he said he was asking some of the new school board members."

"Shit! Logan's on the board now? That means I'll have to see him every month." She wondered if he joined expressly for that purpose.

"That was crazy back there with Mrs. Churlick," Margie said. "I bet he felt terrible. It seemed like he was in shock."

Jane was stunned. Was she the only one who had witnessed the expression on Logan's face? "Terrible?" she said. "You didn't see the look he gave her."

Margie smiled, distracted, and nodded toward the shore. Jane followed her gaze.

Logan stood like a piling in the water. He crouched, with Darcy balanced on his lap, and they could hear his faint counting. One-two-three! She sprang off and belly flopped into the water. Bekah scrambled to be next. Jane stood abruptly, wanting to snatch them away. Margie reached up and pulled her down, as the boat gathered speed.

The twins squawked and laughed. They climbed back onto Logan to be flipped into the lake. The scene transfixed her. All the manipulation, guilt and now the fresh proselytizing at camp. It angered her to see the girls actually enjoying his company. Her daughters, made of her own genes and blood, flourishing at his hands into some strange Fellowship flesh.

The boat sped across the water and Michael, Margie and Bo's enthusiasm caught Jane up and brought her out of her brooding. She and Margie were girls again. Many summers ago with Margie, she had discovered the thrill of racing over water. Finally, the boat stopped, and the air was warm and still, the lake smooth as dark green glass.

"I need a bath," Bo said, and dove into the water, resurfaced and hauled himself into the boat. Hardly a trace of sand was left.

"Ready?" he asked. "You go first. It's real warm."

"Yeah, right." Jane noted the goose bumps covering him.

"Go on, Janey," Margie said. "It's been so long, I can't even remember how." Her face brightened. "Let's do it together. Like when we were kids." She looked at her husband. "You've got another line in here somewhere, don't you, Michael?"

He did, got it out, and threw both ski lines into the water, then maneuvered the boat to straighten the ropes. Jane and Margie jumped into the lake. Frigid water sent shocks through Jane's sun-warmed body. Long tendrils of hair floated around her face, tiny bubbles tickled, and she was twelve again, rebounding toward the light.

Bolivar threw a ski to Margie, then one to Jane.

Teeth chattering a little, Jane caught the ski and worked her feet into the black folds of the boots. She was nervous, but when she glanced at Margie beside her in the water, she knew that her anxiety was nothing next to her friend's. Margie dipped in the water, struggling to fit into the ski, lost hold of the rope. Jane swam after it, and reached her hand back to Margie as the lulling motor pulled her gently away. Finally, Jane let go of her own rope and Margie's, signaling for the boat to circle around to them again.

"I don't think I can do this," Margie said. "It's like I've never done it before."

"Sure you can," Jane assured her. "It's like riding a bike. You just gotta have faith it's still there somewhere."

Margie looked at her doubtfully.

The boat moved slowly past them, trailing the ropes. Michael and Bo watched, Bo waving the red flag in encouragement.

Jane said, "Tuck your feet under your hiney and let the rope pull you up. The rope'll do it. You just hang on."

Margie nodded.

Jane said to her, "Ready?"

"As I'll ever be."

Jane gave thumbs up. The boat roared and threw back a monstrous spray that drowned them. The ropes snapped taut and the force of the lake drove against the women as they struggled to move from crouch to upright positions on their skis.

Jane's arms ached. The drag was almost too much for her, much more than she had remembered as a girl. She felt a slight plucking of the other line. Still crouching, she looked through the deluge of spray and let go of her handles, then swam over to where Margie had fallen.

"I can't," Margie whimpered. "I don't know how to do this anymore."

"Bullshit!" Jane said, and Margie stared at her. "You can't do it because you think you can't. Sort of like how you feel you can't harbor anything but respect for the weasel who runs your church." The words came of their own volition, catapulted by emotions held in too long.

Margie's eyes widened.

"I saw how you watched Churlick being such a 'good daddy' to my girls. You don't really believe me when I tell you he wants to have sex with me again." Her voice quavered. "Margie, he's teaching my girls that I'm an unbeliever. They act so different since he got his hooks into them at church camp. And I don't know what to do. You, of all people, know the real Jane. You have to believe me."

Michael shouted to them from the boat. "What's up? You guys ready?"

As if a spell were broken, Margie shivered in the water. Face contorted with sorrow, she said, "I can't help it. I couldn't really believe Reverend Churlick was capable of—of lying. But I know you're right. You're telling the truth." She paused. "I'm sorry I doubted you, Jane."

"Everything all right?" Bolivar called.

Jane nodded. "In a minute."

She and Margie floated languidly in the water, which suddenly felt like a warm bath. Jane nodded, and gave her friend a small smile. Margie returned it, curled her fingers around the ski rope handles and gave a thumbs up.

A roar. Their ropes snapped taut, the boat's spray engulfed them, and the lake fought Jane and Margie once again. Jane's ankles wobbled and she wondered how Margie was doing. She could barely see her friend submerged in the small pocket of air created by the rush of water against the tip of her ski. Jane locked her ankles, held tight and strained against the force.

She straightened her knees, and in an instant, popped through the water to the surface. She leaned back against the ski, its tip strong and straight, pointing toward the sky. Cheers from Michael and Bolivar in the boat. Jane looked over at Margie, pulling against the rope, legs straining against the water. Suddenly, she popped to the surface. Cheers again from the boat.

The women cut back and forth behind the outboard, skimming Priest Lake. Jane's chestnut hair streamed out behind her, like gold in the sun. They let out wild whoops over the engine's roar.

Jane threw back her head and laughed.

After fireworks signaling an Independence Day in reverse for the educators, a mourning for the end of summer, the children were put to bed.

A huge bonfire popped and sent sparks heavenward. Jane relaxed in one of the beach chairs. The people around the fire pit had divided themselves into two groups, drinkers and non, separation of church and state.

Dallas opened the ice chest. "This crew's not afraid to belly up to the bar." He distributed a few beers. "Gettin' real low. And there weren't that many to begin with." He eyed Michael good naturedly. "Mostly pop, thanks to the Christian coalition. I'll leave these two in here to breed."

"I'll see what's left in the cabin," Jane said.

"Good luck," Dallas called after her.

The wooden screen door slammed behind Jane and she surveyed the cabin. The old beagle, Sergeant, slept curled up on the worn linoleum. Two playpens in the corner held sleeping babies. She tiptoed to where Bekah and Darcy slept in their sleeping bags. Rosy cheeks and noses, colored by the day's sun, hair damp with the heat of sleep. She kissed them. Other children slept around them in a patchwork of sleeping bags and blankets.

The screen door banged, and Bekah flinched in her sleep. Jane turned, a finger to her lips.

"Sorry!" Bolivar whispered. "Need some help?"

She smiled, glad to see him. "I owe you."

"Good." He gave a short nod and tucked thumbs in his waistband in the pose of a man who had just come into good fortune. "For what?"

"Taking such good care of my kids. And me. I had a great time today."

"Yeah, well, that son of mine's out to get me, you know. He got 'em started burying me. Perfect way to impress that little filly he had in tow: kill the father. Very Oedipal. We've got good kids, Jane." He opened the refrigerator, ducked his head and peered inside. "Nothing left."

He shut the door and Jane opened it again. "Hm. What's this?" She reached in the back and pulled out two bottles of premium Kendall Jackson.

Bolivar grumbled a little. "Men are blind. Can't see a thing if it's right in front of 'em. Missing a chromosome. Takes a woman to find anything." He looked at the bottles. "Whoa! Kendall J. More than $3.95 a piece. What we call *decent* in the faculty room."

She felt his eyes on her while she searched for a bottle opener. Over her shoulder she said, "Blue Nun would've been more fitting for Priest Lake, don't you think?"

"When's the last time you took a canoe ride on a moonlit lake?"

"Never," she said, and felt suddenly shy.

"Seems a shame to waste it."

She nodded, not sure how to answer. Such a delicious feeling, this man's high regard for her. Would this be right, in their new, adult-to-adult relationship? She picked up the bottles and went to the door. Bolivar held it open.

"Relax, Jane. You're still safe with me."

She stopped in the doorway, a little shocked at his reassurance that his motives were pure. "Thank you, Bo."

She wondered what it all meant, wondered if she'd be swimming through the frigid waters of her confusion and loneliness to the shore of his affection once again. She chided herself. *Stop it! He's just being nice. I'm going to embarrass myself if I'm not careful.*

They returned to the bonfire amidst cheers. She started the bottles around and happened to catch Logan's sulking glare.

"For thy stomach's sake," she called across the fire pit.

Dallas held a bottle to the light. "Whoa! Saved the best till last, huh? 'Bout time you brought out the good stuff."

Glass raised in acknowledgment, Jane smiled.

Bolivar caught her attention, pointed toward the dock.

Shadows and light played on Churlick's features until it was hard to distinguish by the moving light whether he was animal or human. He gave Jane an odd look.

She headed to where Bolivar waited. *Good,* she thought, knowing Churlick followed her with his eyes. *Maybe he'll finally let go of this fantasy.*

Bolivar sat on the edge of a silver canoe. "Ready? I grabbed some blankets."

"Yup. I asked Margie to peek in on the kids once in a while."

He took her hand and she stepped into the canoe. Soon, they were gliding across the glassy mirror of water. Hazy clouds drifted past the face of the full moon and their eyes adjusted to the night. Balancing in the sleek aluminum vessel was tricky, but Bo was experienced in a canoe, and a good teacher. The ripple of the paddle slicing the water became the rhythmic meter of their conversation.

Jane let her fingertips trail in the cold water. "So, you still like teaching?"

"Sure. English been berry, berry gud to me." Moonlight highlighted the planes of his cheeks; he was grinning.

"Do you like what you do?" He pulled the paddle up, into the lake and back. "What is it you do, anyway?"

"I work in the district office. It's okay. Pays the bills. Keeps my kids fed."

They sculled in silence for a while. Then, the stories, of course, always the stories. She knew them from his classroom, of his childhood in the small town of Bounty, working on his grandfather's farm: he and his cousin, Lee, peeing on the cucumber plants that grew wildly from their organic fertilizing; Grandpa letting the ten-year-old boy disc and harrow the fields; the killing of the vicious, red rooster and roasting him over a spit made of a forked tree limb. She envied Bo his uncomplicated past.

" . . . and when grandpa saw that decapitated rooster, all the feathers and the blood all over the cutting block in that wood shed, well, you never saw any two boys with butts redder than ours."

He leaned into a stroke and pulled against the paddle. She'd never noticed his power before. These were the arms of a farm boy. And this afternoon on the boat, the water on his tanned shoulders, water dripping from his broad chest, the light beard and hair, shining in the sun. The way he glanced at her in her swimsuit when he thought she hadn't seen him. This man, teacher to the core, who she felt so safe with, scared her a little.

What was she doing out here with him? Enjoying his company more than she could remember ever enjoying any man's. There was no doubt that she was drawn to him. But it was beginning to dawn on her that she was drawn to him in a way that made her stomach flutter, as if butterflies cracked out of their cocoons and flew around in some strange and wild formation. What was it with her? Was she doomed to repeat her mistakes? He was a married man, just as married as Logan Churlick.

"Can I ask you something?" He grinned sheepishly. "This is going to sound crazy, but would you mind coming shopping with me sometime? I need a few shirts and I sure could use your touch. I can see you have a lot better fashion sense than Simon."

"Yeah, I'd love to be the one responsible for those starry-eyed juniors talking about what a hunk St. Bernard is."

"If there's anyone I'd like to see starry-eyed, it's you," he said.

The formation of flying insects inside her did a barrel roll.

She recovered and said, "So, what about Mrs. Bernard?"

Bolivar did not respond. The words made a tinny sound through the hollow can of the night. The paddle hesitated.

"Kate died six months ago."

Jane was choked by the uprushing of shock and grief. "Oh, Bolivar, I'm so sorry."

Kate Bernard dead. The reality thundered through her, reverberating from bowels to chest. What a tragedy for Bolivar, only a friend, until now. The safeness of being with this old friend was suddenly yanked from her. What would her integrity say now? Why was she out here, anyway? That sorry, shrunken little place where love belonged had an appetite as big as the Grand Canyon. What was integrity, really, to a hunger as large as that?

"Why didn't you tell me before?"

"It's hard for me. Some days I still feel like the walking dead."

She asked gently, "Was she sick?"

"No. We figure she fell asleep at the wheel coming home from one of her seminars. Wanted to see Simon's baseball game. Just like her. Always was a pushy woman . . . one of the things I liked best about her."

Her throat tightened. The pride in his voice. Simon motherless. It wasn't fair.

"I never knew her, except the stories you told in class. She sounded wonderful."

"She was. It's hard to believe she's gone sometimes. Sometimes, I walk around the house talking to her."

They were quiet for a while. Only the sound of the water and the lonely sky.

"I didn't want to talk about Kate tonight. Didn't want to spoil this," he said, and waved his hand to include the canoe, the lake. "One of the best days I've had in a while."

"Me, too."

He hesitated. "Besides, I didn't want to put it right out there. I needed you to be my friend. If I'd admitted I was a widower, well, I'd have had to turn this into a date with the beautiful queen of the lake. And then, you'd have to be suspicious." The words were serious, but there was a smile in his voice.

She grinned. "Bo, I've always been suspicious of you. So what's new?"

They talked again as friends, planning a shopping trip. Yet Jane was aware that something splendid was beginning between them, and it put a brightness in her voice and laugh that bubbled from her like a clear, cold stream.

They drifted, or cast watery chevrons, moon glinting off silver, sluicing through the wide trough of Priest Lake. Dawn found them before they realized they had spent the night together. The magnificent sunrise touching the tree tops, tracing a ring of fire. They watched the fire broaden into a golden band that lit the sky in purples, oranges and pinks.

Bo stretched and pulled on the paddles, heading the canoe to shore. "You warm enough?" She had settled near him in the back of the canoe, wrapped up in blankets.

"Yes. I just hate for it to end."

They continued on toward shore in the wan light. Birds sounded the new day.

"No more teacher-pupil stuff where you bow to my superior brains or experience anymore. Friends, promise?" But his look was beyond friends.

"Just friends." She paused, wanting to say something significant. Instead, she reached up and took his head in her hands and kissed him.

They bumped onto the sandy bank, and he pulled the canoe ashore. The stillness was broken by the bang of the screen door.

"Jane!" Margie shouted, running toward them.

"Oh, God, something's wrong, Bo."

"Logan!" Margie cried, out of breath, "Logan took the girls."

Twenty-Two

Jane ran to the cabin, grabbed her purse and sprinted to the car.

"You're in no condition to drive," Bolivar said. She pushed past him. In two steps he caught her, grabbed the keys and ordered, "Get in."

The old Ford took the first bend and she braced herself against him. Wild daisies whipped by in the faint light, a white blur along the roadside.

Jane let out a shuddering breath, and grief overcame her. Hands over face, the sobs went on and on, rooted in her depths.

"How can he *do* this?" she asked, and wiped her eyes with her palms. Maternal fears bred in her mind, multiplied and expanded to far-flung consequences. Not simply today, but her children's very characters, their future perspective of the kind of place the world was, and their courage or fearfulness in facing it, were at stake. How could they feel secure ever again, when their own father had stolen them from their mother?

"I just want to kill him," she said.

His gaze left the road. "Everything's going to work out. They'll be okay."

She was sure nothing could ever work out okay with Logan. Around another corner, and they squealed onto the main highway. The day had begun in earnest now, and lit the early morning sky with a slate of blue. The drive from Priest Lake to Rathcreek took two hours. Somewhere along the way, Bolivar succeeded in quelling her panic.

She rubbed her neck and tried to relax, glad for Bolivar's company.

But when they pulled up to the Churlicks' house, faith left her. The curtains were closed and everything locked. Jane and Bolivar ran to the rear of the house, checked the garage. The Peugeot was nowhere in sight.

Her panic rose, along with the pain in her temples, the mighty throb behind her left eye. They made their way back to the front door and knocked. She strained to hear any movement inside.

Jane and Bo stared at each other. His look of despair told her there was no longer anything he could say. No further action would change things. Dead end. If Logan wasn't here, where had he taken the girls?

"You're white," Bolivar said, and put his arm around her shoulders. They turned and started down the walk to the car. She wondered how long it would take her to get to the police department, wondered if they would have any better luck finding her girls. Her head throbbed with every step; the morning light hurt her eyes. She was beginning to feel sick to her stomach.

A window on the second floor opened. The startled pair turned and looked up.

Dolores spoke through the black screen, her tiny voice snide, "You won't find 'em."

"Where are they?" Jane demanded.

"Camping."

"Camping?" she repeated, dumbfounded. "Listen, Dolores, I want my kids. Where are they?"

"I can't tell you." The coquettish way she spoke, the sickening child-ish voice, amplified the hammering that raged in Jane's head. She was close to being sick.

Dolores leaned against the protection of the second story window sill. "Our lawyer instructed me to tell you only that they're all right and we're going for custody."

The word exploded in a haze of red heat in Jane's brain. Custody. A hysterical giggle escaped. "Custody? You've got to be joking. It's more like me charging you with kidnapping."

"We've only done what our lawyer instructed. We're completely within the law." She scolded Jane, "You aren't the only parent, you know. They love their father. And they love me. And I love them like they were my own."

She wanted to vomit, imagining Dolores' whimpering to the girls about how much she loved them and God loved them, but had no doubt she would do anything for Logan. God help her girls if they believed their step mother. Advised by an attorney? Stealing her kids, legal?

"I'm supposed to tell you, our lawyer'll contact you."

She stared up at the screen. "Don't tell me about love, you conniving little bitch." She took Bolivar's arm and strode toward the car. "And tell Logan you'll get my children over my dead body."

They got into the car. The pain stabbed her brain like thorns. She curled up in the seat and closed her eyes.

"Migraine," Bo said. "It's a son-of-a-bitch."

Her first. She had never known such pain.

At home, she took aspirin, threw up, and felt worse than before. She managed to call the police, who told her since this was a custody issue, she would have to produce legal paperwork for the visitation schedule. Where was it? She couldn't think straight. Too sick. Next, she called her lawyer. Out of town. He would call as soon as he returned.

Finally, she persuaded Bolivar to leave. There was nothing he could do; she simply had to be sick, had to rid herself of the bile and fear and outrage. He promised to call. She ran to the bathroom and heard him close the door as she hunched over the toilet. Then she retched until her eyes watered and she was empty.

Two days the migraine raged, clamping down on optic nerves like pliers. Eyeballs ached at the least light. The thought of food made her want to gag. It was all she could do to endure the monstrous pressure in her skull and not go mad with worry about her girls. The curtains were drawn and the house completely dark. She lay in bed in the fetal position. Sleep was the only thing that blotted out the pain.

By morning of the third day, the nausea ebbed. Soon, she could hold down broth and toast. When her strength returned and her head cleared, she remembered she hadn't phoned the office, so she did, to let them know she was sick, not AWOL.

Then, she called home and poured out her worry to her mother and Louise. After their initial shock subsided, Louise offered to find someone to put out a contract on Churlick. Jane politely declined.

Pulling her robe around her, Jane sipped hot broth and shuffled to the mail slot. The bright mid-morning light spotlighted the mail scattered on the floor. Now that she felt better, she contemplated her next move.

She set the cup down and went through the correspondence, hoping to find a letter from Logan or his attorney. Instead, she found a note written in Bekah's childish hand. She ripped open the envelope, read, then slid down the wall to the floor.

Dear Mom,

How are you with the news Dad gave you? I'm really sorry. It's my fault. He said you were out on the lake all night drinking alcohol and would Darcy and me like to go home with him. I said yes. Now he won't let us come back. Mom, I don't know how to tell Dad I don't want to live with him, I want to live with you!

I haven't cried, except when I came across a letter you wrote me this summer when I was at Vacation Bible Camp. It was in my jacket pocket, and said 👁 ❤ U, and you wrote, "See you soon!" Oh, Mom, we've been waiting all summer to see you. We want to be with YOU.

Can you give us some money to come back to Spokane on a plane? Don't let Dad know I snuck this out to you. I ❤ you more than anything!

Love, Bekah

Her poor babies. Naturally Bekah would feel at fault. Logan scared her to death, then took them in the middle of the night. But where? Damn. Damn!

Before she decide how to respond, a courier delivered a letter from Logan's attorney. Mr. Moore requested her presence at an informal meeting that afternoon.

What? She read the letter again, and felt a dull throb above her left eye. Taking a deep breath, she tried to calm herself, to will away the impending headache. *What am I going to do? How can I prepare? My lawyer's out of town.* A call to his office confirmed he would be back the next day. Jane felt naked going alone.

The letter stated she could pick up the children at his office. There were issues to discuss. Nothing about custody. Simply an informal meeting with Logan and his attorney, not a day in court.

Jane had been through the system before and came to the hard conclusion that justice was the biggest crap shoot of all. An important plea delivered badly, a counter-argument overlooked by an attorney, mis-statements of fact, impressions made on the judge, all rolled around equally on the judicial table. But this was not court. And she would get her daughters back. Jane hurried to the bathroom and started the shower.

That afternoon, Jane entered the lobby of Dick Moore's downtown legal firm. Before he could usher her into his office, she erupted in fury. "Where are they?"

Moore held up his hands. "All in good time."

"Good time, my ass. I knew it. I *knew* I should've called the police first. You produce them *now* or I'm calling the police." She waved visitation papers in his face.

"Now, Ms. Powers . . ."

Logan appeared from a shadow of the office doorway, cut in, "Don't worry, Janey, Dolores is bringin' 'em."

"Can we?" Moore motioned to his office.

Jane didn't move. "What the hell do you think you're doing? You advise him to kidnap my children, you get me down here, promising me my kids, and they're not here? They're brought out if I'm a good little girl and do what I'm told?" Her legs wobbled from anger. "I'm out of here. I'm calling my lawyer and the cops."

Moore held out his hands. "Please! Ms. Powers. That's not our intent." He picked up the phone on the recepitonist's desk and handed it to Logan, who dialed.

"Dolores? No, not yet. Bring the girls now." Then in a flat voice, "I said bring 'em now."

"We know this has been hard on you," Moore said, "but they're on their way. Twenty minutes. Come into my office? Please?"

She followed him and sat in a chair facing the desk, hand tapping the purse in her lap.

"You know that Logan took the girls home, and went camping. Why did you tell him to keep my kids from me? Take them somewhere I couldn't even call?"

"I've handled family law for many years, Ms. Powers. I'm considered one of the best in Rathcreek. One reason is because I anticipate well." He leaned back in his seat. "I can tell you, whenever custody issues arise, there are always strong reactions, and you wouldn't be the first custodial parent to bolt. We were merely protecting our interests."

Custody. The reality of it caught her like a blow. She said nothing, not trusting her voice.

He gave her his tight-lipped smile. "However, since I've had more time to speak to Reverend Churlick, we've come to the conclusion that perhaps a more appropriate course would be to mediate a small increase in visitation."

"You're out of your minds!" She pounded her fist on the chair. "Why would I give this man more time to damage my girls?"

She turned and fired at Logan. "You slimy bastard! You steal my kids, then bribe me to meet you here. And you expect me to agree to some plan you've cooked up with your crooked lawyer?" She leaned out toward him, voice rising. "First summer you've ever had them, and you listen to our phone conversations, preach to them that I'm going to hell, undermine me every chance you get . . . and now you ask me to hand you, just *hand* you, more time?"

Her attack had caused some of Logan's natural vitality to ebb, and he spoke rapidly. "First, Jane, I was just doin' what the lawyer told me to. I never wanted to hurt you or the girls. It was *my* suggestion that we leave a message for Dolores to give you personally, let you know the kids were all right."

Moore nodded.

"I know, now, I shoulda never took 'em. It's just . . . I thought they woulda been scared when they woke up to find out you left 'em. Goin' out on the lake, stayin' out all night with that man. I figured it wasn't any big deal to start our weekend visitation a little early. But, I realize, now, I didn't have the right. I apologize, Jane."

She stared at him, jolted and unbelieving. This wasn't the Logan she knew.

He coughed to clear his throat, and the sound irritated her. "I don't see why we can't work this out and save a lot of fuss and expense. We both heard the judge say my visitation could be increased."

She sensed he was posturing. What was beneath it? Then, it occurred to her. Had Moore warned him that he didn't stand a chance of getting custody? Or perhaps after a day in the wilderness, trying to woo Bekah and Darcy to live with him, he had failed?

He coughed several times again, a habit that had always annoyed her. "I love our girls, too, want to spend time with 'em. Their salvation is my responsibility, an' I'm not gonna let my Jesus down."

"Shove it, Logan."

His face was working and his voice, hurt. "I have rights, too. I have hopes for the upbringing of my girls."

"After you took my kids, on my way into town? My hope was to rip your face off to get them back. How's that for hope?"

His laugh was unsettled. "Because I'm onto your tryst with your little boyfriend?"

"You tell him, Moore, tell him he's out of his freaking mind. Just because he's the father of my kids doesn't mean he's the deputy of my love life."

Moore frowned.

"So that's it, huh? All these years?" Logan roared, "They *love* me! Ask 'em!"

"Please, Logan," Moore said.

Logan continued, "But that doesn't count for nuthin', does it? You think you can keep jerking me around. Think I'll always be there for 'em, cooperate, be nice. For the kids. An' never get—" He rose abruptly, waved a hand, went to the window.

Jane glanced at Moore. It felt as if she were drowning in Logan's words, faltering and confused in the make-believe world that was so real to him. She had seen the kids play with him at the lake. And there was no mistaking his capacity for loving children, or his devotion to her. But that wasn't all of Logan.

She stood. "I'm not afraid of you. And I don't owe you another minute with them. I will protect my girls. See you in court."

Logan rushed over, grasped her wrists.

Moore held up a hand. "Logan! Just a minute, Ms. Powers." Moore stood, pulled a piece of paper to the center of his desk. "You'll need to sign this order, which prohibits you from leaving the area."

What? Was this so? Then the whole world was crazy.

Jane stepped into Logan, hard, on his instep, yanked her wrists down and was free. She reached across the shiny mahogany desk and pushed her hand, hard, into Moore's face. Startled, he fell backward into his seat, half cried out, skin turning a deep blush at the collar of the starched shirt. It all happened within seconds.

"Jane!" Logan came at her.

"Stay away from me!" she screamed, backing toward the door. "Don't speak to me! There's no court in the land that'll give you custody of my girls. I'm not unfit. *You* are, you Jesus stalker. I'm not signing anything."

"You can't—" Logan's stony eyes went blank, went underground to whatever desert his emotions resided in, until the rage that drove him surfaced. "You'll regret this day. Trust me on that."

"To hell with you, Logan, and your slimy lawyer." She walked to the door. "To hell with you both, and the Jesus you rode in on!"

In the lobby, Bekah and Darcy ran to her, while Dolores looked on. Jane scooped them up in her arms, hugged them to her, and the emotional charge of the other room exploded into a torrent of tears. This time, it was Jane, not Bekah, who could not let go.

Dolores finally said, "I only did what I was told. Nothing personal."

Jane stood and faced her. "You love them as if they're your own? You selfish, sorry excuse for a woman. What *mother* would do what you've been doing to my children? How could it *be* anything but personal?" She took Bekah and Darcy by the hands and led them outside.

In the car, they buckled up and she started the engine.

Her stomach suddenly wrenched. "Wait a minute."

She lifted Darcy's hair away from her head. Darcy tried to hide her face, but Jane turned it toward her, and pulled the hair back from her ears.

"No!" Jane cried.

Her tears only made things worse, as the girls began bawling, too. She couldn't have been more outraged if she had seen bruises. But his method was manipulation. No marks. Except this time, he had left his mark.

Logan knew Jane had forbidden ear piercing until they were thirteen. She read, by Bekah's glistening eyes, and Darcy's sobbing, the shame of their betrayal. Only when they saw their mother's anguish, could they understand their father had tricked them. There, on each daughter, ringed with the red puffiness of newly pierced ears, were two tiny, gold hearts. They had been bought for a pair of earrings.

Twenty-Three

A week later

Jane avoided Logan during the exchange of the children on the following weekend, an exchange on the advice of her lawyer. Sanchez assured Jane that with the ruse Logan was using about picking the children up "early," and especially since his taking them had never happened before, they hadn't a leg to stand on, as far as taking him to court.

To keep herself busy, Jane tackled the twins' bedroom, always a state of solid disaster. She tore Darcy's bed apart first, snapped off the white eyelet pillow case. A tithing envelope used at The Fellowship fell to the floor.

"Now what?" she muttered, weary of the need to always be suspicious. Why was the thing hidden in the pillow case? Logan, a tyrant when it came to tithing, always felt the need to prove one's love for God. Was he pressuring them to tithe more than ten percent? Then she saw the writing.

A quote from the Bible. Only a memory verse, written in Logan's hand: "Delight thyself in the Lord and He shall give you the desires of your heart," Psalms 37:4 She had memorized hundreds when she was a child . . . so why did this one make her scalp tingle?

Bolivar Bernard pulled the black '78 Cadillac Seville into the underground parking garage and found a space on the third level. He swung his legs out. The supple leather was smooth; however, a wire had broken through the leather piping in the seat to gouge the leg of anyone hapless enough to forget.

"Jesus!" he yelped.

On his thigh, a neat triangle of material showed white flesh along the edges of the flap. The dark gray grew darker, as the blood soaked into the material.

"Slow down, Bolivar, she'll still be there," he said, and glancing at his watch, hurried to the open door of the elevators. He punched the button for the skywalk level, the covered walkway between tall buildings above the busy downtown Spokane streets.

He walked briskly along the enclosed corridor. Below, it was rush hour, and a snarl of stop-and-go traffic. He liked shopping, but never alone. It was a lot like dinner time, meant, first, for social interaction, then for sustenance. In this trait, he was different from most men, and that pleased him. He often chose peculiarity over normality, and found that such odd choices led to a happier, wider experience of life that offset the stigmas endured by a man who enjoyed shopping.

It was not the wound that bothered him, but the necessity of having to buy another pair of slacks. Since Kate died, he had resisted taking over many of the jobs she always did. He was old fashioned, he knew, but their division of labor worked; she liked to sew and he tinkered with cars. She was, in fact, an accomplished seamstress who had sewn half her wardrobe, and his. He had never learned to sew on a button. The association between sewing and Kate was so strong that, even now, he knew he would sooner buy another pair of slacks than take up a needle.

Shirts, pants. At least I'm in the right place, he thought with mild amusement.

He made his way past the women's lingerie to where Jane would be waiting for him in the cafe.

Jane would look good in that, he thought, eyeing a filmy number on the aisle. *Good God, we're just shopping for shirts!* He wondered at his ability to jump into bed with her, then realized that after nearly a year, it was a good sign. Kate's grip was lessening.

Then he spotted her, sitting alone, drinking coffee. Jane held up her cup, flashed him one of her beacon smiles.

In high school, she was such a plain little thing around that smile, he thought.

"Hi! I'd about given up on you."

"I had a parent conference. Finally had to tell her, 'Listen, lady, I've got a shopping date with a goddess. You got thirty seconds to wrap it up.'"

She stared at him and he waited. In a flash, lips parted, eyes crinkled, and the glimmering laugh rolled out of her.

"Bo!" she said, sounding shocked, though they both knew the story wasn't true. She always got his humor, in fact, greatly enjoyed his odd, almost Tourette-style remarks. He had always been mesmerized by her laugh. It was the sound of her abandonment he enjoyed, the surrender to and appreciation of foolishness and sorrow. No matter how small the incongruity, how terrible the embarrassment that was a signal for amusement about the tragedy of being human, she understood. The way her face took on a split-second wounded look before transcending to hilarity, and then, the release of infectious, unselfconscious laughter. He loved it all.

"Ready?" he asked.

"Yup."

They rode down the escalator, passing a tuxedoed man in an alcove at the bottom who played a sleek, black grand piano. Bo bounced a little to the catchy tune. He was a teacher, certainly, but the luxuriant feeling of shopping at Nordstrom's made him feel oblivious to the fact that he had chosen a career for love, not money.

In the men's wear department, sales clerks made their presence known, then hovered nearby.

Jane held up a richly designed burgundy, gold and navy silk tie. "I've never seen you in one of these."

He slipped it over his neck and brought the end into the first loop. "Well, look hard, because the only time I expect to wear one of these again is my wedding and my funeral. And, you know, come to think of it . . ."

She stopped him with a hand over his mouth. "Don't you dare! No rude comments about them being one and the same."

"Can't get away with anything, can I? Forgot about your mind reading." He took off the tie and placed it on the table.

Bolivar studied her. There were many times during her high school years, too many for coincidence, they had spoken each other's thoughts, or blurted them out at the same time. Even Kate, for all her talents, lacked that one.

He was drawn to Jane, yet thinking of her in the old framework, trying to ignore natural impulses, he felt strangely twisted, like a piranha in a bowl with a friendly goldfish, and the realization made him feel suddenly bereft of his manhood.

He rubbed his forehead, ran a hand through his hair, reflecting on the difference in their ages.

What am I doing here? This is one of my students. Was. Was my student, he reminded himself. *She must be—what'd she say? Thirty-something? Guess she's old enough to decide whether she wants to go out with me.*

"What did you have in mind?" she asked. "Dress or casual?"

"I've got a special assignment for you." He pulled at the blood-crusted flap of his pant leg.

"What happened?"

"Saved a '78 Cadillac from the scrap heap, and this is how it repays me. You got any expertise in pants?"

"Certainly." She took him by the hand to a rack of dress slacks. He liked her warm touch, her self assurance in the foreign land of a men's department.

They nosed around the racks and tables, examining various weights and colors of slacks. They examined shirts, took their time, and he appreciated her sense of fabrics and colors, her ability to visualize combinations. He missed that artistic touch.

They talked about Kate. It was difficult to open up, but somehow, Jane's gentle inquiry made him feel okay about it. She questioned out of caring, not crude curiosity, and while she probed his pain, she did not try to take it away.

He spotted an upholstered chair outside the dressing rooms, reclined in it. "Thank you, Dr. Freud, I think my hysteria is beginning to leave me now." He jumped up. "I can walk! I can walk!"

God, how he loved her laughter, and the pride he felt at his ability to turn the key to it. They got back to the task at hand, found two more pair of pants.

"So, how's Simon doing?" she asked. "I can imagine how difficult it must've been for him to lose Kate."

"He took it hard," Bo said. "I think he was close to suicide."

"Oh, God. What did you do?"

"Got him into counseling. I think that counselor saved his life. Anyway, he's practically dropped out of his junior year, but he's alive. It was hard on both of us to stay in the house after—" He squinted out the window at passersby on Riverside Avenue. "Since Simon opted out of school already, we moved to Bounty, to be near my mom. She's one of those crazy Christians, but I don't hold that against her."

"Crazy Christians? You mean there's another kind?"

He held up a shirt. She shook her head, and he put it back on the rack.

"I mean she's one of those fundamentalists, but a good, stabilizing influence. She and Simon have grown pretty close. Bounty's a real commute, but worth it."

Jane stared at him, and then glanced quickly away across the racks of suits before asking, "He's pulling around now? Going to be okay?"

"Uh-huh."

She was silent.

"What?"

She shifted the stack of shirts to her other arm. "I was just thinking. Maybe I should get my kids into some counseling."

He studied her steady eyes, the ones he used to tease her about looking like wide, green fields of Ireland, knowing perfectly well her heritage was Polish and French. He swore they changed from hazel to green when she cried, which was often, after David died. He tried to read from them now what she wasn't saying.

"What's wrong, Irish?" he asked gently.

She filled him in on the scene in Dick Moore's office, the note in the pillow case.

"I don't know how to deal with Logan. I can't tell what's going on over there, but I can bet he's telling them what the delight of their hearts is. It gives me the creeps, but my attorney says there's nothing we can do."

They walked toward the dressing rooms.

"You should get involved in your own church. Combat what he's feeding them."

She wrinkled her nose. "The thought of going to a church, facing some kind of organized religion again, makes me break out in a sweat."

"I know. That's why I left my mom's church." He stepped into a fitting room, poked his head out. "Let's take a break, okay? Be back in a minute. Gonna let my blood pressure simmer down so I can make sense of this new Churlick mess."

He tried on slacks, then a shirt he would never have selected and stared, pleased, at the reflection. The collar and yoke were blue denim, the shirt fronts, muted purple and sleeves a gray-green.

At the cash register, he laid his credit card on the counter. Next to the card sat a handsome wool hat, a fedora, like the one worn in *Indiana Jones*.

Jane wandered over to a table to examine more shirts.

"This yours, sir?" the clerk asked. Bo nodded, and the young man began ringing up purchases.

Bo picked up the hat, looked at it, smiled. He placed it firmly on his head, pulled it down at a rakish angle and turned from the clerk, who was putting the shirts and slacks into a shopping bag.

"Sir? Your total comes to . . ."

But Bolivar's back was to him now, the moment more important. He moved toward Jane with exaggerated steps. She turned in time to see him tip his hat. Then, planting his feet firmly, he scooped her up in his arms.

"Bolivar!" Her arms were wrapped around his neck. She threw her head back and laughed.

The sound was like a chord from his own heart. A fear intruded into the void, then his strong need for her conquered the fear. He examined her laugh lines, no longer dimpling, but the beginnings of creases aging her. He loved the aging, losing the dimples to the lines, turning her from skinny kid to the woman in his arms. This woman was no school girl. He was keenly, painfully aware of the fullness of her. And she did feel good. Eyes crinkled, alive as blades of Irish grass, dancing with the magic of being the woman of his heart. Hope was a choir now, filling the emptiness with an exquisite resonance.

He marched ahead, holding her close, humming the refrain from *Indiana Jones*, as people stared and pointed. "Da-da, da-da-da—"

He pulled the warmth of her closer, walking past the cologne counter now, breathed the spiced mix of musk and sex appeal other men needed, but not Indy.

At the door of Nordstrom's, with Riverside Avenue just the other side of the thick glass, he slowed, turned. He tried to judge if she were taking his little joke all right. The smile was still there, the arms encircling his neck. God, how those arms pleased him. They didn't need to be there, because this woman's strength and resourcefulness were amazing. Yet, there they were, throwing her strength, vulnerability, her capacity for thought and action, over to him, the Bernard who rescues a girl-woman who doesn't need to be rescued any longer. She could save herself—but for his need to rescue, she gave into the game. She was rescuing him now.

"I don't ever want to put you down," he said.

"You never have to, Bo."

He knew he could love her at that moment. Her belief in him, her wonderful sense of the absurd. What kind of woman would tolerate being carted all over Nordstrom's? No one else he knew would have reacted the way Jane, with her dignity, had.

"You're beautiful," he said. She rested her head on his shoulder. The smell of her. He breathed in. Had he been with her all this time and never noticed? No, he realized it was always there, the subtle, fresh, clean smell that kept him in turmoil.

"What's that?" he asked.

"What?"

"What you're wearing. Smells good, like morning. Is it perfume?"

"Yes, new, blue Cheer."

He hugged her close, savored her little joke. The scent was Jane, just Jane.

People were parting for them as they neared the counter, staring at them. The people grinned at the romantic comedy, the way people do when they are brought into the circle of lovers.

Gently, Bolivar placed her down. Removing the hat, he held it aloft, looked at the thing askance. He put it back on the counter and said, "Must've been the hat."

Twenty-Four

Jane and Bolivar met again the following Wednesday, Thursday and Friday after work. Neither saw any reason to go at the relationship slowly. Jane had a "short leash," as she put it, needing to pick up the kids at the sitter's by six o'clock, and Bo had the long drive home to Bounty. Work days in Rathcreek threw them in close proximity, and the brief hours were not wasted.

They kissed, the kind discrete enough for public, but which hung on Jane's lips when she made herself pull away.

"We've become such clock watchers," she said over her shoulder.

Bo followed her through the crowded restaurant to the bar where they would wait to be seated. He pulled out her chair. "Feels like we're going 180 miles an hour. Pretty quick, I'll be using the 'R' word."

She wondered a moment, then broke into a grin. "Relationship?"

He nodded. "Afraid I'm a goner."

It was too much for her, and just enough. She needed to hear him say that she was as important to him as he was to her. Her eyes broke away and scanned the lounge overflowing with people. A collection of odds and ends was suspended from the ceiling, a canoe, mangy moose head, '50s bicycle and more, all to create the dizzying effect of over-stimulated senses. She breathed in the aroma of sizzling fajitas mingled with the smell of beer. She liked the noisy bar and restaurant called Kahoot's, which had managed to flourish, despite The Fellowship's influence. Its activity, din and clutter made her believe she and Bolivar were alone.

"It's crazy for us to be seeing each other every day, isn't it?" he asked.

She leaned forward to be heard over the uproar of happy hour.

"Maybe you're right. A hundred-eighty is pretty fast." The slight unhinging of his smile, the fade to disappointment made her happy. "But it's almost sluggish, with the right driver."

He grinned. "It's not easy being involved with a teacher, you know. We have a tendency to bring our command persona home with us."

"What do you mean?"

"There's always a few that give you your money's worth. Gotta nail 'em without inciting a mutiny. Take command, or they screw around, talk, don't do their work. They'll get their 'F' and take everyone around them down, too."

"So what does that have to do with us?"

"Teachers just naturally take command. When you're not around a mob of adolescents, it can be annoying. Usually took two weeks of summer to get normal so Kate could stand to be around me full time."

Jane wondered what he intended by revealing that quirk. The idea of being bossed around by any man, even Bolivar, was not appealing. She had been on her own for over ten years, and was not about to give up her independence to anyone.

"What were you like by July?" she asked.

"Like a lamb. Kate would lead me around the yard, pointing to places where new shrubbery needed to be planted. Kind of like I do now, when I follow you into the bar, leading me with that luscious ass of yours." He leaned forward. "Baaa-aaaa."

It seemed to Jane she had made a career of misjudging men, and was relieved to see that Bolivar was what he appeared to be. And, more than relieved, she was pleased to be desired by this man.

She said, "Sounds like this strange behavior may require a session with Freud."

"Don't know. Do you make house calls?"

"I wish shrinks made house calls, I'd send one over to Logan's."

"How are the kids? Did you get them an appointment with a therapist yet?"

She grew interested in the table, struggling with her anger and frustration. "They refused to go. I ordered them, but they just broke down, crying, telling me their dad said they didn't have to. When we got there, they clammed up for the shrink. Later, when I called Logan, he swore he never told them not to go."

"How does he get away with turning the Good Book into the Fifth Amendment?"

"He's damn good at it, that's all I know."

The earlier mood was broken. Jane didn't want to talk about Logan. But she needed to vent or explode.

"Everyone thinks he's this wonderful man. Even my own father. Dad's come a long ways over the years, but he still drags Mom to church. I've patched things up with my family, but it's not like it used to be."

Bo raised his eyebrows.

"Abortion, for example," she said. "The family and me, miles apart."

He said, "Edward Abbey said it best. Churlick and the people he incites, they're nothing but a bunch of mother-killers." He lifted his cup in a toast. "Let the known and loved personality die; we must baptize the embryo!" He was silent a moment. "How many girls have I taught over the years who are living miserable, poverty-stricken lives because they dropped out of high school to have babies?"

"Exactly! And Logan uses the abortion issue to the hilt, saying anyone who's pro-choice is going straight to hell." She put her chin on her palm. "He was the worst mistake of my life. I'm sorry, I just can't quit talking about him."

"I'm not."

She frowned.

"You've got two beautiful kids. You could still be with The Fellowship and married to that first jackal, if all this hadn't happened."

"Oh."

"You've slowed down a bit over the years," he said, gently mocking her. "You were a lot sharper in the classroom."

"I'm going to kick you. And where I kick, it's going to hurt."

"Anyone ever tell you you're cute when you talk dirty?"

"Unless I use my toes," Jane continued, and kicked off her shoe. She slid her foot onto his under the table. With her stockinged toes, she rubbed his ankle, lifted the pant leg, ran her foot up and down his shin. "See? It won't hurt at all."

Bo smiled and narrowed his eyes.

She felt content again, and didn't want their short time together to end. "Can we get some coffee? I don't want to go home yet."

"Do they sell it by the pot?"

He left for the crowded bar, and she watched him move. He was unlike any man she had ever known: funny, intelligent, sensitive, loved to philosophize. And a man who actually listened. The way he moved. Sexy. She remembered how it felt to be in his arms, marching through Nordstrom's, shook her head and smiled. Strong, silly, romantic. He was everything she needed. But were she and her problems what *he* needed?

Servers hurried back and forth, their small, cork trays crowded with drinks; Bolivar waited at the bar, glanced over his shoulder at her. Shoe off, she raised her foot and wiggled the toes. He grinned, looked at his lap, back at her toes, to his lap.

By the time he brought their coffee back, however, she was in a serious mood.

She took a sip. "Are you sure you want to get involved with me? I mean, I want you to be sure. It's not just me. It's me and my kids. And Logan."

"I'd fight God*zilla* for you, Jane. Me, Indiana Jones; you, Jane." He paused and said in a serious voice, "I can handle Churlick. I know his kind."

"You do?"

"Sure. When I was a kid, I couldn't listen to the radio on the Sabbath. No dancing, no sports, no movies. A couple times, I snuck in anyway."

"I didn't know that about you."

"Hell, you're not the only one firebombed by the blood of the lamb." He grinned. "I can remember asking an elder once, what about dinosaurs? If the earth was 8,000 years old, like Elder Stead said, wouldn't they have been put on the ark with Noah? Elder Stead said they were on the ark."

She laughed. "Those brontosaurus must've taken up a lot of room."

"After the floods, the cloud envelope over the earth dissipated. That shrunk all the dinosaurs . . . which are still here today. They're just shrunk down to lizards."

She choked between disbelief and amusement.

"'S right. We had our very own prophet to interpret these important events. At one time, she prophesized it was a sin to not wear bloomers!" He glanced under the table. "Just as I thought. No bloomers. Straight to hell, you *wicked* woman."

"You'd know, you wicked man."

Now she understood Bolviar's irreverent attitude came from the same well as hers. She had always admired his level-headedness when it came to religion versus common sense and dignity. He had suffered, as she had, and the trauma had set them both free.

"Got some good things from 'em, though," he said.

"What could you possibly find of value in that bunch of wack-o's?"

Her tone was sharper than she intended; religion tended to bring out the kamikaze in her.

"Well, they were a logical outfit. Always arguing, looking for proof. Do things make sense? Come, let us reason together." He paused. "That's important, right?"

"You've got to be kidding. Seems to me they left their logic at the door. Tyranosaurus Rex, a lizard? Come on." She sipped her drink, eyeing him. "Do you still go?"

"Nope. But Simon does." He lounged comfortably in his seat, ankle resting on his knee. She noticed the tip of his shoe wiggling.

"You let Simon go?" For some reason she couldn't explain, she was deeply disappointed that he had allowed his son to get mixed up in such a group.

"I don't let him go, he just goes." He sighed, as though impatient. "You know, you shouldn't throw out the baby with the bath water. It's been good for him in some ways. When we moved to Bounty, he decided to start going to church with his grandma. Only bad I can see is it means giving up basketball, because he won't break the Sabbath. Games are on Fridays. But it gave him what he needed to get through his mother's death."

She was stunned. How could he tell her about the quirky sacrifice called for by a nutty prophet, the one he endured as a boy, and sit still while Simon suffered the same injuries? What was it with men? Was sacrifice to religion, to other obsessions, necessary to feel like a man?

Then, on top of it all, telling her not to be angry? Slowly, trying to control her temper, she said, "How can you allow him to be sucked into that?"

"Look, it's not a big deal. Besides, wait till your little girls get their own heads, you'll know I'm telling it straight. He's old enough to make up his own mind. And my mom's crazy religion probably saved my son's life."

"He who saves his life may lose it," she shot back.

He spoke loudly, over a group of businessmen and women at a nearby table. "Every parent screws up their kids. It's their job. It's going to be Simon's job to fix it when he gets out on his own. My parents screwed me up, and I'm screwing Simon up. No matter how hard we try to raise our kids right, it's just the way it is."

She wanted to get out of there. The noise and colors and hanging junk were too much for her. This side of Bolivar was too much for her.

"You can't know how helpless I feel watching my kids get 'screwed up' and not being able to do anything about it." She wadded a napkin into a tight ball. "I've spent the last twelve years fixing myself after Logan convinced me that submitting to him was commanded by God. I was taught not to think, but to accept blindly, by faith. I say, it's not a matter of screwing up kids, it's open our eyes and screw blind faith."

Anger verged on tears. She was furious with herself. She didn't want to cry; she was too mad. "Don't brush off the power of religion to screw up Simon, maybe for good. Your job is to protect him. I wish I could protect my kids."

"Don't you think you're overreacting about the girls?"

Slowly, she pulled back. "Overreacting? *Overreacting?* Just like every woman who ever was, now I'm overreacting." She crossed her arms.

"What I . . ."

"I know what you meant." Was her pain so difficult for him to deal with? He knew the severity of her problems with Churlick. Bo's sympathy had become her refuge. Gone, now. A desolation, a great, yawning desert on the map of her broken faith in men.

"Maybe you're right. Maybe I am overreacting," she said quietly. "It's been a gradual thing, though. At first, when they were babies and couldn't talk, came home from a weekend with their new daddy with stomach aches and headaches, I didn't overreact. Then, when he told the kids I was going to hell, I was *ooo*-kay with that. When he kidnapped them and tried to get custody, I got a little testy. And now, this verse that could mean he's leading them along like little sheep to desire who knows what? Yes, you could say I'm overreacting. *But I wouldn't if I were you.*"

Bolivar slumped in his seat.

"I just found this bumper sticker. Couldn't wait to put it on my car. It says, JESUS: Protect Me From Your Followers." She gave him a tight smile. "I mean that with all my heart."

Shit! What'd I say? Bolivar rubbed his head and scowled in misery. He was scared, starting to unravel, lost in trying to figure out what road they were on, how they'd gotten there, where he'd made the wrong turn. Where the hell had that turn come from, when he hadn't seen the curve, for all the gorgeous scenery? And now, grasping at how to recover, with his old mainstay, humor, he quipped, "Does this mean we're not going out tomorrow night?"

Jane studied him a moment. Her look was not humorous.

"I've just made up my mind," she replied. "Dallas called the other day. I think I'll call him back and let him know I *am* interested in going out with him."

She grabbed her purse, glanced at her watch. "I've got to go."

Bolivar stood abruptly, an old reflex was all. He watched her retreat through the crowd, walking to the door.

He sat down, dazed. *What the hell happened?*

Twenty-Five

One Month Later, October

Jane missed Bolivar, but needed time to sort out what had happened, who he really was. She thought of herself as a wunderkind when it came to making bad choices about men. Or was it that all men were doomed to disappoint women? As Lord Byron put it, *All men are intrinsical rascals, and I am only sorry that, not being a dog, I can't bite them.* Coming to the conclusion that she, also, was without canine instinct, Jane decided the fantasy of love could take a hike.

The twins were helping rake the yard when Dallas pulled up. The sitter, a talkative, acned fifteen-year-old, held open the trash bag. Jane had purposely started the task to avoid hearing the phone. Also, the kitchen junk drawer was already cleaned out.

She waved, surprised at her case of nerves. It wasn't at all like the comfortable feeling with Bolivar. But then, comfort was not what she needed. What she needed was distraction, and Dallas was certainly that.

Jane kissed the kids, grabbed her purse and rustled out to the curb through a sea of leaves. Dallas opened the door of the glossy red pickup, and she climbed in. Diesel filled the air and the engine sound warbled through her.

He wore a cowboy hat, tight jeans and scuffed boots. The blonde hair was slicked back and shiny.

His gaze was approving. "Lookin' good. Kinda rustic, out there rakin'. I like a woman who doesn't worry about breakin' a nail."

"Kept me busy," she said. "It's been rough since Logan took the kids."

"Yeah, that's why I gave you time before I called. But you don't fool me. You're no pansy ass. Followed that preacher back to town, kicked butt and got your kids, didn'cha?"

She grinned, nodded.

"Well hang on, your workout's comin' tonight." With a roar and flurry of crimson leaves, he pulled out into Boone Avenue traffic.

An evening of line dancing with Dallas was different than she had expected. Rather than merely putting in time to take her mind off Bolivar, it was absorbing and fun. Kick, together, kick. Grapevine left. Quarter turn to the right and repeat the pattern.

He showed her a good time that evening and other evenings, in a way free of pressure. It was easy to keep her distance emotionally; her heart longed for Bolivar. But unlike Bo, Dallas didn't need to save her, fix her or woo her. They both understood their relationship wasn't eternal. They were friends. It didn't stop his attempts to talk her into bed. He tried, and she gave him his no. He took the no with minimal grumbling.

Dallas was the kind of man who could keep a woman distracted the rest of her life. He was a cyclone with red fenders: unpredictable and potentially dangerous. She wondered at times at her strength in the face of sensuality awakening. Was it possible Dallas might work a yes out of her?

As the weeks went by, Dallas' attentions grew stronger, and the memory of a hundred and eighty miles an hour was just a dull ache. Still, the ache was there, and perhaps it would be Dallas, not Bo, who would fill it.

In the wake of the scene in his lawyer's office, Churlick continued to keep a low profile. Jane bent a watchful eye to her girls, who, remarkably, seemed happy once again. She had debriefed them, of course. They had had a rough time the first few weekends at Logan's, but Bekah and Darcy proved resilient. Still, she worried.

One weekend morning, Jane poured batter on the griddle. Six whole wheat pancakes rolled sizzling over the heated surface. Her father had been the pancake chef of her youth, and now Jane fixed them the way he did. The normal kind, without wheat germ and oatmeal in the batter, seemed unhealthy, and their texture, uninteresting.

She was lifting a corner of a pancake to peek at the bottom when a screech sent her bolting to the bathroom.

"What's wrong, Darcy?"

The dark eyes closed in agony, a hand went to the side of her head. "My ear. Owww! My ear, my ear."

Jane held back the hair and saw the angry, pus-filled lobe. She tried to free a few strands of hair stuck in clumps of green matter.

Darcy screamed and yanked her ear away, feet pattering the floor. "Mo-om!"

"Oh, honey, it looks so sore. Why didn't you tell me?"

"I don't know. It hurts, Mommy."

Darcy hadn't deigned to call her such a juvenile endearment in a while. She was so young, so tender still, and Jane was touched by the name.

Typical. Another mess by Logan for Jane to clean up. She got Neosporin from the medicine cabinet, soaked a cotton ball with warm water and touched it to the flaming earlobe to loosen the caked matter.

Later, after Jane had reminded Darcy and Bekah how to soak their ear lobes in alcohol, Logan called to tell her the girls were going to be in a church play.

"So?" Jane said.

"I thought you might want to come an' see 'em."

"No."

"It's going to be broadcast on my program," he said casually. "You know I've branched out and got into radio, didn't you?"

Logan's vacillation between the rage in Moore's office to this pathetic figure baffled her. Why couldn't he take no? Louise would say the rejection was a challenge.

She was about to hang up when he said, "You know a Dallas Boulder?"

The mention of Dallas' name prickled her skin. Quickly, the implication bore into her: once again, Logan knew who she was dating.

"How do you know about him?"

"Kids mentioned 'im." His voice was barely above a whisper. Dolores must be around. "You're datin' him, aren't you?"

"It's none of your damn business!"

"But it *is* my damn business. These are my kids. Everything you do affects them. This Boulder's a crazy bastard. Blows things up. Lives like a hermit out in the woods." He demanded, "So, you screwin' that son-of-a-bitch?"

She hung up on him. Why, after all this time, was he still harassing her? Or had he been spying on her for years, and never caught?

The phone rang. She jumped to it, not wanting it to disturb the kids.

"Quit calling me."

"I just wanted to apologize."

She drew in a savage breath, let it out, heard him say, "I'm sorry for swearing."

What? With the appalling invasion of her personal life still throbbing in the pit of her stomach, he was calling over a swear word? Then, he said something that made the hairs on the back of her neck stand up.

"Did you know that he and his first wife were involved in a *commune* with another couple? Probably had orgies and stuff like that."

My God, she thought. She fought through the shock and made herself ask in a casual voice, "How would you know that?"

"I got friends. They know about this man you're carryin' on with. Question is, do you think it's healthy for our kids to be around someone with that kind of morality?"

"I'm only going to say this once more. They are your kids and my kids, but they'll never be our kids." Her voice cracked. "Don't call me again. Ever."

A week of blissful silence passed. Fear of Logan's contacting her gave way to excitement over a costume party whose Dionysian leanings were legendary.

The night of the party, she closed herself in the bathroom, appraised herself in the mirror. Bells jingled when she shook her head. She moved the black and scarlet fool's crown to a more rakish angle. Overall, the effect was a look her mother would have called "wanton," and Louise would have amended to "pre-orgasmic."

Inexperienced in flaunting her sexuality, such brazenness made Jane uneasy. Yet, wasn't Louise right? Wasn't pre-orgasmic and beyond what she wanted this night?

The knit tights encased one leg in scarlet; the other in black. Scarlet and black met in a center seam of the tights. She turned and looked over her shoulder. The curve of her buttocks was just visible under the drape of the tunic. Naked, she couldn't have been more provocative.

Mmmmm. Naughty, very naughty. Too much?

"Mom!" Darcy knocked. "You better come out. There's a weird Santa out here."

Santa Claus? Disappointment deflated her fragile panache. She wasn't sure she could go through with this new Jane.

Dallas had told her what to expect, if the past was any indication of the wild, lusty nature of his parties. She had difficulty picturing it all. An indoor hot tub. Guests of past parties were freeze-framed on his walls at school, holding cut glass vases like beer steins. Dallas Boulder's friends did not surprise her. After all, here was a man who, when he took her to dinner, made reservations incognito in the name of Underhill, the only way he could gain entrance to places he had been before.

She looked forward to a night of intemperance with Dallas, felt ripe to experience the other side of life, the side verboten in her youth by The Fellowship. If her early life bore the impression of The Fellowship, the self-righteous abortion clinic protests she took part in, the faith healings gone wrong, then the latter part would be a protest against him.

And Dallas was more than willing to help her in any way she wished. But what of Bolivar? Why hadn't he called?

Whatever. She was restless, worn down by always doing what was right. And by Churlick, about whom she could do nothing. There was no lusty, passionate existence in a life of insipid correctness, besides offering no connectedness to humanity. She was lonely. So. Regardless of Dallas' pedestrian costume, she was in a mood for exuberance. She opened the door.

Dallas spied her first. "Ho, ho, ho! Don't you look *dang* pretty!"

He wore a red suit, but tradition ended there. Tight red pants and a red double breasted jacket. Sleek snakeskin boots. Skinny, black patent leather belt. Hip, expensive sunglasses. But what struck her most was his beard. How had he put his hands on it? He wore a trim blonde beard, a close match to his own hair. Red cowboy hat set back on his head gave him an appearance of a rockin' Marlboro man, like something from L.A., not the north pole.

She grinned, but wanted to get out of there, especially the way she was dressed. The sooner they left, the less chance of the twins supplying information when their father pumped them. Hurrying to the coat closet, she introduced Ruth and Bob, who had come for dinner and to baby-sit.

"Don't worry about bringing her back early," Bob said.

The girls kissed her, and she made Ruth and Bob promise to not let them eat too much Halloween candy.

The shiny red truck sped across town toward the city limit, the red-suited cyclone sitting next to her, bearing her above the landscape of her ordinary life.

"I didn't want to say anything in front of the kiddies," Dallas said, one large hand resting on the steering wheel, the other tugging suggestively at the wide, scarlet ribbon tied at her calf, "but, whoa, mama, you're some kinda sexy jester. What are those things?"

"These?" she asked. "They're my lightening bolts. I've got 'em Velcroed to my thigh. Oh, that reminds me." She dug through her purse, retrieved a name tag, peeled off the backing and stuck it on.

He took his eyes from the road, glanced at it and laughed. "*Hello, my name is—God?* Jesus!"

"Yeah, and the Holy Ghost, too."

Dallas slowed, then pulled to the side of the road. He pointed to the glove box. "There's a button in there, the pin-on kind. Get it for me, would ya?"

She produced the button. "*Santa's Coming.* Cute. Want me to pin it on you?"

With a sly grin, Dallas shook his head, then opened the pin and fastened it to his fly, an inch below the patent leather belt

"Like it?"

Her laugh erupted, gleefully wicked. "Beware dirty old men bearing gifts."

He took her in his arms and kissed her. It was the first time he had tried and she hadn't said no. She enjoyed seeing his surprise at her willingness, enjoyed the feeling again of being with a man.

When they came up for air, he said, "Good God, Jane! If I'da known that was lurking there underneath all that 'good-girl,' I'da—"

"Youda nothing," she said. "I wasn't ready till tonight. Now get us to the party before some state trooper comes along and your teaching credential gets yanked for disorderly conduct on the highways."

When they arrived at his place, she saw no sign of a house, only a huge dairy barn with a rough-hewn yard where a few chickens flew out of the truck's headlights. A bent weather vane and some loose shingles topped a mansard roof. The barn was surrounded by the woolly green bowl of acres of towering pine trees. An owl hooted in the distance. The October air was crisp, the breeze fragrant with the sharp citrus aroma of pines.

She stared at him. "You live in a barn?"

"Yup. Wanted to bring you early so I could give you the royal tour." He gazed at the mammoth structure with pride. Constructed of ten-by-ten, and eight-by-ten timbers, it stood a hundred feet long, forty feet high, fifty feet wide. It looked large enough to house a fleet of 747s.

He walked Jane to the entrance, a pair of gigantic, double doors topped by a rosette window.

"I put a lot of work into getting these doors just right. They're real special. Just use your fingertips to open 'em."

She gazed at the massive doors. Each looked to be about nine feet wide. Fully opened, a hay truck could drive right through them.

"You've got to be kidding. They must be twenty feet tall."

She extended two pinkies, barely pulled, and the doors gave way like a kite on a breeze, gliding soundlessly outward, as she walked them back.

"Amazing! You renovated this place?"

He nodded.

"By yourself?"

"Me and a little inheritance that fell into my lap. Kind of an eight-year hobby. When I finally finished it, I moved out of the travel trailer I was livin' in. Had a party to celebrate. Great party. Dynamited the trailer."

The stillness of the woods absorbed her laugh. The exhilaration she usually felt in his presence was heightened tonight. Could a cyclone be trained? Why train a cyclone?

They entered and she hung her cloak on a peg by the door. Wide-eyed, she surveyed the quarters. The inside of the barn proper was a huge cavern, filled with a dozen sizable wooden platforms built at various levels above the base floor. Beyond, the effect of a multitude of colors and lights, along with hanging artifacts throughout, some plush, some silly or garish, gave the impression of a colossal wonderland.

"You live here?" she exclaimed.

"Like it?"

"*Love* it. I wish the kids could see this."

They climbed the staircase to the largest platform, which held several comfortable couches, a couple of overstuffed chairs, wood stove, some things she couldn't identify and a staggering collection of neon art.

"The living room? Why the glass wall?" A floor-to-ceiling glass barrier, which sectioned off half of the dimly illumined barn beyond, stood at one end of the platforms.

"Code says the living space hasta be separated from the barn, so I sealed it off. Right now, it's sort of my garage. See? A '38 Chrysler. That one's a '41 renovated Willy's Jeep from Belgium. Over there's a '32 Ford double B flatbed."

The place was warm enough, and smelled of dust, timber and an exotic blend of foods. She wandered up a short brace of stairs to the dining room platform, the table spread with a mother lode buffet.

"How many are coming? The whole Strategic Air Command?"

"Enough to make it interesting," he said.

"Did you make all this?"

He held up his hands. "Hell, no! This is Nanette's work. Best caterer I've ever known." He called, "Nanette?"

A blonde emerged from what Jane guessed to be the kitchen, arms laden. She wore a short French maid's uniform, very becoming. The two sized each other up, smiled, while Dallas tossed two hefty logs into a wood stove.

"Nanette? Is that her real name?" Jane whispered.

"Of course. Warm enough? Takes two stoves to heat this monstrosity." He pointed to another wood burning stove, its glass front reflecting brightness.

She felt like a child at an extraordinary amusement park. Everywhere, incredible, fantastically oversized, out-of-place novelties.

Neon art reigned. Impossible sizes, colors. Beer signs, tinsel lightning and signs flashing in other languages. One, unlit, was extraordinary. Twenty feet long, four feet high, double backed, reading *Joe's X-Roads Bar*, it was the focal point of the room.

"My latest acquisition," he said. "Cool, huh? See? Twenty feet above the floor from that ridge pole. Gonna light it up for the first time tonight." He nodded. "See those two transformer canisters?"

"Where?"

"Over there, about five feet tall? Three feet around—"

She nodded. "Where'd you get them?"

He shrugged. "Best to not know. One's got 110 volts to a buzzer, the other's got 110 volt relay to the neon. Just wait'll later." A shiver of danger and excitement ran through her.

Dallas poured a couple of drinks, handed Jane one. Before they could toast, he pulled her toward him, kissed her.

"Nanette," Jane cautioned.

He laughed. "You can take the girl outta the church . . . Dressed like that, you're gonna incite riots tonight, honey, guaranteed. No matter who's around."

She smiled, pleased at Dallas' nod to her new persona.

Jane held her glass aloft. "To the riots!"

Twenty-Six

Strains of Herb Alpert and the scent of chlorine filtered into the livingroom from a hot tub inside a steamy glass barrier on one of the many platforms that made up Dallas' home. Spot lights in the water backlit rising steam. Waist-deep, musicians hammered with their brass instruments.

A chorus of voices rose: "Te-qui-la!"

Above, Jane turned from the railing of the livingroom platform and observed the houseful of people. A hundred or so guests gathered on various levels or made their way along cat walks connecting the platforms. Like roving bands of juvenile delinquents, their carousing seemed to fit. The staff Halloween party enjoyed a reputation that brought educators flocking to Dallas' house en mass each fall.

A dozen carved jack-o-lanterns reflected orange moons in the kitchen windows. Dallas lounged against the counter, engrossed in a discussion. But Jane wasn't ready to be tied down yet. Too much humanity to explore.

At the moment, she was drawn by an aroma that, sooner or later, lured everyone to overindulgence. Nanette and her troop of caterers scurried back and forth from the kitchen, ensuring the dishes were filled. Stir fry, almond chicken, foot-long Dagwoods, casseroles, pizza, salads, lasagna, crackers, cheeses, cakes, pies, cheesecake and more.

"Ye Gods! It's God!" the back half of a horse pronounced loudly. He stood near Jane in a gray dapple, dishing up potato salad. His wobbly head reared back, focused on her, and he put down the plate. "You're not going to curse me, are you?" he said, coming closer. "I mean I am drunk, 'course I'm drunk . . . but I'm not a lush or anything."

She grinned. "Okay, you're not a lush."

"I mean it," the man staggered closer, his leer wandering drunkenly over her. The horse's ass smiled, attempted a nonchalant move and fell to the floor.

He moaned, looking a little gray. "I think I'm gonna be sick."

Jane and another guest, the Phantom of the Opera, lifted him under the arms to another level where the bathrooms were located.

"I'm not sure he really deserves salvation," the man said from behind the mask. The voice sounded familiar.

"Probably not," she replied, as she helped the horse's ass along, "but who does?"

"Thanngs, you're angels," the horse said, and stumbled into the bathroom.

"After you." The phantom held out his hand, offering Jane first use of the narrow cat walk to take them back to the dining room.

"Michael!" she said, suddenly recognizing his voice, "I didn't know you'd be here. Cool costume. Where's Margie?"

"Out there, somewhere." He waved a hand at the throngs below.

They moved over the wooden slats, dodging human army surplus figures. The catwalk was solid enough that an elephant could have tap danced on it without a creak. Dozens of lamps, hurricane lanterns, and the neon that was everywhere, produced an eerie profusion of colors and planes of light, and seemed other worldly.

They made their way back to what Jane's father would have called the Table of Death and finished loading their plates.

"There she is." Michael pointed to a crowd.

Margie, dressed as the Phantom's Christina, stood out against a riotous group converging around a gorilla and pharaoh who played mumble ty-peg. A jackknife quivered in the floor. The gorilla flailed his arms, beat his chest.

Jane made her way to her friend's side, asked, "Know where you can get a little wine for thy stomach's sake around here?"

Margie stared, then giggled. "God, the joker. Leave it to you."

Jane nodded, and her fool's crown erupted in jingling. "Biggest joke of the cosmos: bring us up submissive, God-fearing girls. Bring in Churlick to show us the way. Pretty funny."

"How you doing?"

"Fine, I think."

Margie laughed. "Shouldn't God be a little more certain than that?"

"Sometimes I wonder," Jane said.

"What do you mean?"

"First, He created Adam and Eve. Choice was important to God, and He told them so. But that whole freedom of choice soured God on his creations. They chose the apple, so He changed the locks on 'em. Then there were the kids. Where do these personalities come from? So after all that mess and a few more generations, God decides, erase. Hand picks Noah and his family. Creme de la creme. But the world's as big a mess now as it ever was. Need I say more?"

Margie took a bite of toasted brie and pastry. "Not a good track record, is it?"

They walked to a Plexiglas molded chair and sat side by side.

"Speaking of bad stock," Margie said, "How's it going with Logan?"

"It's not worth ruining a good party," Jane said, then savored a bite of lasagna.

"Ho, ho, ho!" said Dallas, strolling over. "I'll bet you been good, eh, Margie?"

Margie chuckled, nodded.

"And, God, here's been *real* good." He sat next to Jane and slid his arm around her waist. "Why don't you sit on Santa's lap and tell him what you want?"

She glanced at the button, *Santa's Coming*.

"Oh, sure, and what could you give God that She doesn't already have?"

He frowned. "One of those hard-to-shop-for types, eh?" He leaned over and kissed her lightly. "I'm sure I could think of something."

The doorbell sounded, a few swashbuckling bars from *Star Wars*, the doors parted, and a passel of people entered.

"Excuse us, will you, Margie?" He took Jane by the hand.

Jane watched as Dallas welcomed his guests, pleased that he had wanted her at his side as—what? Hostess? Were they a couple?

"MacKenzie, you forgave me!" Dallas shouted. "Glad you could make it, Charlie, Phil! You ol' son-of-a-bitch! Haven't seen you since that messy court thing."

Phil and Dallas slapped each other on the back.

"This your date?" Dallas inquired, smirking.

Phil introduced a veiled harem dancer. "Lulu, Dallas Boulder."

Only the harem dancer's heavily blackened lashes were visible. Steamy and utterly sensual, she returned Dallas' smile with her eyes.

Jane felt a pang of jealousy, then chided herself. She and Dallas a couple? Before this night, hadn't she always told him no? Did she really want tonight to be different?

Lulu raised her hands above her head. Tiny metal cymbals on her fingers and thumbs chinged. Slowly at first, then faster and faster, the staccato ting-a-ling, ting-a-ling, as she undulated through the circle of revelers forming around her.

Hips swayed the sheer fabric that skirted to her bare feet. Her head dipped back and shoulders shimmied. Palms up, she used the cymbals to draw the circle of spellbound men to her, then motion them away.

"I want one of these, Santa!" Charlie shouted. MacKenzie elbowed him.

The dancer twirled, whisked off the filmy wrap covering her shoulders and drew it under Dallas' chin, enveloping them all in a dizzying haze of perfume. Her jeweled bodice heaved in a controlled slow motion, gems sparkling in the neon light. Finally, the cymbals grew faster, the shimmying blurred, until the dance came to an abrupt end.

Applause echoed from the circle surrounding her to the highest platform, where people leaned and whistled. The veiled dancer was breathing hard, and glistened with perspiration. She bowed low on one knee.

In a smooth move that took Jane by surprise, the woman hooked her arm through Jane's and Dallas' and steered them toward the stairs to the livingroom platform.

"Well, what'd you think?" she asked. And to Dallas, "This place yours? Nice. You and Jane know each other?"

The sound of that voice was like a hammer blow to Jane. "Louise?"

"I thought Phil said you were Lulu." Dallas turned to Jane. "You know her?"

"Louise, it's you, isn't it? Oh man! I would've never guessed under that get-up."

The eyes danced, and Louise unhooked her veil to reveal a red-lipped smile.

Jane hugged her. "Dallas, this is my sister, Louise."

"You may have mentioned Louise, but you never told me about *Lulu*."

Louise, arms linked through theirs, stopped. "Mmmmmm-mmmmm. Look at that."

"What?" Jane asked.

Jane and Dallas glanced around at the men, some still leaning over the railings above, others staring openly in knots of appreciation on the stairs and landings.

"Yessir," Louise said, "like walkin' through a field of waving penises."

Dallas twisted into a red pretzel of laughter. He finally managed, "I thought Phil brought you."

"Oh, Phil, the gay Philistine. Girls aren't his type," she said. "I just arrived with Phil, I'm not leaving with him."

"You're not?"

Louise gave him a sultry stare. "No, I'm not. I'm going home with someone else." She unfastened the transparent wrap and slung it across her forearm, baring her jewel-bedecked cleavage. Walking away, she gazed at him over her shoulder. "Feeling lucky?"

At the height of the party, Dallas called for silence. The uproar died back, and the soft trumpeting of "A Taste of Honey" filtered down from one of the platforms. He made an elaborate show of snubbing out his cigar in a 500-pound Air Force practice bomb, whose nose was cut off to hold sand. People from every level hung over the railings.

With a crow bar, Dallas opened a crate marked DANGER! DO NOT ASSEMBLE UNASSISTED! He withdrew a large rubber apron and handed it to Jane, who tied it around his waist.

A thrill of apprehension and excitement shot through Jane. What kind of stunt would he pull tonight?

He bent over the box and removed a pair of lamb's wool gloves. With Jane's help, he donned the protective mitts, pulling them to his elbows.

Next, he took out a six-foot, double-bladed knife switch and held it up for everyone to see. Anticipation crackled through the crowd.

Louise stood off to Jane's right in the company of three admirers. Jane realized she had never been out with Louise in a social situation, where she had seen her sister's brashness in her interactions with men. With Dallas. Of course Jane had been shocked. But Louise didn't know about Dallas, because before that evening, Jane hadn't known herself if she were truly interested in him. Now, she asked herself, *Am I?*

Dallas affixed the switch to a spot on the ridge pole where wires connected to the giant neon sign above. Then, he pulled a welder's mask from the box.

"Don't want to lose my sight." He glanced around, knocked on the mask now in place on his face. "Anyone else bring theirs? Well, that's all right. Just squint."

Several people with weaker constitutions moved back from the railings. The circle around Dallas widened, and he gave the musicians a nod. They played a volley and held it.

Dallas dropped the blade. It clacked into the contacts. He threw the switch. The huge electric buzzer blasted its sound through the barn. The neon sign hummed, flickered and shot to life. Twenty feet above, *Joe's X Roads Bar* emblazoned the raptured, eerie faces reflecting brilliant red, yellow and blue. People looked at one another, perplexed. A smattering of clapping cut through the neon's hum.

That was all. No danger, simply the lighting of a neon sign.

Dallas admired *Joe's X Roads*. "Ain't she a beauty?"

The crowd exploded in shocked laughter and, finally, applause. They had been duped by Santa, who failed to deliver anything but a contrived drama, all over some lighting. Should have known better. They were used to Dallas' sleight of hand.

He signaled, and the brass picked up the driving beat of "A Taste of Honey." Guests laughed, talking about the sheer audacity of the stunt, of Dallas' not delivering what he promised—whatever that was. They seemed to enjoy being snookered by the man in the red suit.

The crowds overlooking from the floors above began to break up. Dallas sought out Louise, grinned at her. Louise brightened, gave a slow shrug, and the siren song traveled down to her hips, where his gaze rested.

Jane watched the tight red jeans retreat, watched Dallas push the red cowboy hat forward. He never looked back, and with Louise on his arm, disappeared into the mass of humanity.

Twenty-Seven

Jane sat on the kitchen counter, a wine glass in her hand, not much wine left in it. The odor of scorched jack o'lanterns surrounded her. In Jane's humiliating retreat from Dallas' desertion, she had stumbled upon the empty room and stayed there. She needed the privacy to whip herself with thongs of disappointment and grief, and for her missed opportunity to change what seemed to be the sorriest little life on the planet.

Grief, for the foolish belief that Dallas could unclog the congested heart that beat in her chest. Disappointment, that she could not be as irresponsible and wild as others around her, who were having so much fun. The weight of morality was a bitch.

She had been watching Dallas and Louise through the kitchen doorway. In his usual cyclone fashion, Dallas teased and joked and flirted, until finally Louise gave in and broke open like a thunderhead, soaking him with her laughter. But what she did then, only Louise could do: she teased and joked and flirted even more outrageously than Dallas, or so subtly he had to work at her meaning, wonder if she were letting him all the way into the joke. Or if he were the joke.

Watching them, a mild jealousy stirred in Jane. Not over Louise having captured him, but envy of how right they were together. Who better than Louise to be with Dallas? Only her craziness, her charming candor and unhinged perspective, were suited to the life of lunacy Dallas offered a woman.

On impulse, Jane cupped her hands around her mouth. "Louise!"

Louise turned, waved at her and playfully pushed Dallas away to answer the doorbell, then beat a sultry path to her sister.

"Well!" Louise said. "Some party, huh?"

Jane nodded, drank the last of her wine. "What do you think?"

"About what?"

"Dallas!"

Louise smiled. "He's fun. Real fun."

"He likes you."

"Moi?" The acknowledgment lit her face, then she frowned and hoisted herself onto the counter, filmy costume fluttering to rest. "Kinda looked like he was your date."

"Not really."

"I'm not stealin' your man?"

"You're not stealing him. I was just borrowing him from you. He's not my type."

"I'm sorry, Janey," Louise fretted. "Men can't help themselves. When you're doin' undercover work, it's just too damn hot for most of 'em to resist. Can't handle the mystery." She craned her neck and whispered, "Seen any CIA?"

Jane shook her head. "You're safe with Dallas."

"Can't be too safe." She fingered her veil. "Sure you're not mad?"

"Yeah. I found out once and for all, I need to be in love. I don't feel that way about Dallas. Thought it could be different, but, there it is."

Louise laughed convulsively. "Love? What's wrong with your hormones, girl? On vacation? Gone into the deep freeze?" Then, a staggering thought straightened her face. "No foolin'? Not in all these years? Good God!"

Embarrassed, Jane turned away.

"Use it or lose it, woman! You're not gettin' any younger."

"Tell me something I don't know."

"Jesus, Janey! You're the only one here perfect enough to play God. But you, with your complexes and striving to transcend, hell, you could *be* God and feel like you weren't doing it right. Besides, He's not so perfect, if you interpolate the word right."

"What are you talking about? And let me tell you, I ain't perfect."

"Hell, God made a flood to wipe out His mistake. And He made us in His image—must laugh His ass off some days. I'm tellin' ya, you can't be The Prankster and take everything so serious." Ting, ting-a-ling. She poured Jane and herself a glass of wine and toasted. "Honey, here's to the plumbing that can wash them blues away!"

Guests drifted into the kitchen. Tweety Bird, the horse's ass and others.

"What about evil?" Jane asked. "We need to aim for goodness, at least."

"When faced with two evils, I always choose the one I haven't tried before." Louise's strong white teeth stood out against red lips. "Stole that one from Mae West."

A matador stepped forward. "Evil is living outside the church, outside God's will."

Louise said to Jane, "Such a doopbyosh," invoking their father's Polish slang, and they grinned. "God's okay. It's the CIA I don't care for."

Tweety Bird said, "Well, you've been outside The Fellowship long enough to have tasted from the devil's cup."

Louise frowned. "Ix-nay, sis, this is bringin' out the nut-sos."

Jane squared on the woman. "God decided He needed a deputy? What a lot of horse shit! The problem with your religion is it doesn't allow anyone else to have one."

"Amen!" cried the horses ass. "Fair is foul and foul is fair. I been there."

"Amen and hallelujah!" said a very familiar voice. "What a piece of work is man, how noble in reason. How infinite in faculty, in form and movement how express and admirable. The beauty of the world, the paragon of animals."

The voice made the little maniac inside Jane's heart beat at the iron bars. Near the kitchen doorway Bolivar Bernard stood in the midst of onlookers.

Desire tumbled through her like a storm, breaking the windows, bending back the iron bars, pulling her down, down, into its frightening tempest.

Bo's smile radiated meaning. Fedora drawn down, tan khakis, a bull whip coiled around a shoulder and hung under his arm. Indiana Jones. He was there for Jane.

The group began to break up.

Immediately, the horse's ass, who looked much less gray, set upon Jane. "I've never been a religious man before tonight, Your Honor, but I believe in you."

Bo staved him off. "She's a one-man deity, pal."

"Is this new reverence some sort of sign?" Jane asked, mocking Bo.

"All I know," Bolivar said, "is we need to talk. There's nothing more important on the face of the earth at the moment."

Jane leveled a cool gaze at Bo, surprised at how his need of her raised her own resistance. "So talk."

Bolivar took Jane to his place, assuring her that Simon was licking his wounds and camped out at Grandma's for the night. He turned on a lamp, started a fire and she curled up in a leather wingback chair. His home had the feel of a bachelor; a tentativeness about hanging onto neatness and order.

"Well?" Jane asked.

"Uh . . . I'm, uh, I - should've called," Bo said.

"That's a hell of a sorry apology."

Was he blind? How ridiculous that he assumed he could get off so lightly, after a hundred and eighty, breaking to a dead stop, and now fizzling along. How dare he think he could command her heart?

Still, Bo said nothing, as if speaking could be dangerous. But his look caressed her, until she softened. After surviving all the catastrophes of the heart, in his eyes she read that the last, great challenge lay before him. He could not fail now. He would do anything for her now.

"You - are in trouble, Bolivar."

"Sweet Jehovah, don't I know it."

"First, you insult me. Then, abandon me. Is this what I have to look forward to?"

"No, no. I blew it. I know that, and I'm sorry. Oh, God, Jane, I'm sorry most that I was a goddam ignoramous, not to see I could've lost you in the time we were apart. But, sorry isn't all there is to it. I know I need to fight for your love. Convince you that I need you." He put his hand on hers. "I love you, Jane."

Her insides swept around, like the upheaval of a hundred pigeons taking to the air, creaking pinions circling and circling. She should be furious—why wasn't she? To think she had prepared herself to be with Dallas this night. If love hadn't been Bolivar's motivation, she would have walked away and never looked back. But it was love—fumbling, stupid, irrepressible love, and that saved them both.

"How could you act that way if you cared about me?" she asked.

"It's complicated. I had some things to sort out, things to take care of. I only know I love you, and don't want to lose you. I've loved you since that night on the lake."

He pulled a slip of paper out of his pocket and unfolded it. "Here. I was going to give this to you tonight. It says it all."

The Lake's Canoe

The moon lighted lake reveals through the trees
Reflecting and smooth.
I sometimes go there and ripple it
With my canoe.
Just put the point in and give a little push.
The water pressing up buoys the silver craft,
Lets it glide until a paddle can be
Dipped and pulled in a gentle rhythm
Oh, so smoothly it moves me.
Rivulets undulating in chevrons to the shore
Tell where the canoe has been.
In the middle of the lake I sometimes pause
To take it all in, sky, moon, trees,
And the mirroring surface, too.
Below, I know the rainbows swim.
I've seen them on mornings when the light's
Just right, moving in circles,
Entwining into themselves,
But that is morning.
At night the lake is lovely, warm and deep.
I love to go there and ripple its surface
Before I sleep.

The paper trembled in her hand. Their first night together, as intimate as if they had slept together. His sexual longing since then, and hers, to make their love complete. This was the only way he could win her, and he had known it. To woo her with words.

"Buy why?" she asked softly. "What in the world did you have to figure out that you couldn't come and talk with me about?"

"The hardest part was Simon, and that was something I had to deal with alone. He hated you, but never knew you. That's why I was so late. The final knock-down drag-out was tonight, trying to make him accept what you mean to me. Weeks of stopping and starting, bringing you out into the light. He was a little shit, but can't say I blame him."

She shivered. Bolivar and Simon fighting. Over her.

Bo pointed out the window at a light snow falling. The half-drawn blinds cut the winter mantle into lines over the soft white that sifted onto the bottom pane.

Jane said, "We've never had snow on Halloween before."

"Going to be a long winter." But the way he said it was comforting.

"So how is it with Simon?" she asked.

"Okay. He can't understand how I can love anyone but his mother. Tried to convince him that my love for you doesn't take away from love for Kate. Kids, they're so loyal. There's no way to tell him how our thoughts clicked like nothing I've ever known before; how you were my turning point, and when I was with you, I could breathe without smelling the stink of grief. I even had a feeling Kate nodded for me to love again. I was alive. You were life — at a hundred eighty."

"For me, too. That's why this month's been so terrible. You should've told me."

"I'm sorry. You're right. I didn't know how cruel it was until tonight when I saw the hurt in your eyes. But Simon's not the only reason it took me so long. You know, you're not like some women who are cute when they're mad," he said, mildly sarcastic. Kneeling, he poked the logs, and the flames leapt, sparks flew up the chimney.

"I had to figure out if you were worth giving up God for." He seemed to enjoy her confusion. "At least my version of God, the tyrannical son-of-a-bitch I grew up with, and allowed to be handed down to my son. I imagine when Eve offered Adam the apple, he gave up his God in one bite . . . couldn't bear the thought of an eternity without the woman he loved." Bo paused.

"You made me proud of myself again. Made me see I had to stand up for my religious beliefs, and for you, no matter how painful it may be for Simon. He knows, now, how strongly I feel. He may still struggle with the idea of my loving you. And he can still choose another way to God. But it won't be because he doesn't know what his father stands for."

She hadn't known such a love was possible. A man who could take her head and heart and pain so seriously that he would re-route the direction of his life, and that of his son's.

He stood and took her in his arms. Mouth barely touching, he covered hers with gentle conquerings and gentle surrenders, both of which grew into a covenant. A hand against the small of her back pressed her against him. The other hand set off the jingling of her fool's cap. She saw with sudden tenderness that his eyes were filled with tears.

His gaze roved over her. "It's good to be back. God, I've been worshipping your strength, your determination and brains and all the rest. I'd almost forgot how beautiful . . ."

She buried her head against his shoulder, smelled the sharp odor of the leather that clung to him and the subtle musk. She grabbed a handful of shirt and held on, unable to believe Bolivar was real. This man was real, more genuine than she had ever hoped for, and he loved her more than the Garden.

Twenty-Eight

For the first time, Jane understood sex beyond rules. Bo could be a sensitive lover, a madman, or an animal. His murmurings in the dark—good God, a man who poured his words into her ear during love making! Dreamy words, erotic, or lit with passion. He brought out in Jane an inventiveness and serenity she had never known she possessed. For the first time, a lusty provoking inspired Jane's ardor.

In November, they arranged for their children to be taken care of, then drove to Victoria, British Columbia. Hand in hand, they roamed the city's streets and browsed used book shops, or enjoyed the fresh scent of winter gardens washed in rain. They found a small cafe with wide windows overlooking the sea, and called it theirs. By candlelight, they leaned over the table and talked of the future. In their room, they ate, read to each other, talked, satisfied with the simple joy of being together—until it was time again. Like animals, they let the natural rhythms and curiosities assert themselves; the animal rutting or tender lovemaking, according to their moods, until Jane clutched Bolivar to her, and he, wanting to make the moment last, murmured, "Don't move, baby."

Drowsy, she lay on him afterward, enjoying the feeling of being encircled in his arms under the warmth of the thick down comforter.

"Marry me, Jane. Marry me, now."

A hot wave of fear spiked through her and a thousand pores opened. Perspiration surged, and though she said nothing, stippled with sweat, her body spoke for her.

"What's wrong?" he asked.

She shook her head. *How can I tell you, darling man, without coming off as more paranoid than Louise? You'd never understand Churlick's ability to wreak havoc with my girls, and through them, hurt me. Just a little while longer, Bolivar.*

She loved Bolivar more than she could ever make him know. He had no need to control her and his love was uncomplicated and pure. Finally, finally, a balance of power, the give-and-take she had never dreamed of. He was willing to take the whole woman, her exuberance, and her anger, if he provoked it. Bolivar was one of those rare men who understood that he could not have one emotion without the other.

What she feared was outside of themselves.

She kissed him tenderly. "I love you, Bo. But we're going to have a war on our hands if we're not careful. Simon's polite, but he's got a long ways to go. And the girls . . . I don't know how they'll react when they figure out you're more than Mom's friend."

Jane gazed out the window at the dark Canadian sky. "I'm really worried about what Logan might say to Bekah and Darcy."

"What's he got to do with us?"

She answered carefully, "You don't know him. This sounds strange, but he's got this weird fixation. I don't know what he'll do when he finds out I'm marrying someone. He comes unglued when he knows I'm dating. Does this make any sense?"

"Mmm-hm." He stroked the curve of her back, ran his hand slowly along her hip. Then he held her face in both hands. She saw his eyes glistening in the moon's light.

He said, "I marry you, I marry you, I marry you."

Her breath caught. He loved her. She loved him. They belonged together. That was all that mattered.

When she could speak, she said in a thick whisper, "I marry you, I marry you, I marry you."

Later, whenever they talked of their marriage, this verbal nuptial was what they meant. The later ceremony was mere formality.

After the Victoria trip, they launched their assault on the children's resistance. They went sledding and skiing. They ate pizza, watched videos, and some nights, simply sat by the fire, the girls nestled beside Bo while he read *The Secret Garden*, and Simon helped Jane make popcorn.

As spring folded into the end of the school year, Jane and Bo were confident they were winning their war of conversion. Mid-June, she called the Churlicks to ask Logan and Dolores to meet her at a Rathcreek restaurant. All she would say was that she had something important to discuss about the children and wanted to do it in person.

Bo stood, and with an effort to be civil, held out his hand. "Hello, Logan."

Recognition of Bolivar gave Logan a strained expression, and he looked suddenly pale. He did not take the hand. "You didn't tell me this was gonna be a conference," Logan said to Jane when he and Dolores were seated. He waved the waitress away from his coffee cup. "What's this all about?"

Jane took a breath. "We thought it'd be a good idea, since we're all going to be involved in the kids' lives, to get together and talk. Bo and I are getting married."

Logan went rigid. For an unprotected instant, over his features emerged an animal ferocity, desperation, as if instinctual from the scent of its own blood.

His fixed stare could have gotten to Jane in the past, but now she simply watched him, intrigued. He was calculating, she imagined. Those cold, black eyes. What was he thinking?

Uncomfortable in the stony silence, Dolores chirped, "Congratulations! I didn't think you'd ever get married."

It was meant to be a slam, something to curry favor with her husband, but Jane saw the relief in her face. She guessed Dolores must have had an idea of Logan's preoccupation with her after all these years.

Jane rested her hand lightly on Bolivar's thigh under the table, and felt the vibration of his twitching foot.

Finally, Logan said, "Where'll you be living?"

"Bounty," Bo said.

Again, the silence, Logan's eyes dull stones. "That's an hour from Spokane, isn't it? Two from Rathcreek."

"Yes, my mother lives there, and I live nearby," Bolivar answered, though Logan ignored him.

Jane was about to broach the subject of how they should arrange visitation at a half-way point between Rathcreek and Bounty, when Logan rose abruptly.

Nudging Dolores from the booth, he cried, "You're doing this on purpose."

Jane and Bolivar stared at him.

"Tryin' to take my kids away."

Bolivar stood. "Nobody's talking about taking your kids."

Jane said, "The visitation stays the same."

"We'll see. We'll just see." He whirled and strode past startled patrons, leaving Dolores to scurry after him.

Bo whistled. "Jesus Christ, Jane. You weren't kidding."

Jane and Bolivar were married in June, as soon as school was out. The informal ceremony in his mother's yard was quiet, and took place under the apple tree Bo had climbed as a boy.

Like the thundering falls of Bounty bathing the town in their mist and beauty and energy, happiness flowed through the Bernard household that summer. The house ran on a river of contentment.

The first weeks of summer were idyllic. Jane and the girls took long walks and bicycle rides in the evenings, exploring their new home. Bounty was a rural community of about three thousand. Living in the country would take some getting used to for the girls, since they were city-raised. Jane, however, quickly found she was in her element, one she had never suspected she could fall so in love with. Louise began calling her Earth Muffin. A small town, an old house with a garden to putter in on the weekend, three children and a man who asked her how her day went while he helped with dinner.

Their charming old home was rambling and filled with staircase, window seat, and a dining room large enough to hold them all. The home was surrounded by a vast, bowling green lawn bordered by wild blackberries. Bo had bought the place from a widow, friend of his mother's, who had lived there years before and decided to move to a condo to let someone younger and stronger take on the two unruly acres on a bluff overlooking a meadow of grazing sheep and the sleepy town of Bounty beyond.

The first week, Bo made Jane cry with happiness when he insisted they keep the housekeeper, saying it had been a top priority for him when he lived alone. Sheepishly, he admitted that though he tried, he and Jane were not equally splitting the laundering, cooking and the rest. Guilt money, he called it.

At the sink one evening, Jane found Bolivar cleaning up the dinner dishes. After a long day's work and commute home to Bounty, she was grateful. Normally the children's job, Bo took over when she left to taxi them to dance and karate lessons. She stood watching Bo's large frame against the setting sun through the kitchen window, set her purse down and picked up a dish towel.

"Thanks."

"What? Didn't know I was so talented?" he asked.

"My ex-husband never helped with the house. Women's work, you know."

For a moment he was quiet, then fixed her with his vivid blue eyes, wry behind his glasses. "I wasn't going to say anything, but was hoping you'd notice. I find myself wanting to do whatever it takes to make you happy." He scrubbed at a pot. "Pitiful, though, don't you think?"

"What?"

"You do the dishes all the time, or the kids. A man does 'em and we've got to have a conversation."

He scrubbed, elbow working, until she took the sponge away from him and said, "This one's a soaker."

They went into the quiet livingroom with tall glasses of iced tea to discuss the new addition to the house that would accommodate two additional twelve-year-old girls.

"Dallas says we won't have to take out a single loan. With him a master carpenter and me doing the grunt work, it'll be close to finished by the time school starts. Between your equity and my savings—" he corrected, "our equity and our savings, we'll be fine."

Dallas, who routinely did construction work during the summer, drew up the plans for adding on two bedrooms for the twins. The back hoe arrived the first of July. Simon assisted Dallas when the cement foundation was poured into wooden molds. He also swept sawdust and ran errands. Bo became a proficient apprentice carpenter after wielding a hammer for a solid week, and eventually began to wash down less Ibuprofen with his coffee. Through the sweltering days of summer, Dallas and Bo hammered and swore and sweat with joyful ferocity.

With construction underway outside, Jane and the girls worked on building a bridge of their own, to Simon. He was cordial to his new stepmother and raved about her cooking—scrumptious dinners every night, compared to Dad's spaghetti fixed six ways. At seventeen, Simon was old enough to recognize time with his father must be shared with Jane, and independent enough to not complain much.

Life with step-sisters, however, was like landing on Mars for Simon. Sharing the bathroom was traumatic for all. And since there was no place for Bekah and Darcy to call bedroom yet, they slept on the couches in the livingroom, which also held their clothes, dolls, books and other necessary articles. Simon was catapulted out of his only-child status into the sensory and emotional tumult of the mysterious and odious life with girls.

For their part, Bekah and Darcy enjoyed having a big brother, although it had its down side. One moment, he and his friend, Ryan, were wrapping them in Ace bandages from head to toe, hoisting the giggling, mummified girls above their heads and marching around the house. Then, like a typical big brother, he was bossing them, territorial and obnoxious.

After dinner one night, when the house had cooled, Jane, Bo and the girls took a tour of their soon-to-be-completed rooms. They walked through the two-by-four framing, pointed out walls, closets, windows.

"I've got a lot of stuffed animals," Bekah said. "Where'll they go?"

Bo said, "See that walk-in closet? You'll have lots of room there."

She nodded.

Darcy pulled Bo by his fingers through the framing to her room. "I need a place for my books."

He grinned at Jane. "Okay, which wall?"

"Mmmm, that one," she pointed.

"Done. You'll have so many shelves, you'll need a ladder to get the dusty ones on top. Are you sure you want to read so much? I've heard reading makes you need glasses."

"I already wear glasses," she said.

"You do?"

She gave him a playful slug.

Jane said, "Now you two go get ready for bed, before Simon needs the bathroom."

After the girls ran back through the plastic sheeting, Jane and Bo walked among the wiring and walls of the yawning shell. They marveled that for a teacher, Dallas was amazingly good, even though Louise would occasionally drop by to distract him.

"I've never seen Dallas so smitten," Bo said.

"She's perfect for him. The only one I know who's crazier than he is."

"And she's not a clinger," Bo said. "He breaks out in hives if he's cornered."

"Louise, too. They're good for each other."

"We're good for each other."

He motioned toward a corner of the structure where a window was framed in. Summer's dusk had colored a pile of nails and two-by-fours a soft salmon. "Maybe we ought to take this room and give Bekah ours. You'd look good over there, the moon gleaming on your nubile body, wisteria perfume climbing in through the window," smirking, he continued, "the echoing canticles of your lusty love song shaking the walls." He gripped a section of the framing and the grin widened. "We could still sound-proof these babies."

Jane gave him a demure smile.

Bolivar's eyes suggested they end the conversation in a room with a door on it. She walked into his embrace.

"The walls do not shake—they just tremble a little," she murmured.

He kissed her. "'Sawright. I like a woman who's not afraid to express herself."

Twenty-Nine

Before the weather turned, Bo gave Bekah and Darcy driving lessons in a beat up red truck he used for hauling wood.

"They're twelve now," Bo said. "It's time, before winter really sets in."

"Twelve, Bolivar? C'mon," Jane said.

"Simon was eleven when he learned to drive, and I was driving a tractor when I was ten," he told her. Then to the girls, "Now, you're only to drive on our property, only around the loop here, between Grandma's and our yard."

Darcy was adept at handling the rig. Bekah, however, was more impetuous. Not satisfied with the monotony of driving in loops, she decided to take the pick-up into Grandma's driveway, and while backing it out, panicked and ran into a mail box. That ended driving for a while.

Jane and Bolivar's first disagreement came after the driving incident. She resented being cast as the bad cop because he refused to discipline his step daughters. Bo, with his soft heart, his inexperience with daughters, was too lenient. But Jane refused the role. He was the one who thought driving at twelve was a dandy idea; she was determined that he could take care of the consequences as well.

"I can't see how a little cracker butt like you can get yourself into such trouble." He glanced at Jane, who sat reading with Darcy on the couch.

Jane swirled her mug of hot chocolate. A fire crackled in the hearth, casting its golden light on the room. She swallowed the cocoa and nodded slightly.

He said, "Now, what should we do about the mail box?"

Bekah shrugged. "I guess we need to replace it. But I don't know whose it is. There was a whole row of them." The idea of mailboxes not attached to the house was still an alien concept to Bekah, and the people who belonged to them somewhere on spurs off the main gravel drive, foreign as well.

"Grandma will know. Ask her," he said. "I saw boxes like that on sale at the hardware store for five bucks."

"Aw, Step. From my allowance?" Bekah winced.

"Think of it as layaway," he said, capitulating. "You can make payments."

Getting in trouble with Step is like going on a picnic, Jane thought. Unable to restrain herself from a firmer approach, she said, "Soon as you find out whose it is, go knock on their door, tell them who you are, let them know what happened and that you'll be replacing it."

"Okay," Bekah said.

"Cracker butt?" Darcy glanced up from her book.

"Yeah, that's what my Uncle Larry used to call all us kids when we were little." He held his fingers up, indicating the size of a cracker, then trained his sights on Bekah's backside. "Yup, both of you, 'bout the size of a cracker."

Darcy said with mock indignance, "Well, if I'm a cracker butt, you're a toaster butt."

"Could be," he said. "Or else Christmas tree butt, or how about Jeep Cherokee butt?"

The twins fell into a fit of giggling.

Jane and Bo exchanged glances. The sight of Bo and her girls ignited a fire in her. It was too much, too perfect, the picture of them all, the golden light of the hearth on their faces, the high pitched laughter. She recognized the miracle of the scene.

The girls had acclimated to their new environment. Bekah was on the softball team at school and took karate lessons. Darcy had a part in the school choir and had decided to take up the clarinet. From the moment Jane arrived home from work, they ran her like a taxi, between lessons and friends.

Fortunately, Simon was not what Jane would call a high-maintenance stepson. Even his grandmother, once so important in his recovery from Kate's death, was seen less often during his senior year. Bolivar and Jane were discovering Simon mainly ate, studied and slept, when he wasn't with friends or playing sports.

By Thanksgiving, they had much to be thankful for. They were beginning to bond as a family. Simon allowed Jane to be a friend, a comfortable role for them both. And the girls, especially Darcy, had an affectionate relationship with their Step.

By December, Jane and Bolivar shopped for Christmas in Spokane, at the gigantic mall at Northtown or downtown, around their busy work schedules, then wrapped presents behind closed doors.

It would be a skimpy Christmas by Bo's standards, with little room to accommodate his generous spirit, since they had spent their entire savings, and then some, on the remodel of the house.

"Bo, we can't afford that," Jane had said. Then she chastised herself for adopting her father's tight-fisted ways. Bo had found snowboards for his stepdaughters. Something they would love, but costly.

"I know, but they're worth it," he replied, admiring the equipment. He laid a couple of accessories around a pair of boots for the full effect. "It's the first time I've had girls to buy for." Seeing the worried look on her face, he added, "I have this philosophy about Christmas—only spend enough to hurt. Hey, we're talking major pain, with what I got for you." He waved a sales clerk over, a victory for fatherhood. "Call it a seasonal disorder. Goes away when we pay off the charge cards in February."

The twins were to spend the first week of the Christmas break in Rathcreek with the Churlicks, and would be home for the second week in Bounty. Before they left, they helped bake fudge and Grandma Mary's five-layer cookies. They sang carols and visited friends.

On the night before leaving for Rathcreek, unable to contain their excitement, the girls presented Jane and Bolivar with a hand-made card and gifts. Along with their hugs, Bo received his first real belly laugh from his step daughters. Inside the reindeer bedecked card was written:

Merry Christmas,
Mom and
Step,
Dad,
Boxcar Butt,
Whatever!
Love ya lots,
Darcy and Bekah

After they had left for Rathcreek, Jane kept busy and tried to ignore the uneasy feeling she was left with after a phone call mid-week from the twins. Bekah's words over the miles between Rathcreek and Bounty still rang in her ears: *I miss the way things used to be. Daddy says you can't really love us as much as you say, because you're so different now that you're married.*

Different? Of course she was different. She was a wife and step-mother, a working woman and the mother of two daughters who thought they should continue to have her every waking moment. Exhausted was more like it. She would certainly have a conversation with them when they came home.

Christmas was postponed until the girls' return on the 28th. Jane bought the largest turkey she could find. They had invited Bo's mother, Joe, Mary, Louise and Dallas for dinner. Gifts were piled under the tree, and it was everything Simon could do to keep his hands off them. It would be their new family's first holiday together.

Finally, the day arrived. Jane got up early. Soon, the aroma of roasting turkey and dressing wafted through the house. Bo peeled potatoes and put together a panful of yams topped with brown sugar and butter. His mother and Jane's were bringing the pies. Louise was fixing her famous topsy tur-vey vegetable casserole surprise.

Simon, in a mood of father-son camaraderie the night before, had asked Bo to go skiing with him. Jane felt vaguely uneasy, left to pick up the girls from the half way point alone. She dreaded hearing all they had picked up from the Churlicks' this time. But she told Bo there would never be another snowfall like the previous night's, or maybe another invi-tation from this senior in high school, and insisted he go with Simon.

"Weather report says roads are all cleared. I'll be fine. Really."

Simon said, "Grandma told me she'd come up and take care of the turkey. And we'll be home by four."

Bo put his arms around her. "You're sure?"

"I'm sure. If you get going now, you'll be back from the slopes before everyone starts coming. You guys can set the table and help your mom. I should be back with the girls around the same time."

"Thanks, Jane," Simon said, clapping her on the shoulder.

Jane was a seasoned winter driver, and the roads had been plowed, making the hour drive easy. She enjoyed the breathtaking scenery, despite her jitters, the sketchy network of tree limbs holding their white palms toward the sky. Pines, magnificently white against banks of gray clouds, endless dark batting, far as the eye could see. The headlights caught a fine mist of snowflakes.

Jane arrived at the parking lot of the McDonald's restaurant, their meeting place. The Peugeot was there, a dark blemish in the dusk against the vast, wintry whiteness.

Hm. That's odd, she thought.

Usually when she pulled into the lot, the girls scrambled out of the car to load their suitcases into her trunk. Jane opened the door. The wind whipped flakes against her cheeks and lashes. Shivering, she zipped her jacket. Still, no movement from the Peugeot.

Snow squeaked under her boots as she stepped across the parking lot. A door of the car opened and Darcy emerged and trod around to the trunk, holding keys. In the fading light, she struggled to get them into the lock.

Just like him to sit in the warm car and let Darcy get the luggage, Jane thought.

"Hi, sweetheart! Merry Christmas! Here, let me help you."

Jane took the keys. Something in the way Darcy didn't quite face her, in the deflection of her kiss to a cheek, sent a stab of foreboding through Jane. The trunk popped open. Snowflakes swirled into the exposed space. Jane reached inside and lifted the suitcase out. One suitcase.

"Where's Bekah's?"

Jane looked in through the rear window.

One head in the dark interior.

In the driver's seat.

Where's Bekah? pounded through her. *Where's Bekah? Where's Bekah?*

"Where's Bekah?" she shouted, strode to the driver's door, yanked at the locked door handle. "Where is she?"

Logan looked out through the fogged window. He rolled it down a crack. Jane could see only his forehead.

"Bekah's not coming back." His tone was not defensive, but righteous, and cold.

She turned to Darcy, still standing by the open trunk. Darcy nodded, tears rolling down her cheeks. He wasn't bluffing. He hadn't gotten to Darcy, but he had pushed Bekah over the edge. Swift subversive conversations swirled through Jane's mind, *Your mother's awful, sweetheart, ignoring you over a new husband. Well, I don't want to tell you what to do, but I want you to know, my door is always open.*

She bit the words, "What the hell do you mean, she's not coming back?"

He rolled the window down a little more. "You can't make someone love you, Jane. Seems you said that to me once. You hurt her, spendin' all your time with someone else. You don't walk on water anymore, and the courts say she's old enough to choose where she wants to live."

Stark raving emotions pounded blood through Jane.

"Get out of that car, you coward! Get *out* here, you son-of-a-bitch, and face me!" When he didn't move, she held up the keys. "You're not going anywhere until you face me."

Logan, for a brief moment, radiated fear, as if he had not counted on this contingency. He may have expected to lord his victory over her, but obviously was not prepared for her fury. How could he not expect her to want to tear his face off?

He emerged from the car, and standing before Jane, smirked like an arrogant victor. Large snowflakes fell around them.

In a lecturing sing-song, he said, "You have no one to blame but yourself. Bekah tried to tell you. You wouldn't listen. She wasn't happy and refused to come tonight."

"What are you talking about?" Jane said numbly through lips stiffened with fear. "This is the end of your visitation. She can't stay. We have Christmas . . ."

His laugh was brittle. "Bekah's in Rathcreek. To live. She's made her choice. And she's not coming back." He opened the door.

She grabbed his arm. "You're not going anywhere," she ground out, teeth chattering. She wasn't sure what she would do next, but she wasn't going to let him go home as if nothing had happened.

Shock and fear darkened Logan's features. The fear struck her as ludicrous. He was twice her weight, stronger by far. What was he afraid of?

He turned to Darcy and barked, "Call the police, Darcy. Call 9-1-1."

"The po*lice?* God damn you! Put Darcy in the middle? Make her call the cops on her mother?" In protectiveness and rage, she called out, "Don't worry, hon. He's just being a jackass. You don't need to call anybody. This is between him and me."

"Do it, Darcy," he ordered.

Darcy looked small, lost in the battle between her parents. Snow was coming down thickly now, and she started to cry. She shook her head.

He shouted, "*Do* it!" and jerked his thumb toward the building.

Darcy wiped her eyes, and bawling, turned and stumbled a few steps in the direction of the building.

Like a sleepwalker coming to on the corner of a busy intersection, Jane's chest beat wildly. A barbaric yell. Her fist, propelled by some invisible force, smashed into Logan's face. The force landed him against the car, where he lost his footing and sprawled on the ground. Jane threw the keys with all her might. They landed with a barely audible chink in three inches of snow surrounding a thick stand of trees and undergrowth at the edge of the lot. Ignoring the blood that was everywhere, she lurched off to Darcy.

She threw her arms around Darcy, who buried her head in Jane's shoulder and sobbed. Her voice sounded thick, padded in emotion, in the vast quiet of snowfall. "Darcy! Oh, God, Darcy." Hot tears turned icy on her frozen cheeks. Thick flakes stuck to her lashes. She breathed in the flakes, gulping air. Her teeth were blocks of ice.

Somewhere in the dim fringes of Jane's perception, Logan was swearing. Somewhere, it occurred to her that she had struck him, that she had never heard such a barrage of cursing from him. It felt almost like madness, the way such inconsequential things were registering.

She caught his movement, and her mind pulled out of overload. This stunned beast was coming to now, and would kill her, or she, him. She hushed Darcy, held her tightly and hurried toward their car. Her eyes stung. She could barely see in the falling flakes and darkness. They made their way to the car. Jane locked the doors, started it.

"What are you going to do, Mom?"

"We're going to get Bekah," she said.

Thirty

Jane stood outside the Churlicks' home, bracing herself against the storm. The wind drove the large flakes so thickly and vigorously against her, she was coated on her right side and head in pure white. The light from the Churlicks' livingroom window was barely visible.

Jane quietly tested the knob, then, cursing, knowing the reception that awaited her, pounded on the door.

The dull orb of the porch light came on through the snowfall. The door opened only as far as the chain let it. In the crack of the opening, Bekah's face appeared.

"Bekah! Honey . . ."

"What are you doing here?" her daughter said in a flat voice.

"Honey, we have Christmas," Jane began stupidly, then, "Bekah, you need to come with me now. Quick, open the door."

The piece of Bekah that Jane could see was rigid, her voice almost robotic, and the glassy hazel eyes stared through her. "I'm not going anywhere with you, Jane. I don't have to. My father's following a higher order than the court's orders."

Jane? Higher order? What the hell—?

The wind's frigid blasts, the whine of the storm, the stinging force against her face, made the brief exchange surreal. Then Bekah was gone, and Dolores filled the crack.

"I've called the police. Logan's on his way," said the childishly high voice. "He's pressing assault charges—"

"To hell with assault—try kidnapping," Jane yelled over the wind.

"I don't have to listen to that kind of language!" Dolores said, and slammed the door against Jane's full weight against it. But the chain kept her out, and the two on the other side pushing steadily, finally closed the gap. The lock thunked into place.

"God *damn* you!" Jane screamed. "Give me my daughter!" She pounded on the door, kicked it. "Bekah!" She looked around for something large enough to throw through the livingroom window.

Jane peered through the whipping flakes toward Darcy, who waited in the car at the curb, and slowly, became able to reason this unfathomable scene into something she could believe was really happening.

How could it be real? Whoever that was at the door was not her daughter. The voice didn't even sound like Bekah. But it had been Bekah alone at the door. And she had called her Jane. Not Mom, but Jane. The sound of her name made Jane want to weep.

Logan would be arriving soon with the police. And she had learned before that the police would not enforce her claim to bring Bekah home without her custody papers. And finally, there was Darcy waiting for her. She had Darcy. Jane turned against the snow boiling sideways from out of the glowering sky and trudged to her daughter at the curb.

Bolivar paced, peering out the black panes of glass overlooking the sheep pasture he knew lay spread out below. There was no moon, and the snow-covered pasture and sky were all one blackness. The night blinded, and Bolivar was both blind and crazed with hours of worry. He strained to see, despite the senselessness of it.

Never should've let her go alone. God—please! Don't do it to me again. You took Kate. Don't take Jane from me. Dear God, look out for her tonight.

Louise joined him, peered into the night's mirror, reflecting their images, blinking Christmas tree lights, family settled in chairs and couches, dog and cat lying before a dying fire. The dining room was set with festive plates, wine glasses and unlit candles. They had put away the turkey and dressing two hours ago.

"She's all right, Bo," Louise said.

He turned to her, distracted, not wanting to take his eyes from the window.

She said, "I can't explain it, I just have this feeling."

Bolivar wished he could feel as sure. He studied Louise. She was looking more—what would he call it? Credible? With hair washed and styled, and the attractive red sweater, Louise hardly seemed herself, except for the mistletoe sprig tucked behind her ear. Dallas had certainly made hygiene and appearance worthwhile. But it was the conviction in her voice, like some report from Jeanne Dixon, that he wanted to believe in.

Dallas came over and put his arm around Louise's shoulder. "Nothing?"

"No." Bo glanced at his watch. "I'm calling Highway Patrol again. If they still don't have anything, I'm driving that piece myself, all the way to Rathcreek if I have to."

"I'm going with you," Joe said from where he stood by the fire.

"Look!" Louise pointed to the window.

They all gathered, stared into the darkness. A pair of headlights shooting past the field of sheep, slowing just enough at the corner to make the turn safely. Then, the points of light were heading toward them, speeding down the snowy road.

Bo spun from the window and was out the door. He was never so happy in his life as he was to see the old beater Ford squirreling up the incline of the driveway. Snow fell in thick blotches on his sweater, hair and beard, clung to his lashes and cheeks. His heart was beating fast enough to propel him to meet her at the base of the drive, but he simply moved from foot to foot, rubbing his hands.

The car's high beams were so dazzling he couldn't see. He lifted the garage door and flipped the light switch. The car slowed, coasted past him and stopped. His breath caught when he noticed a sizable dent and broken window on the right side.

He rushed around to open the door, and was jolted by the sight of Jane's tear-streaked face, her anguish. Fear swelled in his chest. He helped her out of the car, instinctively looking her over for signs of injury. She was freezing.

"Bo!" She couldn't finish. Her arms were around his neck, face buried, shuddering spasms of her sobs ripping through him.

He hugged her to him, tried to warm her. He knew she had held it together until she had gotten them all safely home. Now, she could fall apart. The thought of her driving in that blizzard, alone with the kids, skidding, losing control on a treacherous stretch of road. A shudder shook his shoulders. He held her tightly, rubbed her back, and waited for her to stop, to tell him what happened.

She pulled back, wiped her eyes and said in a shaky voice, "He kept Bekah."

"What?!"

Family waiting in the garage doorway now gathered about them. Dallas opened the car door and a shaken Darcy emerged.

Louise took the girl in her arms. "What? Where's—" She bent to peer into the car, and slowly straightened. "Goddamn CIA."

"What am I going to do?" Jane cried. "What can we do?"

Bo's voice was calm and sure. "You're going to make it through this night, then we're going to call your attorney, get this straightened out and bring Bekah home." He drew her close. "It's going to work out."

"No, you don't understand," Jane cried. "It's Bekah. She's the one who won't come home. Logan wasn't even there. That witch kept Bekah locked in, but Bekah . . . She didn't *want* to come home. And then, Logan called the police . . . But she *wouldn't* come home. Didn't sound normal. He's done something to her. Something's not right."

"Then we'll find out what's happened and fix it. Bekah loves you, and you can't just make love go away."

His voice took on a humorous, worried edge, the one telling her he would like to protect her from all the world's hurt, but knew she would never let him. "I think I'm still strong enough to kick his ass. Can I?"

She closed her eyes. "I already did."

Jane tossed fitfully when she slept at all. She shivered and pulled the comforter over her shoulder. Cold. So cold. Wind rushed in the broken window of the car as it shimmied down the highway. A trucker pulling her out of a ditch.

"You warm enough, hon?" she asked Darcy, seated in the car next to her.

Darcy nodded, bundled in her coat, hat and muffler pulled up around her chin.

Jane slowed, then stopped. The road had disappeared in the swirling snow. Alone, Jane walked through a forest in a blizzard. Had to find a way to get her girls safely home. First Darcy, then Bekah. Finally, she came to a clearing and looked up in wonder. Tall Rathcreek pines surrounded her. Snow piled against the trees and against her ankles in little drifts. The Rathcreek wind was bitter cold. She gathered her coat at her neck.

Odd-shaped lumps filled the clearing, a few as tall as Jane, most shorter, tops rounded off softly with snow. She had a strange feeling about the lumps and was drawn to them, yet held back. Something eerie, other-worldly, frightened her.

At the edge of the clearing opposite, she could see two figures, small and straight, fighting through the snow toward her. The moonlight glistened on them and Jane squinted against the gusts. Each minute the figures moved closer, the more the snow coated them. As it clung to them, they wiped at the crust forming around their bodies. The crust grew thicker and thicker. Eventually, Jane heard them, voices carried faintly in the wind, sounding like kittens mewing.

Still far off, they grew close enough to see their crusty faces and mouths opening and shutting. Were they crying? She couldn't make out the words in the wind or see who they were, yet she was sure they were crying out for help.

Instinctively, she ran to help them. Raising her heavy, snow-caked boots, she pushed forward, one foot after the other, in drifts to her shins now. She worked and worked, but the closer she got, the farther away they were. She struggled against the storm and generated such heat that she sweat with the effort. The snow that threatened to cake her, too, melted and ran off in rivulets to pool at her feet and freeze.

Finally, she stomped through the knee-deep snow, keeping her eyes fixed on the two figures, and the distance between them shortened. She was sweating copiously, and snow sloshed off her like great, spring avalanches. Closer, closer, now she could hear over the freezing blast of the wind. Maaaah! Maaaawww!

The voices seized Jane's heart. Bekah and Darcy. She struggled through the deepening snow, but by the time she reached them, hard, crusted ice capsules had frozen over their faces and bodies. Their pitiful mouths were frozen open in an expression of fright. Arms held out to her. Rigid, white ice cocoons.

Hot tears streamed out of Jane. "No! *No!*" Snow dumped over them from the leaden sky and she brushed it away. She embraced first one figure, then the other, hoping the warmth of her body would melt their encasements. She caressed them, wept over them, ranted and clawed at the ice, smashed it with her fists, until she was raw and bloody. Nothing she could do could change the way things were. Iced inside, Bekah and Darcy were perpetually frozen.

The roads were plowed by noon the following day. By the time Jane and Bolivar drove into Spokane, consulted their attorney and approached a judge, it was nearly five o'clock.

Judge Simons frowned. Gazing down at them from the bench, he said in a stern voice, "Am I correct in understanding you are the custodial parent and this is the second time the father's taken the child without your permission?"

Jane said, "Yes, Your Honor."

"Why hasn't your attorney included in this paperwork a request to find Churlick in contempt?"

She and Bolivar looked at each other.

"I'd like to have his butt thrown in jail, but my hands are tied," the judge said.

"What do we do?" Bo asked.

The judge glanced at the clock over the doorway. "Haven't got much time. You've got to get an order signed by five to take to the Police Department next door. Run downstairs and call your attorney. Have him give you the wording, and you add it to this paper here, then get back before five o'clock."

Bo said, "I don't think there's time . . ."

Jane grabbed the paperwork off the judge's desk. "Stay here. I'll call Sanchez."

"I can't come up with information on demand over the phone," Oliver Sanchez said.

Jane wanted to grab her attorney by the throat. Calming her voice, she said, "Listen, Oliver, it's your oversight. The judge said he was surprised we didn't have this contempt thing included. Just read it to me and I'll take it down."

"I'll have to check my files," he said.

She held her nervousness in check while she waited by reading the document.

Bolivar came dashing downstairs. "It's five! They're going to close up. The judge has to sign the order—with or without the contempt." They raced back upstairs, receiver dangling in the phone booth. Judge Simons signed the paperwork, wished them luck and said he hoped the scoundrel would be before his bench in the future.

The Sheriff's Department was sympathetic, and was able to send an officer to the Churlicks almost immediately. Jane and Bolivar waited at the station. When the deputy returned, they were dismayed to learn nobody had been home.

"It's church," Jane sighed. She turned to the deputy. "Can you check again after ten o'clock?"

"If we've got someone to send, you bet."

At midnight, Jane awoke to someone calling her name. Bo sat beside her rubbing his eyes. An officer held a scowling Bekah by the arm.

"Here she is, ma'am. She's not too happy."

Fresh from her father's, Bekah radiated an antagonism Jane had never seen. Bekah's face was not her daughter's, but an icy image taken over by rage.

Outside the station, Bekah screeched, "How could you send the police to get me in the middle of the night? I won't go with you! You can't make me!" She stopped dead, crossed her arms.

Jane gazed into the familiar hazel eyes, but they were different. Emptiness stared back at her.

Anger meant for Churlick, exploded from Jane. "You will come with us, and you'll talk in a respectful tone of voice, young lady." She grabbed Bekah's arm and pulled her. Bekah struggled to get free. "Don't touch me!" she squealed. "You abuse me and we'll use it in court. I'm telling the lawyer." She twisted and squirmed from Jane's grip.

Jane's hand went to her mouth in shock. Incomprehensible. She couldn't respond, because she couldn't make sense of the scene with the alien girl in the middle of the night at the Rathcreek Police Station.

Bekah made a break for it, and was half way across the snow-covered courtyard before Bo had wrapped his arms around her. They scuffled, her kicking up chunks of snow and writhing, until he tossed her down on a bench.

"You hurt me! I'm . . ."

"Shut up!" Bolivar bellowed. Steam rose from his mouth and nostrils like a bull.

Inside Jane, confusion and fear welled up, and tears came. First Bekah, then Bo—she had never seen him so angry. Nothing was as it should be. She ran over, fearing what he might do. What in God's name was wrong with her daughter?

The courtyard outside the police station was empty, except for the noise of the scuffle, Bekah's shrieks and Bolivar's gruff voice. In the snow-muffled quiet of midnight, their racket seemed amplified. Strong lights towered above, throwing out huge, bright circles carved out of the blackness, and their dark shadows stirred in exaggerated movements. Unreal, like a stage production.

Bolivar stomped back and forth before the shrunken girl sprawled on the bench, his wide shoulders trembling with fury. "Do you have any idea how much I love this woman? I love her with every fiber. She's in my fingernails, in my guts, my soul. And I'm not going to stand here and watch you treat her like this, watch you kill her with that cold voice and those eyes."

Bekah sat, impassive as stone.

He pointed. "Look at her! I said look at her. Your mother's crying over you. And you just want to get away. She's crying because she loves you. All the years she's put into you, and you act like her tears mean nothing. You act as cold as any criminal."

Bekah glanced up, then averted her eyes. "I can't help it. Things are different now. I've changed."

"What's different?" Jane asked. "What's so different you have to run away?"

Bekah studied her, and the look chilled Jane. A different person, distant, voice cold and robot-like said, "I'm a Christian now. I'm old enough that the courts will let me live in a Christian home. I *hate* living with you."

The ragged air tore Jane's throat. Her brain, frozen. No interpreting the nonsense she was hearing. Not simply the words, but words uttered by a voice filled with venom. Their poison was killing her.

This isn't my Bekah.

Slowly, Bo spoke. "I've done some pretty rotten things in my life, but I've never, ever hurt my mother the way you're hurting yours tonight. All she ever did was love you. And how do you pay her back? You run. Then you blame it on your faith."

Bekah crossed her arms, belligerent. "We've been through this already. How many times do I have to hear how good she is and how rotten I am?"

Bolivar stopped his pacing. Clenching and unclenching his fists, he said, "You'll sit here until hell freezes over, if you have to. You're going to hear some truth for a change. I don't know what went on in that house here in Rathcreek, but you've got to be pretty low to buy into a faith that would sacrifice your own mother. It's not Christianity, I can tell you that. How can you call it Christianity when it breaks your mother's heart? In all my life, I've never met a woman who loved her children more than your mother loves you and Darcy. You're everything to her."

Bekah shivered. Her look said it was the frigid weather, not his words—they had no effect on her. She drew her gangly legs up onto the bench, wrapped her arms around herself and turned away, so the courtyard light illuminated her back; her face was hidden in shadow.

He took her chin in his hand. "I'm talking to you. You better have the sense to pay attention."

She yanked away. Posture rigid, hostile eyes glazed, she directed her sight at Bolivar, and stared through him.

His look turned to Jane, arms wrapped around herself. She had stopped crying, and went to sit near Bekah, who ignored her.

He said, "Now, you're going to hear this, even if you choose not to believe it. What you're doing now? You remind me of Judas. You're no better than him. How could you sacrifice your own mother? The woman who gave you life? You know she's never done anything but love you." He held Jane in his steady gaze. "She's the best mother I've ever known—bar none."

Tears sprang to Jane's eyes. The love for this man she had married grew large and warm, until the swelling tightness blocked out the pain, eased her misery.

"I don't understand why you want to act like this, honey." Jane pulled up Bekah's coat collar against the wind.

"Honor your mother and father," Bo said.

Bekah transformed into another beast now, an unhuman thing, impervious to everything. If Jane hadn't known her daughter over the past twelve years, a child who had spoken hardly a word of contempt, she would not have identified the creature before her as her own.

Bekah shouted at them in a choked, nightmare voice, "I honor my father! But my mother? Do not give your children cause for wrath, the Bible says. If you don't let me live with my dad, the Bible says I can hate you. After tonight, I already do. You can't stop me. I'm going to live with my father. I'm not living in your godless house."

Thirty-One

Logan did not press assault charges when Jane agreed not to file kidnapping charges. Staying out of jail to be with her daughter was all that mattered.

During the following hellish days, however, the nightmarish proportions of Bekah's angry rebellion expanded until Jane could barely stand to be around her. Bekah, the stranger who lived with them, wanted nothing more to do with the woman she now called Jane. The monster-child did everything in her power to make her mother want to send her packing. In any other circumstances, Jane would have assented to her wishes, but the devastating change in personality, in voice, in her formerly sweet manner . . . something was terribly wrong. Had Churlick slept with her? What horror could have changed her so? Jane vowed she would do everything she could to protect Bekah. She would fight Logan for her. Their case was quickly taken up by the courts, where the stewards of family wreckage, her lawyer and Churlick's, argued their case.

The judge heard the charge of Churlick's counsel that Bekah, at twelve, was legally of age to decide where she would live. He also had before him documentation from the office of a psychiatrist hired by Churlick specifically for the purpose, testifying to Bekah's aversion to her mother. Thus armed, justice saw a chance to pacify both parties.

The court ruled that Bekah would reside with her father temporarily, and Darcy with her mother. A Guardian Ad Litem, GAL, was to be appointed as legal advocate for the children. After three months, he would make a recommendation to the court about permanent residence, not simply validating the child's choice, but according to what he saw was in the child's best interest.

Swept along by the complexity of judicial forces beyond their understanding or control, Jane and Bolivar were bitterly disappointed at losing Bekah to Logan, even temporarily. Yet, there was nothing for them to do but wait and let the GAL do his job.

Will Barry was a competent Guardian Ad Litem, as far as Jane and Bolivar could see, his limited experience made up for by his openness to Jane in their initial interview. He seemed genuinely disturbed by her account of Logan's religious indoctrination and the friction it caused. An affable man in his early thirties who wore a crew cut and dark glasses because of an eye injury that left him sensitive to light, he was thorough in his questioning and encouraging in his pledge that he never let his own religious beliefs get in the way of doing his job. He meant to be an honest Mormon.

Nerve-wracking weeks dragged on, as the GAL met individually with the families in both Rathcreek and Bounty. Barry would say nothing about what he learned. Out of compassion for Jane, however, who was filled with remorse over what she may have done to prompt her daughter's sudden bitter rejection, he made a small exception.

"I just want you to know," he said, "that if she were my daughter, I'd toss her over my knee and give her the spanking of her life. Her complaints are bogus. I don't know how she's worked herself into such a lather, but it's nothing you've done."

Jane and Bolivar made themselves wait, cautiously optimistic about Will Barry's forthcoming recommendation to the court.

Time wore on, and though she never understood the cause, Jane grew inured to Bekah's insubordinate and abrasive behavior during her reluctant court-ordered visits. And over time, Darcy and Jane grew closer than ever.

"Darcy," Jane said, trying to keep her voice even. She held a small pile of mail. The letters from Dolores troubled Jane; her stepped up correspondence seemed only for the purpose of expanding their influence over this daughter as well. Yet Jane could not simply get rid of them. What would Will Barry think when Churlick told him she stood in the way of his communication with his daughter?

"Darcy, I'm just going to be honest with you. I'm afraid of these letters. I don't know what happened, but Bekah's different now. And these letters . . . I think three letters a day is a bit much, don't you?"

Darcy nodded. "Throw 'em out. They're stupid anyway."

Jane sat next to her, and Darcy put her book down. "I know I've asked you this before, but honey, is there anything you can think of that made Bekah change?"

Darcy's dark eyes were troubled. She twisted her mouth with finger and thumb, and sat silent a moment. Then she shook her head. Nothing. Either she hadn't been privy to whatever had occurred, or it was so horrible she had buried it. How Jane wished her sweet daughter could explain the terrible grip Logan had over Bekah.

When it was Darcy's turn to visit Rathcreek, her loyalty did more to heal Jane's heart than Bekah's behavior could ever do to crush it.

"I don't feel good," Darcy said, waiting with Jane in the parking lot in Spokane.

Jane placed her hand on her forehead. "What's the matter?"

"I dunno. I just don't feel good." She looked at the ground.

Jane tried to read what was going on. "We're here now. If we go back, we'll just have to come all the way back next weekend. It's important that we follow the court order for now. Hopefully, the GAL will make up his mind soon, and this nightmare'll be over."

Darcy seemed to consider this, then dragged Jane to a planter box at one end of the parking lot, chatting about school and friends. The short brick fence surrounded the tips of crocus making their way through the gray snow. She hopped up on the bricks, and, clasping her mother's hand, held her arms out for balance and walked along carefully.

"I don't want to leave you, Mom. I don't like it over there."

Jane stopped. Darcy, still holding her hand, stopped also. Darcy's agitation caused a sickening worry to worm its way through her stomach. Was Logan pressuring her now, too? She almost scooped Darcy up and turned for home. But Jane had to follow the court order. When Jane had revealed her fears, the GAL had told her he would not look favorably at her keeping Darcy from her father.

"Is there something you want to tell me?" Jane asked.

Darcy poked at a brick with her shoe. It rocked loosely in place and dirt spilled out of the crevice. Then, she climbed down and sat on the bricks. Jane sat beside her.

Darcy ran her hand tenderly over the emerging crocus and tulips. "Are you sure you're going to go to heaven?"

It was a familiar question, but it made Jane want to scream. She chose her words carefully. "We've talked about this before. Why do you think I wouldn't?"

"I dunno. Dad says you're in favor of abortion." Darcy tipped her head, her look begging for denial.

Jane was weary of the guerrilla warfare. To protect his place in his daughters' world, Logan steered the girls toward questioning their mother's morality . . . then carefully, Bible in hand, explained to them how he was their only hope.

"You know, it bothers me that your dad thinks he's the only one with a pipeline to God, and God trusts him enough to tell him, alone, who's going to heaven. Doesn't that sound ridiculous?"

Darcy nodded, dark eyes twinkling.

A frightening thought struck Jane: this was an opportunity to finally get out the truth about her relationship with Logan. Her heart pounded with fear, yet it hammered louder with the hope that she could at last address his lies. All these years, he had perpetuated the lie that their parents someday would get back together, that they had been, once, a married couple. He knew that in order to contradict him, she would need to divulge their affair. Now, Darcy was old enough, and the chance to free her with the truth stood before Jane.

"You know, hon, abortion is a very tough decision. Even though I think it's a woman's choice about whether she wants to keep a baby or not, I know I couldn't do it." She hugged Darcy to her. "You're here, and Bekah, because I couldn't . . ."

Darcy looked at her quizzically. "What, Mom?"

"It has to do with me and your dad." She got up. "C'mon."

Arms linked, they strolled through the deserted parking lot, warm enough in their coats and mufflers in the strong sun. Along the lot's edges were the ragged, dirty remains of winter: gray piles of snow that had been plowed aside, clinging in melting mounds.

"I was only twenty when I got married," Jane began. "Fell in love with my high school sweetheart."

"You and Dad went to high school together?" Darcy asked in a shocked voice.

"No," she said. "Your dad's about twice my age. We couldn't have gone to high school together, could we?"

Darcy shook her head. "But I thought . . ."

"I know. It's time you heard the truth. Jake Powers is the man I married."

"Mr. Powers from church?" Darcy exclaimed. "He's your husband?"

"Was. Our marriage was a disaster. We were married a year, then divorced."

"But what about Dad? Is that what you thought we wouldn't understand, that you were married twice?" she asked. "Is it a very bad sin to be married two times?"

Jane kicked a black chunk of ice. It skidded a ways along the asphalt and bounced off an ice gray embankment.

"That's not what I'm trying to say, honey. Let me start over. The reason I moved out of Rathcreek was because I had a terrible experience in The Fellowship. It involved your dad."

Darcy's perplexed look, the slowing of her walk, told Jane she needed to go as easy as she could. She was about to bury Darcy's father, the man who ran the church, the one who could do no wrong in his daughters' eyes.

"When Jake and I were having problems in our marriage, I went to Logan for marriage counseling. I was married to Jake. Your father was married to Dolores."

Her bones were beginning to ache. She tried quickly to imagine what effect the revelation would have on her daughter, but couldn't. The lie had been in place so long, it was unimaginable for their lives to be based on truth.

"During those sessions, Logan was interested in much more from me than he had any right to. That's when I got pregnant with you and Bekah." Her knees were literally shaking, heart pounding. "We were never married. Do you understand what I'm saying?"

They stopped.

Darcy stared at her, awash in confusion. Mouth open, eyes bright with tears, she slowly shook her head. "No! I don't believe it. You'd never do anything like that. Dad isn't that way either!"

"Darcy." Jane touched her shoulder.

Darcy pulled back. "No!"

"Find out next Sunday. Sit down with Jake, uh, Mr. Powers. He probably doesn't think too highly of me, but I think he'd tell you the truth about our marriage."

Darcy wouldn't look at her.

"Listen, I know it's not easy. It's not easy for me to tell you, either. But it's the truth. You need to know that's the reason I could never marry your dad. I could never forgive him for how he took advantage of me. He lied to me, and then lied to get custody of you and Bekah. For years tried to use you to get us together. I'd never, ever marry him. I could never trust him. He didn't marry Dolores *after* me. He was already married."

"But why?" Darcy asked. "He's a minister! How could he . . ."

Jane wasn't sure exactly what to say. Her emotions were running so high. "He didn't want to admit this strange attachment to me or that we weren't married, because what we did was wrong. Just *wrong.*

"But when you talk about a person who has reason to consider having an abortion, you're talking about me. I was a single, unmarried young woman. I thought I couldn't go through with my pregnancy. But when it came right down to it, I knew . . ." She choked up. "I've never - never - regretted keeping my babies."

"Oh, Mom," Darcy said in a shaky voice. "Did you ever love Dad?

This time, Jane turned away. Her daughter wanted to know if she was created out of love, rather than the hatred she had witnessed for so many years.

"When you were conceived, I did love him. But not in a normal way, because I never really knew who he was. Does that make any sense?"

She nodded. "Sometimes I feel like I don't really know who he is either. You always tell the truth. But Dad . . ." She began walking, slowly. "Now it makes sense. There were so many little things."

They picked up the pace, skirting the streams of dirty water that flowed from the melting mounds into the grates. They walked hand-in-hand back toward the planters. "Didn't you ever wonder why your last name was Powers and your dad and Dolores are Churlick?"

"Bekah asked him about that once." She frowned, trying to remember. "Oh yeah. He told us it was a feminist thing. He wasn't happy, but you wouldn't listen, so he just went along. That's not what happened, is it?"

"No."

"After that, whenever we were over there, he made us use—" She gasped, clamped a hand over her mouth. She whispered in a high, scared voice, "Sorry, Mom."

"He made you call yourselves Churlicks?"

She nodded, and tears spilled down her cheeks.

Quickly, she made the logical next step. "And do you call Dolores 'Mom'?"

Darcy nodded, not meeting her eyes.

Jane covered her face with her hands. Weakness that grew into a powerful rage overwhelmed her. Then, tears. She felt like gnawing off the leg held in the trap of her unraveling disclosure. So much hurt, for both of them. Of course it made sense. The canceling of Powers, the last name she had given them, and then *her* name, 'Mom.' She should have guessed. Bekah had been calling her 'Jane' for some time now.

"Bastard! How could he do that? How could he take the name of the person who carried you for nine months, who brought you into the world and give it to someone else? She's not your mother, Darcy, I am. I am! And it's not okay to pretend she is."

Sobs materialized out of the place where comfort for her daughter had just resided. Frustration poured out of her and over the dark eyed little girl who stood before her.

"I gave up everything to have you. My parents were ashamed of me and my church kicked me out. I had to move out of town. But I wanted my babies, no matter what. I wanted to be a mother. So now *she* steps in, just like that?"

Darcy's sudden terrible sobs scared her. Jane gathered her up, and held her tightly, as she struggled against her. "Shhh, I'm sorry, I'm sorry, sweetheart. I'm not mad at you. It's not your fault. I would've done the same thing if my dad did that to me. I know, I know. Shhh."

Finally, Darcy quieted. Jane fished tissues from her pocket for both of them. She brushed Darcy's hair behind an ear.

"There's only one thing I want you to always remember. No matter what, I'll never stop being your mom, okay?"

A phantom smile touched Darcy's lips.

Jane put her arm through Darcy's and steered her toward the car.

"Where are we going?" she asked.

"You said you didn't feel very well. I don't feel so good myself. We're going home."

"But he's already on his way," she said in a timid voice.

"Yes, he's on his way, all right. He's on his way."

Thirty-Two

Will Barry sat behind his desk scribbling down the last of Jane's comments. He put the pen aside and looked at her through the smoky gray wire rims. "It seems things are getting worse."

"A lot worse. More than just teenage rebellion. Otherwise, I wouldn't be here. Whatever it is, it scares the Be-jeezuz out of me."

Studying her with a strange quietness, he took up his pen, tapped it on the lined paper. "Do you often take the Lord's name in vain?"

She blinked, repeated dumbly, "The Lord's name in vain?"

"Be-jeezuz. Do you think that kind of thing is helpful in reconciling yourself with Bekah?"

She burst out laughing. "It's a figure of speech."

"Maybe to you."

"What are you talking about?"

"Those who are more dogmatic about their faith take such blasphemies very seriously."

"You mean Bekah."

He nodded.

"You know what's funny? Darcy's taken up swearing! And she really fights me about having to go visit every other weekend. I tell you, something is not right over there. How much longer is this evaluation going to take?"

He bit his thumb nail. "Tell me, does it surprise you to see the twins growing apart?"

"No. Bekah's an alien to us now. But they used to be very close." She drew in a breath and studied the shelves of a bookcase too small for its contents. Books were crammed on the dusty shelves, more laid sideways on top of those, and more stacked precariously on top of the bookcase itself. Little piles erupted here and there on the floor, like toadstools among the clutter of the office.

She continued, "Twins have a bond, a kind of emotional shorthand. They finish each other's sentences, have looks that mean something only to them. Inside jokes. Sometimes, when Darcy goes to call Bekah at Logan's, she'll find Bekah already on the line, ready to call her."

"That doesn't mean they're not different. Different as night and day, sometimes. It's like they staked out their turf at an early age: Bekah is the artist, Darcy's the sports nut. Bekah's got her animals, Darcy, her books. Bekah's more high strung, easier for me to read, because her emotions are right out there. Darcy buries hers."

Jane wanted to get to the crux of the matter. The GAL's study of the two families had been going on for two months. It was time to make a decision. But she was wary of coming off as a hysterical mother determined to keep her girls from the clutches of their evil father.

"Now it's like she's afraid of Bekah. Definitely uncomfortable about going over on the weekends. Oh, and I told you about the book, didn't I?"

"What book is that?"

"*This Present Darkness*. It paints the most gruesome picture of anyone not associated with fundamentalism. We're all under the influence of Satan and demons."

"So, do you have a faith?" The dark eyes were barely visible behind the smoky lenses of the glasses.

"Does it matter?"

"Maybe to Bekah. And that's what this is all about, isn't it?"

She said miserably, "I can't be something I'm not. What's causing her behavior? It was so sudden, like she snapped or something. Have you ever seen anything like it?"

"No," he said simply. "I've worked with kids of mothers who are prostitutes, dads who are on drugs, kids, who by all rights, should want out of abusive situations. But I've never seen anything like this." He sighed. "It's odd. She genuinely loved you, had a strong bond. I've talked to both girls, seen the little notes, and gifts you've saved over the years . . . Nothing I know would bring about such sudden animosity."

His referral to Bekah's love in the past tense stabbed Jane. She pleaded, "Can you talk to some of your colleagues? Maybe they've heard of something. Please, for Bekah?"

"I'll call around."

She felt a small surge of hope. But she burned to fill Barry in on the full extent of Logan's campaign against her. He'd never find out such details in a one-on-one with Logan, and some things were too subtle for the girls to pick up.

"All the stuff going on over there . . . do you think the court would stand by and allow him to put notions in her head that aren't true about me? My lawyer says this is alienation, and the courts hate alienation."

Barry thought a moment, tapped his chin with the pen. "I understand how frustrating it all is. But alienation is not easy to prove. Let me put it this way: is Logan doing things to purposely hurt your image in the children's eyes? Or does he have a right to express his true feelings when his children ask if their mother is saved?" He shrugged, as if what followed were obvious. "Can you see what a fine line it is?"

Her stomach plunged with the fear that she could lose her daughter. For the first time, she saw that the system, with its court and its GAL, was not equipped to deal with ambiguity. For the first time, the pain of defeat forced hope back.

"So, you're telling me if a religious fanatic states his 'true beliefs' about a child's mother, the court finds nothing wrong with that? There's no protection? My reputation can be destroyed?"

He fiddled with his pen. "What would you do, hang a man for his religious beliefs? Take away his children because those beliefs are too strong?"

"How do you define alienation, then?" she asked icily.

She stared at Will Barry, degrees in law and psychology backing him up, books surrounding him. It was so obvious that Logan had convicted himself out of his own mouth. But apparently, alienation was impossible to prove. What would it take?

"The legal definition of alienation is a pattern of behavior, comments or conduct that diminishes esteem or consideration for the other parent."

She controlled her voice. "Can you give me some examples?"

He stared at the desk, and without looking up, rambled off, "Your mom's a jerk, a whore, she doesn't care about you. When the mom makes decisions and the dad says, 'You don't have to follow her decisions.' When he says, 'Your mom's sleeping with other men, and it's wrong, and you shouldn't be around that. But I'll protect you and take care of you.'"

"And calling Dolores 'Mom' doesn't fall under this?" she exclaimed. "What about the bike incident?"

"What bike incident?"

"Oh ho, they didn't tell you about that? Well, Bekah doesn't like the cheap bike Logan bought her, so her dad demanded I give him the bike at our house while she's living with him, saying it's half his, since he paid child support."

His eyebrows shot up, but he said nothing.

"Anyway, I said it was staying at home with us, and she could ride it when she came to visit. Now, I swear this next is the truth. Ask them. I warned her not to, but Darcy rode the bike to the store and it got stolen. The next time she went to Rathcreek, she told Bekah her bike got stolen. Do you know what Dolores said?"

He waited.

"She said, 'Isn't it a coincidence that Jane wouldn't let you have your bike over here, and suddenly it got stolen?' Then she asked Darcy, 'Did she tell you to ride it?' Darcy said I'd told her *not* to."

Jane felt her anger rising. "Is there a chance *this* could be seen as alienating? She's saying I arranged for the bike to be stolen so I wouldn't have to send it to Rathcreek."

"She didn't say. She asked."

"Are you blind? She's implying I had it stolen, by the question." Jane stopped, breathed deeply, modulated her anger, fearing she may have already crushed her chance for a favorable recommendation. "Is there even the slightest chance I'm diminished in Bekah's eyes as a result of the *question?*"

The GAL's demeanor was wary, as if he resented being pushed into revealing his position. He did not answer.

She leaned forward in anticipation of his answer, or the next piece of harrowing information.

His manner was brisk, as though they were finished. "I appreciate your bringing these things to my attention. Every little bit helps. It's a tough call in these custody disputes, and there's a very thin line between parental indiscretion and alienation. I want you to know, though, we try to serve justice."

"Oh my God!" she said in a voice so shrill it startled her. At the prospect of another manipulation by Churlick, another observer blinded by his position as religious leader, the hostility poured out of her. Bitterness meant for Logan, years' worth of people believing him instead of her. She finally saw that her faith in justice, faith in the truth were not enough to save her girls.

"My God, Will, what does it take? He did everything but call me the whore of Babylon, say I'm dangerous to live with because I'm an unbeliever. Help me here!"

He said dryly, "Have you heard of religious freedom? It's guaranteed by the Constitution."

Feeling like a madwoman, she went on. "So anything's okay in the name of religious freedom? Okay to send two, three letters a day? Call all the time? Does the court allow him to do that?"

"I'll talk to him."

Jane could see she was not endearing herself, pressuring him this way. Then, suddenly, everything else seemed secondary to a very important question that must be answered. "When are you going to make your recommendation to the court?"

"When I'm ready," he stated.

"But what about Darcy not wanting to go over? You may not get what's going on from your interviews with them, but this *means* something." She blurted, "How about eavesdropping devices?"

"You'd better consult someone about the legality before you go to that kind of expense, Mrs. Bernard," he said, clearly annoyed. And then, as if he had found a way to free himself, he said, "You'll remember the judge's words at the outset. It's not what Bekah or Darcy want, it's what's in their best interest. That's what I've been hired to determine." He nodded at her over the file. "Your relations with Bekah are severely strained right now. If I could use that to justify keeping her from either parent, where would that leave you?"

And so Jane waited. But while she waited, she frequented the reference section of the Spokane law library, searching for something that might add weight to their case. Her lawyer, Oliver Sanchez, for his part, had assured her the courts hated alienation, and were usually swift and sharp with anyone who turned a child against a parent.

Sanchez had said, "He's a real weasel, all right. We'll just keep throwing mud until something sticks." Beyond that, he did nothing. "We have to wait and see what the GAL recommends."

Not willing to wait, Jane searched psychological journals, law journals; she hunted down and read rulings in cases similar to hers. At first, she had no idea how to go about it, and her attempts were clumsy. With time and help from the library staff, she was able to figure out how to read the volumes of referenced and cross-referenced indexes and case synopses. Though the venture was mainly futile, she kept up the practice, spending most evenings after work. Bolivar was more than patient with her, and she loved him for it.

As Darcy's next visitation to her father approached, anxiety ate at Jane, yet she knew the GAL would not hear of disregarding the visitation order.

The night before she was to leave for Logan's, Darcy woke, crying. The old mothering instincts still alive, Jane awakened instantly, and stumbled across the hall, practically before she had awakened.

"What's the matter, honey?"

Darcy turned into her embrace, snuffled against her. "I had a bad dream."

"What was it?"

She looked at Jane through dark lashes clinging together in tears. "Someone was trying to kill me."

Jane sat up, suddenly alert. "Who?"

"I don't know. A man who lived next door to Dad's house. Had black hair."

"What happened?"

"He was coming after me, trying to get me, and I knew he would kill me if he got a hold of me. So I ran into our house. But he followed. I was so scared. I tried to find someplace to hide. Finally, I ran into your closet and hid behind your clothes."

Jane stroked her hair. "Did he find you?"

"No, but he almost got me."

Jane held her Darcy, afraid to ever let her go. This innocent's subconscious was telling the world that her black-haired father was murdering her will every time she went over there. But who would believe a dream? Who would believe a mother scared to death for her daughters? Not the blind, court-appointed GAL.

The next morning, Jane sat on the edge of her bed and watched Darcy sleep. Puffy lips. Dark lashes brushed her full cheeks and long, auburn hair splayed against the pillow.

"Darcy." Jane touched Darcy's cheek. It was warm. "Time to get up, hon."

Her eyelids fluttered, then closed. A smile suffused Darcy's face as she waited for the ritual.

"How's my girl?" Jane asked.

"Grrrrrreat!" Darcy reached up and threw her arms around her mother's neck. Waking ceremony over, Jane kissed her and gave her a long hug, then left to fix breakfast.

After packing was finished and Darcy's fears soothed as best she could, Jane sent her to Rathcreek for the weekend.

On the following Monday, Jane picked up a stranger.

Thirty-Three

If before had been a hellish nightmare, losing both daughters' love was hell itself. The house in Bounty was not the same after Darcy returned. A wariness, an angry tension, pervaded everything. And a sadness filled Jane so completely, it left no room for any other emotion, not happiness, not rage, not contentment from the love of her husband.

A part of her could not believe the change that had come over her daughter. Yes, it had happened to Bekah, but she was not living with Jane. Darcy demonstrated every waking moment of every day how much she despised her mother.

Jane asked, of course, what had happened over the weekend visit. Nothing but the same story as Bekah's: "I'm changed. I'm a Christian now, and the court says I'm old enough that I can choose to live in a Christian home." Jane was beyond despair in her hope of bringing Darcy or Bekah back.

The loss of innocence from the sweet face chilled Jane. Nothing in Darcy's face indicated they had been through twelve loving years together. Nothing in her eyes said, *You are my mother.* Most of the time, she looked through Jane. Vacant, glazed, unseeing.

Like her sister, Darcy had undergone a radical personality change. Sometimes in an eerie war with herself, the old Darcy would surface without warning, at times in mid-sentence, seeming herself, with the old attitudes, familiar mannerisms. Even her posture was looser, warmer. She spoke with emotion and even possessed her old sense of humor. But these moments were brief and rare. Just as suddenly, as if yanked back into the black basement of her soul, Darcy disappeared, replaced by the stranger Logan had sent from Rathcreek.

One day Jane stayed home from work because of a cold. After meeting Darcy where the bus dropped her off after school, they walked to the house together.

"I'm curious," Jane said. "You say you're Christian, but you don't follow the Bible?"

Darcy tightened, gave Jane a cold look and shifted the backpack. Her gaze wandered to the trees, to Lucy running beside them, anywhere but to Jane's face.

"I follow the Bible."

"All of it?" Jane asked.

"I said I did. Do you?"

Jane recognized this new style: answering a question with a question.

"I try to, especially the part about honoring my father and mother." Receiving no reply, Jane asked, "Is this how you honor your mother?"

Silent, distant, Darcy walked beside her. When she did speak, it was with her newly-acquired hostile, know-it-all attitude, and her voice assumed Logan's lecturing tone. "You took that out of context. It says honor your father and mother, but it also says not to bring your children to wrath."

Jane was ready. She forced herself to laugh. "Oh! I can see I didn't read the fine print: honor your father and mother . . . unless they piss you off!"

"Christians don't cuss," Darcy said stiffly, and pulled ahead. "Don't bother meeting me at the bus anymore."

Until the GAL made his recommendation to the court, Darcy was stuck with Jane, and so she began her active revolt. She told Jane she had outgrown her jeans and needed new ones. That weekend, when Jane pulled the car out of the garage for a shopping trip, Darcy opened the door and hopped into the back seat.

Jane stared at her. "What are you doing?"

"I don't want to sit in the front."

"Why not?"

"I just don't want to," the girl said, voice flat.

She had always sat up front with her mother, had fought Bekah for the privilege.

Jane asked, "Want to go to the mall?"

"I said I did," she replied in a sulky voice.

"Then get in the front seat."

Darcy's eyes glinted anger. She hesitated, gauging whether Jane meant it or not. Then she got out of the back seat and into the front. They drove toward town in silence, until Darcy, in a fit of pique, addressed her as "Jane." Furious, Jane turned the car around and headed home.

"What?" Darcy cried.

"If you can't figure it out, you're in bad shape."

"I should be able to sit where I want."

"You call me Mom, or you can wear those jeans until they're up to your knees." She swung into the drive and pulled the car into the garage.

Darcy said, "Fine. I'll ask Dad. I didn't think you'd really take me anyway, the way you spend all the child support money on who knows what."

Jane slammed on the brakes and threw the car into park. The momentum shot Darcy forward, and she stared, face full of shock and anger. Jane wondered what it was that glared back at her.

"What did you mean by that little smart ass remark?"

"Just what I said. We never have enough money. You're always saying we have to watch it this month." Her body was rigid, face in a trance, victorious. "You work at your secretarial job. Bo teaches. But you never spend anything on me. Or Bekah. Where do you suppose it goes every month, hm?"

It was all Jane could do to not wipe that smug lack of respect off Darcy's face. But Jane had never slapped her daughters, and would not start now. Besides, this was not her daughter. If it had been, even for an instant, Jane would have gathered her into her arms. She hungered for the real Darcy. The realization that this monster held Darcy hostage and could not be slapped into letting her go helped keep this psycho's contrived upper hand in perspective.

"You are on very dangerous ground here. If I were you, I wouldn't say another word. You have no idea of the bills we're paying off for the construction of *your rooms*."

The face undulated with something akin to enjoyment. "Dolores showed Bekah and me your paycheck stubs from her file. I know how much money you and Bo put in the credit union every month."

Jane was stunned. What kind of parent would pull such a despicable stunt? The Churlicks must have had the stubs from when the court collected information for determining child support. Was Dolores crazy, dragging the girls into the middle like that? All Jane could think was, *Got to write that down, got to document it for the GAL.*

Darcy made to leave, turning the moment into a solid victory with the coldness of her back. Jane grabbed her until she cried out in pain, phony "for the court" squeals that stopped with the look Jane gave her. "I'll tell you what we spend our money on."

Flipping through the check register, she said, "Let's start here. There's a couple pair of shoes you got at the beginning of the month, because you outgrew your old ones."

She wrote down $75.00

"Then there's lunch tickets, that's thirty dollars a month. Oh, and don't forget, we paid *twice* last month because you *lost* your other ticket book." She couldn't keep the sarcasm from her voice. "Payment on your clarinet is thirty-five a month. Gym shoes. Remember, we had to replace the ones you ripped out? Fifty. Eye exam and glasses, a hundred and twenty. School supplies, ten dollars. You left your jacket somewhere after the game and it cost seventy-five to replace it. Gas for two trips to Spokane . . ."

She tallied up the figures. Darcy fidgeted. Jane held up the paper.

"It's far more than the two hundred twenty-five a month Logan sends for you, and I haven't even counted food, hot water for your showers, telephone . . ."

Darcy scowled and threw her long hair to one side with a hand. "There always seems to be plenty to spend on Simon."

Jane grabbed her by both shoulders, face inches away. For a split second, fear registered there, then the third-rate prosecutor fleshed out again. "You're really rude, you know that, Darcy? And you'd better snap out of it. How does weekend restriction from phone calls from Rathcreek sound for starters?"

Darcy faltered. "You can't keep me from my dad."

"Oh yes, I can. It's done." Jane hated the way she sounded, as if she had already lost. But then, hadn't she? Spite, at the moment, was all that was left.

She continued, "You want to see just how rotten it can get around here? Keep it up and there's a lot more where that came from. Now let's get one thing straight, and you can take this back to Rathcreek: Simon gets his mother's Social Security, and not one cent belongs to you or Bekah."

A reasonable explanation to an illogical complaint made Jane feel in control again, and she calmed down. "If it makes any difference to you, we spent everything we had on your bedrooms. That's why it's so tight. But we wanted to. It was worth it, even if we have to scrimp."

Darcy's voice was cold. "You did that for the resale value, not for us."

"What?" How could she possibly know about resale value? Then it hit Jane. Churlicks, of course.

Darcy shouted, "Why don't you just let me live with my dad? Why do you have to fight this?" She flounced out, screamed, "Why?" and slammed the door.

Jane watched Darcy storm into the house. Bereft, she whispered, "Because I love you."

First, Jane called her lawyer to update him, then reported the new information to the GAL. She also made an appointment with a psychologist.

She had called every psychiatrist, psychologist and counselor in the phone book, but none had ever dealt with the bizarre behavior Jane described. None but Ramona Myer, who said, yes, she had worked with estranged children where religion was involved.

The following Monday, Jane and Darcy sat alone in the waiting room of Dr. Myer's office. She called Jane into her office first.

"Now, what exactly do you expect to get from this?" Dr. Myer said in her mild voice.

The question caught Jane off guard. She had expected Dr. Myer to tell her how these things went. She was the one with experience, wasn't she? Jane had been assured over the phone—assured of what? That whatever *this* was, was something Dr. Myer had dealt with before. She had helped others in similar circumstances.

"I need a . . . well, a cure for whatever's caused this change in my daughter."

"A cure for what, exactly?"

"This brainwashing of her dad's that's turned her against me."

"She's how old, twelve?"

Jane nodded.

"Ah, teenage rebellion."

"No! It's not rebellion." She opened a notebook in her lap and recounted a dozen or so notes on Darcy's behavior that she had documented for the GAL. She looked up at the woman, her white spun hair and pursed lips. The doctor was so mild mannered, Jane wondered if she were shrewd enough to get to the heart of things with Darcy in her altered-personality state.

Jane asked, "What do you call it if it's not teenage rebellion? She looks different, acts different, her personality's flat, as if some automated teller had been implanted in her voice and face. It's much deeper than typical rebellion."

"There's nothing typical about teenage rebellion. Each case is different. But it's hard to say until I've talked to her. Why don't I call her in now?"

Jane sat in the dim waiting room. Stacks of papers and mail were piled on an unoccupied desk, and still, nobody else had shown up for an appointment. She was beginning to wonder if the woman had any other clients, beginning to make the uncomfortable connection that the shabby office, lack of staff and patients could be an indicator of her failure in the "mental biz."

After a short while, Darcy emerged. Jane tried to read her for an indication of whether Dr. Myer had been successful. Darcy's small, hard smile made Jane's hope disappear before she returned to the doctor's office.

Dr. Myer began, "Well, I've seen these types before. It's always the same."

Jane groaned inwardly. This woman was out of her league.

"When a child is trying to form religious beliefs and the parent is of an opposing persuasion, the best thing to do is to keep showing love . . ."

"Is that right? Does no good as far as I can see. I told her yesterday that no matter what she did, I still loved her, always would love her. Know what she said?"

Dr. Myer shook her head.

"She said not to bother, because she already had a mother who loved her." Jane paused. "She was referring to her stepmother."

Dr. Myer said briskly, "Why hire a professional if you're not interested in my opinion? Believe me when I say I see this all the time. Children go through these stages every day, dear. And they grow out of them."

"It's not a stage. Most dysfunctional families still have some good times occasionally. There are no good times with this stranger or her sister, who both walk and talk and act differently."

"Of course, I wouldn't be able to tell that in one session."

"Why don't you just say it? You don't know *what* this is. You don't know what to call it. Rebellion doesn't come with an instant, complete personality change. It's all the same to you, because it's not your daughter who's changed into this—" *monster*, Jane wanted to say, but stopped.

"Look, I'm a good mother. At least, I used to be. I'm not sure anymore. But seeing your daughters call you Jane and look right through you can do that. Our bond is gone. There's *nothing* left. I love my daughters very much, and I'd do anything to get them back. But, something very, very wrong is going on here, and if you call it rebellion one more time, I'll scream."

Dr. Myer's face softened. She laced her hands in her lap and sighed. "Well, I suppose you're right, dear. I've never heard of anything like what you're describing, so I suppose we don't know what to call it, do we? Let alone what to do with it."

The doctor rose and went to open the office door. "I don't believe I can help you, in any case." She looked at the clock. "Oh, and one more thing. I won't be charging you for today's session."

Thirty-Four

The strangeness between Jane and her daughters went on, until what was normal faded. The early years, when she was the adored center of her daughters' lives, were the memories Jane clung to. Yet day by day, her confidence in herself as a mother, once so strong, lessened.

"C'mon, Bo, I need a walk." Jane patted the pocket of her hooded windbreaker, checking to see that it was full of dog treats. Along the course of their walk, her new friends sat, tails thumping, or stood pawing at the chain link, tails whirling, waiting for the treats to be passed through, the petting and sweet talk. One, however, would not be wooed. When Jane reached into her pocket and called, "Hello, boy! How ya doin'?" he would not take the dog biscuit, but let it drop to the ground, sniff it and resume barking, as if to say she could not entice him from his post with this paltry treat. Jane noticed it was always gone by the next visit, however.

Bolivar sighed, then said, "I'll get my hat."

She often dragged Bo out for a walk to town. March weather was unusually warm from el niño that year and the road offered them the privacy to share their feelings of helplessness, to try to answer unanswerable questions and talk about the latest bizarre incident. The pewter sky was woven with soft, thin ribbons of pink in the gathering dusk.

In the three months since the judge had assigned the children to their separate homes, Jane had been collecting notes, organizing them in a binder. She thought they may be helpful to the GAL to compare before and after. The notes included the girls' behavior, statements from school counselors, statements from relatives, teachers, and the non-Christian former friends the girls had cut off. She also included a few journal articles from her continuing forays to the law library.

Still, the frustration of living with a hostile child was taking its toll. More and more often, Jane was plagued by headaches and stomach upsets by day, bad dreams at night.

"I don't know how much more of this I can stand," she said, marching double time down the road. "This was the worst yet. It's been building, but today was the worst."

"What's the little Christian up to now?"

Jane took a deep breath. A large crow winged by, its raucous cry the only sound in the early spring evening.

"Darcy told me if it wouldn't hurt their case, she'd run away. But she figured that wouldn't solve anything, because I'd just haul her back, and it would look bad for Logan. She said my heart was made of steel, rock and cement put together, and if I thought she loved me at all, I was dead wrong."

Bo strode beside her, his long legs keeping up with her pace. "Do you really think she'd run away?"

"Oh yes, and find the scripture to back her."

"Do you think a bus ticket would help?"

"Bolivar."

"I can't help it. It's wearing on me, too, you know. To see the way she's cold as ice to you. I wish you'd let me —"

Jane held up a hand. She would have none of his talk of protecting her from Darcy's barbs, her acts of sedition and sabotage. Yes, some days were hard, when Jane yearned to shut everything out and shut down. But the pain made her feel alive. Without taking part in the fight, she would feel as dead as her daughters had become, as they wished her to be.

She said, "I don't mind. We know the day'll come when you're more of a target than a sideline, and believe me, it'll take everything you've got not to lose it. Save your strength."

"Why the hell is the GAL taking so long? The judge said three months. It's been that, and he's spoken to all of us."

"Last time I talked to him, he said he'll make his recommendation when he's ready. Says he's looking for documentation on exactly what this is."

"Still trying to get answers?"

"Yes, but no luck. It's such a slippery thing. All the reading I've done, our visit to the shrink, a dead end. I can't believe nobody's ever seen this kind of alienation thing. And I hate what it's doing to me."

"What's that?"

"I'm getting so defensive. I feel like nobody blames them, they blame me, the terrible mother."

"Who?"

"Anyone who happens to see how I'm acting around Darcy these days. The school secretary, for instance, when I dropped the little brat off the other day. I'm not my most charming when Darcy purposely misses the bus to make me late to work."

"Why do you put up with it?"

She didn't answer.

He walked in silence for a while. "How can you not hate them?"

She stopped, surprised. "What would it take for you to hate Simon?"

"I dunno, but this bullshit would go a long way toward it. Why don't you punish her?"

"This may be hard for you to understand, because with Simon, there's a bond — you punish him and he's still your son. With Bekah and Darcy . . ." Jane hesitated, not sure she could put into words what her gut told her. "There is no bond. So first, punishing doesn't do anything but give her fuel to hate me more, if that's possible. And second . . . I can't explain it, but the worse this gets, the longer it goes on, the more permanent it feels. If punishing alienates her all the more, with her righteous indignation, how will I ever get her back?"

He took her hand and they walked in silence. "So, finish telling me your catastrophe d' jour."

"Well, you know she's been missing the bus."

"What does missing the bus . . . Oh, I get it."

"That's me, chauffeur. I've been warning her not to be late, because I wasn't going to take her to school anymore. This morning, she did it again."

"Why do you fight it, Jane? Make those grades her responsibility. If she flunks out, she'll take it again next year."

"Wish I'd thought of that. But that would mean she'd be alone in the house to do God knows what all day long. Have you forgotten the marks in the livingroom ceiling where you caught her scraping it with your golf club? Or the square foot of rug she trimmed in the middle of her room?"

"Hard to forget those."

"Besides, I was so mad I wasn't thinking. I just screamed at her like a raving lunatic, which is exactly what she wanted. More ammo to report to Rathcreek."

Bolivar stopped as Jane walked over to greet Hector, who pawed the fence. "Hey, boy! Hey, how ya doin'? Oh yeah, I've got it. Slow down. Here ya go."

"Anyway," she said as they resumed their walk, "Darcy came back from the bus stop telling me I had to take her to school. I told her she was on her own. Before I knew it, she was calling me filthy names, shrieking that if I didn't take her, she wouldn't go to school. That she hated me. I yelled back, 'If you're going to throw a tantrum like a two-year-old, I'm going to treat you like one and paddle your butt. Now get on your bike and get to school! And I'll call them to make sure you made it, so don't try anything!'

"She was furious, bawling her head off. She hopped on her bike and the last thing she screamed at me amidst a few choice epitaphs, was that she hated me.

"Jesus Christ," Bo said. "You can't go on much longer this way. We've got to do something." He stopped. "Okay, hear me out. Why don't we look into getting their phones bugged?"

"What good would that do? Besides, I already blew it and got the idea nixed by Will Barry."

"I'm sure we could get enough so even Will would have no problem seeing Logan for the sleaze he is."

"Aren't wire taps illegal?" she asked. "Will made it seem they wouldn't be admissible in court."

"I don't know," he said. "We could ask Sanchez."

"Believe me, I'd love to, but I wonder if it would do any good. You don't know this guy, Will. I've already told him about the bike incident, sulfur-belching demons. He just talks about Constitutionally guaranteed freedom of religion."

Bo didn't answer, but followed Jane to another fenced yard to greet Penelope and feed her dog biscuits. When they were walking again, he said, "The judge will be hearing our lawyer in court, too, not just Will's recommendation. But the real question is this: when's it time to give up? Even if we win, what've we got? A couple of prisoners. Is that what you want?"

"No!" she shouted. "That's not what I want. I want my girls back, the real Bekah and Darcy, the way they used to be. If we get total custody, we can keep them from Logan, find some counselor and maybe eventually they'll come around."

His look was resignation or blame, she couldn't tell which, and made her consider that maybe she was being unrealistic. Perhaps hope was the ultimate delusion.

"I'll never give up on them," she said finally.

"Forget the whole thing. I'm sorry I ever brought it up."

"What's happening to us?" Jane asked. "We're acting like . . . like, my God, like Logan. Wire taps is something he'd do."

"You worry too much. You have enough integrity that even if you lose a little, it'll just put you on the same level as the rest of us."

Jane stopped. "That hurt."

"You think that hurts, try this end, the Step. For months now, we've conducted this war on your terms, as if it doesn't affect me, too . . . and we're losing. You can worry about moral issues all you want, but morality's not going to win your case in court. It's not going to get your girls back. Like Will said, there's no real justice in these things."

Bo's attack wounded her, and she felt all at once alone. "You have all these great ideas, but I'm telling you, you don't know what you're talking about. Everything's in the hands of the GAL, and he *won't* make a decision. Go ahead, bug the hell outta Churlick, and see what light that puts us in when we go to court."

"I'm a man, Jane. A man fights. I want to beat the livin' shit outta Churlick and take the girls back." He turned to her. "You've got to do something."

"What?"

"I don't know. But I can't stand much more."

"So much for testosterone," she said. "And as far as you're concerned, I'll tell you right now, this is about my girls, not you or me. They're being torn apart, psychologically ripped in two, and I'd do anything to save them. If it means waiting for the GAL to make up his mind, we'll wait. If it means keeping Darcy with us, taking her daily abuse, so she's not driven further away, so she can be whole and healthy some day, I'll take it."

Bolivar was quiet for several minutes. Finally, he said, "And what's left for me?"

The loss in his voice was terrible to hear. Now Bo, too, was making her choose, between two girls doing everything they could to make her give them up, and her man, who would not see her crucified to save these hateful brats.

They reached the town's only traffic signal. On the corner stood one of the ubiquitous coffee shops of the Pacific Northwest. Usually, they stopped for a cup before returning home. As if reaching the same conclusion at the same time, they turned without stopping and headed back.

Thirty-Five

Now that Jane's anger had found its voice, Bo grew closedmouthed in an effort not to provoke it. A cold protectiveness grew up between them, tempered by occasional hot spots that flared involving Darcy's behavior and their inability to come to a concensus about how to cope with her.

Darcy continued to lock herself in her bedroom to avoid Jane whenever possible. Four months ago, she would have lounged around the livingroom lost in a novel; now, when she wasn't spending hours in her room, Darcy went zombie in front of the television. If Jane joined her, she left.

The mail, surprisingly, had stopped for the most part. Perhaps the GAL had talked to Logan. More annoying were the phone calls. Sullen and withdrawn most of the time, Darcy brightened whenever a call was for her. Lengthy conversations with Logan, Dolores and Bekah had become a part of many days per week.

Jane knocked on the bedroom door. "Darcy, time for dinner."

"I'm on the phone."

"You've been talking an hour. That's enough for one day."

At dinner, Simon filled the void, as he had become accustomed to doing, with talk of scholarship applications and his part in the school play. The meal was barely finished when the phone rang again. Darcy jumped to get it and went toward her room.

"That's enough for one day," Jane repeated.

Darcy rolled her eyes, and mimicked the edict into the phone. Jane wanted to rip it out of her hand and club her with it. Instead, she called her back into the dining room.

Darcy turned and gazed back insolently. Jane called her over with a finger.

"What?" she demanded.

"Give me the phone."

Darcy held it to herself. "What for?"

"Give it to me."

She handed it over.

"Hello?"

"We're calling for Darcy, not you," Dolores said.

Then Logan came on. "What's going on here?"

"That's what I'd like to know. The GAL told me he was going to talk to you about so many calls, that it wasn't good for Darcy."

"Well, he didn't."

"Then I'll make a decision as her *mother*. From now on, we're limiting calls to twice a week, the way it used to be."

Darcy's features were twisted with tragedy, and she shook her head. Jane pointed, ordered her to her room and she stomped off.

Logan said, "You can't keep us from calling."

"I just did. Listen, Logan, maybe you don't understand. This phone is part of my home. And you're invading my home, stirring things up, making it hard for Darcy to be with us. . . . but, that's your goal, isn't it?"

"She's unhappy there. She's the one that wants us to call."

"Of course she does, now that you've brainwashed her."

"I just want to talk to my daughter."

"No, you don't. You want to make her choose between us, and you're tearing her apart, you son-of-a-bitch!"

"There's nothing in the court order that limits the number of calls we can make. We'll call as often as we like."

"Bet me."

"I'm calling the GAL with this."

"Good," she said. "And one more thing. No more religious crap sent home with her when she comes back from Rathcreek."

"You can't do that! I have the right to bring the girls up in my faith."

"Not in my home. If I see any more of your hocus pocus, speaking-in-tongues, check-your-mind-at-the-door bullshit, I'll burn it."

Darcy's bedroom was the eye of a pubescent tornado. Havoc carelessly wreaked there was a tribute to independence and style. Christian rock singers shared the walls with kitten and horse posters. The floor was a flotilla of various pieces of clothing, books, shoes, pop cans and a partially eaten bag of chips. More clothes, a portable CD player and discs were lost in the folds of the bed. Jane stood over Darcy, recently returned from a visit to her father's for the weekend, watching her unpack.

Darcy stopped. "Do you have to stand there?"

"Yes. Why? Do you have something to hide?"

"No. Don't you trust me?"

"As a matter of fact," she said, and reached into the suitcase, "no." She drew out of a side pocket Sunday school papers, and crumpled them into a ball.

"Those are mine!"

"No. You know what I told Logan."

Darcy flung a pile of clothes to the floor.

Jane pointed to a green plastic frog in the suitcase nestled next to a quart-sized bag of Dolores' home-baked chocolate chip cookies.

"What's that?"

Darcy snatched up the frog. "It's mine. It's a toy Dad gave me." Then in a snide voice, "Are you going to take it, too?"

Jane turned to go. At the door, she stopped and listened. "Sounds like Aunt Louise is here for the picnic. We're leaving in an hour, so get yourself ready."

"I'm not going."

"Oh, yes you are. If you're not ready, you'll lose television privileges for a week."

Taking away the protection of Darcy's isolation was the only leverage Jane had, and the threat did its work, and changed her attitude to sudden humility.

"All right," she said with uncharacteristic meekness. "Aunt Weez is okay."

Jane was taken back. Once or twice over the months, the old Darcy had surfaced. God! Jane hoped this truly was *her* Darcy. From the doorway, Jane watched her take an armload of clothes and dump them into a dresser drawer. Jane had to smile; shortcuts like that one reminded her of herself as a teen. Darcy caught her looking, gave a shy grin. A miracle! Memories of her girl came flooding over Jane, laughing times, affection-filled moments, and her chest tightened and ached with yearning. Her daughter was here now, her own flesh and blood, whom she adored.

Bolivar appeared at the door. "Louise is here. And we need to get out last year's tax returns to fill out financial aid forms. You got a minute?" His gaze traveled over the wreckage before him. "I see the tide's come in again."

Darcy's expression clanged shut. She flung the prisoner of war back into the dungeon. In a flat voice, she said, "Is that all you can do is pick on me?"

Putting a hand to her forehead, Jane closed her eyes. "Shit!"

Bolivar followed Jane to her desk where she sat, arms crossed.

"You are such a jackass sometimes."

"What'd I do?"

She grabbed a folder off the desk. "Here. This is what you came barging in for."

"What are you trying to say?" he asked, impatient, now.

"She'd flipped back in for a minute. You ruined it, Bo."

Louise walked by, then, reading their faces, backed up. "Whoa! War zone! Incoming!" She retraced her steps. "Think I'll go see the little Christian for a bit."

"Good idea," Bo said tersely. "How was I supposed to know? All I saw was a disaster—kind of like your desk." He said it playfully, hopefully. The desk was piled with books she meant to read and a stack of bills to be paid. Pictures of Bekah, Darcy and Simon were posted to a cork board, along with cards she had received from the girls during the good times. A framed wedding picture of her and Bo was pushed aside on the desktop, nearly obscured behind the black binder containing information for the GAL.

"Have you checked out your side of the bed? Or Simon's room lately? It'll be a wonder if any college takes him."

"What's wrong? Is it that time of the month?"

"No, it's *not* that time of the month," she said. "Darcy was normal for the first time in so long . . . God, I miss her."

He stood there, muted by misery.

Jane said, "All I want is for you to say you're sorry. But, judging from our last walk, that's asking the impossible."

Exasperated, he gazed at the ceiling. "Okay, let's have it."

"Let's have it? What's that supposed to mean? This isn't a car estimate, this is your wife. Don't talk down to me, Bolivar. I'm not your student anymore."

"Tell me what's bothering you," he said in a controlled voice.

"I needed you during that walk. And all you could do was make me feel guilty for hanging in there for my girls."

"It's not a matter of guilt. I want us to *do* something. Anything. Can you get Sanchez to lean on the GAL?"

"Will's not ready. He won't budge. And our lawyer is worthless. He won't call."

"The GAL has to commit to something one way or the other. This has got to end."

"Like magic? Make the whole mess disappear?" she asked.

"Stop it! You're acting as though *I'm* supposed to make your pain go away. But that's your job. I've been teaching long enough to know that my taking care of your pain just turns you into pudding. I'm sorry I hurt you," he said in a mincing voice, "let me take it back and give you some butterscotch."

She felt tears gathering, a knot of pain in her throat. "Pudding? That's all my pain is to you? Stop being my teacher! You need to have empathy for my pain, not take it away." She clenched her fists. "Empathy—that's pudding? No, that's when we're most connected to each other. But you want the easy way: 'I hurt you? That's your problem.' It's much harder to say, 'I'm sorry. Let me hold you till you feel better. I don't understand, but I want you to know I love you.'"

Bolivar stared at her. He tossed the folder on the desk, took her hand. At the closet, he grabbed their jackets. "C'mon. I need a walk."

He directed her out the door and down the soggy gravel driveway. The previous night's rain formed rivulets that still trickled all the way to the road. The force of the storm had unclogged the last of the blackened leaves of fall from the path and beaten the tall grasses to reveal green shoots along the runners of wild blackberries over the hillside. The sky was clear, the sun warm, and steam rose off the blacktop.

They didn't march, but stroll, hand in hand. He had put her hand in his, but she couldn't help but feel guarded. How could she allow herself to relax, with her resentment over this fresh loss of Darcy? The walk went on, Bolivar's spontaneous, funny peace offering. Then, despite herself, the strain of emotion began to depart, leaving the awkward residue of going forward.

"Wanna know something?" he asked.

"Hm?"

"Sometimes you rush off, taking care of the list of things you do to manage the house, me, Simon and Darcy. I watch you from up here on the hill, racing over the speed limit. Beauty, mind, soul. I miss you before you get out of sight."

He stopped and faced the mountain. "Someone asked me once if I'd ever seen a sight more beautiful than that mountain. I said, only one."

It stood in the distance, the majesty of the snow covered mountain, glacial ice, volcanic temper beneath the earth's crust. Jane didn't want to be swept away by emotions, wooed back by his words, even to a world more solid than any she had ever known, if it didn't include Bekah and Darcy. Her daughters, life with Bolivar. This man anchored her existence, yet she could neither grab onto him nor let go of her girls. Then, she cracked open inside, trembling, crying. Bolivar held her.

"I'm terrified I'm going to lose them," she said. "I don't want to lose you, too."

"You won't."

"I don't know how to break through whatever this is. I'm scared, Bo."

"Scares the hell outta me, too." He tightened his embrace and gazed at her quietly, bent to kiss her. Crows cawed in the distance, and the sun lolled in the clear sky.

Taking her hand, he turned toward home. "Better get going, we got a picnic."

They walked slowly, and Jane, content with the silence, sun warming her back, relished the odor of damp earth and pine. Then, she noticed his look of amusement.

"What?"

"Know when you get an emotional overload and have to divert it with a joke?"

"Mmhm," she said.

"Well," he said, tucking her arm under his, "I just passed up three pretty good ones."

At the house, Bo packed the car and Jane found Louise in the kitchen fixing tuna sandwiches, her square shoulders moving rhythmically with the chopping knife. Small piles of celery and onions already sat on the cutting board.

Louise wore jeans, sweatshirt, tame earrings—for Louise—and a red hair ribbon. Her ponytail swung back and forth with the chopping.

Jane hadn't seen much of her sister since she had married and moved to Bounty, and all at once, missed their closeness.

"You look great. Letting your hair grow out?"

Louise gave her a smug glance. "Dallas likes it."

"Well, it looks good on you. He's been good for you, hasn't he?"

Scraping the pickles, celery and onions into the tuna, Louise nodded and added a dollop of mayonnaise.

"Is he coming?"

She grinned crookedly. "I don't think so. But knowin' Dallas, I'll bet he's at least breathin' hard."

"You're bad. And he's worse." Jane reached into the cookie jar and took out a handful of ginger snaps. "Speaking of which, how serious are you two? Or is that privileged information?"

"About as serious as a couple of accountants. That what you mean?"

Jane put the sack of cookies in the picnic basket. "Louise."

"I'm sure I do tax him a little on the side. But, he's the best thing I've come across since computer sex." Louise returned to her sandwiches, scraped the last of the tuna from the bowl. "It's easy to be normal on the net. Real time's different. None of us can stand too much reality, can we?"

"What are you saying?" Jane asked.

"What man would want a serious relationship with me? Dallas is crazy, but not that kinda crazy." The stark gray eyes glared at her, dared her to soft peddle her truth.

With painful clarity, Jane realized how hard it must be to feel that love would always be out of reach because of schizophrenia. How alone Louise must feel, not able to control those moments of madness when she went underground and her disjointed twin took over, bringing her terrible, private interior to light. Jane and Louise went back to making lunch, taking solace in the quiet.

"So, how 'bout you and Bo Man?" Louise nodded toward the doorway.

"We're fine. Just had to get some things talked out. Darcy's been so hard to live with, it's really getting to us."

"No kidding! What a perfect little shit Darcy is today."

"You noticed."

"I walk into the room and this little robotic demon child with a voice cold as January, eyes that slice right through me, goes stiff as a board while I hug her, then orders me out. What's with her?"

"I told you before. Logan's turned them against me somehow."

"And me. Guilt by association, huh?" She was silent a moment. "So this isn't just a bad mood?"

Jane shook her head.

Louise said slowly, "And she really doesn't love us? Not you an' not me?"

Eyes suddenly brimming, Jane looked down.

Louise roared, "I changed their poopy pants, cleaned up their *vomit,* for God sakes!" She shuddered. "You know me, Janey, I hate throwing up. Vomit could dry on my carpet and I'd just call it high-low. But for my nieces, I was *there!*" Voice trembling, she asked, "Now they hate their Aunt Weez? How can you stand it? Doesn't it kill you?"

"Sometimes I wonder how I get out of bed in the morning. How I face the little monster when I know she's going to tear my heart out again today."

Long suppressed thoughts exploded from Jane. The kitchen was running, like lava. She ignored the hot flows down her cheeks. "After nine months of feeling my babies come alive inside me, I was a different person. The first time I heard them cry, felt them laid on my stomach, all wrinkled and beautiful and warm . . ." She wiped the tears. "I think this must be what it's like when a child gets killed in a car accident. You die, too. And even though you still function, you're never the same. Never."

Louise grabbed Jane in a desperate hug. "You told me about it, but, guess I really didn't understand what you meant until I saw it for myself. God, I'm sorry, Jane."

They held onto each other, blind, heart-broken sobs erupting from both, until Louise turned away, rubbed her nose and wiped her hands on her jeans.

"I had this crazy plan," Jane said, and paused. "Even Bolivar didn't know."

"What?" Louise asked.

"When I couldn't take it any more, I thought of a way to keep the girls away from Churlick. Permanently. Wait for a weekend when Bekah was over visiting, then put them on a plane and fly away."

"Great plan!" Louise said.

"Yeah, well. My kids've been mentally kidnapped, Louise, and they don't *want* to be rescued. I even got so far as calling to make ticket reservations. Then I thought, how am I going to do this? To get the kids onto a plane, I'd have to drug 'em, get 'em into a wheel chair or something. Okay, sleeping pills, but how many to really knock 'em out? How many's too many?"

Jane was pacing the kitchen. "And even if I were able to keep them asleep on the plane—and *that* wouldn't be suspicious to anyone, huh? Even if that worked out, *then* what? What do I do when they wake up? Keep 'em prisoners? The first chance they had to get to a phone, they'd call him. And I'd be in jail. How could I fight this then?"

"Couldn't you find someone to fix their twisted little minds?" Louise asked.

"No! I've called everywhere. Asked the GAL for a referral, but he says there aren't any experts who know about this. Even took Darcy to a woman who said she was experienced in this kind of thing, whatever it is. A bust. Nobody's heard of it," Jane said, almost shouting. "People in the mental business haven't got a clue about how these kids changed. Or how to get them back."

"I can believe it," Louise said. "They don't know how to fix me, either. But these kids can't be the only ones. Nobody? Nobody's heard of this, this whatever it is?"

"What *is* it? No! Nobody's heard of 'it.' Nobody treats 'it.' At least as far as the fifty or so phone calls I've made trying to track down some sort of professional."

"Jesus! What can you do?"

"I'm open. Any suggestions?"

Louise was silent, brooding. Finally, she shrugged her shoulders.

"It can't be too late, can it?" Jane said, voice breaking. "I should've smuggled them away before it got to this point, but I didn't know. Bekah and Darcy loved me. How could we know they would ever, ever hate me?"

"Powerless. Against the powers that be. It's a conspiracy, isn't it?" Louise asked.

"What? No. Louise . . ."

Louise twirled the ponytail faster and faster. The other hand flitted to stroke her face, her neck. "Sure, as if you're going to admit it." Wild eyes flicked through the room. A strange certainty lit her features. "It's that bastard child-stealer, Churlick. At it again."

Dashing out of the kitchen, Louise shouted, "Well, I'll be burned and urned if he's going to kill any more after David!"

Thirty-Six

The following day, Jane stood at the desk of the Rathcreek Police Station. "I'm Jane Bernard, here to see my sister, Louise Crownhart."

A uniformed woman behind the thick glass consulted a sheet. "Assault?"

"That's her."

The harsh door buzzer sounded and Jane was let in, then led down a hall to the visiting area. She followed the policewoman, keeping her eyes on the squared shoulders in the dark blue uniform ahead of her, rather than the grim cement walls. She felt eerie, like a diver going down into the depths, depending on the air she carried on her back for survival. One could not survive in a place like this without a lifeline.

"Eastern's on their way," the woman said, not turning. "She won't be here long."

Louise had been an inmate of Eastern State Hospital in the past. Jane asked, "How much time do I have?"

"Half hour, maybe." The woman took out keys and unlocked a steel door.

Jane didn't know what she expected to see, but the starkness of the small cement and steel cubicle made her claustrophobic. She walked into the cell. The door locked behind her, a loud, *chung-clatch*. The stale air was strong with the odor of cigarettes, urine and vomit. On the wall was a no-smoking sign. She seated herself in a plastic chair facing thick glass.

Louise sat on a wooden bench facing the glass from the other side. Jane noted the agitated face, the distant look of her luminous gray eyes. The red ribbon was gone, as were the earrings, and Louise wore an

orange, elastic-waisted jump suit. She spun the pony tail around her finger into a tight spiral that knotted back upon itself. She nodded, cursed or
spoke loudly—to no one.

Jane said to the dull glass between them. "Louise?"

Then, remembering her instructions, she lifted the receiver of a wall
phone. The line buzzed with static. She held it up, indicating that Louise
should pick up her end.

Louise twirled the hair around her finger, absorbed in her private
conversation.

The voices, Jane thought, and wondered what it must have been like
for her sister to be hauled off to jail in the state she was in. *How do you
comfort someone who hears voices in her head, but not yours? Or they're
telling her not to listen to me? Or God's talking?*

Slowly, Jane stood up and placed one palm against the bullet-proof
window, then another. She placed her face between her hands on the
glass, as she and Louise had many summers ago at the Seattle Aquarium.
In the mysterious darkness of the aquarium viewing room, plastered to the
glass, the two little girls had been awe-struck by the sensation of being in
the tank with the sharks that swam swiftly by, a tattered wisp of food trailing from a sharp tooth, steely black eyes just inches away.

When the time came, Jane followed the ambulance to Eastern State
Hospital, legal offender unit, where people charged with a crime who
were determined to be mentally ill awaited their competency hearing.
Louise did not come around that day, and so Jane called her parents to
update them, and left.

The next day, Jane returned, was led by the nurse inside the sally port
giving entry to the ward. She stowed her purse in a wooden locker, the
nurse waved a metal detector over and around her, then unlocked another
door leading to the day room for inmates. Jane walked in. Behind her
sounded the ominous, loud clack of the lock.

She waited. There were no chairs outside the day room, and though
she had visited her sister in mental wards before, Jane felt uncomfortable
venturing into the midst of sociopaths and psychopaths alone. So she sat
on the worn checkered hallway floor, her back to the pale green wall. A
couple of nurses walked by, laughing, talking, as if there were nothing
unusual about working in a mental hospital.

Eventually, Louise came into the dayroom. Jane watched her through
the glass. She wore a blue cotton shift, shapeless, nondescript, except that
Louise wore it off one shoulder. On one foot was a slipper; the other was

nowhere in sight, and left bright, red toenails exposed. She circled the room like a dog lying down to rest, and finally lit on a couch, and smiled when Jane approached. During the night, apparently by medication or time, Louise had been restored.

"This ain't the Ritz! Bars on the windows, no cords on the curtains, everything's Velcroed. Worse part is I can't write in my journal. No pens or pencils. And no smoking. I saw this woman on her hands and knees on my way down here. The nurse tells her to get away from the wall socket and takes away her contraband pencil lead she's stickin' in there, tryin' to get a spark so she can light a cigarette. Jesus, buncha crazy people!"

Inmates lounged on couches and chairs around the room's two television sets, and the remainder idly surrounded the green table where two women were at a fast game of ping pong. A scene from a rec center at any park: the sharp tock, tock of the ball, the occasional exclamation of triumph or despair.

"Care to tell me what happened?" Jane asked at last.

Louise picked at a molten hole, a cigarette burn in the imitation leather couch. She looked up with a mischievous grin. "I sloughed him."

Jane broke into a startled fit of laughter. "You hit Logan?"

Suddenly animated, Louise acted out the scene, swinging visciously at the imagined Churlick.

"Found him at church, gettin' ready for service. Got him right in the nose. He just laughs, like I'm nothing," she said, indignant, hands on hips. "So then, I clocked him with my purse." She gave a quick, triumphant nod.

"Oh, Lou-*ise!*"

"Weighs about the same as a sledge hammer, I guess. He went flyin' backwards about three feet, slammed onto the floor. Yup, caught him by surprise with my overhand tomahawk jam." She demonstrated in a windmill of arms, then flopped back on the couch.

"*God*, Louise!" Jane said, and clasped her hands. "Wish I could've seen it. Tell me everything. Was there blood?"

"All over the place. Noses are like that, ya know. He's running around screaming for Dolores to call 9-1-1. Threatenin' to send my little ass to jail. He was gonna get me. Had blood in his eye. Literally. But whenever he'd get close, I'd just do the copter move with my purse." She jumped up, spun around, hands together, arms outstretched. "Messed up the carpet, the pews . . ." Out of breath, she plunked down again.

Jane marveled at her sister's uninhibited streak of violence. A crazy woman tripped into action by a man who deserved such insane wrath. "Must've been just awful for him," she said in mock seriousness.

Louise stated somberly, "Yes, it was."

They broke into uproarious laughter.

"Yeauh," Louise said, holding her breath like some cowboy sucking on a piece of straw, "He'll bruise up purty good."

The laughter was cathartic. The image of Louise swinging her heavy purse, the shock in Logan's eyes, him sprawled on the floor with blood oozing over his unavailing hands. Down payment, anyway, in the annals of poetic justice.

"What about Dolores? Was she upset?"

"Oh, I think you could say she was." Louise chuckled. "She screamed real hard and high, and her voice suddenly broke, kinda reedy-like." Louise screamed, "Get - out - of - here, you crazy lunatic! Sounded like the whistle on a cartoon train. She dropped the phone, had to redial. Couldn't get the words out. No one could understand that broken voice anyway. Ended up, he had to make his own damn 9-1-1 call."

She smirked, then shook her head. "Then, Bekah came outta nowhere, probably finally heard the commotion. She ran in and gave me the most hateful look I've ever seen. Said if I did anything to hurt her mother . . ."

Jane flinched.

"I told her this woman she called *her mother* was no better than a whore. An' Dolores was someone who justifies breakin' up a family because someone else has what she wanted. I told her, 'She's sittin' there gettin' the dirt on your sweet mother, *that you gave her!* Then this bitch blows it all up an' takes your side. She calls it *supportin' you!*' Then I marched right up to her hostile little ass and hollered, *Dolores* is the *enemy*, Bekah! They're BOTH CIA! Run for it! Save yourself! *Run, Bekah, run!*'"

Jane felt the bite of tears. Was it too late for Bekah? Would her daughter ever be herself again?

"Chased Bekah right outta there. Then said my good-byes to Mommy dearest . . ."

Suddenly, Louise hopped onto the couch, jumped up and down, fists balled. "Come on!" she shouted. "Come on, *Mom!* Isn't that what they call you? And the woman who gave 'em birth, you all call her Jane, right? Steal *my* sister's kids? I'm gonna get you, you home-wreckin' slut!"

Jane reached up and took her hand. Breathing hard, Louise sat back down. Jane considered all she had heard.

Louise gave her a tangle of details: Churlick's charge of assault, the competency hearing and what came after that. "You wanna know somethin'?"

"What?"

Louise stared off in the distance, her eyes taking in something only she could see, then she said, "It won't stop Churlick. You know that, don'cha?"

Jane sighed. "Nothing can stop him."

Louise seemed pleased that Jane understood. "Put the mark of the beast on him anyway."

Depressed, they grew silent, the sound of the ping pong game pock marking the complexion of their dreary thoughts.

"Know what bothers me most?" Louise looked at her, and for the first time, Jane saw fear creep into her sister's face. "Dallas. I think I finally did it. I think this time I scared him away."

"You mean jail?"

"No," Louise snorted, "Dallas is the kind of man who's seen the inside of a jail cell once or twice." She pushed her hair behind her ear and sighed. "No. This place. Now I'm certified nuts-o. I don't think he can handle having a girlfriend who's crossed the line into Wonderland."

"Are you sure? That doesn't sound like Dallas."

"I'm not sure, but I'd give it good odds. He's great in his own odd way. Since he really doesn't fit in genteel society either, he's entranced by moi. But he's what you might call shallow. I'm pretty sure he'd fly if he found out just how bad it is with me."

"Well," Jane said, "how's he ever going to find out?"

"While he was still freshly bleeding, the asshole called the papers. If Churlick's lucky, it'll be on the front page of the *Rathcreek Times* and the *Spokesman-Review*."

Jane's stomach plummeted. Louise couldn't care less about public condemnation, because she had already given up caring what the world thought. But had Dallas?

Louise said in a strained voice, "He's the best thing that ever happened to me, sis."

Thirty-Seven

Jane climbed the stairs of the Rathcreek Courthouse, not to fight her own legal battle, but as moral support for Louise as she faced Churlick's charges of assault.

On a bench in the hallway of the second floor, Louise looked chipper. The change in Louise since the six weeks she had been under treatment was noticeable at once. In the hands of a new therapist, she was more self-possessed than Jane had ever seen her after having recovered from an acute schizophrenic episode. Still the nervous wanderings of Louise's hands, but fewer.

When Jane asked what was different this time, Louise replied, "New drugs."

"I thought you hated drugs."

"Not these babies. Thought I'd done it all, antioxidants, B-6, niacin. Loved that rush—felt like I was goin' through the change! I've tried Thorazine, Compazine, magazine . . ." She chuckled. "Navane, Orap. And now . . . Moban." Louise's neck moved side to side. "Mo-ban, man—sounds kinda jivy, huh?"

"You know what I mean," Jane said. "There's something else." Schizophrenia had no cure, only a degree of control, and the hope that the bad episodes were separated by months of normalness. But she was encouraged by such a quick recovery, which had never happened after previous breakdowns.

"Yeah, there's something else." Louise's gaze shot down the hall. Jane turned to see a slender Asian woman striding toward them.

"Jane, Kay Reynalda, my shrink. Kay, Jane, the St. Bernard I told you about."

They shook hands. Louise and Jane moved down on the polished wooden bench outside the courtroom to make room for Kay, who placed a briefcase on her lap.

Louise winked. "Not to worry. Morita therapy's changed me, but I sure as hell ain't gonna start wearing a suit to the office."

Louise's appearance seconded the notion. Fire engine red lips. What she called her slutty red shoes. A multi-colored dress that looked like rayon by the swing of the fabric. All topped by a wide-brimmed hat. Also red.

"Morita?" Jane asked.

"Yeah, playin' ball on runnin' water. Morita is: what are you *doing*? Don't talk about your problem—what are you *doing* about it now? I felt like I couldn't *do* anything to change things like David, the CIA. Only two ways to go: give it up or have this tremendous ability to cope. I did the one, you did the other. Well, anyway, with Morita and this new stuff, Moban, man, it works for me."

"Seems to be working a little too well," Kay observed. "How much did you take?"

Louise gave her an ambiguous grin, then turned to Jane. "See how astute she is? And sweet baby Jesus! She's so friggin' good at what she does. If she wasn't wearin' the white coat, I'd swear she belonged on the inside, rather than out loose."

"Maybe I do," Kay chuckled. "Takes one to know one. That's not to say this recovery fixes everything. But you know you're not alone. Life gets garbled and distorted and everyone goes AWOL in varying degrees, especially during periods of stress."

"Everyone," said Louise, and lit up, hands out, fingers spread wide. "Hey! Maybe we should open up Eastern to vacationers, put in hot tubs, call it Scatter Brain Resort. Run stressed-out people through therapy, from the slightly cracked to flaming loonies. Recreational, occupational . . ." The intense gray eyes softened and she took in a delicious, carefree breath, let it out. "I learned things nobody ever taught me before."

"Like what?" Jane asked.

"Let's see, how did you say it, Kay?"

Kay shrugged. "Go ahead, you're doing fine."

Louise crossed her legs and flicked her stiletto heel. "Mmm. She says schizophrenics have trouble shifting gears when they get stressed, and stress triggers the really bad times. Normally, I'm sorta strange, ya know? But I get along. When bad times come, I don't know how I feel, how to act." She hesitated, "Or even . . . who I am. It's really scary. Ever since

David . . . I always felt so helpless to *do* anything. Seemed there were only two ways to go: the strength to cope, like you have, or totally undone, like me."

"Hooah!" Jane said. "I'm not so sure about that." A dead feeling drifted through her. Bekah's instantaneous metamorphosis into hateful brat outside the police station with Darcy following suit. And try as she might, she could do nothing to stop her girls from choosing Churlick. Jane felt about as far from strong as she could imagine. She was crazy with grief over the loss of her sweet daughters. Nothing strong there.

Kay's been teachin' me not to be so afraid, how to avoid stress, an' ways to cope when things are getting away from me, turnin' me inside out."

Kay said, "She's done marvelously. Now that she's trained to better see stressful situations coming, and with this new medication that suits her so well, she'll have more control to avoid psychotic episodes. We've even discussed the possibility of a low-stress job."

"A job?" Jane said. "Great! What do you want to do?" Even while she said it, she recalled previous attempts at working. Louise? Report to a boss?

Louise beamed. "I've already done it. Got my first rejection last week. But I got a real nice personal note." She dug through her purse. "*Not quite right for us. Enjoyed your very different perspective, though. Send along any other pieces you've got.* See? The world needs me, they just don't know it yet. I've always been a writer. An' with freelancing, I don't have to deal with an ugly overlord. Email, baby!"

"Writing?"

"Fiction, news stories, exposé, however the muse moves me."

Kay said, "She's reading, writing, working on craft. Taking it slow, no pressure. Mental health is an ongoing process, a whole lifetime of recovery."

"Yeah, a life sentence," Louise said. "She's always cheerin' me up like that. But I figure, hey, like nobody else has stress? You can do it, I can, too."

Louise's lawyer poked his head around the door of the courtroom. "Ladies? It's time." Jane liked his manner. Louise said Kay had recommended him, and like the psychiatrist, he was forceful, yet understated. Something about this attorney inspired confidence as Sanchez never had.

The women made their way into the courtroom and Jane asked, "What about Dallas?"

Louise paused. "I called when I was first admitted, told him I was going away for a while. Then, I chickened out, avoided the stress of dealing with him until this is over. I mean, what do I say, I'm goin' crazy, wanna come with me? Woulda been nice to see him today, though."

Louise walked into the courtroom, accentuated hips causing the dress to flow in kaleidoscopic colors around her. "Look, there's Mom and Dad. He said he'd try to get off work." She waved. "The troll's gettin' old, Jane. He's even talkin' you up over the CIA these days. Imagine that."

Jane stopped at the door. "Be back in a minute." And she dashed downstairs to a bank of phones.

Dallas arrived twenty minutes later. He crept in, tiptoed to the front row of benches and sat beside Jane, directly behind Louise. Jane could only guess at the speed barriers he had broken to get there.

He whispered, "Bo kept me posted. But I didn't want to screw things up if she wasn't ready." Jane nodded, relieved he could make it.

The judge was delivering a brusque statement to the defense counsel. Although the man at the bench had appeared, so far, to be fair minded, he was not of the opinion, he stated, as so many of his colleagues were, to turn a blind eye on accountability. The mildness of Louise's schizophrenia worked against her. To disagree with someone did not confer the right to violence.

Dallas frowned at the judge's words. Finger to his lips, he motioned to Jane for something to write with. She dug through her purse for a pen and small notebook.

Jane watched Dallas put the pen to his mouth and stare at the bright red hat before him. He began writing, stopping to listen to Logan's testimony or watch with dismay the gory color pictures presented showing the extent of the attack.

Dallas' note went on and on. Finally, he tore off the paper, handed it to Jane. Grinning proudly, he tapped the pen to the page, indicating she should read it. Dallas, always playing for the audience, like a certain stunt he had pulled for a houseful of people with a certain neon sign extravaganza.

To the Lady in Red,

I was just down the hall fighting a traffic ticket, and thought I'd drop in. I was in a hurry to get out to Eastern State Hospital to visit a friend. No sane woman could do the things this crazy woman does to me. She's ruined me for anyone else.

Anyway, after the siren and lights, I pulled off the highway—sorta. Left two wheels on the road. Told the officer I didn't have off-road insurance. So there he stood, plastered against my truck, cars whizzing by, asking to see my license. I rolled the window down a crack—it was raining—asked to see his badge. He got a little testy at that. But we finally made the exchange through the crack of the window. He copied down my number and I copied down his.

Anyway, that's how I got here today. Hope you don't mind my dropping in to be part of your cheering section.

Love, Dallas

He nodded toward Louise.

Jane leaned over the partition and tapped Louise's shoulder.

Louise took the note and returned her attention to the front of the court. Then the head dipped.

The bright red hat turned. Louise wore an expression of shock and delight, fingers straying uncertainly to her cheek.

"Dallas!"

"You told me you went on a trip."

Louise's gray eyes were merry. "Well? Isn't it?"

A slow grin spread over his face. "Take me with you."

In the end, it was obvious that Louise, a first-time offender who had been successfully treated by Dr. Reynalda, was not a danger to the public. Crowded facilities may have also been a factor. The judge suspended Louise's sentence, placed her on probation and ordered damages and continued treatment.

Thirty-Eight

First the kids, then Louise. Jane was hardly herself lately. It was April, four months since the court assigned the GAL to the case, and he refused to make a decision. Work was a distant third to Jane's daily dealings with the twins and Louise.

After lunch, the office staff gathered in the lunchroom to celebrate Grace's birthday. Middle aged and experienced at school district matters, Grace had taught Jane much that had resulted in her rapid advancement in the Superintendent's office.

"Who made the cake?" Grace asked.

Jane sliced up and dished out platefuls of cake to other staff and answered that Irene had rustled it up in her spare time.

"Rum cake, isn't it? Mahn, you got the gift," Grace said.

They ate and talked, and for a little while, Jane forgot problems outside the office.

Russ, from Finance, approached Jane. "Hey, I got a bone to pick with you. You know the consortium everyone went to yesterday? The one all the school and city finance people were *supposed* to go to?" Russ' voice was loud and angry enough to stall other conversations. Jane's stomach fell. She had sent out the meeting notices.

"Well, I wasn't part of it." Russ stood, cake in hand. "And you know why? Not because you didn't get a notice to me. No. I got it. Only it didn't say the consortium wasn't meeting in Rathcreek or even Spokane, where they normally do. By the time I drove downtown, then south to Spokane, then all the way to Moses Lake, where *someone* in the office told me it was, since you were at lunch by that time . . . it was over."

"Russ, I'm sorry," Jane said, glancing around. It was an important meeting. No denying the mistake was her fault. "I'm so sorry."

"Being sorry doesn't get me there. Screwed up again. You been doing that a lot lately." He turned and walked down the long hallway that led to his office. The room was quiet. Jane put her plate down, gave Grace a look of contrition and left.

At her desk, Jane forced herself not to cry. Shit, her whole life was turning to shit. Something had to break soon. How much longer could she hold everything together? She strode down the hallway to Russ' door, knocked, and before receiving a reply, entered.

"You've got some nerve," she said.

"What the hell is this?" Russ asked.

"You listen to me," Jane said. "I just want to know how all the *other* finance people made it to the meeting, despite my error. So I goofed. I'm sorry. Did you have broken arms? Couldn't pick up a phone and call the office earlier? I admit I made the mistake, all right? But yours was worse, Russ. You think because you're a boss you can take my screw-ups and parade them in front of everyone, humiliate me?" Her voice shook with anger. "You've got no right to do that. As if you never make mistakes."

Russ' jaw was set. He watched with a look that measured Jane's volatility. "Who are you, telling me how to behave, little secretary?" Jake would have called her that.

Jane planted her hands on the desk. "I'll tell you who I am. I'm the one necessary to your existence, little man. I'm the *position* in the office that types up your goddamned financial reports, pushes something you've generated from one side of my desk to the other, so that it sees the light. Without me, everything you do is meaningless. And I have feelings. I'm flesh and blood. Human, not divine, like some poor deluded suckers."

The tiny office was quiet. Then Russ said, "Jesus." He closed his eyes and shook his head. "Only a jackass would've made a public spectacle like I did out there. Sorry. I was mad. I should've never done it out there in front of everyone." He looked at her evenly, smiling a little. "You got balls, Jane. And you've been a damn good secretary, too. Even if you have been a little sketchy lately."

"Sketchy?" She sat in the chair. "You don't know the half of it."

Jane and Russ had a conversation that should have taken place months ago. Before she left, Russ told her that despite her screw-ups, she was the best secretary he had ever had, bar none. "So get this thing settled," he told

Jane on her way out, "and then get to work on that finance report for the Board I left on your desk this morning."

Later, Jane called Bo, who met her after work. Before they headed home to Bounty, Bolivar detoured into Spokane, to their favorite bookstore.

"Sky's the limit," he said. "Buy anything your heart desires. You deserve it after a day like today."

"*Anything* my heart desires? Like the Bible verse?" Jane mocked.

She walked down the aisles of Auntie's Bookstore, nosed through the psychology and philosophy sections, while Bo found *The Fifth Child*, a book he had always wanted to teach. With an armload of books, Jane moseyed around until she found a rocker.

Before long, the lights were flashing to signal the shop would soon be closed. Bolivar found Jane, laughing that even the flashing lights had not disturbed her, but she hardly heard him.

"Honey?" Bo said.

Jane felt as though she were on fire. She held up the book she was reading.

RELEASING THE BONDS
by Steven Hassan
America's Leading Cult Counselor

Like a spring thaw after a brutal winter, the book on mind control was the beginning of an avalanche of breakthroughs. Shortly after she discovered it, at the law library Jane unearthed something called *Parental Alienation Syndrome*. Another bingo. And this one had been used in court in the past.

Together, Jane and Bolivar read the book on brainwashing, which soon became a mass of dog-eared pages and highlighted passages. At last, hope. Their experience was defined and documented by an insider, himself brainwashed by religion, personality erased, identity stolen. Bekah and Darcy's victimization was no longer a mystery, and this single sober fact gave Jane and Bolivar a fighting chance to win their case in court.

The information on parental alienation detailed behavior of children alienated from one parent by the other, and its pages clearly laid the blame with Churlick. An ignorant observer would believe the girls' hatred of Jane was due to some hidden abuse. But the information, in fact, proved the opposite, cautioning the courts and psychiatric professionals *against* lending credence to the children's hatred and fear of Jane. The author warned against placing children in the home of their choice. To do so would risk permanent alienation from their victimized parent.

Like two hungry law students, Jane and Bolivar took their real-life case study to Oliver Sanchez, confident he could put together an unbeatable plan of action, regardless of Will Barry's recommendation. Sanchez took the material, but cautioned them that to pressure the GAL before he was ready would prejudice him against them. And to attempt to move forward without the advocate's recommendation was foolhardy. So they waited.

"I needed this night out." Bo leaned back in the plush seat of the Garland Theater.

Around them, the theater was filling, couples walking arm in arm in the dim light, and women of all ages, coming to see the classic, *Joy Luck Club*.

"Me, too," Jane said.

After the movie, they sat in the dark, emotionally wrung out. The house lights came up and young attendants collected trash in their giant plastic bags.

"How you doing?" Bolivar asked.

Jane blew her nose. "So sad. It's our story, sort of. The emotion, at least. They hate me and don't even know what's made me what I am. And all this time, I didn't know that Logan trashed their sweet personalities and turned them into what they are."

Outside, stars dotted the black night's yard. They hardly noticed people passing by. They walked to the Milk Bottle Cafe and ordered steaming cups of Americano, found a booth and watched the sparse traffic of Garland Avenue through the window.

"You think Bekah and Darcy will ever come around?" Jane asked.

"I don't want them back if they're *not* normal. That would be hell."

Anger and fear froze her insides. She snapped, "Don't you think I know that? Do you suppose I'd put you through it, or that I could stand to live with these hateful little fanatics forever?"

He seemed to compose himself before answering. "I'm saying it's destroying me to see you keep taking it. You're the kind of mother whose love is so good and decent, you'd let them break your heart. A man's gotta protect the ones he loves. I've quit loving them. There's nothing left to love . . . that leaves you. You're the only one I'm protecting anymore."

Jane understood only too well what he said, because it was written on her own heart. She was protective of him, also. The antagonism between them ratcheted down, until the look she sent him was returned by an uncertain smile.

"The parental alienation information says we have a chance if we get them out from under Logan's influence," she said.

"We *have* to get them out of Rathcreek. But even therapy won't get 'em back to normal if they go visit him every other weekend and in the summer. He'll keep love bombing 'em and telling them lies about you and using God to scare the hell outta them."

She ran her hands through her hair. "How can Logan do this to them?"

"He wants to win. Remember the mind control book? He's actually broken down the twins' personalities, given them a *new identity*. Logan's. Paranoid and fanatic."

Passages from the book could have been written about her daughters and their new identities. Neither the girls' intelligence nor their love had saved them from Churlick.

Bo took a swallow of coffee. "The author goes into it step by step. Even though we don't know what went on over there, now we know *how* he brainwashed them."

"I don't understand when Hassan says they have two personalities. And at war. With themselves? He talks about the submerged, real personality dropping hints, coming down with psychosomatic illnesses, having revealing dreams. If the real Darcy and Bekah are there, why can't they just—oh, hell." She wrapped her hands around the coffee cup. "Does brainwashing mean they could become like Louise some day?" Studies showed mental illness as hereditary. The thought was heavy on her mind.

"Don't worry about that. This is different. Louise is never going to be what you'd call normal, not completely. But the girls can be de-programmed, or desensitized, whatever the book calls it."

She shook her head. "I can't believe it, I almost forgot—Steven Hassan called me back today."

Bo gaped, then said, "Great. You found his number. Is he for hire?"

"No. He flies all over the country—kind of a cult buster. He's completely booked. He gave me the number of a man in Colorado. I called and we talked for a while. Then, I gave him Will Barry's number."

Bo grinned and kissed her lightly. "You've been busy."

"Yes," she said, then frowned. "But from what I could tell, talking to this guy in Colorado, there's something wrong about the way our lawyer's handling our case."

"What?"

"I don't know. But I have a phone appointment with Sanchez tomorrow."

"Have you had a chance to read the book yet?" Jane asked into the phone.

"Well, I've been very busy," Oliver Sanchez replied. "But, I've got it right here."

Her shoulders sagged. "It shouldn't take long. I've highlighted the important sections."

She was desperate for a commitment to a clear strategy, regardless of how the GAL's recommendation went. Four months. It had to end soon.

Holding the receiver with her shoulder, she flipped to a section. "How about if I read a quick passage or two?"

Reluctantly, Sanchez agreed.

"If we define mind control with Hassan's definition, then show how the girls changed abruptly to fit that definition, kind of a before and after . . ." She sounded lame, even to herself, a layperson telling a professional how to do his job.

"Listen to this: *above all*, it should be noted that mind control is *a very subtle process*. A person's beliefs, behavior, thinking and emotions are disrupted and replaced with a new identity. One that the original person would strongly object to if he or she knew in advance what was in store."

"Jane," the attorney said in a cross between patience and patronizing, "what you're saying may or may not be the case here. But you can't say your minister—"

"Ex-minister."

"Your ex-minister is running a cult, that he's brainwashing your kids. Is he having sex orgies? Any evidence of physical punishment or coercion? No. The courts aren't going to buy it. It's too far out."

"Okay, okay. We've agreed to call it 'undue religious influence' anyway, right?"

"Yes. But we still have the issue of constitutional protection of freedom of religion."

"But there are all kinds of references at the back of the book . . ." She flipped to the index. "'Mind Control or Intensity of Faith: The Constitutional Protection of Religious Beliefs,' *Harvard Civil Liberties Law Review*."

Silence at the other end of the line, then a rustling and a click.

"What was that?" she asked.

"What?"

"That noise on the line. Are you recording this?" Then, *My God, is my phone line tapped?* Jane admonished herself. She was becoming as paranoid as Logan.

He spoke stiffly. "No, it's not from this end. It would be unprofessional to tape conversations without informing a client, not to mention illegal."

Who else was home? Was Darcy eavesdropping?

Jane bid Sanchez good-bye. Impulsively, she ran to her daughter's room.

Darcy stood against the wall near her night stand, eyes wide with fright, plastic frog in her hand. Her guilty look told Jane all she needed to know. Jane grabbed the frog.

"That's mine!" Darcy shouted and lunged for it.

"Get back!" Jane shouted, gritting her teeth, and felt the barbaric part of herself. Pitted against her morality, the barbarian was willing to do anything to save her children, was ready to spring forth if she didn't control it. The other-Darcy backed away.

"A phone?" Her gaze followed the cord from the back of the flip phone she held in her hand, to the wall. When they had built the extra rooms, Jane specifically asked for phone jacks. What teenage girl could live without talking on the phone for hours to her friends? She had forgotten the decision until that moment. "You were listening."

"So?" Darcy folded her arms and plopped onto the bed.

"And your dad calls you every day, doesn't he?"

"You can't keep me from my dad. The courts say he has a right to call me."

Calls coming to her from Rathcreek every day. Forbidden, rotten, proselytizing.

"But not every *day!*" Jane shrieked.

She realized, then, there must be more. More evidence. Church materials, still making their way into her home. Memory verses. Evidence that would prove, as Hassan's book stated, that Logan was bombarding Darcy, subtly influencing her against her mother.

Jane yanked open dresser drawers. Darcy screamed. "No! What are you doing?"

After rooting through drawers, Jane went through the closet, until she found what she was looking for: a mountain of church material bundled in a corner. Enough memory verses pinned to the back wall of Darcy's closet to serve as map to all the uncharted regions of her alienation. Jane stripped the walls, to add the materials to her collection of incriminating evidence for the GAL.

Next, Jane knelt, opened the bottom drawer of Darcy's night stand, and stared, open-mouthed at hundreds of letters carrying Dolores' spidery writing. When had they come? How could such a heavy flow of correspondence go unnoticed? She gazed up at Darcy, dumbfounded.

"Those are mine!" Darcy raged, but stayed out of reach.

"How did you get them?"

Face flush with victory, she stared straight through Jane. "I cut school at lunch, picked up my mail and took it back with me."

"My God." Jane ran her hands through the letters. "Oh my God."

That night, when she couldn't sleep, Jane wandered through the house, until finally, she found herself in Darcy's bedroom.

By the hall light, Jane could see Darcy sleeping, her breathing regular. Angelic.

Jane sat on the edge of the bed, ran her fingers over the soft, full cheek, the line of her chin. "How's my girl?" she whispered.

Darcy's eyelids fluttered, then opened. The movement startled Jane, and she jerked her hand away, poised to retreat. She didn't want another scene.

Darcy sat up. Her face shone with a sweet, empty, night-smile. Bright eyes shone with love. In her dreamy trance, she held out her arms.

Jane, hardly allowing herself to believe in such a miracle, quickly, fiercely, took Darcy into her embrace. Jane's breath caught, she squeezed her eyes shut and savored the joyous sorrow of the moment.

Eventually, Darcy pulled away, dark eyes still wide and loving, smile radiant. Her look was so alert, Jane could hardly believe Darcy was dreaming. Finally, her daughter lay back on the pillow. Jane tucked her in and kissed her softly on the cheek.

A sob caught in her throat. A dream. Against the anonymous night, she didn't exist for her lost daughter. But Darcy *was* there.

She whispered, "Darcy, it's Mom."

There was a brief hesitation, the eyes fluttered open, the radiant smile again.

"I know."

"Look at these," Jane said, and opened the black binder to a section tabbed, *Alienating Letters, Etc.*

Oliver Sanchez leaned back in the leather chair, fixed his reading glasses and tucked in his chin as he scanned the correspondence. The stack was two inches thick, all in the same spidery script, all a variation on the same theme.

He flipped the pages. He turned to one on pink stationery. At the top in bright, bold letters was printed #1 Mom, and under it, There is no better friend than a Mother. He read aloud in a voice filled with disgust:

Dearest Darcy,

How's our girl today? Our call to you yesterday was so sad. But it'll get better soon, just you wait and see. Talk to Jesus about your feelings and about your desires. Listen to your music and read your Bible every day. The Lord is there with you and will help you, so don't be afraid.

Boo hoo hoo! We all miss you, even Bowsie. We love you very much, and Jesus does too. We're very proud of you. Remember, Jesus never fails, Jesus never fails. You might as well get thee behind me, Satan, because Jesus never fails. Keep your eyes on Jesus, sugar plum, the battle is the Lord's, not ours.

He's the one we'll stand before on Judgment Day. Keep serving Jesus with everything you have, no matter what anyone says.
Here's your Sunday school papers and your memory verse: "Seek ye first the Kingdom of God and its righteousness and all these things shall be added unto you." Matthew 6:33

Love, Dad & Mom

"Nauseating." Sanchez closed the binder and pushed it away.

"Can we get a copy of Logan's phone bill? How do we do that—subpoena?"

"Phone bill? What for?"

Every time I talk to this guy, it's like he doesn't know anything, she thought. "Remember? The GAL talked to him about limiting the number of calls. It's obvious now that Darcy's been getting these calls and letters from them all along."

"Yes, of course. I'll take care of it."

She held up the pages on parental alienation. "What do you think about this?"

He leafed through his copy, not answering right away. "How did you manage to dig this up? Nobody I've talked to has seen this stuff. Nobody. Legals or shrinks. By the time your case is finished, you'll have a law degree."

"I ought to." She got up and paced the office, which was crowded with too much furniture and not enough bookshelves. She went to the window and looked out.

"Well?" he said, "What strikes you?"

It irritated Jane that Sanchez always looked to her. She found a spot and read:

> The children of these parents are similarly fanatic . . . they share the parent's paranoid fantasies about the mother. They may become panic-stricken over the prospect of visiting their mother Their blood-curdling shrieks, panicked states, and hostility may be so severe that a visitation is impossible. If placed in the mother's home, they may run away, become paralyzed with morbid fear, or be so destructive that removal becomes warranted. Unlike children in the moderate and mild categories . . .

In a quiet voice, she said, "They've broken it into three categories: mild, moderate and severe. Bekah and Darcy fit the severest alienation."

Turning from the window, the interior seemed even darker. From a tote, she drew out a letter and handed it to him.

"Another one?" he asked.

"I found it this morning, before I called you. Apparently a hint from her alter ego. She left it where I couldn't help but run across it."

Dear Mom and Dad,

I hate Jane! I hate her so much I feel like killing her 1,000 times!! First she takes me away from you, and now she found my frog phone and took it away. She said I can't talk to you! She also found my memory verses and your letters and won't let me have them. It's getting so bad around here—I can't stand it anymore. I hate Jane! If I don't get out of here soon, I'm going to kill her or myself. Get me *out* of here! She makes my blood boil over! I hate you, Jane! I need you, Mom! Bekah was here last weekend and it helped, but not enough. I NEED YOU! I love you very, very, very much!!

Love, Darcy

Troubled, Sanchez lifted his eyes from the letter, but said nothing.

Without knowing she had come to a decision, Jane suddenly said, "What would the court do if I changed lawyers in the middle of all this?"

"Jane. You don't want to do that. Wouldn't be taken as favorable, that's for sure. Might be conceding that you aren't able to make a strong case. After four months, you're suddenly scrabbling to find - ah - someone who can work with these crazy accusations."

"Crazy, huh?"

"Well, you know what I mean. You keep trying to pin this man who has a high profile as a pillar in the community as a sleazy cultist, and *can't prove it.*"

"No, *you* can't prove it, Sanchez," Jane said, rising. "I'm the one combing the law library, the book stores. I'm the one who's turned up any evidence at all that can link our girls to this unheard of phenomenon in mainstream psychology and courts of law. You haven't done a damn thing. For which you'll be paid accordingly." She opened the door of his office. "You're fired," she said, and left.

Thirty-Nine

Jane met Bolivar at the courthouse, where the appointment with Will Barry was to take place.

"We're looking out for the girls' interests today, right? So we need to be civilized," Bo said.

She grinned. "Are you saying I'm too blunt for my own good? Not to worry. Today, sweetheart, I'm the friggin' Sphinx. And with a new attorney, maybe we'll get somewhere."

After making arrangements for Louise's defense against Churlick, Jane learned from Kay Reynalda of a book, *The Best Lawyers in America*, in which Oscar Sanchez was not mentioned. Hiring Arthur Vidal had pushed their credit cards to the max, but it was the only way they felt they had a chance to get their girls back.

Jane and Bolivar entered the conference room on the third floor and took their seats at the table. Jane was flanked by Bolivar on her right, Arthur Vidal at her left. Will Barry faced her. An uncomfortable feeling settled on Jane. She had grown allergic to legal maneuverings, whether in court or not. In her opinion, the upstairs lounge of the restaurant, Dewey Cheatum & Howe would have been a better meeting place. Some good wine and a pool table were all they needed to spread out the notebook bulging with letters, articles and notes that now lay open before the GAL.

Arthur Vidal was a large, square man. His face, through an amazing suppleness of the planes of his African-American features and expressive gold-brown eyes, complimented the mind that had shown itself thus far as strong and able.

Vidal said, "We appreciate your taking the time this week to familiarize yourself with parts of the Hassan book and the parental alienation article. You can see the way Jane's organized the letters in that notebook. And she has another important piece of information, from just yesterday, that bears on the timeliness of your decision. Our aim is to establish culpability in the alienation. Hopefully, we can come away today with a clear sense of how to act in the best interests of the children. After four months, it's time a decision was made."

Jane noted that in this dark-paneled, windowless courthouse meeting room, Vidal seemed in his element, an attorney at law, who could state that a decision must be reached and lay out the reasons why. She thanked God for her luck in finding him.

Will Barry recognized the significance of the letters at once. Leafing through the notebook, the GAL took his time examining them. Finally, he massaged the bridge of his nose, directed the lenses of his dark glasses at Jane. "This letter where Darcy wants to kill you a thousand times. I've said it before. I'd like to take her over my knee and spank her. You haven't done anything. These kids are blowing little things all out of proportion."

Vidal interrupted. "From everything I've seen, I agree. But it's much more than kids acting out. You're right, Mrs. Bernard hasn't done anything to create such hostility. And however hard it is to believe, Hassan's book and the alienation article make it abundantly clear Churlick has taken over their minds," Vidal stated. "These children aren't blowing anything out of proportion that he hasn't already programmed them to believe about their 'Satan-influenced' mother."

Vidal's remarks astounded Jane. She glanced at Bolivar, whose look told her he had heard it too. Finally.

"So convince me they aren't alienating themselves. *Prove* they're brainwashed," Barry said.

At once tense and expectant, Jane had been waiting for this moment, hoping Vidal could open new regions in this man's professional experience. Backed up by the golden words of brainwashing experts, they should be able to prove their point.

"Why don't you tell Mr. Barry what happened yesterday?" Vidal said to Jane.

"Well, Darcy wouldn't eat breakfast unless I allowed her to talk to her dad, and then, only if *he* told her she should eat. Since I discovered the phone she smuggled into the house, phone privileges are gone."

Vidal handed a subpoenaed copy of the Churlicks' phone bill to the GAL.

Jane continued, "So I told her she could choose not to eat, but she was still on restriction. Then I gave her an ultimatum: clean up her attitude by the time I got home from work, or she'd be cleaning windows. She went ballistic. She was *physically* different! Body rigid, eyes glazed over. Before she left for the Churlicks', it would've been impossible to imagine my sweet Darcy's face so filled with hate."

"All kids go through periods of intense feelings toward their parents," said Barry.

Jane said in a solemn voice, "I said she *looked* different. The school called later to ask if she were sick. She never showed up. Didn't come home last night. She's run away."

Barry frowned, shook his head, as if it shouldn't have happened.

"Kids don't hate their mothers enough to run away for window washing," Bo said. "They hate Jane because *he* made them hate her."

"Have you called the police?" Barry asked.

"Of course. We went over to Churlick's this morning. Police demanded he hand her over, and we brought her kicking and screaming home." Jane said ruefully, "My sister Louise is guarding her at the house right now."

Vidal continued. "The point is that now there's evidence of what's happened."

"What's happened has never been in contention," said Barry. "Can you prove in a court of law how the alienation happened?"

Jane tried to control the terrifying, sucking vacuum that threatened to take her. Of course no evidence had been uncovered tying Churlick to the alienation. Neither he nor the twins would ever admit to his poisoning them against her.

"You've talked to that specialist in Colorado, haven't you?" Bolivar asked.

"Yes. His name's Justin Smith," Barry said. "He called me, and I have to say I found little validity in his views. By his criteria, all mainstream religions are cults. They all contain elements of brainwashing. Let's take the love bombing he talked about: members make new converts feel loved and cared about, give them unconditional approval and surround them with church members who reinforce that message."

He spread his arms, grinned. "I'd guess every one of us here has engaged in brainwashing, if it's that simple." He tapped his pencil on the table, a steady, nervous Morse code that filled the silence. Jane looked at Barry sharply. After she had finally found a brainwashing expert, Barry was discrediting the subtle ways in which cult activities take place. Dismay ate at her.

"Be that as it may, no parishioners in my church are estranged from their loved ones," Vidal said. "I'd like to suggest Smith evaluate the girls, Mr. and Mrs. Bernard and the Churlicks. The Bernards have been searching for months for a qualified expert; Smith is the only expert they've been able to find with experience in brainwashing. He could assess whether undue religious pressure has been used on these children."

Jane squeezed Bolivar's hand under the table until he winced. His chin quivered when he grinned.

"I would consider doing that," Barry replied, "but I can't. Only a psychiatrist or psychologist's testimony can be used in court." He scanned the sheets on the table. "My notes say he's a counselor."

Vidal said, "So you're saying there's nothing we can do. The courts won't accept information from just anyone who hangs out a shingle and calls himself a therapist. It has to be a psychologist or psychiatrist."

Jane closed her eyes. Then to Barry she said, "So basically, we have no expert. And you still insist the 'smoking gun' doesn't mean anything? And that you'll never find a connection between my two zombie daughters and Churlick?"

"Frankly," Barry said, "every time I've met with Reverend and Mrs. Churlick, I've never seen anything but two attentive, caring parents. That's what's so puzzling."

Arrows, needles with giant eyes, dark-lined daggers covered the borders of Jane's yellow note paper. She looked up from the paper arsenal. "How can you chalk off a professional legal journal, where page after page of behavior looks like it was written about my daughters?"

"How can you ignore its advice?" Bo added, picking up the article and reading:

Well-meaning therapists sometimes give the advice to 'respect' the children's desires not to see the rejected parent. This is a grave mistake. Such removal will generally be detrimental to the children. —Let's see, I'm just giving you the flavor, now—Even telephone calls must be strictly prohibited, because there's the danger of using the phone for programming the children.

While in the father's home, the children are going to be exposed continually to the bombardment of denigration and other influences that contribute to the perpetuation of the syndrome. Accordingly, the first step toward treatment is removal of the children from the father's home and placement in the home of the hated parent.

The court's therapist must have a thick skin and be able to tolerate the shrieks and claims of maltreatment that these children will provide. If the court is naive enough to allow the children to remain living with such a disturbed father, they'll be doing these children a terrible disservice. It is likely there will be lifelong alienation from the mother."

In the silence that followed, Jane hoped the Guardian Ad Litem was absorbing the full impact and the terrible seriousness of the decision he must make.

She said, "That notebook in front of you is full of letters calling me Jane, while Dolores calls herself Mom. The Churlicks phoned several times a day for months to keep things stirred up. They imply we're an enemy to fight, and with the help of the Lord, they'll win. I'm going to hell because I'm not a Christian. For crying out loud, Logan baptized me! Yet, my daughters say I'm not a Christian because I don't go to their church, because I believe in a woman's right to choose abortion." She said slowly, through her teeth, "If these things don't prove he's turning them against me, *what does it take?*"

Barry was silent a while, then his tone was unemotional, professional, and it filled her with fear. "Both sides make accusations about the other in cases like this. I base my decision on what I see and hear, and I haven't seen any behavior of the Churlicks' that could cause alienation of your children."

"Do you think I've alienated them?" She held her breath.

"No, but I don't deal with probabilities, I deal in realities. What I see and hear. So far, all I've seen is their love. I see the Churlicks taking time out of their busy lives to go to school functions, take Darcy and Bekah to church . . ."

"And turn those girls against their mother," Bo said. "My wife should be talked up to those children whether she's an atheist or a sun worshipper. Logan's poisoned them, saying they'll go to hell if they stay with her."

Barry said, "Logan claims he doesn't have power over them. Says he only backed up their decision to stay with him. He can't get them to come back, I can't. I've tried."

"He laid the groundwork years ago," she cried. "When he told my girls they're in a battle, and God's on their side. And me? I'm the poor pawn of the devil, never mind that until Bekah and Darcy cracked, until they went zombie, those girls loved me with all their hearts. Logan twisted their beliefs years ago in a web of nightmares and stomach aches when they were toddlers. According to him, Satan and demons are real, and they've invaded my brain, got their talons in me, because I *think* I'm a Christian, but I'm not. So here's your fine father, trying his best to get them to cooperate with me. Logan will *tell* you he begged them to come and visit—but he's already done everything he could to make sure that doesn't happen."

Will Barry sighed. "All I'm saying is Logan has a right to raise his daughters according to his faith. Nothing can change that, not even that article on parental alienation; which, by the way, carries no weight at all in a court of law."

Jane was stunned. "What do you mean?"

"I mean it's a study, a piece of paper. A judge won't accord any weight to a so-called alienation syndrome, if you have no expert—a living, breathing expert—who can testify there's a connection between that syndrome and your daughters."

"You trashed our expert," she said. "So now it's your job."

"I have limits to my expertise, and this is outside them. I've done all I can to locate a qualified professional who's had experience with this. I've done my best—truly. But, there's just no one with the proper credentials out there. Including Smith in Colorado."

Jane was about to strike back, but something stopped her. She wasn't ready, yet, to jeopardize their relationship with the GAL. Will Barry, appointed by the judge, was the person who could help get her daughters back.

"You don't understand what you're doing," she said softly. "You don't take a mother's children away. You sit here and talk about how Logan has the right, but these are my *children*. I'm a good mother, a very good mother. How can you say what's happened to my kids is okay? They're like zombies, even their personalities have changed. The book and article on alienation say *he's* the culprit, even though nobody can see it. The fruits, Will, the fruits of his actions."

"This isn't getting us anywhere," Barry said wearily, and glanced at his watch.

"Will, just listen—" Bo began.

Something snapped inside Jane, and the leash tethering her civility flapped behind as she slid down into the chaotic room of emotion, walls bulging with hot words.

"Christ, Bo," she shouted, "can't you see what this - this, advocate is saying? He's saying he's too chicken shit to make a moral decision."

Bo opened his mouth, grabbed her hand under the table. He looked at Barry, then Vidal apologetically. With the patronizing sting of her husband making amends for her, Jane slipped a little further into the structure of her trembling emotional balance.

Vidal said, "This is a very stressful time . . ."

"It's okay—" Barry began.

"No, it's not okay, you asshole. That's what I'm saying. It's not okay to just wash your hands of us." She turned to Bo. "Can't you see? He's got all the information he could ever hope to have to make an informed decision 'in the best interest of the girls.' Letters, hell, hundreds of letters. Camp letters: we love you, Mommy. Alienating letters: I want to kill Jane a thousand times. That kind of annihilation of personality is almost a direct quote out of Hassan's book."

She rounded on Barry. "Do you know I lock our bedroom door at night? Ever read about kids like this who attack their parents while they sleep?" Her voice cracked in bitter laughter, "And here's the insane part: I'm not afraid of dying—as much as I'm afraid Darcy's going to prison!"

"Jane." Bo put a hand on her arm. "We're not here to work against Will. We're here to help him do the right thing."

"No!" she said. "No, he's not going to do the right thing. He's already told us that. He hasn't got the balls to stand out there alone. Not with the expert we put him in touch with, or all the information in every book or article ever written. No, he sees Logan and Dolores as credible witnesses with a respected attorney, who'll cause the judge to question ol' Will's professional judgment." Her voice rose, quavering, gathering, fueled by an anger that would not be controlled after being held back so long. "This thing on cults or mind control, or whatever you want to call it, is just too weird. Or is it too close for a Mormon?"

Bolivar gave her a morose look. Vidal just stared.

Barry fixed her with those bleak, tinted eyes, confirming the end had come.

Jane teetered on a fine edge. Or had she already gone over the edge? The freedom was terrifying. She had insinuated that Will Barry could not, would not, come to a conclusion in their favor because he was Mormon, a member of a religious group whose history was sprinkled with charges of cult influence.

Jane realized fate had brought them all here. God had brought these points together, their do-nothing lawyer, then valiant Vidal, but most importantly, the cowardly GAL. No matter how much evidence she had, how much she pleaded for him to see the evil the Churlicks committed, nothing could prevent her girls' destruction.

In that moment of utter despair, Jane decided she would do the only thing she could think of to save Bekah and Darcy. It was a decision that made her soul quake.

Forty

Jane sat in Arthur Vidal's office. The office reflected the man: books from counter to ceiling along one wall, bound in red leather, neatly arranged. Two leather chairs faced the large desk. "What can we do, Arthur?"

Vidal rested his chin on folded hands and was silent. "I've had only one other case like this. They are rare. In that one, a young boy's mother lived in Texas, his father here. We did everything we could, but ended up giving her full custody. Tragic. Felt we had no choice, considering how far gone the situation was."

"What are you saying?"

"Jane, you're sending me mixed messages here. You say you want to do whatever you can to save your children from a nervous breakdown. Then you want me to go after them, when we know it's virtually impossible to win."

"But why can't we win?"

"I can spend every last penny you have, put you into debt—"

"I don't care! Can you get them back?"

"No. I can't make that promise. I can possibly be successful at persuading the judge to go against the GAL's recommendation. But even then, without the expert testimony on your behalf to tie the end result to their father . . ."

"I'll drag Steven Hassan here by my teeth, if I need to."

"In what—six months? And by that time, how far gone will your children be? How much more guard duty is Louise capable of? It boils down to this, Jane. The twins are twelve years old now. They're of age. According to the courts, they can choose to live with either parent. That's Churlick's trump. They've made their choice."

"No, they *haven't*. He's made their choice for them."

"In the end, you can't save them if they don't want to be saved."

Tears welled up. Her voice was helpless with grief, and it was everything she could do to smother her sobbing. "Then why did I bother to get a new lawyer?"

"I know mothers. You wouldn't stop unless you'd come to me. You had to hear this from someone who's been through it, so you could trust there was nothing left to do. There's nothing left to fight with. Trust me."

Trust? Was there any left in her? Why hadn't she fled with her sweet daughters when there was still time? When they wouldn't have taken the first opportunity to contact their father to rescue them. An old fantasy. She had been through it a thousand times. Oh God, how had it come to this?

And after all these months, what did she feel? She had loved her daughters, more than her own life. But now? Now, if she were able to face the truth, she would know that after all the large and small attacks of these monsters against her mother's heart, without realizing it, even such a love was turning to hate. But she did not know this yet. The love she held onto over-rode everything, and that deep part of herself, to preserve that love, was telling her to let go, before she could have no other feeling toward Bekah and Darcy but hate.

Arthur's voice brought her back. "There is one way. The reason you came today."

She stared at him, afraid, knowing what he would say.

"You can save them by giving them up."

"I know," she sobbed. "I already faced that choice. I'm - I don't know if I can go through with it."

"Lots of families are religious. They've got a chance to live a somewhat normal life if their father doesn't need to scare them, if he quits ripping their psyches in two."

Jane shivered, dread tingling through her from throat to groin. "You're asking me to sacrifice them, too, not just me. They won't be normal coming out of *that* house."

"How normal are they now, believing they're headed for eternal fire and damnation if they're loyal to you? Severe psychological disorder's what they've got so far. Screaming to the GAL they want nothing to do with you, yet part of them wants nothing more than to be with you, even if it means hell. How much more can they take?"

Jane plucked a tissue from a box on his desk. She thought about her sister's fragile mental health, her mother's sacrifice for Jane when she had wanted a divorce. Who knew what would put her girls over the edge?

"I know what you're saying. Every book and legal paper I've read says my little girls won't come back . . ." She broke off into hard crying. Then, voice barely holding together, said, "How can I desert them?" And in her most hallowed recesses, where her heart had healed after Rathcreek, and faith had flourished after leaving The Fellowship, a faith that went hand-in-hand with reason, she asked, *How could God desert us?*

The following day, Jane sat in Arthur Vidal's office again. Bolivar was with her.

The attorney spoke into a phone to an assistant, hung up. Then to Jane, said, "It's a hard decision. It's the most heart-breaking part of my job, drawing up papers, seeing the parent who's best for them give up the children."

In a few moments, there was a knock on the door, and a legal assistant brought in a sheath of paperwork, then left. Vidal handed the adoption papers and a letter addressed to Churlick's lawyer to Jane to read.

A fresh flow of tears blurred her vision. She touched a wadded ball of tissue to the corner of one eye, then the other. It all felt so unreal, to be holding in her hands the papers that would, by law, cut loose the daughters she was tied to by nature. But the tears would not let her read. She handed the letter to Bolivar, who read aloud.

Jane's head jerked. "New birth certificates?"

"I'm afraid so," said Vidal

"But why?" Bo said. "It's just cruel."

Vidal studied Jane. "Second thoughts? Are you sure you're ready to go through with this?"

"I love them! I'll never be ready. You said if Churlick adopts my girls, he won't tear them apart trying to get to me. And I know you're right. But adoption means I'll be completely obliterated as their mother. You didn't tell me that. *I* gave birth to them, not her. Their original birth certificates should stand. This isn't the same as a teenager giving up a newborn. I raised my girls for twelve years."

"It's just the way it is. It's part of the process," the lawyer said gently.

She took the document from Bolivar that would wipe her out, not only from her daughters' future, but from their past as well. It was agony. These papers rearranged history, they were a lie.

He answered her other questions about "lawful issues," "testamentary disposition" and other language she was not familiar with. Then she read the letter.

Dick Moore, Attorney at Law
Re: Bernard v. Churlick

Dear Dick:

Please be advised that I have now been retained to represent Mrs. Jane Bernard. I have enclosed a copy of my substitution of counsel.

In view of the circumstances that are involved in this case, my client has decided, much to her regret, that the best interest of the minor children would be best served if they were legally adopted by Mr. Churlick and his present wife. This is strictly confidential, however, and must not be divulged to your client until after a final meeting is arranged between my client and the children. I will call to work out details.

This decision was reached, not out of any denial of love or degree of self interest. It is solely a recognition that the children have been so alienated from their mother that it would be an engagement of futility to continue this struggle, and it would generate more hatred than affection. I commend Mrs. Bernard on her decision. It requires the courage and wisdom of Solomon, and most people I know are too selfish to do what Jane Bernard is doing.

This is conditioned upon the adoption being filed forthwith and completed as quickly as possible. In view of the fact that a Guardian Ad Litem is already in existence in this case, he should stay involved and prepare the necessary post-placement reports.

Sincerely,

VIDAL LAW OFFICES, P.S.
Arthur Vidal

Jane wadded the tissue, dabbed her eyes and gazed out the window at the gray afternoon. She handed back the letter. Arthur picked up the phone and called the Guardian Ad Litem.

Will Barry made arrangements for Jane to see Bekah and Darcy one last time. No explanation was given to Logan, other than the GAL required the meeting to conclude his findings. It was set up to be a single, supervised visit held at a place of the Churlicks' choosing. Both girls had been living with Logan for the previous two weeks, since Darcy's second run away attempt. Jane and Bo agreed there was no sense in bringing her back to Bounty.

On the day of the meeting, Jane pulled into The Fellowship parking lot. The church of her youth was much more than the last time she had seen it. The familiar building had new additions, and sprawled over a half-acre lot. Narrow stained glass windows lined the main chapel. On the new steeple, a thin metal cross replaced the old wooden one. What used to be gravel was covered with smooth asphalt. And the tree, the lightning rod, was in the process of being removed. Two workmen hacked pieces of it off with their chain saws, threw them into a chipper.

She pulled into a space next to the Churlicks' new Mercury. The girls stood at the entrance to the church with Logan and Dolores. Heads bowed, they were praying.

Jane's father sat next to her, squeezed her hand. "Looks like they all showed up."

Joe had offered to accompany Jane and she gladly accepted. Logan and the girls had vetoed Bolivar's presence, and Louise had declined, saying she would be glad to come, but could not guarantee there wouldn't be a fracas, which could jeopardize her return to civilian life. She was determined to serve her stint at community service so that she and Dallas could take off on an extended vacation in June.

"I'm nervous," Jane said. "I don't know what to expect."

Her father got out of the car and came around, opened the car door. "Ready, Jane?" His eyes were bright with emotion, the corners of his mouth turned down in firm resolve. He nodded. They walked toward the Rathcreek Fellowship of the Holy Bible.

Her father patted the arm that was linked with his, and in his voice was an unaccustomed tenderness. "I want to tell you how proud I am of you. This is the dirtiest thing in the world. We've had our differences, but that's done now. I don't know how—" He drew in a breath and bunched up his chin. "I love you, Janey."

"I know." Then through tears, she replied, "I love you, too."

They reached the building and Jane said, "Where are the girls?"

"Why the tears?" Logan asked, then when he received no reply, said, "They went to wait for you inside." He held out a hand. "Good to see you, Joe."

Joe gazed coldly at the extended hand, slowly raised his eyes to Logan's face. "We have nothing to shake about."

Logan took it silently, but seemed surprised at the solidarity aimed against him.

Jane's father waited in the lobby while Dolores led her and the girls to what was called the Prayer Garden, a new structure off the rear of the main chapel. Gloating, she walked, one arm around each girl, leaving Jane to trail behind.

Darcy whispered to Dolores, who searched her pocket and pulled out a stick of gum. Dolores moved to follow the girls into the room. Jane stepped between her and the doorway. Round face inches from her own, an impasse.

Jane murmured, "Why don't you go into church and talk in tongues, you home-wrecking slut, because you're not coming in here. No evil in the garden today."

Startled by the fierceness of Jane's voice Dolores stood frozen, then called to the twins over Jane's shoulder.

"It's okay, sweetie lambs, your dad's already turned on the alarm, so there's no way for her to leave without us knowing. And remember, Jesus is with you. He'll protect you." With quick steps, she hurried down the hall.

Jane gaped in amazement after her, waited for the humiliation and outrage to wash through her. Fresh reminder of why there was no other way. She closed the door and approached the twins, wondering what she had gotten into.

Darcy regarded her with raw anger. Her eyes were stony, lids drooping insolently, arms crossed. Bekah's gaze was fixed on the floor, and she twisted a strand of hair. Jane realized with sadness that they had not made even the suggestion of a greeting. She hadn't either. The old pattern of defense was already in place.

An overpowering emptiness seized Jane and she longed to embrace them. She swallowed. They sat in the uncomfortable silence of the room, she shut off from her daughters, and they from the mother who loved them so much this moment was killing her. From far away, the chain saws roared, the howl changing pitch when the blade bit into the wood.

"How are you?" Jane asked.

"Fine." Bekah's gaze flickered up, then returned to the floor.

Darcy said nothing, but chewed her gum.

"It's good to see you . . ." She stopped, the emotion too much. Good was nowhere near what Jane felt, good was a shadow of the joy she felt simply to be with them. She steadied her voice. "I can't believe how tall you are. Almost as tall as I am."

Bekah gave her a blank smile, then stared across the room at a spot on the far wall. Jane was miserable, but the misery injected her with new energy. "You can look at me, you know. I'm not going to bite. And I'm not going to take you away. I just wanted to talk with you one last time. Let's just relax, okay?"

"What do you mean?" Darcy asked.

Jane studied them, drinking up the changes time had brought to her little girls. They were on the verge of becoming women. Bekah's face had lengthened, the roundness of childhood was gone. Her cheekbones gave her a classic loveliness. Light brown hair brushed her shoulders and she wore wispy bangs to the side, framing her hazel eyes. She wore the leather jacket Jane and Bo had given her for her birthday.

Darcy's permed hair fell loosely past her shoulders. Thick bangs shadowed eyes peering out from their protective blind. Her loathsome stare wounded Jane's fragile courage. Darcy was beautiful in a way anger couldn't hide, strong brows, black eyes, like her father's. Scorn on the full lips. An orange tee shirt had the name of her new school on the pocket, and she pulled at the gum in her mouth, bringing the string out and chewing it back, bringing it out, chewing it back, until Bekah elbowed her and said, "*Dar*-cy."

"What I mean is I wanted to see you one last time, before I went out of your life."

"You mean the GAL's made a decision?" Darcy said, seeming pleased to hurt her.

"No, I have." Then she asked, "You call Dolores 'Mom' and me, 'Jane.' I haven't been Mom in your eyes for a long time now, have I?"

They shook their heads, definite. Her soul grew heavy with the truth of the situation, with the futility of any further fighting to save these souls she had created of her own flesh who would not recognize her. The pain was infinite.

"The reason we're here today is that I'm giving you up for adoption to Dolores. I'll be out of the picture and you can be with Logan and Dolores for good."

There was a stunned silence.

"What's the catch?" Darcy asked.

"No catch. I've already signed the papers."

"You'd give us up just like that?" Bekah snapped her fingers. "No strings?"

The girls exchanged pleased glances.

Nodding, Jane watched them closely, and saw by the twins' silent communication that more than anything, they yearned for their fantasy family. They had been praying for this miracle.

"I'm giving you up because I think it's the best thing for you. You may find this hard to believe, but I'm doing it *because* I love you. We can't go on any longer this way."

In a voice filled with contempt, Darcy said, "If you love us so much, why are you putting us up for adoption?"

Jane stared at the angry child and held back a sob. Was her daughter, her dreamy-eyed daughter, speaking again? Now the sorrow was too much to bear. She wanted to take Darcy in her arms and say, *How's my girl?* and hear her say in her groggy morning voice, *Grrreat!*

No, this blame was simply another way to hurt Jane. Months of alienation stood between her and the little girl of those mornings. A hostile, bitter Darcy glowered.

"I'm giving you up because you both divorced me a long time ago." Her own bluntness shocked Jane.

"That's right," Bekah said. "When you married Bo, you divorced us."

"That's not true!" Jane cried. "Your dad's the one who made you feel like you had to choose between us."

"You used us to get back at him."

Logan again, twisting things. Anger boiled up. Again, Jane was to blame, always would be to blame *if she were in the picture*. And that was why she could not be.

She said tiredly, "It's time the war was over."

Darcy was quiet, eyes averted. Bekah stared at her sister and played nervously with her hair.

"You're being pulled back and forth, until you rip apart. It's gone too far." Suddenly her voice broke, "I don't want to see you ripped apart. Understand?"

Darcy chewed her gum furiously. "Oh, we understand."

Jane did not avoid the hard eyes, and she nodded at Darcy, head barely moving. She thought of how much grief Darcy would have, carrying her anger for years, perhaps, which would blind her to the need to forgive herself for cruelty to her mother, and to forgive her mother and Bo for being human. Jane longed to protect the quiet, auburn-haired girl from the pain, but knew she couldn't.

"Do you have any idea how hard it is for me to let you go? You can't imagine how much love I have for you."

Saying the words to her beloved daughters, their last moments together in this forever good-bye, so intense, overwhelming, she almost couldn't speak. She listened to the words emerge from a bottomless place that used to be her mother heart. Tears rolled down her cheeks.

Bekah, too, was touched. Tears splashed from her chiseled cheeks, and long, slender fingers wiped at them, first one eye, then the other.

The sight shocked Jane. Did Bekah still have feelings for her at some deep level? Yet, even if the shock of her news to them were to break loose an emotion momentarily true, she knew as soon as Bekah left the sanctuary of the Prayer Garden, Logan and Dolores would fill her with poison again.

"I didn't want to cry today," Bekah said.

"What do you mean? If you can't cry today, the last time you'll see your Mom, when *can* you cry?" She touched Bekah. "You can't imagine how much. There's no words that can describe . . ." she collected herself. "There's no piece of paper that'll ever change the fact that you are my children. I'll always love you." Then, fiercely, "Always."

Jane wondered how she could ever forgive herself. Two reflections, one dark-eyed, the other light, two halves that made up the whole of her reason for being.

Darcy stood, hostile and edgy to be gone. Stiffly, she allowed Jane to hug her, then left the Prayer Garden. Jane turned to Bekah. The hazel eyes so like her own were green from crying.

Jane gathered her daughter into her arms, and felt Bekah's breathing. Felt the heavy leather jacket over the thin frame, put her nose into the silky strands of hair. Sweet, tangy perfume. Jane hungered to remember everything about this moment. Then she held Bekah at arm's length to memorize everything. How tall she was. The particular color of her eyes, the wetness of her smooth cheeks, the pink of her lips, the fair skin, the soft angle of sunlight from the window, bathing her in its light. It was all she had.

Forty-One

Jane stepped out of the dusk of the Prayer Garden and walked down the long hall toward the light. Her father waited for her.

Logan, Dolores and the girls joined them, and the light threw their heavy shadows against the wall. They all watched to see the effect of the meeting on Jane. Logan's righteousness, Dolores' arms enclosing Bekah and Darcy, girdling them against sin. Darcy glared. Bekah's cheeks were dry now.

Jane felt invisible walking among them. Bekah and Darcy were not hers anymore. The thought of never seeing them again made her light headed. She felt an other-worldliness, as if everything in her life had led to this moment.

She looked at her watch. "It's time, Dad."

He nodded and left.

"Time for what?" Logan asked. "What's going on? The girls were talkin' some nonsense, an' I couldn't make sense—"

"Patience. It's the Good News, as you like to say."

Dolores stood tense, arms protecting her girls.

"By the way," he said, and cleared his throat in an escalation of post nasal hacking. "I went to put their stuff in the trunk. Your dad told me to load all of it in there. Looked like everything they owned. What's that all about?"

Dolores tightened her grip on the girls, shoulders rigid.

It occurred to Jane that for people who believed they were covered by God's grace, Logan and Dolores were more riddled with fear than anyone she knew; and out of their complexes, more dangerous than any atheist.

"I think we all know it's over," Jane said. "Both girls want to live with you. They call Dolores, here, Mom." She turned to her. "How'd you like to be their mother legally?"

Dolores, attempting ingenuousness, blinked several times. "What do you mean?"

"I mean I've signed papers terminating my parental rights—I'm giving them up to you for adoption. If you want them."

Dolores blinked again, turned to Logan, smug victory in her face.

The girls broke away and gathered around him, chanting, "Yeah! Yeah!"

When he said nothing, Dolores sputtered to life. "Yes, of course I want 'em! We sure do want 'em, don't we, sugar bear?"

At his look, her face fell. She rubbed a fleshy arm, shoulders rounded, defensive, as if she had been tricked.

Logan was pale, mouth a stark line. He stared at Jane, wide-eyed.

Bekah grabbed his hand. She yanked and hung on it like lead weight, needing his affirmation. Absently, he shook her off.

She took hold again and chanted. Darcy joined in. "Do it, Daddy, do it! Do it, Daddy, do it!"

He roared, "Shut the fuck up!"

They let go, faces wreathed in astonishment. An involuntary little bleat of a cry escaped from Darcy, but Logan, so focused on the cataclysm facing him, didn't even bother to excuse himself or cover up the word. Perhaps had not heard himself utter it.

His voice trembled. "What's this? What're you sayin'? You're their mother . . ."

"No," Jane answered. "She's their 'Number One Mom.' Right, Dolores?"

Dolores did not respond.

Churlick cried, "How can you talk about orphaning our daughters?"

Jane didn't answer, but came forward to the table in the foyer decorated with Easter lilies. The skylight above opened the ceiling, and the sun streamed in. Bathed in its light, she touched one of the lilies. A deep red garnet, her wedding ring, sparkled. Jane's only jewelry, a part of her.

Joe Crownhart entered with Will Barry.

The Guardian Ad Litem greeted them, snapped opened his briefcase, rummaged through it, then began laying out documents. He brushed the yellow pollen off the table.

Jane said to Logan, "Maybe you and I should discuss this privately."

Bewildered, Logan followed her into the sanctuary. They seated themselves in a pew out of earshot.

He whispered, "What kind of garbage is this? You think you can scare me?"

"You're terrified, Logan," she said grimly. "You've won."

"You're some kind of mother. You'd give up your children, for what? To choose him over me?"

"I don't know what's going to happen to Bolivar and me." She thought of her self-imposed isolation, her trek into the wilderness of her vast interior, a place where Bolivar couldn't follow. She emerged a solitary figure. Bolivar could never take the place of her children. The idea of not touching Bekah and Darcy again, not filling them with her version of truth, with the kindness, tolerance and resilience that made for strong, principled people. The idea they would now resemble Logan and Dolores. *This* was why she had brought them into the world? The irony of her decision to bring them into such an existence. Even now she didn't regret it.

The *Nnniiiyinnngg* of the chain saw rang out. She looked out the narrow window. A large limb of the split oak fell and the ground shook, the windows trembled. The old dead half was already disposed of. The great oak's trunk had been cut back enough that she could see even the good part of the tree had finally become rotted from exposure to disease or insects boring into the soft, unprotected flesh. The raw April wind whipped the tree's starched, brown leaves, still clinging to the limbs in their death grip. Suddenly, the massive half trunk squeaked, teetered, then crashed to the ground.

With the gashed-opened oak disposed of, Jane could see grass on the hillside. An exuberant expanse of green. As if she were seeing creation's personality. Earth's covering, lush and lime-green, bursting with new life, hurt her eyes.

"Jane. Listen to me." Logan ran his hand through his hair, and the fingers trembled.

She noticed, then, the crooked set of his nose, the jagged scar Louise had marked him with. The broken nose had healed, but he still had the raw line of the wound. The crepey skin around his eyes was tinged with the last yellow of the faded bruise.

"This isn't right. You got me all wrong. It's not what I wanted. All I ever wanted was to fulfill our union, the thing God started in us. You, me and the kids happy, together. You can't just leave me with Dolores and those girls. *It'll drive me crazy.*" His voice grew more frantic. "It's *you* I live for, Jane. You're my only love. I'll make you happy, I swear. We're not so different."

She ran a hand along the fine wood grain of the pew. Arm outstretched, blood red garnet at the end of it. "You're wrong, Logan. There's a huge difference between us. I believe the Bible when it says Jesus was first a teacher."

Churlick's hand kneaded his mouth.

She continued, "But you've always acted like Christ was, first, an insurance salesman. You and the insurance companies. Anyone has a claim, like Dolores? Like my girls, who've lost their minds? You cancel 'em. You are the slime of the earth."

Logan drew air into quivering lips and faced the nightmare he had brought to life. An almost palpable mental darkness gathered and surrounded him. His face. His terrible face, anguish coating it like a thick, black grease. And he was backlit by the incredibly bright light outside the narrow stained glass window.

"That's crazy! Insurance?" he cried. He leaned toward her, as if the terror of his life, beyond any human comprehension, scorched him. "You're the sleazy one. Give up your own flesh and blood! Why?"

"You still don't get it, do you? It's not my choice, but theirs. They've already left me." She pointed toward the vestibule, and his gaze followed her outstretched arm. Will Barry gathered the girls to him, squatted to be at their level. Dolores was stooped over the table signing something. Will finished reading a paper to the girls and laid it on the table. He asked something and they nodded. Then he gave Darcy a pen.

"What's he doing? What're they signing?"

"My attorney told the GAL I'd give up my parental rights of the girls so he could recommend to the court that you and Dolores be given full custody." Again, she watched the shock roll through him. "If, for any reason, you decline Will's offer, then full custody reverts to me."

He was half out of his seat, rigid, as he watched Bekah sign the document, jaw moving in small jerks, as if to speak. But he was too unnerved to string words together. When Bekah finished, he slumped back in stunned silence.

Jane saw that Logan could never imagine a love so great it would sacrifice itself—and that was what had defeated him. He could never know such a love.

The black eyes filled with tears, brimmed over in genuine anguish, as things he had no control over surpassed him. With infinite sadness, she watched the moment of Logan's defeat.

He turned to her. The voice, once so strong, like a magnet, drawing others to him, had no clarity, and the body no vitality. "No! God, Jane, no!"

The desperate truth of his situation stood out in his face. All these years of fighting her, hope of having her, had kept him strong. The oldest need of man. Someone separate from himself, but like himself. Without her, there was only God, and to God, Logan Churlick knew, he was as filthy rags.

Like the first man, he needed woman. Needed someone as imperfect as himself, someone he could even worship in his way, not as an incorporeal deity, but someone with form and substance who kept his soul alive.

In that moment of sorrow there was beauty. It was the beauty for which the human race had sacrificed the garden. Out of Eve's pain, knowledge was born, and out of Jane's, God's grace.

Forty-Two

Bo came upon her in the kitchen, hair bedraggled, room dark, except for the glimmer of the computer screen in front of her. He watched his beloved wife for a moment, the light from the screen absorbing her, and thought, *She looks like hell, exhausted, circles under her eyes.*

He opened a drawer, took out a large plastic fishing tackle box containing a myriad of vitamins and shuffled across the kitchen in his slippers. "You okay?"

Clad in a thick robe, Jane looked up from her laptop on the kitchen table.

"It's quarter after three."

Jane shrugged. She glowed in the light of the computer's screen.

Bo handed her the fishing tackle box. "Thought maybe you could use some vitamin C for your scratchy throat."

She laid her hands on the box. "I think I was about nine or ten when I found out how vitamin C works," she said softly. "I had a cold, and Dad gave me this little vitamin A, which was easy to swallow. But a thousand milligrams of C was too big for me, so he crushed it between two spoons, and mixed it with honey. Then with my throbbing throat, I ate it off the spoon . . . it was good, kind of sour-sweet. Dad said the C draws all the bad germs to it, like a magnet, from all over your body. Then, when you pee out the vitamin C, it takes all the bad stuff with it, until there's none left and you're all better."

Bo gave her a little smile. She spoke about her father fairly often now, always fondly. He handed her a glass of water.

Jane fished out a vitamin C, zinc, B complex and vitamin A, threw her head back and washed down the pills.

At least he could do that for her. She had taken a medical leave of absence from her job a month ago, but at least he could keep her healthy while she was in his care. And he did baby her and fuss after her, as soon as he raced home from work each day, for all the good it seemed to be doing. He didn't know what to say, so said nothing, until the silence between them became oppressive.

He stared at his wife reflected with the glowing light in the dark window, then took a seat next to her. "I know you're suffering. I'm suffering, too. Not like you are, but I loved those girls. The way Bekah used to run ahead when we went for walks, like a race horse." He chuckled. "And Darcy would grab me by two fingers and pull me along, drag me into book stores. God, that girl did love to read."

He paused. No response. No will to respond, he imagined. Where was his bride? "I'm going crazy, seeing you this way. You're more and more inside yourself. You look, but you don't see —"

"I see everything," she answered quietly, taking her eyes from the screen.

There she goes again, he thought, *talking in riddles.* "Look, I know I can't help. Nobody on earth can . . . he gestured vaguely, "but it's just . . . if you're not alive, I'm not either." He tenderly cupped Jane's tired face in his hands. "I'm right here beside you, as long as it takes. As long as it takes. You need to understand that. And I need to say it to you out loud."

Mildly, Jane shook her head. "Bo?" Her voice was frightened.

"What, Janey?" He took her hand and held it tight. The coldness shocked him. How long had she been up? He closed his warmth around her.

"I keep asking myself what I could've done to stop it."

He shook his head. "It should've never happened."

"But it did. It did, and I couldn't save my girls," she said, voice quavering, and the last, desperate, "because they *chose* him."

He felt powerless, and saw in her anguish that planets could be aligned on the pull of her guilt. She was drawing away from him again.

"You let them go because you couldn't live with the alternative. If it had kept on, the war between you and Churlick would've torn them in two."

"I know, I know," she said hoarsely. "Why didn't he know that?"

He couldn't answer. Her grief moved past him, dwarfing and darkening his own in its shadow. That was the question. How could he be so blind, stealing these girls from their mother? How often did a mother like Jane come along?

Jane's fingers were clicking over the keyboard, and the light brightened, changed, and drew her to it. She read, "Chief Joseph said, *We do
not want churches, because they will teach us to quarrel about God.*" Her
gaze searched his face. "Got it?"

He nodded. "I like it. What site is that?"

"theprotest.org," she answered, facing the light again. "And get this.
Here's the latest bomb: Churlick's going for more. Rathcreek's not
enough. He's on the Internet."

"You're kidding."

"Louise came over the other day and plugged into a search engine
that shows there are three and a half million religious websites: cyber
prayer groups, inspirational messages, Sunday sermons. Click here and
you can listen to devotional music, click there for guided meditations.
Then Louise plugs in C.I.A. And there he is, bigger 'n hell: Reverend
Logan Churlick and the *Christ In Action* Weekly Gospel Hour. Don't get
it confused with another churchy C.I.A. site, Churlick's is the C.I.A.
Weekly Gospel Hour."

"Incredible."

"God help us all," she said. "The web, he says, is the body of Christ.
Calls himself the New Missionary. You should see it." Her fingers scrambled over the keyboard, which then pulled the site into focus. Words flew
at them from the screen, dissolved into the week's webcast, complete with
doe-eyed Dolores and their daughters in the background. "Singing their
lungs out for the Father," Jane said. "Like television, only better. You can't
accept charge card donations through t.v. like you can over cyberspace."

Suddenly animated, Jane said, "Something's got to be done about this
horror. Now he's all over the world. This C.I.A.'s *dangerous.* I've got to
warn the courts, the psychiatric field, everyone. It's time for someone to
speak out against Christianity—"

"Jesus, Jane, sweetheart—"

"Are you afraid?"

"No—yes! For you."

"There are millions of people out there like us who've been firebombed by the blood. Moral as the day is long—and quiet and cynical,
sick of the hypocrisy, sick of being put on the defensive because they're
considered goddamned heathens in a Christian nation."

The website C.I.A. flashed off, and the screen turned black, leaving
the screen-saver to wander randomly.

Bo said, "Even if you tell people about Churlick, they won't see themselves as that kind of Christian. How will they know who's using Christianity for their own agenda?"

"For starters, people can tell they're in with the wrong faith if their beliefs are breaking people apart. Love of an all-powerful God should strengthen relationships, not destroy them. How powerful *is* their God—if peace—is beyond God? That doesn't mean staying in an abusive relationship—that's a step backward. If God shapes the meaning of our lives, and we can't get beyond a fear of those with different ideas, then our God is nothing more than our own shadows on the cave wall." She was quiet, and he waited.

"We need a set of guiding principles that are more than: my church is better than your church. So that our meaning isn't tied up in perfection beyond, but the imperfection we've got to live in. *How* we live gives our existence meaning. It's all we've really got. So that when you come to the end of your life, you can look back at what you did and say, 'Yeah, I was mostly a moral person.' Huxley was a big brain, and he said it all boils down to, 'Be kind.' I don't care if you call yourself Baptist, Lutheran, Catholic, Muslim, Hindu, Buddhist or Sun Worshipper, your religion is what you *do*, not what you say."

"Are you talking *mainstream*? Jane—"

She waved his objection away. "So I shouldn't attack mainstream churches because it's all too big? The Fellowship was mainstream. Part of a huge network. Only Churlick had his own quirks layered on top of church doctrine. Just like those horny priests who interpreted Catholicism by giving it their own twist. Poor kids—they listened, and look what happened to them. And the church has been protecting these guys. No, I have to do it because it *is* so big. People involved in churches are not exempt from the consequences of their actions.

"I have to stand for something so big, so universal that it's the truth in the heart of hearts. Good people will *feel* the truth I tell in their human dignity, their morality. That it makes sense, and will give them strength to confront people like the Churlicks, Swaggarts, Bakers, al Qaida, pedophile priests, abortion protesters who say they *know* I'm going to hell because I believe abortion prevents child abuse and neglect, over population. Christians have to allow others to have different views without condemning."

Hesitating, Bo said softly, "But how do you *do* this without sounding like a raving lunatic?"

Her sharp eyes picked up on his skepticism, and when he looked away, embarrassed, she did also. An underground chaos rippled through the room.

"Lunatic?" she said, and laughed, strange and glittering. "You think I'm crazy?"

He faltered. "I never said that."

"Maybe that's what it takes. I'm talking about a revolution, a spiritual uprising of the silent masses of *good* people, like you and me and Ruth and Bob, against the tyrants who'd condemn us. Listen, Bo. What if one judge or one GAL hears me, and so one mother or father doesn't lose a daughter or son?"

"That's noble," he said. "But going after churches is dangerous."

"No. Know what's dangerous? Those fish on people's cars."

"What?"

"They can't just have their little fish and let us have Darwin. On car trunks all over America, there's a war going on. And watch out for that church camp that sends home your little Christian soldier. Or how about this? God help the child whose parent spouts off about sulfur-belching demons invading the brain of his abortion-loving New-Ager wife, as he tucks his little darling into bed at night. For God's sake! The story's *fiction*."

He sighed. *Where* was she going with this?

"Dangerous, Jane. Did you hear me?" *Shit!* he thought, *What can I do? Who do I call? How do you stop a breakdown?*

She said, "And what about our father who art in his website, with his games and his dirty little secrets? By his fruits you shall know him. I'm going to tell people they have a moral responsibility to scrutinize the fruits they're handed. From this day forward, blind faith is the only sin."

Jane calmed down, fixed him with those steady eyes, green in their shimmering emotion. Bolivar shivered. She looked suddenly hallowed. Or unbalanced? Would she do it?

The silence about them was a promise, cutting off the outside. Only Jane was with him, her solid breathing, her passion. The early morning slate gave way to the sun's fiery outline of the mountaintop. The kitchen seemed like a holy place, like a beginning.

He said, "You're serious. Are you serious?"

A small smile graced her serious lips.

"Christ, you could be killed by those religious nuts."

And he saw in the slight rise of her eyebrows and steady gaze what she had been trying to tell him. How, generation after generation, God was politicized, used, and how few throughout history had the courage to confront it. Hadn't he taught the great writers who had tried? And how, in this generation, Jane was the one to suffer, and offer herself out of her suffering. Why? Why his Jane? God's grace, his Jane, she was the way.

Then in his stubborn, selfish heart, the question arose that Bolivar feared most: would *they* survive?

He felt the crack inside begin, felt the tears sting his nose and eyes, and swallowed them, until he couldn't hold back. He reached for Jane and held her until the kitchen was silent again.

Forty-Three

Almost without sleep, from Friday through Sunday, Jane worked on her fledgling website, theprotest.org, until a vicious flu took hold. In her run-down state, it nearly killed her. The strain of her daughters' leaving, coupled with the flu, instead, took her pancreas.

In the months of recuperation, she, in turn, learned to take insulin, learned to eat differently—stingy amounts of healthy food at calculated times—according to the amount of insulin she shot into her system. Now, she walked for exercise, and Bolivar walked with her. Jane survived the loss imposed upon her by her body, but she never recovered from the loss of her daughters.

In the ten years following Bekah and Darcy's leaving, Jane never heard from them. Any correspondence she sent, a birthday card or Christmas letter was sent back unopened, marked, Return to Sender. Only once did she receive correspondence, from Logan:

Dear Jane,

 Enclosed you will find the letter you wrote to Bekah and Darcy. In the past, both girls have requested you not to contact them. You apparently have not heeded their wishes. In the future, I will not accept any letters written to Bekah and Darcy from you. They will be intercepted and destroyed. In addition, if you decide to telephonically contact them, the calls will not be accepted. The children are free to contact you once per year, as per the adoption order.

It was signed: Cordially, Logan Churlick, Bekah Churlick, Darcy Churlick. Cordially! Jane wondered if he knew what the word meant.

Jane heard from Margie that Logan looked old and sour, and his ministry, which had risen from small town to flourishing, including his expansion into radio and Internet, was faltering. Schisms were splitting the empire he had built. There was talk of his leaving town to bring the word to another state. Texas? That was all Jane knew. Margie and her husband, along with as many others as they and Jane's parents could influence, had quit the church.

Through the years, Jane survived on hope that had become her religion. She rarely talked about her fervent belief that some day her girls would return. Her thoughts on the matter were met by a patronizing acknowledgment by friends and relatives that she was still going through emotional stages of recovery.

Her recovery truly began when she entered the classroom. Bolivar had just taken a teaching position in their own small town of Bounty, leaving Rathcreek schools behind.

From the Rathcreek district office, Jane saw how badly teachers were treated there and across the nation, in salary, outrageous class sizes and the politics of *the education biz,* as she called it. What bothered her most was the money sent to ease the dire needs of these teachers and their classrooms. Like third world countries, the aid dissipated into the unknown layers of bureaucracy until the few dollars reaching students were like cups of rice.

So Jane traded in her typewriter for an emergency teaching certificate and became one of thousands of substitute teachers who were able to earn miserable pay, no sick leave, no health benefits, and kept the kiddies from killing each other. Eventually, Jane's love of teaching led to a teaching degree and a class of her own, also in Bounty. What she found surprised her: teaching was in her blood.

With only the overhead projector shining, Jane took role in the dim, cave-like room, noting who in her sophomore honors class was absent. Students wrote in response to the daily journal prompt on the screen:

There were some ancient Japanese ceramic cups. These rustic cups were once the property of a holy monk, one of the few possessions he permitted himself to keep. Centuries later, one of the cups was dropped and broken, but even in this condition, it was too precious to simply destroy. So it was repaired, not with glue, which wouldn't hold for centuries to come, but with thin seams of gold solder, thus repairing the break in what could never truly be repaired perfectly. The gold solder added a beauty to the cup, making part of its history quite visible.

—Author Unknown

Jane noticed several students whose journals lay open blank before them.

"Okay, let's shed a little light here to get the ink flowing. Think of bad little things that've happened to you," Jane said. "Now, think big—something so bad, it's broken your heart. You're the cup. But since you're so precious we don't want to throw you away, we'll repair you—but with *gold*. Those gold seams that hold together those pieces of your heart? What does the metaphor say you look like to other cups—to the rest of us? Check out the last part."

"Beautiful!" Keith said, then unsure, added, "Historical?"

"And that means," said Sable, "the gold is the hurts, and everyone can see how beautiful they make us. It's part of each person's history."

"Right," said Jane. "It's our pain that marks us, and when we piece ourselves together, we're different, and beautiful, in a whole new way. No one would ever throw away that cup, eh? So write about the 'gold' that's in you, and in everyone."

"Everyone, Mrs. Bernard? Even you?" asked Casey. "I've never seen *your* gold."

Holding up her hands Italian style, Jane said, "Whatsa matta witchu? You blind or something? Mama Bernardo, she gotta so many golden cracks, you gotta squint, I'ma so bright. That's how come Mama Bernardo, she can love alla *you*. An' believe me, it takes a *lotta* gold for that."

When the lights were on again, students got out their writing. Jane went from desk to desk, offering critique and encouragement.

Eventually, Bolivar slipped into the room, put a finger to his lips. Students tore their eyes from him, trying not to be obvious, but failed. Jane, however, was engrossed with a student who was asking questions about his parody of *Lord of the Flies*.

"By God, you've got it, Ty," Jane said. "This is hysterical."

A student raised her hand. "Mrs. Bernard, what's that American Novelist class you'll be teaching next semester?"

Jane glanced at the clock on the far wall and began collecting papers. "Well, that's where we read books by writers, some of 'em alive and some of 'em dead. And then we try to figure out if we're glad they're dead or not."

A split second of silence, then comprehension, laughter. She loved all her classes, but honors English was a treat . . . they *got* her jokes.

Jane paper clipped, then tossed the stack of papers onto her desk with the others.

"All right, we've got time, and it's Friday. I've been promising this. How about a reading by an American writer who's not dead yet?"

"Okay if I stick around?" Bolivar asked.

"Bo!"

"They ran me out of the office after I broke the copier. I decided to come by and watch you do what you do best." Then, softly, "Bloody well impress me."

She grinned. It was an inside joke with them by now: *Bloody teacher! Is there ever a time you're not in teacher mode?* he'd say when they were out together, watching her pick up some book or music or piece of art she could use in the classroom.

"You know Mr. Bernard from down the hall," Jane said to her students. "All right, now let's impress the nice man, shall we?"

She turned to write names on the board: Jane = God's grace, Logan = little hollow, Louise = renowned fighter and Will Barry = another way to spell Barry?? With her back to them, she said, "It's what he'll *do* to the protagonist."

She turned to face them. In a sort of domino effect, students had put their elbows on desk tops and chins on their bent fists. The room was a sea of Rodin's Thinkers.

She looked at Bo and laughed. "Okay, okay, so stop impressing the nice man."

Jane went to her desk and took a sheath of papers out of her briefcase. "All right, here we go. You gotta promise me, though, you're gonna let me do my teacher thing first. It's important." She had them. The students sat quietly.

"I keep telling you that reading between the lines is important, that literature has more to it than you get on first glance. You have to be detectives, because any writer worth his or her salt isn't going to make it easy.

"This writer named her protagonist Jane." She pointed to the board. "The author chose the name on purpose. Look it up in a baby name book, and it means God's grace. Now she's a Christ figure in this book like Jim Casy in *Grapes*. Remember? The significance of J.C., the light around his head and sacrificing for the good of humankind?"

Students nodded.

Mama Bernardo added under her breath, "Don' *worry*. Steinbeck's next year. Plenty a time to get totally confused. Now where was I? So this J.C.'s got a double whammy going: she's going to need God's grace after what she goes through, and she *is* God's grace.

"Now, her maiden name is Crownhart. Crown. What's it mean? Heart. Huh? Can you put together what the writer wants you to get out of Crown-heart?"

Hands waved in the air like seaweed, undulating in an invisible current.

She called on a student in her formal British accent. "Britney?"

"Could it be King? King of love?"

"Good show, my dear! And if this character is a Christ figure and Crownhart's her last name, who's her father? Who *is* the King of L—?"

"God!" Mauricio shouted.

Jane nodded. "Bingo. Now, that's not complicated enough. Jane marries this jerk by the last name of Powers . . ." She paced back and forth before students, avoiding Bo. "How do we find our power, how do we get in touch with how powerful we really are? When good things happen to us, or when we overcome the bad stuff?"

The classroom was a roaring chorus. "Bad stuff!"

"Right, and man does she come into her power. Now, she meets her true love, oh, about the last third of the book. Name's Bernard. She gives him the nickname of St. Bernard. Who knows what a St. Bernard does?"

"Rescues people," said Winson with shy certainty.

"Brings 'em booze!" Faith laughed.

"Right. So, Faith, how does the name fit?"

Faith's dark eyes grew serious, then she shook her head.

The class was silent a while. Jane scanned the room, tried unsuccessfully to avoid the nodding head of Bolivar, his look of Uh-*huh!*

A tall, Black student in the front row, off to the side, raised his hand, and she called on him, all English. "Mr. Blakeson?"

He spoke as if everyone should have gotten the point long before he had brought it up. "Christ saves people. Like a St. Bernard. Uh, Mrs. Bernard, is this book autobiographical?"

She looked to Bo. He grinned, waited for her reply. Her eyes brimmed, and she blinked back the pride. Her kids. God, she had taught them well.

"All fiction is a mixture of truth as the writer sees it and flaming lies. Writing is simply another means for truth to escape, besides crawling out the hole it's eaten in the author's belly. And the good stories have just the right mixture of startling truth and bodacious lies to keep you reading to the end."

Jane and Bolivar drove home that afternoon, and observed a rare phenomenon. Hovering over the mountain, colored pink and purple by the setting sun, a cloud formation forced them to pull the car over to the side of the road like a couple of tourists. The newscaster on the car radio called it rare, breathtaking. An altocumulus standing lenticular cloud. Only happened when the air that usually flowed over the mountain was forced back down. Jane and Bolivar savored the phenomena, knowing they would likely never see it again.

In the kitchen later, Jane cooked tacos for dinner, fixed guacamole and slaw.

"I think I liked the singing best," Bolivar said, taking plates to the table. "Sum-m-m-mer time . . ."

"Oh, shut up! They loved it."

"They love you, Mama Bernardo. Why didn't you tell me you were working on a story?"

"I don't know. Therapy, I guess. Better if I don't have to defend my writing from your red pen. Keep an eye on the tacos, will you? I'm going to get my kit and shoot up."

Bolivar grinned, and the love and admiration she read on his face made her pleased with her little joke.

She sat on the side of the bed, waiting for the glucometer to register her blood sugar level. She nodded, satisfied with the nearly perfect 105.

The phone rang, and she sprawled full length across the bed to grab it. "Hello?"

The line was silent a moment, then the sound Jane heard took her breath away.

"Hello, Mom? It's Bekah."

Appendix A

If you or someone you care about has been involved in circumstances similar to those Jane Crownhart and her daughters experienced, you may find the following information helpful in illustrating that: 1) bad parenting has not brought about the alienation from your child you are experiencing, 2) the nightmare you are enduring is explainable and 3) there is hope (psychologically and legally).

At the end of this appendix, you will find information to assist you in obtaining the book from which the following information has been obtained.

In 1985, Dr. Gardner introduced the term *parental alienation syndrome* (PAS) to refer to children who are victims of a parent consciously and subconsciously programming the children to hate or judge the other parent with accusations that are unjustifiable and/or exaggerated. Furthermore (and this is extremely important), it includes factors that arise within the child—independent of the parental contributions—that play a role in the development of the syndrome. Children with PAS see themselves as having only a "loved" parent and a "hated" parent, although there is still much love for the so-called hated parent and much hostility toward and fear of the allegedly loved one.

In many cases, therapy for PAS families is not possible without court support. Only the court has the power to order a parent to stop the manipulations and maneuvering. Dr. Gardner emphasizes that therapists who embark upon the treatment of such families without court backing are not likely to be successful.

Case Studies: In an evaluation Dr. Gardner conducted with Billy, a seven-year-old boy in his parents' tug-of-war, the following exchange took place:

Gardner: I'm very sorry to hear that your grandfather died.
Billy: You know, he just didn't die. My father murdered him.
Gardner: (incredulously) Your father *murdered* your grandfather, his *own* father?
Billy: Yes, I know he did it.
Gardner: I thought your grandfather was in the hospital? I understand that he was about 85 years old and was dying of old-age diseases.
Billy: Yeah, that's what *my father* says.
Gardner: What do *you* say?
Billy: I say my father murdered him in the hospital.
Gardner: How did he do that?
Billy: He sneaked into the hospital, at night, and did it while no one was looking. He did it while the nurses and the doctors were asleep.
Gardner: How do you know that?
Billy: I just know it!
Gardner: Did anyone tell you any such thing?
Billy: No, but I just know it.
Gardner: (now turning to the mother, who is witness to this conversation) What do you think about what Billy just said?
Mother: Well, I don't *really* think that my husband did it, but I wouldn't put it past that son-of-a-bitch!

The scene above illustrates that children are capable of creating scenarios of their own, above and beyond what their programming parents provide. This mother had created a PAS in her child, yet in the presence of a reasonable adult, she could not, except by implication, go along with her son's allegation.

In another case, two boys (six and eight years old) denied in family session that their father had ever taken them to any enjoyable events. The father produced pictures, showing the boys with him at the circus, at a rodeo, at the zoo, in Disney World and Disney Land, and a wide variety of other extremely enjoyable activities. In every picture the children were smiling and it was obvious they were having a good time. Whereas at first the boys denied vehemently any enjoyable experiences, they were old enough to appreciate that these pictures were "proof" of their fabrication. The following interchange took place in the course of a family interview:

Gardner: What do you guys have to say about these pictures? It seems to me that they're proof you had good times with your father at many different places.

Eight-year-old: That's just trick photography.

Six-year-old: Yeah, that's just trick photography.

Gardner: (to mother) What's your opinion about what the boys are saying? Do you believe these pictures are trick photography?

Mother: No, those are real pictures. But those are only the things that *he* wanted to do. He never asked the boys before we went whether they wanted to go to these places.

Eight-year-old: Yeah, he never asked us. He just made us go. All those things are things *he* wanted to do, not us.

Six-year-old: Yeah, and we didn't want to go. He just made us.

Above is an example of not only frivolous explanations for the campaign of denigration, but the mother's programming. The idea of the boys being forced to attend these enormously enjoyable events is absurd. But absurdity is one of the important manifestations of PAS. Notice also, the parroting of a younger child of an older sibling.

In a case involving religion, one six-year-old girl told Dr. Gardner she hated her father because he was not "a *real* Christian."

Obviously, these parents came from different Christian religions, the mother viewing the father's creed as not *real* Christianity, and the child herself could not possibly have made the judgments necessary to come to such a conclusion. She was clearly parroting her mother.

Another mother repeatedly criticized the father, always in front of the children, that he did not respect *their* feelings when they said they did not want to visit him because they don't like him.

Here, the mother planted in the children's minds the notion that the decision not to visit their father was *theirs* and that she was only reinforcing *their* feelings. In this case, the programming parent contributes to the independent-thinker phenomenon by telling the children that the animosity is not from her, so it must come from them; where else could it come from?

Often these children are exposed to other independent-thinker induc-
ing statements such as "Stand up to your father, you have rights, too,"
"Don't let him do that to you," or "He's brought it all on himself," or
"What can you expect from a child abuser; of course they hate him."

One child told Dr. Gardner, "I've memorized my lawyer's telephone
number just in case I have to call him when I'm at my father's house."
When Dr. Gardner asked him if there ever had been a situation in which
he felt he needed to call his lawyer, he said, "No." However, he stated that
it was good to have that number in his pocket. He claimed that his mother
gave him a card with the lawyer's number on it, "just in case." He then
related that his mother reminded him to take that card before each visit.
    Here is an excellent example of the mother's programming and the
child's delusion that he needed such protection.

Another child, during a court-ordered visitation, told his father as soon
as he got into the car, "The only reason I'm here is because the judge said
I have to come." The father invited the child to select a restaurant, to
which he responded, "Choose any shit-hole place you'd like to eat in. I
don't give a shit." The entire ride to the restaurant, the child said nothing
to the father. When they arrived, he poked his nose in the menu for about
10 minutes without saying a word. He then got up and said, "I've got to
call my mother. She told me to call her to make sure I'm all right." When
the father asked politely to make it quick, he responded, "I'll speak to her
as long as I want, and what I'll be saying is none of your fucking business."
He made two calls, 10-15 minutes each, during the meal. Not surprisingly, he refused to eat the elaborate and expensive meal he had ordered,
claiming, "This food tastes like shit; why don't you bring it home in a doggie bag and give it to your girlfriend?"
    The scene above illustrates the complete lack of guilt that PAS chil-
dren often exhibit when mistreating the parent they're programmed
against. This father, like most PAS parents, suffer a terrible dilemma: the
choice of serving as scapegoat or removing themselves from maltreatment
and thereby risking complete loss of their children.

Referring to a parent by first name is a common form of denigration.
When in the programming parent's home, PAS children may be taught to
refer to the other parent by first name, the implication being that (s)he is

not worthy of traditional respectful and affectionate terms such as "Mom" and "Dad."

When the children publicly vilify a parent in the presence of the alienating parent, the children may be told, "Now you know that's not the way to speak to your mother/father." The children, of course, pay no heed, because they know quite well that this is the parent's public stance. They recognize there will be absolutely no follow-through and no threat of disciplinary measures.

Of the mild, moderate and severe categories, Jane Crownhart's daughters suffered from Severe Parental Alienation Syndrome. In cases of severe alienation, the alienating parent may be fanatic and even paranoid, and does not respond to logic, confrontations with reality or appeals to reason. They will readily believe the most preposterous scenarios. Often the paranoia did not exhibit itself prior to the breakup of the marriage, but is a psychiatric deterioration frequently seen in the context of custody disputes.

The *children* of these parents are similarly fanatic. They have joined together with the alienating parent in a folie à deux relationship in which they share the paranoid fantasies about the victim parent. They may become panic-stricken over the prospect of visitations. And in fact, their blood-curdling shrieks, panicked states and hostility may be so severe that visitation is impossible. They may run away, become paralyzed with morbid fear, or be so destructive that removal from the victim parent's home becomes warranted.

With regard to the *therapeutic approaches* in this category, traditional therapy is often not possible. A court order that the alienating parent enter into treatment is futile. Most judges are aware that they cannot order an impotent husband to have an erection or a frigid wife to have an orgasm. Yet, they somehow believe that one can order someone to have conviction and commitment to therapy. Accordingly, the evaluator does well to discourage the court from such a misguided order.

Therapy for the children, as well, is most often not possible *while the children are still living in the alienating parent's home.* No matter how many times a week they are seen, the therapeutic exposure represents only a small fraction of the total amount of time of exposure to programming against the victimized parent. There is a sick psychological bond here between the parent and children that is not going to be changed by therapy as long as the children remain living with the alienator. The children are going to be exposed continually to the bombardment of denigration and other influences (overt and covert) that contribute to the syndrome.

Accordingly, the first step toward treatment is *removal* of the children from the alienating parent's home and placement in the home of the allegedly hated parent. This may not be accomplished easily and the court might have to threaten sanctions and even jail. Following this transfer, there must be a period of decompression and a debriefing in which the alienator has no opportunity at all for input to the children. The hope here is to give the children the opportunity to re-establish the relationship with the victimized parent — without brainwashing. Even telephone calls must be strictly prohibited, slowly increasing contacts, starting with monitored phone calls, to forestall re-programming of the children.

In extreme cases, one may have to sever the children entirely from the alienating parent for many months or even years. In such cases, the children will at least be living with one parent who is healthy. *If the court allows the children to remain living with such a disturbed parent, it is likely that there will be lifelong alienation from the victimized parent.* Emphasis, D.K. Bunnell's.

The mothers and fathers who have been good moms and dads, and significantly involved with their children, need to be helped by a professional therapist to see they do not deserve the animosity being vented upon them. They have formed with their children over the years a healthy psychological bond, and should develop a "thick skin." Some parents become quite discouraged and think seriously about removing themselves entirely from their children, so pained are they by the rejections. Many have even been given advice (sometimes by well-meaning therapists) to "respect" the children's desires not to see them. This is a grave mistake. Such removal will generally be detrimental to the children

Last, a special comment about Guardians ad Litem (GAL). In most of the custody evaluations Dr. Gardner conducted, he found that the guardian ad litem could generally be relied upon to assist in obtaining documents that a parent might have been hesitant to provide or to enlist the court's assistance in getting reluctant parents to cooperate in the evaluation. However, there is a definite risk in recommending that the court appoint such a person. A GAL who is not familiar with the causes, manifestations and proper treatment of children with the PAS may prove a definite impediment in the course of treatment. The GAL generally takes pride in supporting the children's needs. Unfortunately, many are uninformed, and reflexively support the children's positions and may not appreciate that they are thereby promulgating the pathology. Some have great difficulty supporting coercive maneuvers (such as insisting that the children visit with a parent who they profess to hate). For guardians ad litem to effectively work with families of parental alienation syndrome children, they must accommodate themselves to this new orientation toward their clients.

Information in Appendix A has been excerpted from *The Parental Alienation Syndrome*, Second Edition, by Richard A. Gardner, M.D., Clinical Professor of Child Psychiatry at the College of Physicians and Surgeons at Columbia University.

For more information: *The Parental Alienation Syndrome*, Second Edition by Richard A. Gardner, M.D., Clinical Professor of Child Psychiatry at the College of Physicians and Surgeons at Columbia University ISBN# 0-933812-42-6

To Order, Contact:
Creative Therapeutics, Inc.
155 Country Road
Cresskill, NJ 07626
1 (800) 544-6162

or

www.rgardner.com (Creative Therapeutics' online catalog and site on which updates on articles on the subject, recent court cases, etc. are available)

Appendix B

Following are resources for those struggling with fanatical religious behavior. While some books are more general in nature, many are specifically targeted at breaking down addictive religious behaviors.

Some are out of print, but available through libraries, local used booksellers, and over the Internet through sources such as Advanced Book Exchange and Amazon.com. The books I was able to get my hands on before press time have quoted material. Others, I was simply intrigued by the titles, as they seemed to indicate appropriate resource tools.

Addiction and Grace by Gerald G. May

A Gospel of Shame: Children, Sexual Abuse and the Catholic Church by Elinor Burkett and Frank Bruni
(Page 101: It's hard to overstate the awe the Catholic church inspires in children who kneel before the crucifix on God's altar. Page 102: One victim was told, "our magic bubble would break," if she revealed her sexual relationship with her minister.)

Answering a Fundamentalist by Albert J. Nevins (1995)

A Thousand Frightening Fantasies: Understanding and Healing Scrupulosity and Obsessive Compulsive Disorder by William VanOrnum

Battle for the Mind: Obedience to Authority by William Sargent

Breaking the Chains: Understanding Religious Addiction and Religious Abuse by Father Leo Booth
(Page 69–70: There is nothing wrong with praying, going to church, missions, crusades or talking about God — but all of these actions can be taken

to dangerous extremes of abuse . . . To be compulsive about any of the above, to the detriment of family, friends and employment is, in a very real sense, a neglect of discipleship.)

Captive Hearts, Captive Minds: Freedom and Recovery from Cults and Abusive Relationships by Madeleine Landau Tobias and Janja Lalich

Churches That Abuse by Ronald Enroth

Coercive Persuasion by Edgar Schein

Combatting Cult Mind Control: The #1 Best-selling Guide to Protection, Rescue and Recovery from Destructive Cults by Steven Hassan
This book saved my sanity. We stumbled across it after nearly nine months of nobody in the legal or psychiatric professions knowing anything about how my daughters could have changed so drastically overnight in their relationship with me. While Mr. Hassan's book focuses on cults, the descriptions I found jumped off every page as behaviors, physically changed looks (such as glassy eyes staring straight through me and stiff, board-like posture) and rhetoric my "Christian" girls exhibited.
(See also, *Releasing the Bonds* by Steven Hassan.)

Cults in Our Midst by Margaret Thaler Singer

Destroying the World to Save It: Aum Shinrikyo, Apocalyptic Violence and the New Global Terrorism by Robert Jay Lifton

Faith that Hurts, Faith that Heals: Understanding the Fine Line Between Healthy Faith and Spiritual Abuse by Stephen Arterburn & Jack Felton
(From Pgs. 283–284): Addiction is not just something the addict does. Addiction is a part of the character and nature of the person . . . If a person is to recover from religious addiction, it will be done with the assistance of a group of caring individuals. It cannot be done alone. And from the book jacket: "A bold confrontation . . . Integrating the principles in this book will be a major step in restoring spiritual and emotional health." — David A. Stoop, Ph.D., Clinical Psychologist. "The hot topic! The urgent issue! All tackled by the right man for a GREAT book!" — Dr. Robert Schuller, Pastor)

Farewell to God: My Reasons for Rejecting God by Charles Templeton

The Guru Papers: Masks of Authoritarian Power by Joel Kramer & Diana Alstad

Healing Spiritual Abuse: How to Break Free form Bad Church Experiences by Ken Blue

The Hidden Persuaders by Vance Packard

How Good Do We Have to Be?: A New Understanding of Guilt and For-giveness by Harold Kushner
(Quote from pg. 109: The quest for righteousness estranges people from each other; the quest for happiness enables them to get past their short-comings and connect with each other. And strange as it may seem, hap-piness may be a more authentically religious value than righteousness.)

Leaving the Fold: Testimonies of Former Fundamentalists by Edward T. Babinski (1995)

Making Peace with Your Parents: The Key to Enriching Your Life and All Your Relationships by Harold H. Bloomfield, M.D. with Leonard Felder, Ph.D.
(Book jacket quote: No matter how old you are and whether or not your parents are alive, you have to come to terms with them. This wise and practical book will show you how to deal with the most fundamental rela-tionship in your life and, in the process, become the happy, creative and fulfilled person you are meant to be.)

Out of the Cults and Into the Church: Understanding and Encouraging Ex-Cultists by Janis Hutchinson

Releasing the Bonds: Empowering People to Think for Themselves
by Steven Hassan, America's Leading Cult Counselor
(Inside jacket: Unlike past methods which rely on short-term, and some-times coercive, educational sessions by "outsiders," Hassan's approach, called the Strategic Interaction Approach, is a goal-oriented, therapeutic course of action that can be initiated and implemented by motivated rel-atives, friends, and anyone who wants to help. Step by step, they learn how to work together to help "awaken" the cult member to the pervasiveness of the group's control over his life.)

Sleeping with Extra-Terrestrials: The Rise of Irrationalism and Perils of Piety by Wendy Kaminer
(One book review: Wonderful Wendy Kaminer! With wit and style and cold hard facts, she skewers contemporary credulity, from New Age spiri-tuality and alien abduction to the growing public power of organized reli-gion and our refusal to reexamine the ill-considered 'war on drugs.'")

Spirituality and Recovery by Father Leo Booth

Spiritual Vampires: The Use and Misuse of Spiritual Power by Marty Raphael

The Apple & the Snake: Challenging the Fundamentalist Mentality by John Colozzi (1999)

The Dark Side of Christian History by Helen Ellerbe

The Gay Agenda: Talking Back to Fundamentalists by Jack Nichols (1996)

The Happy Heretic by Judith Hayes

The Search for God at Harvard by Ari L. Goldman
(One book review: Is it possible to honor the truth of one's own religion while being genuinely open to others?)

Toxic Faith: Understanding the Fine Line Between Healthy Faith and Spiritual Abuse by Stephen Arterburn and Jack Felton
(Formerly, *Faith that Hurts, Faith that Heals*, now in print as paperback). Helpful resource for people who want to retain their Christianity, but release the choke-hold it has on their lives. Also affiliated with New Life Treatment Centers. Has a self-test to determine whether the reader's faith is unhealthy. Also has referrals to organizations dedicated to helping people suffering from harmful practices of faith.

When God Becomes a Drug by Leo Booth

When Good Things Become Addictions by Grant Martin
(Has a self-evaluation for religious addiction, pg. 144. Recommends Richard Foster's *Celebration of Discipline*. Gives a great Bible passage, Colossians 2:6–23 for meditation and contemplation.)

When Prophecy Fails by Leon Festinger, Henry W. Riecken & Stanley Schachter

Why I Am Not a Christian by Bertrand Russell

Internet

www.freedomofmind.com
Website of Steven Hassan, author of *Releasing the Bonds: Empowering People to Think for Themselves*, and director of Freedom of Mind Resource Center. The center offers a *wealth* of information shedding light, and offering help, for victims of religious fanaticism.

www.rgardner.com
Website of Dr. Richard Gardner, author of *The Parental Alienation Syndrome* excerpted from as Appendix A. Check their online catalog and updates on articles on the subject of parental alienation, recent court cases, etc.

Internet, In General

Yahoo
Key Word: Fundamentalists Anonymous

Check out sites: "Sorry, But I Don't Buy That," "Skeptics' Corner" and "Walk Away," an important site for victims recovering from fundamentalist Christian tyranny. Lots of links and support.

There are a wealth of sites, information and support through the Internet. While I found several interesting entries using the formula above, you may want to try another search engine than Yahoo to locate others.

Legal Resources

One of the most difficult tasks of those dealing with children alienated due to religious brainwashing is to find legal representation that is knowledgeable about the process and can put together a coherent, convincing argument of why the children now "hate" their parent. While this is a very short list, you may find other attorneys listed on the website *www.rgardner.com* (cited above) by state and by case, which would leave you the task of tracking down the attorney after obtaining the case he or she was representing from the law library.

West Coast
Ford Greene, Bar No. 107601
HUB LAW OFFICES
711 Sir Francis Drake Blvd.
San Anselmo, CA 94960-1949
(415) 258-0360
Fax: (415) 456-5318

East Coast
Herbert L. Rosedale, Esq.
affrose@aol.com

ORDER FORM

➤ Telephone Orders: Call WordSmith Publishing, Inc. **toll free** 1(800) 232-9790 or (360) 458-2324. Have your Visa or MasterCard ready.

➤ On-line orders: Through the website, www.theprotest.org

➤ Through the mail: WordSmith Publishing, Inc.
                             P.O. Box 1576
                             Yelm, WA 98597

Please send a copy of _The Protest_ to me at the following address:

Name: _____

Address: _____

City: _____ State: _____ Zip: _____

Please send a copy of _The Protest_ as a gift to the following address:

Name: _____

Address: _____

City: _____ State: _____ Zip: _____

The Protest	Number of Copies	Price of Each	Amount Due
The Protest: Address #1		$24.00	
The Protest: Address #2		$24.00	
Subtotal	~~~~~~~~	~~~~~~	
Washington residents add 8% sales tax	~~~~~~~~	~~~~~~	
Shipping @	$4/first;	$2/add'l.	
Total Amount	~~~~~~~~	~~~~~~	$

Payment:
      ❏ Check
      ❏ Visa
      ❏ MasterCard

Card Number: _____

Name on Card: _____ Exp. Date: ___/___
               Please Print

Signature: _____

Call _toll free_ and order now